The Wish

Alex Brown was born in Brighton, Sussex and ran away to London when she left school at sixteen, where she found the streets she lived on for a while weren't paved with gold. After twenty years working in a variety of jobs as a live-in nanny, cinema usher, T-shirt printer, telephone operator, bank cashier, sat-nav voice recorder and beauty salon owner, Alex started writing and found she couldn't stop.

In 2006 she won a competition to write the weekly City Girl column for the *London Paper* and her first novel, *Cupcakes At Carrington's*, was published in 2013.

Now living in a beach house on the Kent coast, with her husband, daughter, and two very glossy black Labradors, Alex is working on her tenth book. When she isn't writing, Alex enjoys knitting, watching Disney films with her daughter and going to Northern Soul nights, and is passionate about supporting charities working with care leavers, adoption and vulnerable young people.

Alex loves hearing from her readers, so please visit her website – www.alexbrownauthor.com or join her for chats on Facebook at www.facebook.com/alexandrabrownauthor, Twitter and Instagram @alexbrownbooks.

Also by Alex Brown

Cupcakes at Carrington's
Christmas at Carrington's
Ice Creams at Carrington's

The Great Christmas Knit Off
The Great Village Show
The Secret of Orchard Cottage

Short Stories
Me and Mr Carrington: A Short Story
Not Just for Christmas: A Short Story

ALEX BROWN

The Wish

HarperCollins*Publishers*

HarperCollins*Publishers* Ltd
The News Building
1 London Bridge Street
London SE1 9GF

www.harpercollins.co.uk

A Paperback Original 2018
1

A catalogue record for this book
is available from the British Library

ISBN: 978-0-00-820669-7

Set in Birka by Type-it, Norway

Printed and bound in Great Britain by
CPI Group (UK) Ltd, Croydon, CR0 4YY

MIX
Paper from
responsible sources
FSC™ C007454

FSC is a non-profit international organisation established to promote
the responsible management of the world's forests. Products carrying
the FSC label are independently certified to assure consumers that
they come from forests that are managed to meet the social, economic
and ecological needs of present and future generations.

Find out more about HarperCollins and the environment at
www.harpercollins.co.uk/green

For all of you, my magnificent readers,
with luck & love xxx

'If you want the rainbow, you gotta put up with the rain'

DOLLY PARTON

Prologue

As the hot evening air furled around their bare bodies hidden among the medley of wild flowers in the meadow, the two young lovers lingered for one last kiss before parting and hurriedly pulling their clothes back on.

'We can't carry on like this,' the man murmured, catching a frond of the woman's wavy blonde hair and twiddling it between his fingers. Nuzzling the side of her neck, he drew in the sweet, sultry scent of her new Blasé perfume, knowing that, no matter how hard he tried, he just couldn't seem to resist her. And it had been this way since the very first time he had caught sight of her, when he'd started at the senior school in nearby Market Briar. Thirteen years old and pulsing with teenage boy hormones, he had fallen for her beguiling ways, the teasing, lingering looks, letting him think he was in with a chance, when all the while he never was. Not really. He knew that now. But that had made him want her all the more, so when she had eventually given him a kiss behind the old abandoned caravan in the Tindledale

Station car park, he had thought he'd died and gone to heaven ... and he had been kept dangling, trapped in the never-ending cycle of lust and loathing ever since. Simply unable to resist coming back for more whenever she wished.

'Why not?' she pouted and pulled her hair away from his fingers before pushing it back over her shoulders. After slipping her clogs on, she dashed over to the layby to retrieve a packet of Player's cigarettes from the glove box of a coffee-coloured Ford Cortina.

'You know why ...' he started, swiftly swiping the Afghan coat that they had been lying on out of the grass and going after her, vowing to call it a day. He lifted her wrist and traced his thumb over the big, shiny engagement ring on her finger. 'You're getting married.'

She snatched her hand away and flipped open the Zippo lighter, sucking on the cigarette until the tip sizzled and glowed flame red. 'And you're not! So stop worrying.'

She made a circle shape in the air with the cigarette before blowing a couple of smoke rings into his face. 'We're having fun, aren't we?' She handed him the cigarette and he managed a couple of puffs before she gestured to get it back.

'Sure,' he shrugged, slinging the coat onto the back seat of the car before pushing his hands deep into the pockets of his flared jeans. 'But—'

'No buts! Come on, why spoil the moment?' They

stood in silence, side by side, resting their backs against the car doors as they took in the view. Tindledale. The little village they had both grown up in. 'Help me with this,' she instructed, lifting her hair and indicating for him to fasten the buttons at the back of her floaty blouse. 'I deserve a bit of fun. And you ... my love,' she paused and gave him a lingering look, 'are far too nice. That's your problem! Always has been,' she laughed, almost mockingly.

And as the golden glow of the sun dipped down on the horizon, framing the fields full of strawberries, sheep, cows, apple, pear and plum trees, he knew that it was time to face the truth. She was about to marry someone else and he needed to tell her straight. He had to, because he couldn't carry on feeling this way. It was wrong. And he needed to be free. Free to find someone else. Someone to love, properly, and not in secret, feeling brimful of shame and confusion.

Chapter One

Present day

Sam Morgan pulled over into the muddy gap beside a five-bar gate that led into the fields behind Tindledale Station and switched off the engine of his tank-like old Land Rover. He undid his seat belt and tried to relax as he sat in silence, watching a plump robin perched on the gate, its stout crimson breast in stark contrast to the virginal white of the spring evening frost. Sam was sure he'd read somewhere, years ago, that robins signified 'new beginnings' ... well, he sure hoped that was true. He wound down the window and inhaled, drinking in the surroundings, as if drawing strength from the familiarity of the sycamore trees that led down to the train track. The place where he had always come to think, right back from when he was just a young boy.

Peering into the rear-view mirror, he pushed a hand through his messy dark hair and then pulled his lower eyelids down to inspect his conker-brown eyes, which were bloodshot and dry after the ten-hour flight from Singapore. But it was going to be worth it – a new job, a year-long contract, which he hoped would be more than enough time to fix things. He would be right here, redeveloping the Blackwood Farm Estate. He'd have less responsibility than he was used to, but it meant being back home in Tindledale. And it would be the perfect opportunity to put everything right with his family. His daughter, Holly, would be fourteen soon. Her birthday was just around the corner, so he really wanted to do that … more than anything.

His phone buzzed in his pocket, making him jump. *Since when did Tindledale have full mobile coverage? Things sure have changed since I was last home*. He couldn't believe it was almost a year. Why on earth had he left it so long? On seeing that it was Dolly, his gran, he pressed the button to take the call.

'Hello Sam, love. How are you getting on?' she asked, in her familiar country accent.

'I'm almost home, Gran, shan't be much longer.' He glanced at the clock on the dashboard and quickly calculated that he'd arrived at the airport over three hours earlier, which was when he had called her to say that the plane had landed safely.

She had insisted he let her know immediately when he touched down. Dolly didn't trust aeroplanes, having only ever been on one in her lifetime, and it had taken two attempts to land on the tiny holiday island of Mykonos before reaching terra firma. Dolly had never forgotten it, and had vowed to stay in the village ever since, or travel to faraway places only by coach. So it was the least he could do to put her mind at rest, especially as she and her second husband, Colin – a coach driver she had met on one of those trips to a faraway place – had kindly offered Sam their spare bedroom to stay in for the duration of his new contract, if need be. But it had taken ages to find the long-term parking place near the airport, and then even longer to defrost the lock on the driver's door so he could actually get in to his car, which had been standing outside in all weathers since he'd last been home to Tindledale. And the parking bill had been astronomical, almost as much as the ancient old Land Rover was worth. But it served him right, Sam figured, he really should have come home sooner.

'Oh well, that's very good now,' Dolly chuckled kindly. 'We're really looking forward to seeing you, son ... I've got your favourite cottage pie with a cheesy mash topping keeping warm inside Beryl, all ready for your dinner when you get here.'

Sam grinned, fondly remembering the extended name of his gran's buttercup-yellow Aga, Beryl the Peril, on account of her being quite temperamental, often needing a tweak to get going, making her perilously unreliable at times. One Christmas, when he was a boy, they had eaten their turkey dinner with all the trimmings at nine o'clock in the evening, thanks to Beryl conking out at the crucial moment. They'd had to take the tinfoil-covered turkey in its tray round to the neighbours next door to cook in their conventional oven. And Dolly had been devastated. Christmas dinner was always at one sharpish in her house, and quite a magnificent affair ... except that year.

'I can't wait. Thanks, Gran.' Sam smiled fondly, momentarily feeling like that twelve-year-old boy again and, given that he was pushing forty-two, there sure was a certain comfort in that.

'Right you are. Cheerio, Sam,' she said, and then added, 'and don't go haring off down those lanes. It's been very wet this spring and then chilly in the evening, so they become coated in frost. Take your time, the pie will wait.' And, after a big intake of breath, followed by an even bigger sigh, she was gone.

Using the elbow part of his jacket sleeve, Sam wiped away a circle of condensation from the windscreen, big enough to look out across the lush, undulating fields leading all the way down to the valley. The valley he knew like the back of his hand, having grown up right here. Number Three Keepers Cottages. A neat row of tiny two-up two-down converted old workers' homes, situated at the top of the unmade lane near the orchards, and not far from the woods. Violet Wood, they used to call it, on account of all the purple flowers that covered the ground in springtime. Where he would play and fish for pike and trout on the banks of the stream with his younger brother, Patrick, and the rest of the boys from the village – Matt (he was the village farrier now) and his older brother, Jack. Not forgetting his good pal, Cooper (who now had the butcher's shop in the High Street), plus a load of other kids who always turned up in the school summer holidays. It was idyllic. And a shame in a way that life couldn't stay like that for always. Sam often wondered why it all had to be so complicated.

Talking of which ... his thoughts turned away from the past, where he had avoided the implosion of his marriage rather than dealing with it and trying to do something, and to the reason he had finally returned to Tindledale after so long away. His wife, Chrissie. Well, his soon-to-be ex-wife, if she had meant what she said when they had spoken on the phone that time. 'Right now, divorce feels like an inevitable eventuality for us, Sam,' she had told him, frankly.

That conversation had been soon after he hadn't made it back home for Christmas. There had been a last-minute near-catastrophe at work, when their largest investor had almost pulled out, and Sam and his team had spent anxious weeks trying to keep the project on track. He was the architectural engineer for a Pan-Asian company, building a prestigious chain of new hotels in Malaysia, Hong Kong and Singapore. He'd cancelled his long week-end home, and knew that both Chrissie and Holly had been devastated. Chrissie had told him it was the final straw the last time they had spoken on the phone.

'If it was this one thing in isolation, Sam, then I might have been able to deal with it. But, on the back of everything else, I just can't. It's all the other weekends when you could have come home and didn't, the phone calls you could have made and didn't, and the five-minute Skype calls that we've had to make do with – or without – most of the time. It's the culmination of everything …'

'Chrissie, I'm honestly doing my best here. I just want this project to be a success and then it could set us up for the rest of our lives. It could really put me on the map and make a huge difference to all of us.'

'And what about me? And our daughter? What is the point of all that success if we're not together to share it? It's meaningless. Empty and lonely.' Sam could hear the frustration and anger in her voice and roused his own to meet hers.

'I'm doing this for us – for you and for Holly, can't you see that?'

'No, Sam, that's not what I see. All I can see is a sad young girl whose heart is broken because her daddy isn't coming home for Christmas, and a permanently empty space next to mine in bed. The empty space where my husband used to be.' He heard her voice crack.

'Chrissie, please, it's just going to be a few more months …'

'I'm sorry, Sam, but I can't take any more of this. As far as I'm concerned our marriage is over. Holly and I have been at the bottom of your priority list for too long and I've had enough.'

Since then, they'd communicated only via email. Sam had called and tried to talk to Chrissie on several occasions, but she had refused to speak to him. He couldn't quite work out when the reality of it had hit home, but he thought it struck him hardest when a Facebook memory popped up on his timeline and he was confronted with the awful, stark reality that he hadn't actually seen his daughter for almost a year. The picture had glared out at him accusingly. He, Chrissie and Holly, on top of the Sentosa Sky Tower in Singapore, with Holly pulling faces for her numerous selfies. He'd clicked through some more. He and Holly, their faces contorted in wild excitement on the Jurassic Park Rapids Adventure ride at Universal Studios, while Chrissie had a look of controlled terror. Then his beautiful daughter cuddling a baby elephant on a magical trip to an elephant sanctuary in nearby Malaysia. Sam had welled up with emotion on seeing Holly so absolutely enchanted – the look of pure joy in her eyes was too much to bear; he missed her and blamed himself for shattering her happiness, so had then gone out and got very, very drunk. The next morning, hungover but with more resolve than he had felt in ages, he had called the

CEO of the company he worked for and handed in his notice.

The situation he was now in had unsettled him like nothing ever had before, prompting him to put the feelers out for a job closer to home. The truth was impossible to ignore. He and Chrissie had been drifting apart for a while, long before he ever went away to Singapore.

Sam had been working hard for years to build his reputation as an architect. He was never the cleverest at school, but he'd been a grafter – it had taken him three years of evening classes, and working all day as a labourer on a building site, to get the exams he had needed before eventually being able to pursue his dream of training to be an architect. Then, frequently working late into the night to qualify had paid off, and he had got a job in a large practice. Since then he'd steadily worked his way up over the years.

Ever since he was a boy, he'd loved building stuff, designing it from scratch and seeing it materialise, magnificent and strong, much like his marriage before the cracks set in. His father Rob had bought him his first Meccano set when he was still in short trousers, and the two of them would spend hours over it. Sam had thought that he and Chrissie were as tightly bolted together as his Meccano constructions, but last year, despite the smiles on Facebook, their Singapore trip had only highlighted the fractures that were becoming apparent ...

*

'Wow! This place is awesome!' Holly had bounced down backwards on the king-sized bed in her dad's Singapore apartment, pushing her legs and arms out wide into a star shape. 'This bed is like a giant marshmallow! It's so soft and squishy.'

'Hey. Don't get too comfortable, your bedroom is down the hall,' Sam had laughed, going to scoop her up into a big bear hug.

'But that's not fair! How come the grown-ups get all the best bits for themselves?'

'Well, you won't be saying that when you see your bedroom. Let me show you.' Sam's apartment was on the twenty-fourth floor of one of the most iconic developments in the city, and the view from each room was stunning. Holly's room had an inbuilt entertainment centre, which included Apple TV and a karaoke machine, her own en-suite shower room and a mini-fridge, well stocked with chilled water and sugar-free drinks on account of Molly being diabetic. Delighted, Holly had instantly whipped out her phone to ensure she captured every detail for her Instagram account, taking the time to select the perfect filters, before then telling him she needed to give herself an insulin injection.

'Oh, right, of course. Want me to do anything?' he'd offered.

Holly shook her head matter-of-factly. 'Nope.'

'OK, I'll be outside with Mum.' He leaned over and gave her a kiss on her head, as she pulled what she needed from her needle case. 'Love you, darling.'

'Love you too, Dad. This holiday is going to be so amazing!'

While Holly slept off her jetlag, Sam and Chrissie had reacquainted themselves with each other in the master bedroom. It had felt so good to have her in his arms again – they'd always been really into each other, and for Sam their lovemaking felt like the monsoon after a drought. They dozed lightly afterwards and Sam wrapped himself around his wife, burying his nose in her soft blonde hair, drawing in the familiar scent of her strawberry shampoo. Uncharacteristically, she had seemed a bit detached. He couldn't put his finger on it but something wasn't quite right.

'Hey,' he said gently. 'What's up?'

'Nothing …' She'd hesitated for a split second before answering.

'You sure?' He could tell when something was on her mind.

A beat of silence followed.

'It's just …' she stalled. 'This place … I wasn't expecting anything like it. It's incredible. I'm not surprised you haven't come home.'

'What do you mean?' Sam asked, leaning up on one elbow. 'This place is great, but that's not the reason I haven't …'

He stopped talking as Chrissie turned around to look up at him, her blue eyes scanning his face as if searching for the right words. 'You've been here for three months and this is the first time we've seen you since you left. When we talked about you taking this job, you promised that you'd be home every six weeks. That's what we agreed.'

'I know, love, but things have been difficult to get off the ground. There's been a lot of bureaucracy and trouble with getting the right contractors. We've been working around the clock to get everything up and running, there's been lots of schmoozing and lobbying … and then there's the time difference to factor in.'

'While Holly and I sit at home watching TV and sharing a cake from Kitty's Spotted Pig café in the village, wondering when you're going to come home?'

'But Chris, you know I'm doing it for us. A few more jobs like this could set us up for life.' He moved his hand from her back and brought it round to the front, where it cupped her breast and his thumb played lightly with her nipple. He waggled his eyebrows suggestively. 'Come on, let's get rude again.'

Chrissie grinned, but took his hand with her own and moved it back to where it had come from.

'Seriously Sam, promise me things won't stay like this. Every job you've had over the last few years has taken you further away. First it was Frankfurt for six months, then Dubai for the best part of a year, but you came home far

more often then. And now you are here in Singapore and
we're still back home in Tindledale, missing you like mad.
If I didn't know better, I'd say you were trying to stay away
from us.'

'How could you even think that?' Sam shook his head.
Chrissie raised her eyes at him.

'OK, I see what you are saying, but we've always known
my work would take me away.'

'You know, it's been much harder since Holly's diabetes
diagnosis.'

'Everything's all right though, isn't it?' Sam checked right
away.

'Yes, as far as it can be, but it's changed things. You feel
further away and I feel less … I don't know … it's just
getting harder without you at home.'

'Hey, Chrissie, you've always been strong, you can cope
with this,' he said tenderly. 'And I'm only ever a phone call
away. No matter what the time difference is.'

'Maybe,' Chrissie faltered, her eyes welling up. 'But I
feel like your career is taking you away from me here,
Sam.' Chrissie touched her chest, in the place where her
heart was. She wasn't the overly sentimental type, but as
he caressed away her worries, he felt her soft tears on his
own cheeks and, like her words, their memory stayed with
Sam for the rest of the holiday.

*

Sam wished now, more than anything, that he had listened to what Chrissie had said that day. She had always been the strong one of them, holding it all together while he built his career. He was solid in his own way, of course. He'd worked hard, given them a beautiful home, sent Holly to a fee-paying secondary school – though of course it had been Chrissie who'd put the effort in to get her through the entrance exams, especially as the exam had been around the same time as Holly's diabetes diagnosis. They were a team, weren't they? Each bringing their best points to the marriage and the whole being more than the sum of its parts. That's what he'd always thought – until now.

They were still married, though, for better or worse … and that had to count for something. It was a starting point at least, and he wasn't about to give up on everything they had together, even if it seemed that Chrissie might already have.

And Holly, he couldn't wait to see her, having missed her so much. Skype calls were OK for keeping in touch, although nothing compared to the real thing, like a proper bear-hug cuddle followed by a tickling session until she begged him to stop. But he had a chance to change that now; he'd be able to see her properly and make up for all those moments that he had missed.

Sam sat back in the seat and allowed himself a moment of contemplation. Time to go over his plan to put everything right. He had thought of nothing else for months now. Ever since he had made the decision to come back for good, and broken the news to his boss. He'd had to work some notice and hand over to his deputy but he'd finally made the break. And it was spring now, a time for new beginnings, he thought optimistically.

Looking back over the last few years, he understood that he had got things badly wrong. He believed that he and Chrissie knew what their priorities were but he could see now – too late – that Holly's diabetes diagnosis had changed so much more than just the blood sugar levels in his little girl's body.

Chapter Two

Jude Darling tucked Lulu, her grumpy old caramel-coloured cockapoo, under her arm, and inhaled the crisp, spring air infused with a glorious aroma of fresh paint. Smiling, she stared at the black timber-framed, white wattle-walled shop with tiny mullioned windows in the middle of Tindledale High Street. Home. After several years of travelling around the world, before settling in Los Angeles for a while, it now felt surreal – but at the same time ever so good – to be back.

'So what do you think?' Tony Darling asked. Jude turned, and with her free arm she gave her dad an enormous hug.

'I love it, Dad. Really I do.' She stood back on the pavement, her rumpus of red curls bouncing on her shoulders as she beamed up at the swirly gold lettering above the window. 'Ooh, it's perfect! *Darling Antiques & Interiors*. Has a certain ring to it, don't you think?'

'It sure does! Though sorry again for the silly surname you've been lumbered with … it's the family curse.' He rolled his eyes and shrugged before going to give Lulu's curly head a stroke, but thought better of it when she growled and lifted her nose up into the air. 'Well, *excuse me*,' he laughed.

'Sorry. She's still sulking over this wet weather – you know what a diva she is; looking down her nose at these muddy puddles everywhere after the heat of the streets in Los Angeles.' Jude adjusted Lulu's little tartan coat. 'And don't be daft! It's a brilliant surname. It's our family's name, and I love it, always have, you know that … ' she replied, nodding her head as if to punctuate the point.

'Hmm, if you say so. But three guesses who's doing the Mr Darling's Magic Show gig *again* this year for the kids at the May Fair?' Tony sighed.

'Ahh, Dad, you love it really. You're the real deal, a *proper* magic man … especially now you're turning into a silver fox. Very distinguished for when you don the velvet Willy Wonka suit and whip a rabbit out of a top hat. And you'll have a full white beard and barnet in no time, the way you're going!' Jude laughed, giving his salt-and-pepper hair a quick ruffle, and remembering as a child how she loved having a magician for a dad, or the 'Magic Man' as her school friends used to call him. And she never tired of telling new people she met along the way that her dad was a magician. That he could do proper tricks, like make a white dove fly out of her ear. Of course, years later she had worked out that it was all an illusion. But back then, when everyone in Tindledale and the surrounding villages loved Mr Darling's Magic Show, it had made her feel special. Proud and safe ... and God knows she had needed that after her mum had died. Nine years old she had been when she'd got home from school one day and found her lovely mummy, Sarah, slumped over the sofa, lifeless after suffering a fatal asthma attack. And that was how it became just the two of them, Tony and Jude Darling. A unit. An unstoppable team.

Tony had been a brilliant dad. Still was. And that was why Jude had come back home to Tindledale, after her wanderlust had petered out, much like her relationship with Scott, the American businessman she had dated for a year or so before he'd announced that he'd 'rather not be exclusive any longer'. Fair enough. Jude hadn't been that into him in any case; plus she had come to the conclusion that what had suited her in her twenties and thirties – fun with no ties – didn't really cut it any more. No. But whilst she had never really been the 'settling down' type, she reckoned she'd be open now to the possibility of a proper committed relationship, with a mature man who would put the effort in. Not an immature guy clinging on to his youth, who only wanted to hook up when he was in town.

Plus Dad wasn't getting any younger – not that sixty was old or anything these days, but still ... there were never any guarantees in life, Jude knew that only too well, with losing her mum at such a young age. And she'd had enough of being away from her home, the place where she had grown up, and the place she loved, Tindledale. She had always planned on coming back here, but the urge to travel, as if to find out who she really was, had always been a driving factor. Growing up without her mum had been difficult at times, especially during her teenage years, when she had yearned to find a connection, a tangible way to know all about her mother, Sarah. To find out who she really was. The dreams and aspirations that were cruelly snatched from her at such a young age. Of course, Jude had never forgotten her mum, and the memories she had of their time together. But having been so young when it happened meant that the hazy snippets of events, feelings, even the scent of her mum's favourite perfume on a treasured scarf had faded. So when Jude was in her twenties, and after a string of disastrous relationships had disillusioned her, she knew it was time to go for it. She travelled to LA to meet Maggie, her mum's cousin, who lived there.

Maggie even looked like Sarah, and had similar mannerisms, but, better still, she remembered vividly growing up with Jude's mum; the silly antics they got up to, the daft things Sarah had said and done. Maggie was able to give Jude a real insight into who Sarah really was. And another wonderful thing for Jude: Maggie was able to share how Sarah had felt about her only child. The love she had felt for Jude, and everything she had hoped she would grow up to be. This had given Jude a tremendous sense of peace, that tangible connection she had yearned for. To feel an affinity with her mum and to know she would have been proud of her. And Jude had wanted to harness that affinity and never let it go, so she had stayed in LA with Maggie, who had moved into Sarah's maternal role with ease, giving Jude a comfort that she hadn't had for so long. And, in doing so, Jude had also felt close to her mum.

LA had become Jude's base, her haven if you like, and after travelling to as many enchanting places as she could afford to on her modest savings, she had then started the antiques and interiors business in order to properly pay her way. And this, in turn, plus loads of hard work, had taken her from Maggie's little spare room in the condo to a plush, mink-colour-carpeted studio in one of LA's most exclusive business districts.

It had been a wrench to leave that studio behind, but Jude had missed her family here too – Dad (though he'd come out to visit every year for at least four weeks), plus the three rambunctious golden retrievers called Betty, Bob and Barney that Lulu had hated on sight. But then Lulu was used to being the centre of attention, and certainly wasn't going to share Jude's affections with any other dogs, so had taken to growling if Jude so much as glanced at one of the retrievers. A properly pampered pooch, Lulu had been a welcome cute-puppy gift to Jude from one of her grateful LA clients, who bred pedigree cockapoos. Small enough to travel with Jude on her very own pet passport, Lulu was used to first-class treatment at all times, often perched, regally, on her lap during flights, or nestled inside a designer pet carrier, as was the norm in LA. It was no surprise, really, that Lulu was finding it tricky to acclimatise to her more modest living arrangements – with her bed in the corner of the kitchen alongside the other dogs.

Jude had also missed her best friend, Chrissie. She had missed her so much. And Chrissie really needed her right now. Jude still couldn't get her head around the disaster that was her best friend's marriage. Last time she had been home, about four years ago, Chrissie, Sam and Holly had been doing OK – they had been a happy family unit. And Chrissie and Sam had always been one of those couples you imagined were set to be together for ever. Like butter and crumpets. The two just go. And it was unthinkable to have one without the other. But somehow that had happened. And Jude was horrified at the situation because, if Chrissie and Sam's relationship could fall apart, then what hope was there for everyone else still searching for their perfect match? That's how solid they were, or had been. It was shocking. More so, as Jude hadn't realised just how bad things had become – Chrissie had always had a tendency to batten down the hatches, make out that she was coping, that everything was fine, that she had it all under control, even when she didn't; that was her way. But Chrissie really had glossed over the startling truth about the state of her marriage during the numerous phone calls and Skype calls they'd had together all the time Jude had been in LA. And her goddaughter, Holly, she needed Jude too. The whole family – Chrissie, Holly and Sam – had been having a tough time this last couple of years or so, and Jude wanted to do all that she could to support Chrissie, who was more like a sister than a best friend. It was the right thing to do. Chrissie had been there for Jude all those years ago when her mum had died, as well as ever since ... and so now it was Jude's turn to be here, close by, for her.

'And I love you too,' Tony smirked, shaking his head some more and cutting into Jude's thoughts. 'But less of the "old man" jokes please ... if you really are planning on staying around for good.'

'Yep, this is me, back home in Tindledale for good ...'

'Well, I sure hope so, love, because it's not safe out there any more. Not with all the horrors going on around the world. You can't switch the telly on these days without seeing some other awful incident unfold. No, it's no good you gallivanting around the globe picking up all that junk ...' He gestured inside the shop, which was crammed full of unique artefacts from far-flung places.

'Oh Dad, it's not junk! Come on, let's take a look

inside.' She looped her free arm through Tony's and practically skipped him inside, she was so excited.

Inside, and after placing Lulu carefully on the rug, Jude wandered around, oohing and ahhing as she took in the gorgeous Farrow & Ball painted walls.

'And, see, I was right about this one, Elephant's Breath ...' She darted towards the main wall that ran the length of the back of the shop, her red curls flaring out behind her, and ran a hand lovingly over the smooth wall, 'and with this one too, Calamine. The perfect match, don't you think?' She dashed over to the adjacent wall to stroke that surface too. Tony couldn't help himself, and his sun-baked, brown crinkly face broke into a big smile, only just managing to stop short of actually laughing at the absurdity of the paint names. He was old school, and these new, fancy, fandangled colours bemused him.

'Yep. Of course ... it looks nice,' he shrugged, before gathering up his brushes and tools to tidy away into his white work van parked outside the window.

'*Nice?*' Jude pretended to be put out. 'Just *nice*, Dad. Oh, come on ... you've done a *brilliant* job, used the exact hues that I asked for, and it looks amazing.'

'Well, it's grey and pink at the end of the day, love.' And after placing his tool bag down on a nearby chair, he held out his hands, palms up, and laughed, 'but if you want the flash stuff that costs an arm and a leg and has to be specially ordered off the internet, when the cheap stuff from the builders' merchants down on the industrial estate would have done just as good a job, then who am I to argue?'

'But it has to be right, Dad. It's important to create the right ambience.' Jude folded her arms and chewed the inside of her cheek as she scanned the shop once more. She'd put her heart and soul into this new venture, not to mention a tidy sum of money that she had saved up over the years for this exact moment. 'And look …' She carefully picked up an exquisite, multi-coloured glass Art Deco lamp. 'This is an expensive antique. It was my job to scour the globe for special items for my clients. They're very discerning you know.' Jude gave her dad a playful punch on the arm.

'Yeah, well they can "discern" or whatever with someone new now. I'm not letting you leave Tindledale again.'

'There's no chance of that. My "gallivanting" days, as you say,' Jude paused to do silly quote signs in front of her dad, trying not to smile when he pulled a face and batted her away, 'are well and truly over. I've gathered enough stock of my own now for the shop, and once the soft furnishings arrive in the next day or so for the interiors section, I'll be having a grand opening.'

A short silence followed as father and daughter exchanged nods, with intermittent glances around the tiny but perfectly formed shop. 'Well, maybe a not so *grand* opening,' Jude shrugged and grinned gamely, knowing this wasn't London's Mayfair. No, Tindledale was a tiny village in the middle of nowhere, 'but certainly a few friends round for an Aperol spritz or a flute of pink Prosecco and a scrumptious fondant fancy or three from Kitty's café over there, that's for sure.'

Jude pointed across the street towards The Spotted Pig Café & Tearoom, looking all cosy on the corner with the glow from the pretty little tea lights sparkling in the windows and the floral bunting buffeting in the breeze. On her return to Tindledale, she had been delighted to see the café still here, having fond memories of visiting after school with Chrissie to drink big mugs of hot chocolate and feast on slabs of Battenberg cake. This was back in the day, and long before Kitty took over; Kitty now lived with her daughter Teddie and boyfriend Mack in the adjoining cottage. So Jude had made a beeline across the road to introduce herself and see if the café had changed very much during her time away. She was delighted to see that it hadn't.

Jude waved when Mack pulled up outside in his car and opened the boot to let two gorgeous dogs jump out – a beautiful, glossy black one-eyed Labrador and a lovely little cocker spaniel, the spitting image of that dog in *The Lady and the Tramp* film. Kitty's daughter, Teddie, came bouncing out of the café to greet them, closely followed by Kitty, who took the dogs by their leads so that Mack could swing Teddie up into his arms for an enormous cuddle. Ahh, she smiled at the wonderful sight, a part of her musing on how nice it might be to have a family of her own.

Tindledale really was a wonderful little village, and she was proud to have grown up in such a picturesque place, but she was under no illusion that it might take the villagers a little while to warm to the idea of paying a fair price for an exquisite antique. They could be very provincial and quite unworldly at times, but more than made up for this with their warmth and generosity. She'd had a number of cards welcoming her back home and wishing her luck with her new venture – Mrs Pocket, parish council stalwart and Jude's old headteacher at the village school years ago, had been the first to call in. Then Mrs Cherry, aka Brown Owl, from the 1st Tindledale pack that Jude had been a part of as a child, and then lovely Molly from the butcher's a few doors along had popped in with one of her famous steak and ale pies. And Jude knew it would take time for things to really take off, but she had built up enough clients around the world to take care of the antiques side of the business in any case – she'd ship the items to them. And that's why she had opted for soft furnishings too – cushions, curtains, door stops, blankets, throws, quilts, and some heavenly-scented candles and trinkets, so there would be something for everyone's budget.

'Good. And you can stick me down for a Bakewell tart

and a pint of beer from the Duck and Puddle pub,' Tony laughed. 'None of this pink fizz for me at the party. Call it payment for the decorating.' He placed his free arm around his daughter's shoulders and pulled her in for a solid cuddle.

'You're on. But I'll still be paying you the proper rate for all the work you've done, Dad. I have the money,' Jude grinned, giving her dad a nudge in the side. 'I'm not fifteen any more and on the scrounge.'

'More's the pity. Are you sure you're going to be forty-one on your next birthday?' Tony lifted his eyebrows. 'Makes me feel properly old.'

'Awww, well ... at least you'll have me here now to make your cocoa and tuck your tartan blanket in around your old weary knees, eh Dad?' Jude laughed.

'Oi, wotchit, cheeky! I'm not that old.'

'Ahh, you know I'm only joking – sixty is the new forty these days,' Jude laughed as Tony pulled a roll-up from behind his ear and popped it into the side of his mouth.

'Come on; let's go to that new Indian restaurant over by the village green. You can buy me a Balti with all the trimmings!'

Chapter Three

Sam devoured Dolly's delicious cottage pie in record time. Then, after a quick catch-up over a cup of tea with her and Colin (to be polite, but not wanting to wait another minute to see Chrissie and Holly), he had jumped back in his Land Rover. With Dolly's words of, 'Please don't be expecting too much,' and, 'It's going to take time for you and Chrissie to sort out your differences,' still ringing in his ears, he had driven through the village, the spring bloom much in evidence as he drove past the villagers well-tended front gardens crammed full of buttery lemon daffodils. He was carrying a big bag of presents for Holly as he apprehensively pushed open the gate of The Forstal Farmhouse, a beautiful sixteenth-century, tile-hung cottage, set on the edge of farmland, which he and Chrissie had bought over ten years ago, after saving for ages to get the deposit together.

Holly had been a toddler, all fair wispy hair and big wide smiles, when they had first moved in, living in a caravan in the garden while they renovated the whole house. They had done most of the work themselves. Sam had designed and built the kitchen units from scratch, lovely soft scrubbed pine for the perfect country farmhouse kitchen. He had plastered the walls, painted, decorated, laid the carpet and the tiles, and had even waterproofed the crumbling old cellar to turn it into a cosy family room. A den, with a TV and a big comfy sofa for watching films and football at one end of the room, and a long table for all of Chrissie's crafting paraphernalia at the other end. The room was also fitted with shelves for her sewing machines; she liked to collect the vintage Singer ones with the brown wooden curved covers and little carrying handles. Sam had even made a special cabinet to house her rolls of wallpaper and fabrics, beads, ribbons, and all kinds of colourful knickknacks that might one day come in handy to decorate a gift, or give their Christmas tree a unique style, perhaps. Chrissie was really thoughtful and generous like that. Sam had thought this was the perfect house for the both of them, Holly too – she had her play area with the replica dolls' house that he had made for her fifth birthday, and the wooden rocking horse for her sixth. Everything had seemed happy and perfect back then.

Sam paused, smoothed back his unruly brown hair, using the moment to get himself together. A smile. Not flashy, or cocky. No, he didn't want Chrissie to think he didn't care about the state of their marriage that – quite frankly – was hanging together by a single thread. He wanted her to know that he now understood the impact of focusing on his job and not on his family. He had to get it right. And, if he did, then maybe, just maybe, she would be pleased that he was back to make an effort to try to sort it all out. To put things right. He'd explain about the new job. The big changes that he was planning. That was another thing she had said during that fateful phone conversation. She'd said it would take something really big to make a difference now. And she was absolutely right. But he was back now, even if he did feel like a guest, a stranger even, as he walked up the path, glimpsing the warm, welcoming lights through the lounge window, to the front door of the house that they had created together, as a family.

So many wonderful memories were wrapped up inside this house. Sam cast his mind back to their first Christmas here. Holly had been a toddler and the three of them had been really happy. On Christmas morning, he had let Holly open every single one of her Christmas presents first thing when she woke up, the two of them running downstairs and ripping open the carefully wrapped gifts under the tree. The entire living room was deluged in piles of wrapping paper and boxes of toys, games and treats. Holly had squealed in excitement and Sam had loved the chaotic fun of it. Chrissie had come downstairs in her dressing gown, perplexed and frowning at the anarchy unravelling in front of her. She'd told Sam off for letting Holly go nuts; now she didn't know who any of the presents were from and it wasn't instilling in their daughter the value that the people who had bought the presents placed on them.

'It's Christmas Day, you can't take anything too seriously, love. And look how much fun Holly is having.' The sight of Holly's face, lit up in excitement, had allowed them to laugh it off, with chuckles of 'it's only once a year'. But with the benefit of hindsight, it was those polar approaches to parenting that highlighted the differences between them, foretelling the cracks in their relationship.

Sam went to retrieve his key from his jeans pocket, and stopped. He wasn't even sure why he still carried the key to The Forstal Farmhouse around with him ... it wasn't his home any more, not now. Chrissie had also made that quite clear with a reticent, 'Maybe it would be better if you stayed with Dolly the next time you come home', a suggestion that was definitely not optional. Followed by something about not wanting to destabilise Holly, as she was used to it being just the two of them now. Sam felt a momentary flash of anger. Chrissie had always tried to drive home to him that he had needed to take his responsibilities seriously – once they'd had Holly – and wasn't that what he'd been trying to do over the last few years; and now Chrissie wasn't even going to let him come home? He took a deep breath and tried to calm down. No, Chrissie was right – he hadn't listened when he should have. But all he wanted now was to see Holly.

They were close. They always had been. He knew that Holly had missed him being there, just like he missed her, but surely he would have known if she was unhappy with him, wouldn't she? Or if she was angry that he hadn't been home in ages. They spoke all the time, on the phone, on FaceTime, and she'd always been her usual bouncy and happy self. But then Chrissie always did have a tendency to want to control situations. Not in a nasty way ... it was just her natural coping mechanism after having experienced no control as a kid. Her childhood had been very chaotic, with her mum an alcoholic and dad seeking solace at the bookie's until they died within a year of each other when Chrissie was in her twenties, shortly before she and Sam met.

Sam pushed his hand into his pocket again. Having the key there felt comforting, like a talisman of some kind, something to hold on to, something to give him hope that this house he had so lovingly restored for his family would be his home once more.

He pressed the bell on the centre of the black front door, and then it struck him, the door had been yellow before. A gorgeous sunshine yellow. A happy colour; that's what Chrissie had called it when they had chosen the paint together in the hardware shop in the village. And he had loved every second of preparing and painting the front door for her ... their happy home, together. And for some reason this made Sam catch his breath. He folded his arms, as if to warm his body, or was it to comfort himself? Either way, he needed to get a grip. He couldn't dither here on the doorstep like some kind of idiot. No, he needed to get inside and sort things out.

He rang the bell.

Seconds later, although it felt like an eternity, the door opened.

'Dad!' Holly was standing in front of him, her face wreathed in a smile. Gone were the little girl bunches and gappy grin that he always pictured in his mind's eye when he thought of his daughter, even though bunches hadn't been a thing for a while now. Her shoulder-length bobbed hair had sophisticated-looking caramel and honey-blonde bits running through it, which accentuated the sparkly shimmer on her eyelids. Her gappy grin was now complemented by a brace on her teeth. Sam felt his forehead crease; the skirt, if you could call it that, was way too short. It was her usual tartan school skirt, but it barely covered her bottom. Surely that wasn't the regulation uniform? How could she have grown up so fast? And how come he hadn't noticed these changes during those FaceTime calls? It just went to show that nothing could beat a proper old-fashioned face-to-face conversation.

'Hello, darling!' Sam beamed, and Holly threw herself into his arms. He picked her up and swung her around, like he used to when she was little. 'Ooof, steady on,' he joked, pretending to be winded as she squeezed him tight.

'Oh Dad, you're not *that* ancient.' Holly stepped back, giving his arm a playful punch. Sam was aware of Chrissie standing aside, allowing father and daughter their moment together.

'Hi, Sam,' Chrissie said. Sam caught his breath as they made eye contact. She looked amazing in a clingy black top and tight jeans. Her blonde hair was a little longer and wavier than it used to be, and she had lipstick on, something she rarely wore. And she smelt gorgeous, like honey and almonds. But it wasn't her usual perfume. Sam instinctively wanted to reach out and touch her, but managed to resist. He and Chrissie had always been affectionate and touchy-feely with each other. To hover here, with her so close but just out of reach, was almost too much for him to bear.

Chrissie held his gaze and Sam noticed a slight flush on her cheeks, a sure sign that she was struggling to keep her emotions in check too. He took a step towards her, but an almost imperceptible shake of her head stopped him in his tracks. In her eyes, Sam could see resolve, but conflict too. Damn it, how had they got to this point? When he adored her. And he was sure that she ... at the very least ... still cared.

'Come on, Dad, come in. I've got so much to show you.' Holly quickly sidestepped around her mum, holding Sam by the arm. 'You'll never believe how good I am on the guitar now. Better than you, I bet.' She laughed, but her smile faltered a little when Chrissie spoke.

'Dad can't stay for too long today, Holly. Perhaps you can have tea with him on Saturday at Granny Dolly's house. Plus, you need to go and finish your homework now ... it's getting late and you have school tomorrow,' Chrissie said, not looking Sam in the eye.

'But it's only Tuesday. I want to see him now. Saturday is like nearly a whole week away.' Holly folded her arms.

Sam could see, despite feeling as if he'd been punched in the stomach, that this wasn't the moment to challenge Chrissie's decision and risk starting an argument.

'Maybe it's best if you do as Mum says. We'll have loads of time together just as soon as Mum and I have had a good catch-up,' he intervened, smiling and keen to keep his cool. 'Here, these are for you,' he said giving her the bag of knick-knacks that he'd picked up from the airport – keyrings, a cuddly toy, bath bombs, sticker book; there were no sweets, though: for Holly they were strictly rationed.

'Oh, thanks, Dad!' Holly grinned, taking the bag and peeping inside it before turning to Chrissie. 'Mum, can I just show Dad my room, I want him to see the blanket I knitted.'

Chrissie eyed them both warily. 'OK, Hol, but just ten minutes, you and Dad can have a proper catch-up at the weekend. I'll be in the kitchen, Sam, if you want a quick chat before you go.'

Ten minutes later, and Sam was sitting on the chair beside Holly's desk. She had hurriedly told him absolutely everything that had happened in her life since they had last spoken on the phone. Plus, proudly shown him the blanket which had taken her two weeks to knit. It was a mixture of pansy colours – purple, pink, blue, yellow and white squares all sewn together.

'This is amazing,' Sam said, holding up the blanket and keen to show an interest in his daughter's new hobby, but then inadvertently spoiled the compliment by adding, 'did you knit it all by yourself?'

'Of course I did, Dad. I'm not a baby,' she told him, rolling her eyes dramatically. 'I learnt how to knit on YouTube. It's really cool.' She took the blanket from him and carefully positioned it over the duvet across the bottom of her bed.

'I see.' Sam nodded. 'So it's not all gangsters demonstrating dodgy dance moves and people telling you what stuff to buy on there, then?'

'Oh Dad, you're so lame sometimes,' Holly laughed, shaking her head at him. 'But, it is brilliant to have you home.'

'It's brilliant to be home,' he smiled and stood up. 'But I'm going to pop down and chat to Mum now.'

'But what about the guitar? I want to show you how good I am?'

'I know, darling. How about we get the guitar out at Granny Dolly's when you come over?' Sam appeased, but thought the whole situation just felt so wrong. And none of it was fair on Holly. She was still just a kid ... even if she was dressed up like Taylor Swift.

'OK.' Holly sat down on the bed, looking resigned, but just as he bent to give her a kiss goodbye she asked, 'Everything is going to be all right ... isn't it, Dad?' And in that moment, she was the little girl with the bunches. The image he always held in his head from when she was about six years old and everything was happy and good. And long before his marriage had started to crack. He hesitated before answering, unsure if Chrissie had explained anything to her.

'It's complicated, Holly.'

'But you will make it right, won't you, Dad. You'll sort it out with Mum?'

Sam saw the heartache in his daughter's eyes and felt a swirl of emotion. 'I'm going to do everything I can, I promise you.' Holly gave him a smile, reassured. And he wished he felt as confident as he sounded.

Heading downstairs, Sam sneaked a glance at the master bedroom as he passed by, briefly pausing to take in the familiar soft grey walls with the original black wooden beams and shabby chic furniture that Chrissie had sourced from various country fairs, and then lovingly restored. The handmade crushed velvet curtains. A stack of books on her bedside cabinet, her intoxicating perfume punctuating the air. The neatly arranged hand-crochet-covered cushions on their enormous bed. The bed that he and his wife should be in together.

Sam found Chrissie in the kitchen, standing against the red Aga. She handed him a mug of hot black coffee. 'Strong and sweet. The way you like it,' she said, tilting her head to one side.

'Thanks.' As he took it, his fingers brushed hers and an electric spark shot up his arm. 'Strong and sweet ... just like you.' He eyed her over his coffee mug, trying to be playful, but on seeing the look she gave him, a knot of doubt crept in. Did she think he was being patronising? It was hard to be sure. There was a time when he could read her like a book, but not now, it seemed ... and that just compounded his feelings about this whole situation. It was almost as if they were two strangers.

'Hmm, it's a good job I am strong, Sam. Seeing as I've had to manage on my own for the last few years.' He smarted. Chrissie had gone straight for the jugular.

After gulping down a mouthful of the coffee, he replied.

'Look ... Chris,' he started, 'I know that I haven't got things right. I realise now that I should have seen that you needed me here, but you've always been so ... capable. And self-sufficient.'

'Self-sufficient?' Chrissie's voice rose an octave. Her cobalt eyes flashed as she quirked an eyebrow. And the uncertainty Sam had felt earlier vanished in an instance – he knew exactly what she was thinking now; her hackles were well and truly up. 'Is that how it works then? I'm the self-sufficient one, just getting on with it all, while you're the one who travels around the globe, having only yourself to think about? Like, what gourmet meal you're going to choose from the restaurant in your luxury hotel-apartment complex, or what film you might enjoy as you kick back and relax on the super-king bed the maid has made for you? While, meanwhile, I look after our daughter – make sure she keeps on top of her diabetes, her homework, friendships, guitar lessons, gymnastics, packed lunches, school uniform, cake sales, netball matches, sleepovers ... and all the rest of it.' Sam watched as Chrissie counted off the list of tasks on her fingers. 'And I make sure all the bills are paid, the house is kept running, the garden is tidy, the bins are emptied, the hedge is trimmed, the lane isn't littered with leaves, the monthly parish magazine is paid for, the village charity collections are contributed to, the May Fair cakes are baked, the summer school show costume is made. Honestly, the list is endless! And I do it all. I keep everything going!' Her voice cracked. 'But who's keeping me going?'

Sam immediately wished he could go back out to his

car and start this all over again. This wasn't what he'd had in mind at all. Of course, he knew that Chrissie was going to be hostile, that was her way ... their fight pattern, if you like. Whenever they had fallen out in the past, had an argument, she would be super-cool with him afterwards, and as soon as he'd calmed down and invariably realised what an arse he was being, he'd apologise. They'd talk it out, do something nice for each other, and they'd make up. That was the way it was. His dad, Rob, had shown him long ago that it was best to back down and be the appeaser – 'happy wife, happy life'; that's what Rob had always said. Sam remembered it clearly – Dad invariably in the back garden, his favourite domain, snipping some roses to take into the house for his mum, Linda, even though she'd been scolding him only moments earlier for not having done something or another exactly the way she liked it. But Rob never seemed to hold a grudge and always let it wash over him. Maybe that was the key to happiness, Sam had surmised, but he wasn't sure he managed it as well as his dad had. He and Chrissie had different ways of doing things – it wasn't always possible to keep the peace and maintain a state of continuous calm.

But Sam had tried hard, always apologising, even if he felt he was in the right – Chrissie could be very black and white, not always able to see things from the other person's perspective. So he'd pull Chrissie in close for a nice cuddle on the sofa, followed by making love as soon as Holly was asleep, and they would wedge the laundry basket behind their bedroom door so she couldn't barge in unannounced, as had happened one time when she was about three years old. Thankfully, she had still been young enough for them to pass off Chrissie bobbing up and down astride him, naked, as 'mummy dancing'. And they had giggled silently together like a pair of silly teenagers for ages over that afterwards, whenever Holly had asked to see 'mummy dancing' again.

Sam put the coffee mug on the kitchen counter and dropped his hands down by his sides, his heart sinking at the sadness of the current situation. He and Chrissie at loggerheads, no mummy dancing on the immediate horizon and their daughter upstairs bravely hiding her heartache. The feeling was quickly followed by an even greater determination to fix things.

'Please, Chrissie, I don't want to fight. Can we talk, properly? I'm back for goo—'

'It's too late for that,' she said quickly, as if instantly throwing up a brick wall to protect herself. Sam wasn't sure if she even really believed the words herself; it was as if she was saying them on autopilot, without conviction, just to keep him at a distance ... or maybe that was just wishful thinking on his part. 'Besides, now isn't a good time ...' Chrissie's eyes flicked to the watch on her left wrist.

'But I've just got back. I thought we could try and have some time together ...'

'There have been plenty of opportunities for us to have some time together over the last year. But you didn't take those chances, Sam.'

'But I'd like to now ... if you'll let me?' Sam tried.

They stood in silence momentarily, until Chrissie took a big breath, exhaled and then added, 'I honestly don't think there are any chances left.' She fixed her gaze on the kitchen floor tiles.

'Come on, Chris, that isn't fair. You know as well as I do that this job was 24/7. I was doing it for us. It was what we agreed.'

There was sadness in Chrissie's eyes now, as well as the anger, and her voice was more gentle as she spoke this time. 'No, Sam, I never agreed not to see you for months and months on end, and that isn't what you thought either. Why did you stay away so long? Why didn't you come back months ago when you knew I'd taken as much as I could? I still don't understand, and you gave me the impossible job of explaining it to Holly.'

Sam scraped his hands through his hair. Trying to find the right words. She was right; he knew that he was avoiding something, but he wasn't sure he could even explain it to himself, let alone Chrissie.

'Well?' Her eyes were full of questions. Ones he couldn't answer.

'I don't know.' They stared at each other. 'I just don't know the answer, Chrissie, but I'm trying to work it out – I want to work it out, you know how much you and Holly mean to me, don't you – how much I—'

But before he could tell Chrissie how much he loved her and Holly, how he desperately wanted to sort things out, she stepped towards him and placed the tips of her fingers over his mouth. 'Don't say it,' she whispered. 'Please. I can't bear it. You need to go back to Dolly's house now.'

Sam could feel the situation slipping away from him. He reached out to Chrissie but she gently pushed him away.

'Please don't send me away, Chris. You know how good we can be together,' he said, the desperation in his voice impossible to hide.

'I used to, Sam.' More silence followed. 'But now ...' She paused and briefly closed her eyes before carrying on, 'I'm not so sure.' Silence swung in the air between them like an enormous pendulum pushing them further and further apart. 'It's time to go,' Chrissie continued. 'Maybe you should take some time to really work out why you didn't come home until now.' She looked away. 'Because I'm not sure about anything any more.'

As Chrissie followed Sam towards the front door, both of them turned on seeing Holly standing on the stairs. They looked at each other, united briefly in concern in case their daughter had overheard the conversation..

'I don't want Dad to go!' Holly stated, her voice a mixture of petulance and fear.

'Dad *has* to go now, Holly. You've got your homework to finish.'

'But that's not fair. Dad has just come back and I got hardly any time at all with him.'

'Holly, will you please do as you've been asked?' Chrissie said tightly, fiddling with the crystal drop necklace that he and Holly had chosen together for her fortieth birthday. At least she was still wearing it – that was something, Sam thought, resisting the urge to play peacemaker; he didn't want to undermine Chrissie. He knew how much she hated that, trying to remember all the rules around bedtime or screen time; he'd always been useless at keeping on top of all the boundaries. But before either he or Chrissie could play their next move, Holly suddenly exploded.

'*Fine!* But I HATE you!' And then, after glaring at Chrissie, she shot back up the stairs to her bedroom, two at a time, and slammed the door, making the mini-chandelier hall light jangle precariously above them. Sam instinctively stepped towards the foot of the stairs and called after her.

'Come back here and apologise, you mustn't talk to Mum like that—'

'Just leave her, Sam.' Chrissie indicated with her head after Holly, before turning to look him in the eye. 'She doesn't mean it ... Besides, there's been a lot of that lately. I'm hoping it's just a phase and she'll grow out of it.'

'But she shouldn't say stuff like that to you. Or slam doors.'

'True.' Chrissie lifted her left shoulder. 'Maybe not. And having you around to tell her so every now and again might have been quite helpful, don't you think?'

Sam knew that Chrissie had a point. He hadn't been around to do his proper share of parenting. And, on top of everything else, this tension between her and Holly was another worrying development.

'Look, I'm sorry but I really need to get on ...' Chrissie glanced at her watch.

'Err ... OK,' Sam said, baffled by her distraction now. 'But we really need to spend some proper time together – tomorrow, the day after, any time,' he urged, keen to have a plan, however tentative...

'Yes ... we'll sort something out,' Chrissie said, quickly glancing at her watch again. *Why does she keep doing that? And why does she look so edgy now?* Sam followed her line of sight and saw her staring at the door.

And then a weird feeling shrouded him. He inhaled sharply. And then the proverbial penny dropped. He got it.

'Are you expecting someone?' he asked, turning to go.

Chrissie nodded quickly, as if keen all of a sudden to get rid of him as swiftly as possible. She even darted around him to pull open the front door, standing by it to make it absolutely clear that his time was up. Sam went to leave and then something inside him – a feeling, a hunch in the pit of his stomach, he wasn't sure, he couldn't quite put his finger on it, but whatever it was made him stop, abruptly.

Of course! The perfume, the lipstick, the new hairdo.

'Is it a bloke?'

Sam's heart lurched as he stared at her, willing the pulse in the side of his neck to stop flicking like an overcharged piston. But it was all too much to take in.

His wife?

Another man?

'Is that really any of your business?' Chrissie's face was hard to read, but Sam could feel a jumpy anger rising inside him, making his own face smart.

'Are you seeing someone else?' As soon as the words were out of his mouth, he hated how pathetic and whiny he sounded. He had to pull it back. Chrissie was never going to give him a second chance if he carried on like some kind of possessive teenage boy. But Sam often felt as if he was muddling through when it came to women and properly understanding them. His mother had always been the boss in their house when he'd been growing up, and sometimes unreasonably so. Yes, his dad had always been the peacemaker, but he had also pandered to her too, almost as if he was overly grateful to be her husband and would do whatever it took to keep her. As if he was punching above his weight. But Chrissie wasn't like his mum at all.

'I can't believe you have the nerve to ask me that question,' Chrissie said, clearly annoyed now too ... but she hadn't denied it.

Sam suddenly felt a strong urge to run, a feeling he always had when things were going badly. 'Look, I've gotta go. But we really need to talk.' He backed away before turning on his heel and setting off down the path towards his car.

Chrissie called something after him. But Sam couldn't really hear any more. He had to get away. Suddenly, he felt like a teenage boy again, out of his depth, making it up as he went along, trying to get it right.

Sam reached his car and, after quickly diving in and pulling the door closed, he sat for a second before letting his emotions spill over. His heart was pounding with panic and anger and fear and sadness ... Chrissie with another man. It didn't bloody bear thinking about. He loved her. And he was almost certain that she still loved him.

Or maybe not.

Maybe she had moved on already.

After willing himself to get a grip, he managed to

shove from his mind the thunderous thoughts of hunting the other man down and ripping his arms off. It could happen, the mood he was in now. But Sam wasn't a violent man, never had been. So he clenched his jaw and drove away, heading back to the five-bar gate that led to the fields behind the station. He knew where he was there. It was his spot, ever since he'd been old enough to cycle to it as a kid.

As he sat there, he tried to figure out how things had gone so catastrophically wrong between him and Chrissie, but the answers wouldn't come. He had thought things were bad before he came home, but he now realised ... they were much, much worse than he could ever have imagined.

Chapter Four

Holly Morgan swept the bedroom curtain aside and looked out down to the path. She pressed her hand to the window, wishing she could bang on the glass or, better still, push the window wide open and shout out after Dad. Beg him to come back. But the window was double-glazed and locked, plus he was gone and inside his car before she had a chance to do anything. She thought about going after him, but it was pitch black outside in the lane and across the fields. And Mum would only go mental if she caught her sneaking out instead of doing her homework. She felt her eyes fill with tears as she whispered, 'I still love you, Dad. And I know Mum does, deep down in her heart. She does, I'm sure of it – why else has she been really moody since you went away? Please come back and fix it. Tell Mum you love her, that you really do ... and then we can all be happy.'

After lifting her headphones from her head and scrubbing her face dry with the paw of a big white teddy bear, Holly lay down on her bed and stared at the ceiling, counting the numerous luminous rainbow and unicorn stickers, as she came up with a plan. If her parents were going to behave like children, then it was going to be down to her to be the mature one, the sensible grown-up around here. She wasn't a kid any more. She was a teenager. Thirteen years old, and that was practically an adult. She'd be able to drive a car in a few years' time. So she was pretty sure she could navigate her parents' marriage onto steadier ground.

Yes, her mind was made up. Holly leapt up off her bed and rummaged around in her desk drawer for a new pad. She had loads of half-used pads, mainly with stories in, she liked making up stories … usually about animals – she loved animals, or girls going on adventures to exotic, faraway places like the moon, or Hawaii, or even Antarctica. And sometimes she wrote magical, mythical stories about a magic unicorn called Lily. But this called for a brand-new pad. She retrieved a pen from her fluffy pencil case – a *Finding Dory* one with a big blue feather on the end – hmm, it was a bit babyish, but it would have to do under the circumstances, as there really was no time to waste.

It would be her birthday soon, and there was no way she was going to let it be ruined because they couldn't all be together at Granny Dolly's house like they always were every year. It was tradition. And it would be no fun at all if she was stuck at home with just Mum on her own, moaning about everything and bossing her around all the time like she had been ever since Dad first went away.

And Mum had been in a bad mood ever since Dad had missed her forty-first birthday. And it wasn't like Dad did it on purpose ... not coming home like he had promised. He couldn't help there being a last-minute emergency at work. Dad had explained it all, and he was so sorry, Holly could see for herself how upset he'd felt when she'd FaceTimed him. And also he had sent Mum the biggest bunch of flowers to make up for it. But Mum hadn't been the same since. Holly had overheard her on the phone to Auntie Jude, saying, 'he knew things were bad and he still didn't come back, not even for my birthday. I feel so let down, yet again.'

Ever since it had all gone wrong with Dad, Mum had been a nightmare to live with, and she didn't even try to remember Holly's feelings before saying mean stuff to Dad and upsetting him. *I bet that's what she did just now. Ruined it all ...* And Mum should also remember who pays for everything. If it wasn't for Dad, they'd have nothing, Holly surmised, glancing at the new iPhone in her hand, which Dad had sent her, and she absolutely loved. She had customised it with pink crystals. Then there was the computer on her desk, the TV/DVD player, iPad, laptop, and all her lovely shoes lined up by the wall near her wardrobe that Mum had bought for her ... using Dad's money. Exactly.

Holly opened the pad.

Get Mum and Dad Back Together in Time for My Birthday.

On the fifth of June.

She wrote the words at the top of the second page (she never used the first page, not ever, because it just ruined the whole pad) underlined the date and flipped the feather against the side of her nose as she thought about what to write next. *Yes! Good idea.*

Granny Dolly and Aunty Jude. Holly wrote down their names and underlined them. *They're bound to help me. Dad is her grandson, after all. And Aunty Jude, not that she's my real aunty, but she's Mum's best friend and was a bridesmaid at their wedding, so the last thing she will want is for them to split up properly. I know that for a fact as I heard Mum telling her on the phone about Dad coming home, but staying at Granny Dolly's house instead of coming here, and Aunty Jude had said it was such a shame. Mum had the phone on hands-free in the kitchen cos she was making some jam and it had just reached the 'crucial bit', she had said, where she daren't leave the saucepan unattended or it would boil over.*

Holly numbered the lines one to ten down the left-hand side of the page, figuring if she could come up with ten things that she could do to get her parents back together in time for her birthday, then that would be a brilliant start.

Send Mum a bunch of flowers. BUT write on the card that they are from Dad!

Send Dad some flowers. BUT write on the card that they are from Mum!

Holly wasn't sure about number two. Dad wasn't really the 'getting flowers delivered' to him type of man. No, she had better come up with something else. Beer. Or brandy – Dad likes 'three fingers full', as Granny Dolly always says on special occasions when she pours from the decanter on the sideboard into a tumbler. But Holly knew that would be hard to get. Even if she tried the supermarket on the industrial estate, they were bound to see she was too young to buy alcohol. She tried really hard to think of more ideas. A bag of wine gums ... hmm, not much of a present. Socks ... boring. Phone case. A good leather one would cost a lot. And it had to look like it had come from Mum. But she wouldn't buy Dad a new phone case after the way she just was with him.

A few seconds later, Holly had it. Chocolates! Yes, Dad seemed to love those sea-salt truffles from the sweet shop in town, the one in the square in the centre of Market Briar. She remembered how he had eaten nearly all of them in the box he bought for Mum on Valentine's Day about two years ago, the last time he had been properly home. Mum had teased him about it and they had laughed together, saying that he really wanted the chocolates for himself and that's why he had bought them for her. But that was when Mum was still being nice to him. Yes, it was the perfect present. And Dad might even think that Mum was thinking about that Valentine's Day and wanted to get back with him, so it would be a romantic thing too. Brilliant. Holly would buy some on Saturday when she went there on the bus with her best friend, Katie Ferguson. She could wrap them up and take them to Granny Dolly's house to give to Dad and pretend that Mum had sent them. To say sorry for being so horrible earlier on and sending him away. How evil is that?

And then Holly wondered if she should bother sending flowers to Mum from Dad. She wasn't sure Mum deserved them, after the way she had carried on ... And she must have said something really nasty to Dad before he left to make him nearly run down the path to get away from her. Holly wished she hadn't been watching a Zoella make-up tutorial on YouTube with her headphones on, because she'd been so angry with Mum. Maybe, if she'd been paying attention, listening on the landing or something, then she would have heard what had happened and could have done something to stop it all.

But it wasn't too late, she was convinced of that. And first thing tomorrow she was going to put her 'Get Mum and Dad Back Together in Time for My Birthday' plan into action. Obviously she'd have to come up with some more ideas, too, because just sending flowers and chocolates was a bit of a rubbish plan. But Aunty Jude was bound to have some really cool ideas ... she used to live in LA. And everyone knows that LA is the coolest place on earth. Apart from Disneyland, that's super-cool too. Holly hadn't been to either place; in fact, apart from visiting her dad in Singapore and Malaysia last year, there were so many places she still hadn't been to. But she'd Google-Earthed loads of towns all over the world and none of them was as nice as Singapore ... in fact, if Mum didn't stop being so angry at her all the time, then that could be her back-up plan. Go and live in Singapore with Dad. It had to be better than being here on her own with Mum in a rubbish mood all the time.

Holly looked at the page again and underlined the words 'Get Mum and Dad Back Together in Time for My Birthday'. That was her wish! Even though she was thirteen years old now and knew deep down that wishes probably weren't actually a real thing ... she still believed in them sometimes. Surely, if you wished hard enough, anything was possible? She had already wished for ages that Dad would come back home, and here he was! So, it could happen. It was just positive thinking and all that. They had a lesson about it at school. In Personal, Social and Health Education. Or PSHE as everyone said. All about mindfulness and the power of thought and focus. And *Pinocchio* was still one of her favourite Disney films. Especially the bit at the end with the 'When You Wish Upon a Star' song ... she loved singing along to it.

She remembered the first time she saw the film, on the sofa snuggled up in between Mum and Dad. They had watched it and sung along together with a big bowl of popcorn, which Mum used to make in the microwave, and then let her tip sprinkles all over it. This was before the diabetes, of course. And before Dad worked away all the time. Now Mum never wanted to watch Disney films. Perhaps if she did, then she'd chill out a bit and feel a whole lot happier, Holly surmised.

She thought of the *Pinocchio* song, going through the lyrics in her head. Pausing on the part about 'anything your heart desires will come to you'. And she knew this was what her heart desired … to get Mum and Dad back together! And it was her birthday soon … and you were never too old to blow candles out and make a wish. She wondered if she could have the wish early and use it right now.

Holly looked down at the words and double-under-lined them one more time. The Wish … Get Mum and Dad Back Together in Time for My Birthday.

Chapter Five

'You make me feel so young, you make me feel as though spring has sprung ...' Jude twirled her auburn curls up into a big bun and secured it with a hairband as she sang along heartily with Frank Sinatra on her Spotify playlist. She really was happy to be back in lovely Tindledale with Dad and her friends, relishing the earthiness and realness here, but she'd be lying if she said it hadn't also come as a bit of a shock. Back down to earth with a bump after all the fakery and full-on fast lane of her life in LA ... And she really missed her mum's cousin, Maggie. They had spoken on the phone last night and she could tell that Maggie was putting on a brave face, being stoic and selfless in telling her she slept well at night knowing Tony was happy having his daughter back. Dad had called Maggie shortly after she'd got home, to thank her for everything she had done for Jude, and especially for bringing Mum's memory alive. Also for the keepsake box that Maggie had entrusted Jude to give to him. The box had been her mum's, and inside were notes and cards that Dad had given her when they'd first started courting. A pressed rose secreted between the pages of a pamphlet advertising the first dance he took her to in the old ballroom in Market Briar. Even a faded old photograph of them both cuddled together under a tree on the village green. It had near taken his breath away, he had said, when he saw it all.

Jude wandered across the shop and rearranged the scented candle display for the trillionth time. Business had been slow for the first week since she'd opened and she had spent most of her time either knitting yet another square to add to the pile waiting to be stitched together to make a blanket, as that was the extent of her knitting skills. Or moving cushions and candles from one side of the shop to the other. But, in contrast to the last few days' weather, the sun was shining today, bathing the narrow, cobbled lanes and surrounding fields full of springy white lambs in a warm, golden glow. So the lovely villagers of Tindledale were either supping ice-cold beer in the Duck & Puddle pub garden, or on the village green paddling in the pond and not bothering themselves with shopping of any kind.

Just as Jude wondered if she'd made a mistake in opening the shop here, and maybe should have focused on selling antiques online, as that part of the business was thriving as it always had done, the phone rang.

'Darling Antiques and Interiors,' she answered cheer-fully, practically falling on the phone, such was the novelty of it actually ringing during business hours. It often rang shortly after five when she had turned the sign on the door to CLOSED, but typically it was her dad, Tony, asking if she wanted a lift home, or Chrissie to see if she fancied a glass of Prosecco and a catch-up. Which reminded her, she wanted to call in on Chrissie later to see how things had gone with Sam. Chrissie had told her that he was coming back and that they were going to be seeing each other for the first time in ages. Jude wished she could understand where things had gone wrong between Chrissie and Sam. They had so much going for them. Of course, no marriage was perfect, and they were quite different people. Chrissie was much steadier than Sam, who Jude secretly thought was a bit of a dreamer; a carefree, creative, surfer type, if they'd lived near the sea. She could see him now in a pair of shades, sliders on his feet, a MacBook under his arm and lots of ideas. He was an accomplished architect, but had always been a bit unfocused. That was until the last few years when he'd really thrown himself into work, especially after Holly's diabetes was diagnosed. Jude wondered if that was where the connection was? She couldn't even begin to imagine how it must feel to have your thirteen-year-old daughter with a serious condition like diabetes; it was hardly surprising that it had put a strain on their marriage.

Jude let out a long breath and shook her head, as if to create a feeling of equilibrium once more.

'What?' A gruff male voice asked to open the conversation, bringing her back to the moment and the telephone call.

'Pardon?' she replied, taken aback.

'Is that the antique shop?' the man demanded in a London accent.

'Yes.'

'Are you sure?'

'Err, yes, quite sure,' Jude confirmed, wondering if this was some kind of prank call.

'But you just called me darling—'

'No I didn't.'

'Yes, you did!'

'Darling is my name and I sell antiques and ... things for interiors such as—'

'What kind of a name is that?' the man cut in rudely. 'Are you having me on?' He sounded as if he might be laughing at her. Jude contemplated hanging up, but before she could decide, he added, 'Can you come and see me? I might have some work for you.'

'Depends,' she said, not missing a beat.

'*Depends!* What sort of way is that to talk to a potential customer?'

'The sort of way that means ... I don't know who you are, or what work you would like me to do. So, until I have that information, I can't decide if I want to come and see you.'

Silence followed. Jude caught sight of her face in the gilt-framed mirror on the wall near the little desk where the phone was and mouthed 'idiot' to herself. He might be cocky and rude and making fun of her name, but here was a potential customer. That's what he had said, and she was being flippant. 'Err, what I actually meant was,' she quickly pulled back the conversation, 'how can I help you?'

'That's better!' And he actually laughed again. A big belly laugh this time. Jude hated him immediately. 'So will you come or not?' She looked again at her face, her cheeks all flushed and florid like two bruised tomatoes. How dared he? Who the hell did he think he was? And then, as if telepathically accessing her mind, he announced, 'I'm Myles King. Rock legend! Will that do you?'

A short silence followed. 'You've probably heard of me ...' More silence. Jude's jaw dropped. There had been a rumour going around in the village. Her dad had told her last night over drinks in the pub that the megastar of the Noughties, albeit faded now, had bought the old Blackwood Farm Estate. Lord Lucan (not the infamous one who disappeared all those years ago, of course) and his wife, Marigold, had sold the estate and retired into the lodge house at the edge of the wildflower meadow, for a slower pace of life.

'Can't say I have,' she said nonchalantly, unable to resist. Of course she'd heard of Myles King. Everyone had.

And here he was on the end of her phone proclaiming to be a 'potential customer'. But she'd seen it all before in LA. The obnoxious behaviour and oversized egos.

'Where have you been then? Living in a cave?' Myles chortled at his own joke. 'Or, oh don't tell me … you haven't been banged up, have you? But then again, I thought they let you have radios and tellies in there for good behaviour.'

Jude exhaled, willing herself to get a grip. 'Namaste. Namaste,' she chanted over and over inside her head, as she been taught to do by her yoga teacher back in LA, for when dealing with unexpected 'moments of heightened stress'. But, feeling like an utter arse, she promptly stopped, balling her free hand into a boxer's fist instead, perfectly poised to land a right hook.

'When would you like me to come and see you?' She almost choked on the words, before adding, 'Mr King,' as sweetly as she could muster.

'Now. See you in ten.' And the line went dead. Jude stared at the receiver, just like they do in films when somebody hangs up unexpectedly, as she got her head around what had just happened. *Is he for real? Talk about rude. And entitled. And pleased with himself.* She'd never heard anything like it. And she had met some very high-maintenance characters in her time, travelling around the world working with exceedingly wealthy clients, some of whom seriously thought manners were just for the minions and not something that they needed to be bothered with at all.

But she had to admit that her curiosity had been well and truly piqued. Plus, she really couldn't afford to pass by an opportunity to get her fledging business off the ground. So, she reluctantly blew out the fabulously fragranced candle, slipped her handbag over her shoulder and scooped Lulu off an armchair and into her arms.

After putting the *Be Back Soon* sign in place and locking the shop door behind her, she headed over to the Duck & Puddle pub to track down Tony. He was bound to be in there with his best mate, Barry, owner of the locksmith and hardware shop, with it being a Saturday afternoon. If she was lucky, he wouldn't have started on his second pint, so would be in a position to give her a lift in his van down the lane to the Blackwood Farm Estate. But she knew she would need to be quick – Tony and Barry had been friends since school, in other words, donkeys' years. So when they got going in the pub, there was no stopping them from reminiscing about the much-feted 'good old days', when nothing bad ever happened in Tindledale. Or so their respective memories seemed utterly convinced of. When, in actual reality, those days were most likely pretty much the same as – or similar to – how they were now. Tindledale was hardly a buzzing metropolis at the sharp edge of popular culture, always one step ahead of the current trends.

An hour later, and Jude had just got off the bus at the nearest stop to the entrance of the estate. Tony hadn't been in the pub. 'Got called away to sort out a potential leaky pipe over in the village hall,' Cher, the pub landlady, had told Jude as she put his silver tankard back behind the bar for later. So, after trekking back across the village green, and past the paddlers by the duck pond, Jude had just missed the bus. *On the hour every hour.* She cursed herself for forgetting this important reality of growing up in the countryside, whilst marvelling at how some things never change, especially in the sleepy, rural idyll of Tindledale. She'd then had to wait for the next bus, all the while vowing to buy a car as soon as possible, which wouldn't be any time soon, seeing as she had sunk all her cash into getting the shop up and running.

She gingerly went to push open the mildew-covered old wooden gates at the entrance to the estate, then thought better of it on seeing how dilapidated they were. The gate on the right-hand side was half hanging off the hinges. So she stepped through the little arched side entrance that was barely bigger than a Hobbit's front door and went to put Lulu down on the soft grass. But the pampered pooch sniffed around disapprovingly, probably getting a whiff of the crusty, dried-up cowpats dotted around, and promptly went to scrabble her way back up Jude's jean-clad legs in a bid not to get her carefully groomed paws dirty.

'Oh, come on then, you spoilt madam,' Jude laughed as she helped Lulu up and under her arm. 'I'm going to have to get you one of those pet carriers if you keep on like this.'

'What are you doing?' A blowsy woman appeared from behind a hedge and stood squarely in front of Jude, making her jump. Lulu growled and bared her little teeth. Wearing a tweed skirt and a navy padded waistcoat, with a peacock print headscarf over a thatch of static grey hair, the woman struck a formidable pose. And with her ruddy complexion as she clasped a clipboard to her ample bosom, she looked as if she'd just stepped out of a Thelwell cartoon.

'I'm here to see Myles,' Jude smiled keenly as she batted a persistent bumblebee from her face.

'What's your name?' the woman demanded, consulting her clipboard.

'Jude Darling.'

A short silence ensued.

'Are you sure?' The Thelwell woman stared for a second, before frowning.

'Err, yes. Quite sure.' Jude sighed inwardly, wondering if Dad had a point after all. But back in LA nobody had ever batted an eyelid over her unusual surname, so she had kind of forgotten about it, to be honest. 'So adorable. Quaint. And like totally British,' is what they had said over there.

'Well then, that's a nice name. Very jolly.' And the woman actually smiled, which momentarily threw Jude, given her sudden switch in temperament.

'Oh, thank you.'

But the thaw was short-lived when the woman snapped, 'Sorry, you're not down here, I haven't had any notification of your visit,' and tapped the clipboard. 'I can't let you anywhere near the house if you haven't been booked in. I'll have to ask you to leave.' The woman gestured with her hand for Jude to go back the way she had come, in through the Hobbit door.

'But, Myles ... ' Jude's voice came out way too high, so she paused, swallowed, and then continued calmly, 'Mr King just called me and asked me to come to see him. I'm a bit late. I was going to get my dad to give me a lift down here, but he couldn't and then I missed the bus and ... well, I'm here now.'

'Hmm, sure he did,' the woman smiled dismissively, reverting back to her frosty setting. 'Come on now, my dear, you really do need to leave.'

'It's true!' Jude folded her arms, irritated that she seemed to have wasted her time on quite frankly the rudest man she had ever spoken to. And no guesses as to who this woman was – his mother, no doubt, must be, given that she was just as rude. It was clearly a family trait.

'My dear, if I had a penny for every time a girl like you had tried that one on just to get inside and up close to Mr King, then I certainly wouldn't be standing here, dodging the cowpats, talking to you. Certainly not. I would be sipping a Dubonnet and gin cocktail on the deck of a yacht moored somewhere on the banks of an Italian hideaway. Good day to you!' And the woman went to walk away. How bizarre. Jude stared after her, slack-jawed and furious. Then, after swiftly reuniting her chin with the rest of her face, she hoisted Lulu firmly under her arm and dashed after the woman, determined to salvage something from the trip. She had paid out for the bus fare, not to mention her time spent away from the shop, which could quite possibly have consequences for her fledgling business – like losing paying customers if she wasn't there to actually serve them. Well, maybe ... if she was really lucky, but that wasn't the point. She had come here in good faith, and was damn well going to see Myles King, even if meant fighting this tedious woman right here in the garden.

'Wait,' Jude said, and the woman turned. 'Please, check again. He really did call. I'm Jude Darling from Darling Antiques and Interiors in the village. My shop is in the High Street ... Tindledale High Street.' Jude tried to get a look at the clipboard, but it was no use, the woman was having none of it and immediately pulled a walkie-talkie from the pocket of her padded waistcoat. 'Yes, please do call him, I'm sure Myles will be able to clear up this misunderstanding.'

Jude pressed her spare hand around Lulu's little chest, inwardly cursing herself for forgetting to bring her shades or indeed slather herself in SPF cream as she always did back in LA. But she had forgotten how changeable the British weather could be and the sun was dazzling out here in the open grounds of the estate. Her fair, freckly complexion was already starting to warm up. And Lulu was panting over-dramatically, as if she was about to keel over from dehydration. Plus Jude could feel a dampness on the arm she had underneath Lulu's bottom, which felt suspiciously like she had relieved herself. Oh no. That was all Jude needed. To turn up to her first potential commission with an incontinent dog in tow.

'Security?' the woman bellowed into the walkie-talkie and Jude's heart sank. Not only had Myles King wasted her time, but she was now also about to be arrested, or whatever it was security personnel did to intruders on private estates.

'OK. I'll go,' Jude conceded, plonking Lulu on the ground, and holding up the palms of her hands before trudging towards the Hobbit door. Then she stopped and turned, 'But you can tell Myles King to expect an invoice for my time ... which he has wasted!' She nodded, pleased with herself for remaining professional, but then ruined it all by adding, 'and the bus fare. Both ways!' She cringed as she pointed a sweaty index finger at the woman, before quickly shoving it inside the pocket of her jeans to mask the ominous whiff of dog wee that was now permeating the air between them.

Jude had just stepped back out through the Hobbit door, when she bumped right into Sam.

'Hey, Jude!' Jude could immediately see, despite his face lighting up when he saw her, that he was tired, with dark circles under his eyes. He looked gaunt, as if he had the weight of the world on his shoulders. Which he did, of course, with his marriage in tatters. Chrissie said they had talked but it hadn't gone that well. He'd accused her of seeing someone and that things had been tense. Jude wondered if she should say something to him about it. But what? She wasn't sure if she should – not here, when he was coming to work – Chrissie had said he told her a few weeks ago that his next contract was back in Tindledale on the estate, but she had also told Jude that she would need to see it to believe it. And it was his personal business, after all. And what if it opened the floodgates? But they had known each other a long time and were friends. Maybe she could help; perhaps she could do something to try to repair their marriage. Mediate somehow. Anything to bring her dearest and oldest friends back together again.

'Sam!' Jude gave him an enormous hug, being careful to keep the damp patch on her arm from touching him, just in case. 'It's so good to see you. And I'm really pleased that you're back. How are you?' she asked, figuring positivity was best, and she certainly didn't want Sam thinking she blamed him or was taking Chrissie's side. No, she was here for both of them, Holly too. And would do whatever she could to see a once-happy family put back together again.

'Not too bad, been better. But, it's good to be back … to sort things out, with a bit of luck.' He didn't elaborate, but Jude knew exactly what he meant. Sam never had been one for long, emotional conversations, and now certainly wasn't an appropriate moment to discuss things further in any case.

'I know, Sam,' Jude said softly, placing her hand on his arm. 'But you're home now.'

'You're right. And thanks, Jude. It's great to have you here too. It'll make a massive difference to Chrissie, and to Holly. You're just what they need right now.'

'Anytime.' Jude looked at the grass, and then back up at Sam. 'And you. We're friends as well, remember.'

She loved Sam. With Chrissie being like the sister she never had, she had always seen Sam in a similar way, a bit like a brother. And so she cared about him too. Plus, she knew how good he was for Chrissie – they had been so happy together for a long time, before their marriage came apart at the seams. If she could help them stitch it back together again, then she would do it. Whatever it took.

'Thanks.' He nodded. They had known each other since primary school, and her dad, Tony, had been friends with Sam's dad, Rob, before he died. Tony was still close to Rob's mum, Dolly, and had always looked out for Sam, her grandson, sometimes stepping in for Rob when Dolly had thought a dad's influence had been required over the years. Jude remembered when Sam had got roaring drunk in the Duck & Puddle pub on his eighteenth birthday, and had ended up nearly drowning in the village pond after larking about in a makeshift boat made out of an old dustbin. Dolly had called Tony in to have a proper chat with Sam about responsible drinking. And how not to make an absolute idiot of yourself in front of the whole village, who had turned out to see him staggering and gasping for air, as he battled the bin off his head and waded back to the pond's bank, before collapsing on the grass and throwing up all over the place. So Jude felt it important to try to keep as much of an open mind as she could regarding Chrissie and Sam's marriage difficulties. She'd been around long enough to know that there were always two sides to everything, plus nobody really ever knows what other people's personal relationships are like.

Sam reached down to give Lulu a stroke. Surprisingly, she let him, and then even rewarded him with a quick lick on the back of his hand.

'Ooh, she likes you. Lulu mostly growls at people, or simply ignores them.' Jude rolled her eyes and shook her head in exasperation.

'In that case, I'm flattered,' Sam said with a small smile. 'So, what are you doing here?'

'Well, I had come to see Myles King, but ...' Jude lowered her voice in case the woman was still within earshot, 'that battle-axe of a gatekeeper won't let me in.'

'Ahh, yes, so he called you then?' He smiled and nodded.

'He did! But how do you know?'

'I recommended you. Dolly told me all about your new venture in the High Street, and Myles is looking for some help with furnishings, artwork, interiors stuff and suchlike, so ... well, here you are.'

'Ahh, thanks Sam. That's really kind of you.'

'You're welcome. Always happy to help out a mate if I can. Talking of which, here ... take these, you're squinting.' And Sam pulled a pair of shades from his breast pocket and went to hand them to her.

'Oh, no, I can't take your sunglasses,' Jude said, thinking, typical Sam, generous as always, he'd give you the shirt off his back if you let him. Just a shame he didn't equate his time as being as important as material things ... Chrissie had often said that Sam loved spoiling her and Holly, but when it came to just turning up or being there, being present in the moment, which he invariably wasn't, he didn't seem to think that was such a big deal.

'OK, if you're sure.' Sam reluctantly pushed the shades

back inside his pocket. 'So, how come she won't let you in?'

'Must think I'm a fangirl or a gold-digger.' Jude shrugged, and Sam laughed.

'Come on, I'll sort it out.' He motioned for Jude to step back though the Hobbit door.

'I thought I'd told you to go!' The woman practically pounced on Jude.

'Sylvia.' Sam swiftly took control. 'This is Jude, from Darling Antiques and Interiors. I recommended her to Myles, and he called her this afternoon ...'

'It's true, Sylvia. He did, just like I said.' Jude side-stepped around Sam and grinned.

'Hmm. Well, if no one gives me her name then I can't let her in.' Sylvia eyed Jude up and down, as if seeing her properly for the first time. She then turned back to Sam. 'You do understand, don't you, Sam? You see, it's more than my job is worth ... Myles is very fastidious about me apprehending ...' Sylvia coughed and stepped in a little closer before adding, 'groupies!' Jude inhaled sharply, thinking what a charmer Myles must be. Not.

'I assure you I'm not a groupie. In fact, I've never hassled a pop star for a selfie in my entire life, thank you ver—'

'Look, I'm sure this is just a misunderstanding,' Sam cut in. 'Why don't you call Myles, or better still let's go to the house and find him, and I'll explain. I can introduce Jude properly then.'

'Stay there.' Sylvia whipped out the walkie-talkie again, pressed a button, and within a few seconds Myles was on the line and she had asked him about Jude.

'Yes, that's right. Bring her in.' A short crackly silence followed.

'Right you are.' Sylvia snapped the button to end the call. After stowing the walkie-talkie back inside her pocket, she muttered, 'He really is *quite* hopeless some-times!' before marching off towards the main house, her sturdy brown brogues snapping furiously through the crusty, cowpat-covered grass. Jude scooped up Lulu and scarpered after Sylvia, eager to get inside to take a look at the most obnoxious man on the planet.

Chapter Six

Sam threw his jacket onto the back seat of the car. It had been the first really warm day since he'd come home and he could feel summer in the breeze. It was nothing like the heat of Singapore, of course, but he'd always loved summertime in Tindledale when the village looked its best. He was looking forward to seeing the gardens in full bloom, the fields festooned with a rainbow of wild flowers, a nice cold pint in the pub garden, the kids queuing to get a 99 from the ice-cream van on the village green ... he'd grown up with it all. And it felt really good to be back home.

But there was something missing today. Perhaps it was being with Myles on the Blackwood Estate – he was certainly an interesting guy, a bit out there perhaps, but Sam could sense that the man was lonely and direction-less. He seemed to spend all his time rattling about in that big house by himself, surrounded by gadgets. And the thought had crossed Sam's mind ... what if he ended up like that too? After pondering for a moment, he shuddered, not wanting to explore the reality of a life like that.

Puffing out a big breath of air, as if to shift the thoughts of doom and gloom, Sam pulled out his phone and called Chrissie. They really needed to talk.

'Hiya,' she said on answering and, despite his anxiety, Sam smiled. She sounded upbeat and he had always loved the sound of her voice ... soft and rich, comforting too, like a smooth spoonful of warm, runny honey.

'Hey, Mrs Morgan,' he replied, slipping into his old habit of calling her that; he simply couldn't help it. She didn't answer, but Sam was sure he could hear a smile somewhere in the silence between them.

'Look. I'm sorry about the other night, Chrissie. I didn't want us to get off on a bad footing.' He meant it. He'd had time to think about things and he realised that whatever was going on in her life, he still needed to keep a cool head. He hoped he'd got things wrong about there being another man. *Please let me be wrong*, he had prayed. But deep down he still trusted her to be honest with him.

'I know. And I didn't either, Sam,' she started. 'But you can't expect just to turn up and for things to be the way you want them to be.' There was a short silence.

'I understand,' Sam trod carefully. 'But I need to see you, just the two of us, let's talk about things together – try to find a way through. We owe it to each other, surely.' He was pushing his luck a bit there, knowing that she was likely to throw his prolonged absence back at him, but to his surprise she didn't.

'Just give me a bit of time, Sam. We can talk, but I'm

not ready. My feelings feel muddled ... seeing you again is ... really hard.' And there it was, a small chink of hope amidst the gloom. 'Anyway, I need to focus on Holly right now ... her health.' Chrissie hesitated.

'What's happened? Is she OK?' he felt the familiar shot of fear through his stomach.

'I honestly don't know, Sam ... her bloods haven't been great; her blood sugar is all over the place and she's been having more tests.' He could hear the tight anxiety in his wife's voice.

'But how long has this been going on? And why didn't you tell me?' he reacted accusingly, as a mask for his own anxiety.

'It's hardly something I could just blurt out in a long-distance phone call!' Chrissie reacted right back. 'Besides, you know how strained things have been. We've barely spoken to each other properly for so long now. And the last time you promised to call on Skype, I waited for over half an hour ... and you know it wasn't the first time you've let me down.'

Sam felt a hot anger itch its way into his own voice.

'If Holly was ill, I'd have come straight home. You know that,' he said.

'No!' Chrissie had raised her voice now. 'No, I didn't know that. I can't rely on you any more and haven't been able to for a long time.'

'OK, fair enough. But you could have told me when

I came to see you and Holly. Why didn't you? Or were you in too much of a rush to go out?'

'That's not fair! I wasn't in a rush. It's like I said before, you can't just turn up and ...' She paused, and Sam heard her take a deep breath, as if bracing herself for more conflict. But he didn't want to fight. And he was beginning to wonder if calling had been a good idea. All he seemed to be doing was antagonising her further. 'Anyway, it's tricky to talk about in front of Holly,' Chrissie cut into his thoughts. 'You know how she is when it comes to the diabetes ... it's hardly her favourite topic of conversation.'

Sam fell silent, knowing that his anger was misplaced. It was his anger at Holly's condition that was making him snappy. He'd always struggled with it ... the sadness and frustration at his little girl getting such a raw deal and there being nothing he could do about it. He'd often wished that he could take the diabetes away and have it himself instead of her ... he would gladly have done so without a moment's hesitation.

He swallowed hard and tried again, keen to turn the phone call around.

'I'm sorry, Chris, I'm not blaming you. I'm really not ...'

'Well, our feelings don't matter right now.' Her barriers had gone back up. 'I just need to be on the ball for Holly.'

'*We* do ... *we* need to be on the ball, Chris,' he reminded her.

'I know what I meant,' she retorted, sharply.

Sam felt the situation slipping away from him again. A familiar feeling of being at sea, where the tide dragged him out, his limbs flailing against the strong current as he desperately tried to swim back to the shore and onto steadier ground.

'So what happens now?' he asked, still battling the surging tide inside his head as he also tried to come up with a solution to fix everything.

'I ...' Chrissie started, and then corrected herself, '*We* ... just have to wait for the test results ... And, in the meantime, we keep a close eye on Holly.'

*

'There you go, love. Sit yourself up over here.' Back at Dolly's cottage, Sam settled into the cosy patchwork-covered armchair next to Beryl, aka the buttercup-yellow Aga, as Dolly handed him a cup of tea and a plate with a very large and delicious-looking homemade slice of Victoria sponge heaped upon it. 'You look shattered. That'll be all that tramping out and about through the sprawling grounds on the Blackwood Estate.' She tutted and shook her head. 'Never mind, you'll get a bit of time off work soon enough for the annual May Fair on the bank holiday. That reminds me, will Chrissie and Holly be coming over this year for Holly's birthday tea? Only, I didn't want to assume ... not with everything that has gone on. And I was wondering about Tony, well, and Jude too, now that she's back home. I know he's been coming to us for years on all the special occasions like Christmas, bank holidays and birthdays, what with him being on his own ... and he was friends with your dad so it's always been lovely having a bit of a reminisce over the years. But with Jude being Chrissie's friend, it might be a bit awkward if she isn't coming and ...' Dolly paused to ponder on the situation, creasing her forehead and fiddling with her silvery grey hair. 'Maybe I'll get in all the ingredients for a lovely afternoon tea in any case, and then at least we'll be properly prepared whatever happens. Holly has been talking about wanting to do afternoon tea for ages ... I think it's quite the rage these days with the young girls. We could have scones with jam and cream, diabetic options of course! And sausage rolls, dainty sandwiches, mini-quiches – and she was showing me rainbow candyfloss on that YouTube film show too ... but that might be full of sugar. Oh well, I'd best get planning ...' She stopped talking suddenly and gave her grandson's shoulder a reassuring squeeze. 'Oh dear, I'm sorry son, I let myself get carried away without a second thought to how you might be feeling about the state of things between you and Chrissie ...'

Sam took a gulp of the tea as a distraction. But it was no use; he couldn't stop his left eyelid from twitching as he desperately willed the scratchiness in the back of his throat to bugger off. Jesus, what on earth was wrong with him? He felt like crying he was that miserable, which was unlike him. Usually he was pretty good at going with the flow, trusting that the good stuff will win out, but with Holly it was completely different. He didn't think he would ever forget the diagnosis of Type 1 Diabetes. The feeling of ice in his stomach and the lurch in his chest as the doctor in the hospital delivered the devastating bombshell that would change Holly's life forever.

He knew it was from his side of the family. Sam's dad, Rob, had been diabetic, and that was why Holly had it – hereditary factors, the doctor had said. Their daughter would be insulin-dependent for the rest of her life. The doctor had talked on, the words barely registering in Sam's mind, saying stuff like 'developments in research are moving so fast' and 'there are now more efficient ways to manage the illness'. But all he could think of were the complications that could happen, the stress on her organs and the rest of her body, the things that could go wrong.

His father, Rob, had been a brilliant bloke, whom Sam had thought the world of, the best dad ever, but it still broke Sam's heart that he had been taken too soon. Sam had been just a boy, younger than Holly was now, when his dad had died, and he had never really come to terms with losing him. He wished his dad was still around, so that he could turn to him now. Rob had always seemed to know the right thing to say.

And Rob had always been there. Sam certainly had no memory of his dad ever going away, not for a weekend, or even to a football match followed by a night in the pub with his mates; he wasn't that type of bloke. Family first – that had been one of his mottos. So unlike his mother, Linda, who would give Cruella De Vil a run for her money. Yes, Sam's dad had been the type of man who had done everything he could for his family. Wasn't that what Sam had been trying to do: be the provider, the man who looked after his family? Just like Rob had.

And the look in Chrissie's eyes when they got the news sitting there in the doctor's office at the hospital. Blame. Written all over her face. She didn't say anything, of course, but that was what she must have been feeling. She had still been unable to make eye contact with him when the doctor had sat back in his chair, made a steeple with his fingers and observed that, 'An earlier diagnosis would have been advantageous.'

Sam knew, knew deep down, that he should have considered it a possibility earlier. He should have realised what was wrong as soon as Holly got ill – the tummy aches, the headaches, the getting up in the night to go to the loo, and then her being too tired to go to school the next day, being thirsty all the time. Until Holly experienced her first hypo, he had passed off her getting up in the night as messing around, assuming she was angling for a day off school to hang out down by the river in Violet Wood, just like he had done at her age. If he had been more vigilant, then maybe Chrissie wouldn't have felt so let down.

If Sam had been on the ball, had involved himself more in Holly's care, in the day-to-day minutiae of their family life, instead of burying his head in the sand and thinking mostly about himself and his work, then maybe he would have spotted it. Not maybe – yes, he would have spotted it. But he didn't. He hadn't been there when he should have been; hadn't seen the warning signs, so that was his fault too.

'Want to talk about it?' Dolly asked gently, sinking down into the chair opposite him. Sam took a deep breath, sighed it out and stared into his tea as he pushed a big wedge of jammy sponge into his mouth. 'Better out than in,' she coaxed, in direct contrast to the sponge cake, which was very much better in than out, Sam mused miserably as he savoured the comforting sweetness. 'Come on, let it all out, love – why didn't you come back before now, you know … to sort things out?'

Sam put the mug and plate on the side before pushing a hand through his hair. 'I wish I could explain it, Gran. But after Holly was diagnosed, I just felt like I was in the way. Chrissie seemed to have it all under control. I felt useless, a bit like a spare part, getting in the way and making it all worse, when it was all my ... well, you know I've always been rubbish at that sort of thing.'

Dolly reached out a pale, age-weathered hand to him, her diamond engagement ring above her gold wedding band still glinting proudly as the early evening sun bounced off the kitchen table. 'You must let go of this guilt, Sam. I know it's still eating away at you. Life deals out these horrible things sometimes, but no one's to blame. We just have to get on with it, and that's that.'

'That's what I was trying to do, Gran, get on with it ... keep working, keep going.'

'Keep going? Or burying your head in the sand?' Dolly topped his tea up from the big knitted-cosy-covered teapot, letting the question sink in.

Sam picked up the plate, took another bite of the cake and looked up at Dolly's lined but still beautiful face. Dolly, who had been more of a proper mum to him than his own mother, Linda, ever had.

When his dad had died, Dolly had been stoic, forging ahead with the funeral arrangements for her only son, Rob. She had even looked after Sam and Patrick, full time, in the days following, when their mum, Linda, had taken herself off on a holiday to Spain, supposedly 'to deal with it on her own', or so she had said at the time. But how come Sam had found a pile of photographs in a shoebox some years later, of her sunbathing, smiling and sipping cocktails with a big group of people he didn't even recognise?

Linda ... the mother who'd barely batted an eyelid when he'd got into trouble at school for bunking off, who would rather sit at her kidney-shaped dressing table applying lipstick than make sure he and Patrick had breakfast before they went to school. Once their dad was gone, there had never been much food in the house and the last time Sam had pinched a bun from the baker's basket outside the shop in the High Street, he'd very nearly been caught. If his brother Patrick hadn't distracted the woman who worked in the bakery shop then he would have ended up at the police house on the far side of village green for sure.

After that, Sam had invariably bunked off school, figuring it was far easier than trying to concentrate with an aching, empty stomach ... counting the hours until he could pass by his gran's on the way home for his tea. A cheese doorstep sandwich, a big slice of chocolate or fruitcake and a packet of Smith's crisps in front of his favourite television programme, *Crackerjack*. He and Pat would put off going home for as long as possible, knowing that their tea at Dolly's was likely to be all they would get until after school the following day. He suspected that Dolly knew this too as she would often pack a sausage roll or two in their satchels – he was also vaguely aware of arguments on the phone after he and Pat had gone to bed and his mother's raised voice exhorting Dolly to mind her own business. But now it was all muddled up in a miserable jumble of sad memories of his childhood years.

Meeting Chrissie was the first time he remembered being really happy since his father had died. And when they'd had Holly, he had a burning wish to make sure she would never feel the same as he had as a child: to have to go without meals, or to miss out on a full education because no one cared. Patrick had built a new life for himself as far away from his mother as he could get, in Australia. Too far for Linda, who had hardly ever been back to Tindledale since taking herself off to live in London. But what about Holly? She was going without now. Going without two parents pulling together.

'Any chance of something stronger, Gran?' Sam lifted his empty mug as he tried to process all his thoughts. Dolly gave him a look.

'Come on now, Sam. Alcohol isn't the answer. Tea was good enough for your dad at dinnertime and it will be good enough for you.' Sam gave her a mock salute.

'You're the boss.'

Dolly batted him gently.

'Now stop mucking about!' she pretended to admonish. 'And think about what you're going to do to make things right with you and Chrissie? Marriage is a marvellous thing, but you need to work at it. Put the effort in,' she added, glancing at her own engagement and wedding rings.

'And I fully intend to do just that. I'm going to be here, Gran,' he said with resolve. 'I'm going to really be here for Chrissie and Holly. And I'm going to try and work it out myself, so I don't mess it up again – if they'll give me another chance.'

Dolly took the now empty mug from his hands before standing behind him and putting her arms around his back to hold him in a hug. Silence followed and Sam had to swallow hard a few times to stop his emotions from bubbling up and swirling his eyes with tears.

'It will be OK,' Dolly eventually said, very softly. 'You're home, for starters. That has to make things easier,' she told him, echoing Jude's sentiment from earlier. 'You didn't have a hope of talking to Chrissie properly from the other side of the world. It's just not the same, son. A woman wants the closeness. To see your face in front of her in the room. Not on a screen, or just to hear your voice down a phone line.'

'You know, Chrissie still won't see me properly, just the two of us.' Sam shook his head. 'And I know she and Holly aren't getting on. It's such a mess.'

'But you have to give her time. Remember what I said about not expecting too much too quickly. This situation between the two of you didn't happen overnight, and it's not going to be fixed overnight either. For what it's worth, I know Chrissie does still love you.'

'Do you really think so?' Sam asked. 'You'd tell me if she was seeing someone else, wouldn't you?'

'Why on earth would you say that?' Dolly frowned.

'I dunno. It's just the other night when I saw her … well, she looked really great, dressed up and with perfume on. And the effort wasn't intended for me. She kept looking at her watch and couldn't wait to get rid of me. She was expecting someone. Someone she didn't want me to see, I reckon.'

'Don't be daft.'

'Why daft? I didn't imagine it.'

'Well, you know how people talk in the village. Not to be mean, I should add.' Dolly patted her hair. 'But we all tend to know everyone's business, and I'm sure someone would have mentioned something to me. None of that matters anyway; you know that old adage, if something is worth fighting for …' She inhaled sharply before letting a long breath of wisdom out as she moved her head from side to side. 'You must stop feeling sorry for yourself and take action. Arrange a date with Chrissie properly. Have a look at what went wrong, and work out what you need to do – both of you; you're in this together and you both need to be honest. And, in the meantime, Holly has a family who all love her and we'll make sure she is OK while you two sort things out.' Dolly smiled. 'Your dad always used to say, "A father carries photos where his money used to be." Family is what counts, Sam.'

Sam smiled, this had always been her way. Pragmatic with a no-nonsense approach.

They were interrupted by the old-fashioned bell jangling in the front porch.

'You sit there, Gran, I know who this is.' Sam bounded out to the doorway like an excited puppy and a few seconds later Holly was in the kitchen with an enormous grin on her face.

'Hello sweetheart, this is a nice surprise.' Dolly stood up and pulled her in for a big cuddle.

Sam was overjoyed to see his daughter and wrapped his arms around both Holly and his gran into a group hug. Holly yelped that she couldn't breathe and as Sam pulled away he instinctively smoothed a hand over the top of her head as he always had.

'Oh Dad, watch out,' she laughed, checking her hair with her hands, 'it took me ages to get it straight.'

'Don't be daft. Your hair is lovely just the way it's meant to be,' Sam said, then instantly wished he hadn't when he saw the look on his daughter's face. He coughed to clear his throat and changed the subject. 'Fancy a drink?' he motioned for her to sit down.

'Yes please, Dad.'

'Orange juice?' he asked, without really thinking.

'Um, no!' Holly pulled a face at him. 'Unless you

want my levels to rocket through the roof. Dad, what are you like?' she laughed.

'Oops, sorry.' Sam smarted, instantly remembering the early mistakes he had made, when he had inadvertently bought her a can of Coke at the May Fair once, without realising it wasn't sugar-free. Chrissie had intervened just in time by swiping it from him as he handed it to their eleven-year-old daughter, whose face had lit up like a Christmas tree. Holly had still been getting to grips with managing her diabetes, and accepting that she couldn't have the treats that she had been used to, so ended up crying and shouting at Chrissie for being mean and 'ruining her whole day.' Chrissie had got irritated with him for not concentrating properly, and the incident had put them all in a bad mood that afternoon. He realised now that it must have been hard for Chrissie ... she was only trying to do her best by Holly. No wonder she had walked off in a huff when he had suggested she lighten up. Dolly was right ... he had to look at what went wrong and work out how to fix it. He turned to Holly. 'Milk or water, what would you prefer, love?'

'Daaad, I'm not a five year old,' Holly huffed, slipping her patent pink satchel off her shoulder and down onto the tiled floor. 'I do know how to choose a drink all by myself.'

'Your dad just cares, that's all,' Dolly appeased, giving Sam a sympathetic smile.

'Sorry, Dad,' Holly said, grinning sweetly, and then, 'I'll just have water, please.'

'No worries, sweetheart. So, how are you? And how is Mum?' Sam asked, and then quickly added, 'Did she have a nice evening out after I came to see you?'

'Mmm-hmm,' Holly responded noncommittally, avoiding eye contact as she took the glass of water from Dolly. 'Mum is good. She asked me to bring you these.' Holly knelt down to her satchel and pulled out a lovely, gift-wrapped box covered in navy tissue with a red ribbon wrapped around.

'Wow,' Sam took the box, puzzled at this seeming change of heart. Chrissie sending gifts? What had brought this on? Sam felt confused, but tried to keep an open mind as he undid the ribbon and then unwrapped the tissue paper. 'Very nice,' he said, on seeing the logo on the box.

'That's right, salted caramel truffles, she went all the way to Market Briar to buy them specially,' Holly said, nervously not drawing breath and wishing she'd bought that primer in Boots when she'd been there earlier – the one that is supposed to stop your face from going all red and blotchy.

'Did she really?' Sam's heart lifted a little as this was quite a big olive branch. Expensive truffles were more

Chrissie's kind of thing than his. Not that he was complaining. He liked chocolate, but a bog-standard bar of Dairy Milk would have been just as welcome.

'Yes, that's right, Dad.' Holly grinned, her heart swelling now as she got into the swing of things, figuring her fibs were for a good cause, after all. 'She must have remembered when you bought them for her on Valentine's Day that time,' she eyed him, hoping he'd get it, 'do you remember?' He nodded. 'So romantic,' she added for good measure.

Sam smiled. Maybe Dolly was right, and there wasn't another man. Maybe Chrissie was just meeting a friend after all, and actually did want to sort things out. And she had every right to be angry and disappointed with him after the way things had unravelled over the last year.

'And she said that she's really sorry for being so horrible to you.' Holly drank some more of the water, before wiping her lips on the back of her hand. *In for a penny, in for pound … that's what Granny Dolly would say if she knew what I was trying to do right now.* And she grinned some more, marvelling at how well her 'Get Mum and Dad Back Together in Time for My Birthday' plan was going. The wish was going to come true. At this rate Mum and Dad would be back together in no time at all!

'Here.' Dolly handed her a piece of kitchen roll and then turned to Sam. 'Well, that's very thoughtful. How about you drop Holly back home later and then you can thank Chrissie in person?'

'Good idea,' Sam nodded, suddenly feeling better than he had in ages.

Chapter Seven

On the Blackwood Farm Estate, Jude was fuming. After all the commotion outside, the officious Sylvia had insisted that she take off her muddy boots and leave them by the back door of the main house. And Lulu had been confined to a utility room where she could still be heard growling and yelping from somewhere over the other side of the house. Sam had gone home to make sure he was back in time to have tea with Holly, so Jude was on her own.

'Myles, this is Jude Darling,' Sylvia said as she ushered Jude into an enormous wood-panelled drawing room. 'I didn't have her name on my list, so if you could let me know next time,' she added, rather pointedly Jude thought, before turning on her heel to leave (yes, she had been allowed to keep her brogues on, Jude noted).

Jude looked around. If Myles King was in this room, then he must be hiding, as she couldn't see him. Sylvia must have made a mistake. Jude wasn't sure what to do. Should she go after her? Or wait here? She knew what she'd love to do, and that would be to go and release Lulu from her makeshift prison cell, and then get the hell out of here. Fast.

The place was spooky; she had seen all the empty rooms on the way here as Sylvia had marched her through the corridors from the utility room. And there were weird, creaky noises, as if ghosts were hiding just out of sight. Despite the warm day outside, Jude shivered. It unnerved her. The Blackwood Farm Estate manor house felt neglected, as if the life force had been sucked out of it and it had been left to go to ruin. It really was a great shame, as she remembered coming here in the past, and the house had been truly glorious, with such beautiful furniture and exquisite paintings, and with nice, cosy, homely touches such as silky throws on the backs of the sofas. Fresh, fragrant pink lilies in giant vases had graced the many occasional tables dotted around.

This had been when Marigold and Lord Lucan had lived here. They used to have the May Fair, summer weddings and charity parties in the gardens for the villagers, and when Jude and Chrissie had been in the 1st Tindledale Brownies, and then Girl Guides, all those years ago, they had come to many of the events. Chrissie had dared Jude one time to sneak inside the house to use the toilet, instead of the Portaloos that had been set up to save everyone from having to traipse all the way over from the marquees, across the vast grounds to the house. Jude, never one to turn down the chance of a dare, had relished the challenge and sneaked in through a side door that the caterers were using, to give herself an impromptu private tour. She had even taken an old newspaper from a box beside one of the fireplaces as proof, to show Chrissie that she had actually been inside the main drawing room and not just a toilet near the service entrance. The very same room that she was now in, standing in a pair of holey old My Little Pony socks that Holly had chosen for her as a birthday present several years ago. Jude had loved them, and worn them to death, but they were hardly suitable attire in which to meet a potential customer, hence her frustration at having to take off her boots. She glanced down and saw her big toe peeping out of one of the holes, and cringed. *Oh well, nothing I can do about the socks now. And after the effort I've made to be here, Myles King will just have to take me as he finds me!*

Jude sat on one of the sofas, wondering if this was the only room that had been furnished. She reckoned it must be. And maybe a bedroom or two, unless Myles was sleeping at Lawrence's, the only B&B in Tindledale. But that was highly unlikely, given his celebrity status and Sylvia's desire to keep groupies well away from him. No, he must be living here and making do until he could get the house properly furnished. And she felt excited at the prospect. Maybe that's why Myles had called her, to help him fill the whole manor house with gorgeous antiques and special pieces to really make it a lovely, welcoming home once again.

She smiled as her anger dissipated, and glanced around. The room was nice enough, with shards of spring sunshine streaming in through the four floor-to-ceiling windows that overlooked what was once the lavender farm – named because in summer time it had been packed with an abundance of perfectly perfumed wild lavender as far as the eye could see. A purple field, Jude had thought when her mum had brought her to one of the open days as a child. She remembered it well, as Marigold and some of the Women's Institute ladies had organised a teddy bears' picnic afterwards. Jude had been sick on too much chocolate cake all over the tartan blanket laid out on the immaculate lawn, and her mum had been mortified.

Tony had taken to retelling the story many times over, usually on Jude's birthday, each time with extra embellishment, just to add to the amusement and poignancy of the moment. But, she also realised retrospectively it was a nice way of keeping Sarah's memory alive. Her dad had always been very good at that, and they had enjoyed many phone calls while she was in LA, where Sarah's cousin Maggie had come on the phone to reminisce with Tony too. She remembered how Maggie had laughed as well on hearing about the teddy bears' picnic, and had said how she bet Sarah's face had been a picture.

And then lovely Maggie, after the call had ended, had especially made a chocolate cake, and they had lain in the LA sun together, on a blanket, eating big slices in tribute to Sarah ...

Suddenly, the door bounced open, breaking Jude's reverie, and she leapt up.

'Here she is! The Darling girl. What took you so long?' A tall, rakish man, in his early forties perhaps, came bounding into the room like an overexcited Labrador. His sandy blond hair was pulled back into one of those silly man buns (she groaned inwardly) and he was wearing a *Star Wars* T-shirt teamed with designer jeans that were hanging halfway down his hips, flashing a pair of tight black boxer shorts with Superdry stamped on the waistband. And he smelled gorgeous, expensive too ... Chanel if she wasn't mistaken. An evocative scent for Jude – she'd kissed a guy wearing it at a beach party in the Maldives, and the glorious smell alone had been enough to make her nearly succumb to his suggestion of a one-night stand. They had been interrupted when a waiter came to bring them more cocktails and the moment had vanished, but still ... Jude had always thought the power of scent an incredible thing.

'Um, err ... well, the bus,' she stuttered, irritation rising inside her again as she pulled her mind away from the man on the beach in the Maldives and back to the moment. For a man she had only just met, Myles seemed to have a special ability to rub her up the wrong way. And that was really saying something after some of the egos she had encountered while living in LA, Jude concluded. Even if he did smell absolutely divine!

'Bus! You came on a *bus*?' Myles said the word 'bus' as if it was some kind of alien concept that had never occurred to him before now.

Jude took a deep, steadying breath and tried not to let the Chanel scent sway her from feeling anything other than focused on putting him right. 'Yes, that's right. I haven't sorted out a car yet. You see, I've not long been back here in Tindled—'

'Where have you come from then?' he cut in, folding his arms and then cupping his chin between the thumb and index finger of his left hand.

'Los Angeles,' she replied casually, playing him at his own game, as he clearly thought he was a really big deal. The global superstar he'd been all those years ago. But not now. Times and tastes had changed, and Jude had kept herself up to date with pop culture. She had to, in order to be taken seriously by her superstar clients, so she knew it was all androgynous boys with pale skin, messy hair and skinny black jeans who were on trend now, with no place for over-tanned has-beens with silly topknots. 'And before that, I travelled all over the world, sourcing antiques for a portfolio of very discerning clients,' she added airily, thinking, *ha, see how you like that!*

'But I thought you were a local. I need a country girl. You know, someone who can sort out this crib.' *Did he really just say 'crib'?* And he waved a hand grandly around the room. 'Make it a proper rural retreat. And I'm thinking chickens, pigs, and goats and sheep, the ones with the black faces and the curly horns ...' He paused to place cupped hands either side of his head, as if to demonstrate what horns were.

'Blackface,' Jude interjected. 'They're called Blackface sheep.' She just about managed to mask her sigh of contempt.

'Yeah, whatever. I want them. Loads of them.' He paced around the room, clearly fired up with enthusiasm for his country living project.

'OK,' she said slowly.

'But LA living isn't what I'm after.' Myles turned away and then muttered something about yoga and wheatgrass gunk. Jude tried not to smile.

'Well, I'm not a fan of yoga either. Or wheatgrass gunk, come to think of it,' Jude retorted, wandering over to one of the windows. She ran an index finger along the windowsill, and then made a point of pulling a face at the coating of black grime that now covered her finger. 'But I do know about country homes. All kinds of homes, in fact. You see, I've worked with some of the biggest names in the world.'

'Like who?'

'Oh, I couldn't possibly breach a client's confidentiality, but I can tell you that my last commission, to furnish a holiday retreat in Mauritius, was for a global superstar,' she said, turning away and trying not to giggle as she kept her face firmly towards the window, enjoying playing with him. She wanted this job. She needed it to get her fledging business, back here in the UK, off to a flying start. Plus, she knew that she'd really enjoy restoring the Blackwood Farm Estate manor house back to its former glory. And she had met enough people like Myles to know that the best button to push with them was the celebrity status one. Insecurity and fierce ambition fuelled it, that fear of tumbling down the list and ending up at Z.

'Hmm, well, can't you give me a rough idea of who you did the gig for?' Myles probed, and Jude knew he was hooked and most likely only wanted to know so that he could boast about having the same interior designer.

'Not really,' she teased some more, 'but I could give you a clue …'

'Yep. Go on.' Myles nodded, stepping forward.

'OK. Is that *lemonade* I spy in that drinks cabinet over there?' Jude pointed and nearly choked with the effort of trying not to laugh on the word 'lemonade' as she gave him the clue – the name of Beyoncé's world-famous album. She hadn't really worked for Beyoncé, but was banking on Myles King, aka faded rock star from the Noughties, not actually having any real connection to the famous singer or anyone in her circle of trust. So he wouldn't know that Jude was 'massaging the truth', might one say. Because she had actually helped source some antiques to go in the holiday home of a well-connected friend of a friend of Beyoncé's, so it was quite possible that Beyoncé would go to the holiday home one day, perhaps.

'Beyoncé! Well, if you're good enough for her, then you'll do all right for me.' And for a split second Jude saw a glimmer of a much younger, cheekier man in Myles's face. His sapphire-blue eyes lit up and the rakish façade from earlier had vanished, leaving him looking innocent and really enthusiastic. A bit like a devilishly cute puppy, as he nodded his head. If he'd had a tail, then Jude imagined that it would be wagging like mad right now. She treated him with a smile.

'And country living is in my blood. You see, I grew up here. In Tindledale. In fact, I was a regular visitor to the Blackwood Farm Estate as a child.' Jude figured a little more 'stretching' of the truth wouldn't be so bad. 'So I could help you restore the manor house to its former glory. Imagine, a proper country estate ... very fitting for a farmer.'

'Hmm, well that's good, I s'pose, and I'm not going to be any old farmer ploughing corn or whatever. My pigs are going to win prizes, so I'll need a decent gaff for when *MOJO* and *Q* magazines rock up for photoshoots,'

Myles said in all seriousness, rather pleased with himself, and reverting back to the cockiness from earlier on. 'But I don't want you blabbing about the inside of my home. Or taking pictures to the press. If you've worked with big names then you'll know all about that.'

'Indeed I do,' Jude turned to face him.

'Good. That's settled then. I'll get Sylvia to sort out the paperwork.' Myles stuck out his hand awkwardly, and Jude stepped forward to shake it, wondering why he wasn't more adept at dealing with people. Surely, he must have been interviewed all over the world on TV and in newspapers and magazines, and met thousands of fans in the past. Or maybe his mother was just very good at keeping everyone at arm's length like she had with her.

'Ahh, yes, about that. I know Sylvia is your mum, but really, would you mind asking her to back off a bit? She's locked up my dog, you know. *And* she was very fierce when I first arrived here.'

'My mum?' Myles laughed, as if this was the most hilarious thing he had ever heard. 'Sylvia isn't my mum. She's my manager, PA, sometimes cook – but not often, thankfully,' and he rolled his eyes. Jude bristled, wondering what Sylvia would think about her cooking being criticised. 'And don't worry, I'll have a word. She does get a bit carried away with that Rottweiler thing she has going on.'

'Thanks. So, when would you like to go through some

ideas?' Jude fished in her pocket for her phone to check dates in the diary app. 'I could put together some mood boards by the middle of next week … if you like?' She stopped talking on seeing Myles frown and fold his arms again.

'I have no idea what mood boards are … but they sound a bit, um well, *moody* to me, boom boom!' he paused and laughed, 'get it?' Jude nodded. 'So I'll just leave the ideas for the house stuff up to you. Tell me what you think will look good and I'll buy it. And then you can give me your bill.'

'OK …' Jude started slowly, figuring it was unconventional, but if that was how he wanted it, then it was fine by her. Free rein to design the interior of the Blackwood Farm Estate manor house. She felt as if her lucky stars had been aligned all at once. Even if it was going to involve working for an obnoxious and, quite frankly, overgrown schoolboy, whose sense of humour, if you could call it that, was playground. But there seemed more to Myles too. 'If you're sure?' she checked, wondering why he behaved like this … or, more to the point, who had made him this way. He was watching out of the window now. His eyes scanning the grounds. On hyper-alert almost. Jude had seen this sort of behaviour before … celebrities in the public eye who put on a front. It came from being surrounded by people who weren't always genuine, and years of experiencing it would make most people struggle to trust and act normally around others. Maybe after a while he'd start to let his guard down and she'd get to see the real Myles. She felt he was playing a part and in time she might find the real Myles King was quite different. She really hoped so, as the glimpse she saw earlier had been quite endearing.

'Yep. Quite sure,' Myles quickly turned away from the window. 'Now, come on, I've already got the pigs. They've just arrived – that's what Sam is sorting out right now. I'm going to be a pig farmer.'

'Oh!' Jude said, a little perplexed at how Myles intended to make such a transition ... from rock star to farmer.

'Yep. Large Blacks they are. Come and see them.' And he hared off down the corridor, making Jude have to do a kind of running-walk just to keep up with him.

Chapter Eight

Holly glanced up from her mobile as she unclipped the buckle of her seat belt and smiled at her dad sitting next to her in the front of the Land Rover.

'Mum's going to be so pleased to see you,' she said, faking happiness and hoping he wouldn't notice that she was feeling a bit panicky about saying Mum would be home when she wasn't. But Holly hadn't reckoned on Dad actually bringing her home from Granny Dolly's house and wanting to come inside and thank Mum in person for the chocolates ... because she'd be found out right away. No, she had hoped that her intervention by way of gifts for each of them would help her parents calm down and start being nice to each other when they next saw one another. And earlier, when it had come to home time, she'd tried to get Dad and Grandma Dolly to let her catch the bus on her own, but they'd been having none of it. Grandma Dolly had said that it was too dark now. Even though the bus journey was only twenty minutes along the main Stoneley Road from Granny Dolly's house back to Tindledale, and then the walk from the bus stop to home was, like, only one minute. Anyone would think she was still a little girl the way they monitored her. Granny Dolly had said it was important they keep an eye on her, what with the diabetes and all. And Holly got that, but still ... family could be so annoying sometimes.

Mum had said she was going to be out until nine o'clock and to make sure Dad dropped her home after that time, or waited with her until Mum got back so she wouldn't be on her own. But realising that the ruse with the chocolates would be rumbled if Dad came in now, Holly hadn't told him what Mum had said. But at least she had managed to get him to drop her home a bit earlier – before Mum got back. So that was something at least. If she could get Dad to leave now before Mum turned up, there was no way her Get Mum and Dad Back Together in Time for My Birthday plan could go wrong! When Mum got in she could tell her that Dad had only just that minute dropped her off and she hadn't been on her own at all.

Anyway, Holly reckoned Mum worried far too much. But at least she let her go on the bus all the way to Market Briar by herself ... well, with Katie, but she was the same age as her so it didn't really count, and that was miles further away. Plus Dad had sided with Gran, and two to one was just so unfair.

And her left leg was killing her. She'd been too impatient with her last injection, just jamming it in quickly in the loo at Grandma Dolly's house, and now her thigh was covered in a massive bruise. She gave it a rub, wishing her skinny jeans weren't so tight as they were pressing on the bruise and making the throbbing feeling a million times worse.

'Actually Dad, I've just remembered ... Mum said she was going out and wouldn't be back yet, so there's no point you coming inside with me. I'll go in and tell her you said thank you, later on, when she gets home.' She grinned some more, pleased with her plan, but wishing she had thought it through more thoroughly. If she was really going to get them back together again in time for her birthday, then she'd have to up her game. Oh well, Dad was happy thinking the chocolates were from Mum and that was good, as he had looked so sad earlier when she'd walked into the kitchen at Granny Dolly's house.

'Oh, but it's getting late, darling. Are you sure?' Sam asked, and then added, 'When will Mum be back?'

'Yes, quite sure. She won't be late. In about half an hour, I think she said.' Holly surreptitiously crossed her fingers to guard herself against the consequences of telling a lie. But reckoned that it didn't really count if it was for a good reason, like getting your mum and dad back together so they could be happy in time for your birthday – and for ever after. A proper family again. And Mum was bound to be happy with Dad now, as the flowers would have been delivered while she was out. They were her favourites too, big pink lilies that smelled lovely, even though they had cost Holly nearly all of her monthly allowance. But she had figured it would be worth it. In fact, it was just a matter of time now until everything would be back to normal. Mum would stop being cross all the time and that man, Gavin, from the village choir … the one who had started picking Mum up on the way to choir practice, wouldn't need to bother any more. Because Dad would be at home to drop Mum off wherever she wanted to go, and pick her up again. And that was definitely a good thing as Gavin from the choir was way too smiley and flirty with Mum. *But Mum really likes Gavin. Fancies him. She must do, seeing now that she's doing her hair and putting lipstick on and all that. She never used to make all that effort just to go to choir practice.*

'So you'll be on your own for about half an hour?' Sam quizzed, glancing at the clock on the dashboard.

'Yes, but it's no big deal.'

'Hmm, maybe not to you, but—'

'Oh Dad, it's totally fine.' She flicked her hair back. 'I am thirteen, you know. I'm not a baby any more. Mum lets me be home alone all the time. She trusts me,' Holly ventured, knowing this wasn't actually true. But reckoned it should be. Mum made such a fuss, just because of the diabetes, saying, 'Anything could happen if you are alone – you could have a hypo,' which was so unfair as she knew how to look after herself. Katie Ferguson was allowed to babysit her little brother for a whole evening on her own, so it was totally ridiculous that she wasn't allowed to be home alone for half an hour.

Sam wasn't sure. Was just-turned-thirteen really old enough to be left on your own? He didn't know, and swiftly racked his brains to try and remember how it had been when he was thirteen. But then he was a boy, so it was different. Or was it? And then he felt a pang of unease for having old-fashioned, gender-stereotyping thoughts. And he was sure Chrissie would accuse him of being sexist, or not being a feminist, for suggesting that Holly wasn't as capable of looking after herself just because she was a girl. He'd made that mistake once before when Holly had wanted to try out the rugby club at school a couple of years ago, and he'd panicked, imagined all sorts, including serious spinal injuries rendering her paralysed. It happened, he knew. And he'd said something about it being a bad idea, and that rugby was really for boys. Well, he wouldn't make that mistake again. The last thing he wanted to do was to antagonise Chrissie, with the way things were at the moment, and just when she had extended an olive branch with the chocolates too ... he'd be mad to jeopardise that. And if Chrissie was OK with Holly being at home on her own, then she'd accuse him of undermining her, surely? And it was only half an hour. So he made his decision.

'I trust you too, sweetheart. If Mum says it's OK, then that's fine by me.' He smiled, nodded his head as if to confirm his decision, and then leant across to give Holly a kiss goodbye.

'I love you, Dad,' Holly grinned, and his heart melted. With her eyes wide and lit up, she was still so naïve in many ways, even though she thought she was all grown up.

'I love you too, sweetheart.' And then he had a thought. 'Why don't you stay for a few minutes? There's no need to rush off. Especially if Mum isn't home. We can have a chat ...'

'A chat?' Holly gave him a hesitant look, wondering how long the chat would take. She liked talking to Dad, but she had better keep an eye on the time to make sure he was gone before Mum got here.

'Yeah, you know ... a conversation, I'll say something and then you'll say something and we'll repeat the process all over again,' he laughed, shaking his head. 'Like we used to before—'

'You went away?' she asked, quietly.

'Yes. Like that,' he paused, 'if that's OK?'

'Sure,' she shrugged. 'What do you want to chat about?' she asked, casually.

'I dunno. Um, maybe I should start by saying sorry for not coming home more often,' Sam ventured.

'Oh, Dad. You don't have to say sorry. I totally understand. You were working to pay for everything.' And she gave him a very serious, grown-up look this time.

'I still missed you ...'

'And I missed you.'

'Did you?' Sam asked, not for vanity, but to try to gauge how much his absence had affected her.

'Of course! Mum is so moany when you're not here. She's always been moany, but now it's even worse. She's a complete control freak too.'

'Well, you two always did clash a bit,' Sam said carefully. 'Mum loves you very much and tries to do her best by you, always,' he added. It wasn't in his nature to criticise Chrissie. No matter how things were between him and her, where Holly was concerned, he felt it important to show a united parental front. It wasn't fair for him to collude in criticising her mum ... what kind of man, or indeed father would that make him? And what would it teach Holly?

'Hmm, well, she could try being nice sometimes though.' Holly twiddled the cuff of her sleeve.

'And you must be nice to her too, love. Saying you hate her isn't very kind,' he reminded her, albeit tentatively, of how she had behaved that evening when he first got back. Chrissie and Holly had always managed to rub each other up the wrong way. He remembered when Holly was just a toddler, and her wriggling and wrangling whenever Chrissie tried to put her in the bath. They had laughed when Sam had taken a turn and Holly had giggled and bounced right on into the water with a big smile all over her face. And then when Holly was older, Chrissie had tried to show her how to tie her laces, but Holly just wouldn't be told and the pair of them ended up bickering, to the point where he had seriously thought one of them would get hit on the head with the stray shoe that Holly had been waving about in protest. So he'd intervened again and managed to calm the choppy waters between them by finding an online tutorial for Holly to watch.

'I know, Dad. But it's easier when you're here. You always sort it out.'

'And I'm sorry for not being around as much as I should have been. I really have missed you, and Mum.'

'But you're back now,' she said enthusiastically, 'and who actually sees people for real any more, anyway?'

'What do you mean?' Sam creased his forehead in concern.

'Oh, Dad. You're so ancient,' she laughed. 'Katie's dad lives in Australia; she was seven when she last actually saw him in real life. Skype is a totally normal thing. You don't have to touch people to still love them, you know.'

'Right,' Sam said, feeling bemused by her seemingly total acceptance of this modern-day phenomena. But then how different things are for her generation – a life lived online. Virtual reality for real. It was crazy, really, when he thought about it. And a bit sad too, if he was honest. It only made him feel worse, knowing that his daughter had accepted his continued absence as normal.

'And most of my best friends are online these days. Except for Katie, of course.'

'Doing what?'

Holly laughed at his ignorance. 'YouTubers, Dad. Online places, group chats, that kind of thing.'

'And they're safe these places, are they? You never know who—'

'Yes, Dad. I know all about weirdoes and pervs. And trolls. I learnt about it at school ... ages ago. In like Year Two or whatever.' She pulled a face.

'Good,' Sam nodded, deep in thought, realising how much he had missed. Holly might be cool with him not having been around, but still ... 'So what do you talk about in the ... online places?'

'All kinds of stuff. Makeovers. Music. Products.'

'Products?'

'You know, like soaps and bath oils and make-up, and there's this dry shampoo ... a new really cool one, which has pink flamingos on the can and it smells of the Caribbean.' Her eyes lit up. 'Like Barbados or somewhere. Coconuts and papaya and stuff, and it has over five hundred five-star reviews. But it's out of stock everywhere. Even the new mini Superdrug attached to the doctors' surgery in the village doesn't have any cans left and nobody ever goes in there.'

'Really?' Sam jumped in, his mind boggling at this

whole new world of product importance that was opening up to him before his very eyes.

'Yeah, so now I've had to go on a wait list.' She sounded devastated as she pushed her bottom lip out, presumably to express just how awful this unthinkable situation was for her. Sam coughed to cover up the laugh that almost escaped from his mouth.

'A wait list?' he then managed.

'That's right.' She turned to him with a very serious look in her eyes. 'To be the first, or nearly the first, depending where I am on the wait list,' she paused and pondered pragmatically, 'so I can get one in the next phase of stock release.'

'Next phase of stock release?' Sam muttered, channelling a parrot now as he tried to get himself up to speed with it all and, for the life of him, try to fathom why his thirteen-year-old daughter sounded as if she worked in the corporate head office of some enormous consumer product conglomerate. What happened to riding bikes in the woods or jumping up and down all day on a trampoline without a care in the world? He let out a long breath. 'So is this what you talk about, products?'

'And boys, sometimes,' she gave him a look, as if testing to see how he'd react. So he made sure to keep a laidback face on. The last thing he wanted was to make her think all that was off limits. Who knew when she might really need to talk to him about something more serious? Sam figured it best to be open so she didn't end up doing stuff behind his and Chrissie's backs and potentially putting herself in danger when she was old enough to have sex with a proper boyfriend. Which he seriously hoped wouldn't be for absolutely ages yet – a decade or two, in fact. 'And what happened at school,' she added, 'we talk a lot about that too ...'

'Even though you've been with these children all day at school,' Sam clarified, relieved to be off the subject of boys.

'Yes, Dad. And they're not children,' she shrugged.

'Of course, my mistake. Teenagers.' Sam elbowed her playfully. Holly's mobile beeped and she flicked the screen to take a look.

'Oh my God. Gotta go. Zoella is going online in five.' She waggled her phone in the air to signify his slot in her busy social schedule had come to a close.

'OK, love. You had better go ... don't want to miss Zoella.' He made big eyes in anticipation and gave her a quick hug before kissing her on the cheek. 'And don't run, you might trip.'

'Stop fussing, Dad. I've been walking up the path at least twice a day ever since we've lived here, which is like eleven years at least.' She rolled her eyes and laughed.

'Go on you, cheeky.' Sam laughed. 'I'll wait here until you're inside.'

A few minutes later, and Sam saw Holly turn to wave

before she closed the front door behind her. Smiling, he reversed, and then turned the car around to drive on to the Duck & Puddle pub in the village. He fancied a pint, and perhaps a game of darts with Matt and Cooper, if they were around; it would be just like the old days.

Things were looking up now. Chrissie was obviously thawing, why else would she be sending fancy chocolates to him? The exact ones he had bought for her on that Valentine's Day. So maybe there was hope that she might give him another chance. And things were great between him and Holly, just as good as they had been before he went away, and that was definitely something to be extremely grateful for.

*

Inside, and Holly tapped the screen on her mobile, but it was no use. She'd lost signal. No service. Not even Wi-Fi. So she was missing Zoella now. Her heart sank at the prospect of being the only one in the world not watching, which meant she wouldn't even be able to join in the after-show chat with all her friends. And what's the betting they'd all get to buy whatever product Zoella was sharing, right now! It was bound to be sold out by the time she got to see it. She tapped the screen a few times more. But still nothing.

And why wasn't the light in the hall working? She

flicked the switch again. But nothing. Using her left hand to feel along the wall, she wished she had night vision or a pair of those night goggles that they wore in those nature programmes when they were looking for badgers. And she wished Mum was home. The house felt different and scary in the dark, almost like it wasn't the same place as it was during the day. But that was silly – she was thirteen years old now and reckoned she was too old to be scared of a few shadows.

'Ow!' Holly bashed into the umbrella stand that was actually an old copper milk churn that Mum had picked up in one of the junk shops in Market Briar. Now her leg was hurting where she'd banged it, and right on the spot where it was sore from the injection that morning. She was supposed to vary the spot where she injected, but sometimes it was just easier to do it in the same place. But then the skin would go hard. Sometimes she hated the diabetes so much. Like it was a monster that had taken up refuge inside her body just to be mean and ruin every-thing. When she'd first got diabetes she had struggled to do the injections on her own. She'd tried to get it right, but putting the needle in was difficult. She'd hated needles when she was little and remembered screaming in terror every time she went to have her immunisation jabs. Not even the sticker they gave her afterwards could stop the tears. The only thing that helped was a big cuddle from

Mum. Hmm, thinking about it, Holly realised that she could really do with one of those now.

The nurses at the hospital had explained what she was supposed to do, but it wasn't until Nurse Polly from Dr Ben's surgery in the village had shown her how to do it properly that she had got the hang of it. And now it didn't really bother her at all.

Mum thought she didn't know what all those tests she was having were for, but Holly knew that things weren't quite right. She'd been going low a lot recently and she'd overheard the doctor talking to Mum about it the last time they'd been in Dr Ben's surgery. She had gone off to get her weight and blood pressure checked with Nurse Polly next door, but had heard the end of the conversation when she went back in Dr Ben's room. And it's what those last couple of visits to the hospital had been about too. But she didn't mind going there as she got to see Lauren, the girl who always had her appointments at the same time as she did, so they had sort of become friends.

Holly wondered if Dad knew? Maybe she should tell him? Hmm, on second thoughts, he seemed worried enough at the moment, with Mum being horrible to him, so probably best not to. And she didn't want him to go away again ... like he had when they'd first found out about the diabetes. Plus, if Mum got even more horrible, then she might be able to live with Dad instead, at Granny Dolly's house. Or she might even get to go to

Singapore if Dad had enough of it back here and decided to leave for good.

Holly made her way into the lounge and tried the light switch there. Still nothing. Next she tried the kitchen, but those lights weren't working either. Another power cut. Typical. Tindledale was always having them and she knew it was just the way it was in tiny villages surrounded by fields, but trust it to happen when she was home alone for the first time ever. Or maybe it was a fuse? That had happened before too, loads of times. Mum said it was because Dad bodged up the electrics when he wired in the spotlights in the kitchen ceiling, so every now and then they cut out and turned the whole lot off by themselves and you had to flick it all back on again.

Holly switched on the torch app on her phone and used it to navigate around the kitchen. She'd get a chair to stand on so she could flick the switch back on the fuse box, just like she'd seen Mum do loads of times. So, after positioning the chair beneath the fuse box, set high up on the wall in the hall, she dumped her satchel on the floor and kicked off her boots – they were covered in mud from walking across the field to Granny's house, and Mum would go mental if she made the seat cushion all dirty. She slipped her mobile into the back pocket of her jeans, climbed up onto the chair and reached her hands up to the cabinet that housed the fuse box. After pulling open the little doors, she lifted up the cover and felt with her hands to find the switch that had tripped, but it was no use, she couldn't seem to do it. She had another go, but it was still the same. The row of little switches were all in the up position, which meant it must be a power cut affecting the whole village.

Holly puffed out a big gust of air and went to pull her mobile from her back pocket to put the torch app back on, just to be sure. But as she twisted her waist to reach behind, the doorbell buzzed. The seat cover swivelled and the chair toppled as she tried to steady herself. The wooden legs went from under her and, no matter how hard she tried to grab on to the fuse box, and then the radiator which was now at eye level, it was no use. She fell and landed on the floor in an awkward heap, with the chair on top of her legs. Seconds later, the blackness engulfed her. And what was that smashing noise whizzing around inside her head?

Chapter Nine

Jude hoisted Lulu onto her other hip and pressed the bell again, wondering where Chrissie was, because it was unlike her not to be in when they'd made arrangements to get together and have a Lykke evening in on the sofa. She had read all about Lykke in a magazine article. A Danish concept. A recipe for happiness, if you like; she reckoned it was just the thing Chrissie needed with everything that was going on in her life right now.

So Jude had come to The Forstal Farmhouse with a big bag of provisions – a bottle of Prosecco to liven up flutes of elderflower cordial into St Germain cocktails, a couple of DVDs – the lovely, summery film, *Mamma Mia*, and the feel-good classic, *Grease*, which she and Chrissie used to watch all the time when they were young girls, singing along to the songs, with Chrissie channelling Sandy to Jude's Rizzo. A giant bag of Twiglets, an enormous Yankee candle in the Happy Spring scent and a pair of handknitted crimson socks for everyone to snuggle up in, Holly included, courtesy of Hettie's House of Haberdashery on the other side of the village. Sybs, the manager there, had called in to Darling Antiques & Interiors the other day to say hello, and after they had got chatting, Jude asked if she'd be interested in creating some items for her new Happy Homewear section. It was an initiative she had come up with after reading the Lykke article and, seeing as her own knitting skills were extremely limited, it made perfect sense to get a crafting expert in to knit some beautiful bespoke bed socks, cashmerino wraps and cardies, plus make fabulous floaty nighties and tea dresses too. Jude reckoned the new additions to the shop would go down a treat in the run-up to the summer holidays, and she'd been absolutely right, having nearly sold out of all the cardies and dresses already.

Jude buzzed the bell again, but had to put Lulu down on the doorstep, as the weight of her and the big bag of stuff was near crippling, sending her back into a spasm. Jude offloaded the bag too, and turned to see if Tony was still waiting – some habits die hard, as he was still there, looking to see her in safely, as if she were still a young girl going for a sleepover. He'd kindly given her a lift to Chrissie's, and was then going on to Dolly's house for a catch-up and to see how Sam was getting on, not having had a chance to see him yet since he returned from Singapore. She grinned and motioned for Tony to go and leave her to it.

'I'm a grown-up now, Dad,' she mouthed, shaking her head and grinning. He shrugged and carried on making a roll-up. 'Hey, stop that, you naughty girl.' Jude turned her attention to Lulu instead, who was now scratching at the door, nosy as ever, no doubt. Jude tutted and picked the dog back up, but Lulu was having none of it, and leapt right out of her arms and resumed pawing and clawing at the black front door. 'Lulu, stop that. What on earth is the matter?' But it made no difference.

Sensing something was amiss, Jude crouched down to the letterbox at the bottom of the door and lifted it open, but it was too low for her to actually see inside. Lulu went berserk and started howling and barking, in between pawing at Jude's legs now, as if trying to communicate something to her. Jude stepped across the path to the little window that looked into the hallway and, after pressing her hands up to the sides of her head, she peered through the glass. The house was in total darkness. But something wasn't right. Jude just knew it. And where was Chrissie? It really was unlike her not to be here.

Jude looped the handle of Lulu's lead over a nearby fence post to prevent her from running off, and then dashed over to Tony's car, where he was still savouring his rollie.

'Dad, can you pass me your torch from the glove box, please?' she said as soon as he wound down the window.

'Here you go, love.' He handed the torch to her. 'Is something up?'

'I'm not sure. But I'm going to find out.' And she ran back to the house and peered again through the little window, this time with the torch on full beam. Her hunch was right! Well ... thanks to Lulu realising that something was up, and then actually having the gumption to alert her, which was a blessing in itself as Lulu was usually quite pathetic when it came to galvanising herself into action and behaving like a proper dog.

Holly was lying on the floor at the far end of the hall with a kitchen chair on top of her legs.

Jude quickly found her handbag and was just about to rummage inside it when she was swiftly pushed aside from behind.

SMASH.

Tony had booted in the front door, making the bevelled glass mirror on the wall behind it fall and shatter everywhere.

'DAD! What are you doing?' Jude hissed, horrified.

Holly was moving now and trying to stand up. Tony grabbed the chair off her back and swiftly stood it upright. Then carefully steered the young girl towards it.

'There now, sweetheart. You just sit still for a minute. You've had a fall by the looks of it.' And he patted Holly's arm before turning to Jude. 'We couldn't just leave her lying there, what if she was having a hypo? Diabetic comas can be fatal!' he said by way of explanation for the now-broken door lock and splintered wood frame. He tried the hallway light switch, and turned it on and off again to no effect.

'I have a key! That's what I was looking for in my handbag. Chrissie gave me one years ago … for emergencies,' she quickly explained, making big eyes and lifting it to show him in the torchlight, before dumping the key and the handbag on the stairs and crouching down in front of Holly. 'What happened, darling? Are you OK?' She rubbed the tops of Holly's arms to comfort her. Holly nodded and stared back, her eyes wide with shock and fright, but she seemed to be OK, no bumps or bruises that Jude could see.

Seconds later, the lights came on.

'There we go. It was just a trip. All fixed now,' Tony said, closing the fuse box and turning his attentions to the front door; then, after muttering something about getting his tool bag, headed towards his van.

Holly was crying now, fiddling with the hem of her Katy Perry tour T-shirt and refusing to look Jude in the eye.

'It's OK, Holly,' Jude soothed, sensing there was more to this than her goddaughter simply standing on a chair and then toppling off it. It was unlike Holly to be so distraught, she usually seemed quite resilient, but now she was almost choking on her sobs. 'Come on, sweetie, surely it's not that bad …'

'Mum is going to go mental,' Holly sobbed in a stilted, breathy voice. 'I thought it was her ringing the doorbell. That she had forgotten her door key again. She'd go mad if she saw me climbing on a chair. And she already hates me!' The young girl put her head in her hands and sobbed some more, as if she had the weight of the whole world on her shoulders.

'No she doesn't,' Jude said instinctively, taken aback, followed by, 'why on earth would you think that?' But before Holly could say anything more, Chrissie came hurtling through the open front door, her blonde hair flying out in the backdraught and her face full of horror.

'Oh God, what's happened?' she gasped, dropping to her knees next to Jude. 'Holly, are you OK? Can you hear me? Is it a hypo?' she shouted, panicking and lifting Holly's chin so she could look into her eyes.

'No, Mum. It's not. I'm all right. Not everything is about the diabetes, you know. Stop making it a big deal.' Holly lifted her feet up onto the chair and, with her knees under her chin, she clasped her arms around her legs, shrinking away from Chrissie.

'Your mum just cares, sweetheart,' Jude said, seeing the look of hurt flicker across Chrissie's face.

'I fell off the chair trying to fix the fuse, that was all,' Holly mumbled into herself.

Chrissie's eyebrows shot up into her forehead. 'You were doing what?'

'I was just trying to help!' Holly looked up, her chin wobbled as her bottom lip quivered.

'But why wasn't Dad here with you?'

'He dropped me off just a few minutes ago.' Holly knew that she was going to get her dad into big trouble, but she couldn't tell the truth about what had really happened – what would become of her Get Mum and Dad Back Together in Time for My Birthday plan then? Chrissie tutted and sighed, shaking her head in frustration.

'Don't blame Dad, just like you always do!' Holly was practically shouting now.

'Don't take that tone with me, Holly. I come home to find my daughter lying on the floor, looking very upset, and it's not a big deal?' Chrissie and Holly eyeballed each other for a moment – both of them furious with the other, before Chrissie crumbled and wrapped herself around her daughter in a relieved hug. Holly started off on a fresh round of sniffles, but hugged her mum tightly in return.

Jude smiled. Holly might be thirteen years old and as headstrong as anything, but at times like these she was still just a little girl who needed her mummy.

'Look, I'd better call Dr Ben right away, I need to make sure that you haven't actually brained yourself.' And Chrissie leapt up and darted into the kitchen to grab the landline phone from the holster. Jude could tell that Chrissie was really upset, but was trying not to show it in front of Holly.

'Go on, love.' Tony was back with his tool bag. 'Check she's all right,' he instructed when Jude glanced up at him. 'Holly and I will be fine, won't we girl?' He gave Holly a reassuring pat on the shoulder as she buried her face back into her knees. 'Let's go and put the telly on in the family room. I can fix the door later, no problem,' he suggested cheerfully, at which Holly looked up and managed a weak smile as she nodded her head and rubbed her tears away on the back of her sleeve.

Jude dashed after Chrissie.

'She seems fine, Chrissie. It doesn't look as if she's done anything worse than given herself a bit of a fright. I don't think she actually knocked herself out. She was checking the fuse box. A power cut,' Jude explained, quickly bringing her friend up to speed. She put her hand on Chrissie's arm, concerned at the grim set of her jaw and the spark of anger in her eyes. She was pacing around the kitchen now with a thunderous look on her face.

'Power cut? Fuse box? But what was she even doing standing on a chair? Where the hell was Sam?' Chrissie said through gritted teeth, holding the phone in mid-air.

'I don't know. But he wouldn't have left her on her own without good reason,' Jude said desperately, not sure what Sam had been thinking, but wondering what Holly had told him. And she didn't want to get Holly into even more trouble than she already seemed to be. Plus, Holly's comment was bothering her ... why on earth would Holly think Chrissie hated her? Chrissie and Holly had always had a bit of a fiery relationship. They clashed. Because

Chrissie could be strict, driven by routine and rules, and Holly was headstrong and typically a child who pushed the boundaries. In fact, Holly reminded Jude quite a lot of how Chrissie had been as a teenager. Spirited and fun too; she knew her own mind. Holly idolised Sam to the point where she had cast Chrissie as the demon, blaming her for her dad not being around, for being the reason for her mum and dad's separation – Chrissie had told Jude all about it during their Skype sessions when she was in LA; how Holly had never so much as once uttered a bad word about her dad. Even when he didn't show up for her thirteenth birthday weekend.

'It's not Dad's fault he's busy working to pay for everything,' was what Holly had said to her mum, absolutely delighted with the expensive new laptop that Sam had delivered to her as a birthday present. Along with the two hundred pounds he put in her bank account so she could treat herself to some new clothes. Not that Chrissie wanted Holly to hate her dad, but it did seem unfair for her to get all the blame because she was the boring one, as far as Holly was concerned. The one who made her do her homework. The one who made her pick up her clothes instead of leaving them on the floor. The one who made her make her bed. And so on. But then Sam was always the easy-going one. The one who let Holly do pretty much what she liked. The one who thought material things made up for missing special occasions.

So no wonder Chrissie was desperate to pull back some control. Jude imagined her friend felt as if everything was slipping away from her. But in her desperation to hold on, she was inadvertently pushing Holly, and possibly her husband, away. It was a mess.

'Bloody typical.' Chrissie was still fuming. 'Why the hell was she even here on her own? I never leave her home alone. She was supposed to be at Dolly's house visiting Sam. And he was supposed to drop her home after I got back. He could have at least waited with her ... No, this shouldn't have happened.'

'Look, why don't we just call Dr Ben on his out-of-hours number,' Jude suggested, in the hope that reassurance from a medical professional might defuse Chrissie's concerns. 'Let's see what he says and then get Holly to bed. She's had a fright falling off the chair and could probably do with a bit of TLC.'

Chrissie sighed, deep in thought, as if mulling over what to do for the best. Then, 'You're right, Jude. First things first; we can talk about this later,' she decided.

*

Chrissie had left Dr Ben a message and he had called her straight back. Jude saw that his lilting Irish brogue had soothed her friend's anxieties, her shoulders relaxing as she told him what had happened. He'd also talked to

Holly to gauge how she was feeling, and Holly told him that she was absolutely fine. She hadn't even blacked out. She was just shocked when she fell off the chair.

'Holly sounds like she has come out of the episode unscathed,' he had reassured. 'But make sure you monitor her for signs of concussion – headaches, vomiting, confusion ... anything out of the ordinary. I'll text you the full list, and please don't hesitate to ring me back. Or you can call 999 if you have any indicators at all, OK?'

Later, feeling reassured but watchful, Chrissie had put Holly to bed. She had tucked her in like she had done when Holly was a young child. All the while she had listened to Holly grumble and fret about Sam and how she shouldn't upset Dad or 'he might go away again.'

Jude had waited downstairs, pulling out her bag of goodies and hoping that something of their Lykke evening could be salvaged. It looked to Jude like Chrissie needed to offload her feelings more than she had realised.

'I'd better only have a very small cocktail. I need to keep my wits about me,' Chrissie said when she came downstairs and into the lounge to join her friend. She had found Holly's old video baby monitor in a cupboard, and plugged it in and set it up on the coffee table in front of them. 'I can keep an eye on her tonight for peace of mind.'

'Good idea. But all seems well,' Jude said, looking at

the little screen on the monitor. Holly was snuggled up in bed reading a book.

'Thankfully,' Chrissie sighed. 'I know it's late for her to still be awake. But, tonight I'd rather she was alert and reading. That way I know she's OK.'

'Sure, and it's a Saturday evening, so it's not like she has school tomorrow. Now, sit back and take a sip of this,' Jude smiled, handing her friend the Prosecco cocktail and hoping she'd try to relax.

Chrissie settled back on the sofa, sinking into the deep cushions.

'Mmm, I really need this.' She took a mouthful. 'You should come around more often if you're going to make me cocktails like this.'

Jude laughed, 'I intend to.'

'But I'm really sorry about all this.' Chrissie shook her head.

'What do you mean?' Jude tucked her legs up on the sofa and turned her head sideways to look at her friend.

'You know, being thrown into my marriage breakdown. I feel like it's got in the way of my excitement at having my best mate back. I'm so sorry.'

'Oh don't be daft, I just want to be here for you, to try and help you and Sam – and Holly – figure things out.' Jude gave Chrissie's arm a comforting stroke.

'I know.' Chrissie smiled gratefully. 'And thank you. It's just ...' She leaned her head back and closed her eyes.

'Just what?' Jude coaxed, taking a sip of her drink.

'Sam! He's so infuriating. You know, when he came here the other day – after all this time – actually standing here in his own house, I just wanted to wish away the last year and pretend it didn't happen. Take him back, right there on the spot. It was the hardest thing I've ever had to do, Jude, to send him away like that. When all I wanted was for him to hold me and make it all better.'

'Then why didn't you?' Jude offered the bowl of Twiglets to Chrissie.

'Thanks.' She took a handful and popped one into her mouth. 'Because I still don't get why he wants to be there – Singapore or wherever the latest contract is – when he could be here.'

'But he's back now,' Jude pointed out.

'Yes, but for how long? He might say he's here for good, but what if he changes his mind? He could be gone again in a few weeks. And then where does that leave Holly, and me?'

'Well, he does drive himself quite hard, Chrissie. And he's never thought he was good enough for you ... so maybe all the high-earning jobs have been so he could provide. You know ... to prove himself, perhaps,' Jude suggested.

'Hmm,' Chrissie replied, pondering Jude's words. 'When has he said that? About not thinking he's good enough?'

'Oh loads of times, back in the day. Don't you

remember? It was usually when he'd had four pints of Tindledale's finest cider down at the Duck & Puddle.'

'You've never told me that before.'

'I thought it was just drunk talk, or self-indulgence – he is quite emotional.' They both laughed.

'True. He did cry at *Finding Nemo* when he watched it with Holly when she was little,' Chrissie said.

'Well, there you go!' Jude grinned and finished her drink.

'And those big soulful eyes of his welled up at Holly's Harvest Festival when she and her classmates took to the stage and sang "All Things Bright and Beautiful".' They sat in silence for a little while and Jude could see that Chrissie was deep in thought about Sam.

'I remember once,' Jude broke the moment. 'I think it was at Holly's christening. He was so proud. The happiest I'd ever seen him, and he was buying everyone drinks and seemed to be really revelling in all the slaps on the back. But later on, he said to me, "Jude, what have I done to deserve this? How could someone like me have ended up with Chrissie and Holly? One day I think I'm going to wake up and it will all be gone."'

'Really?' Chrissie stared at the bottom of her glass, swilling the liquid around.

'Yes, really.' Jude nibbled on a few more Twiglets.

'That mother of his has got a lot to answer for.' Chrissie shook her head. 'She starved him of affection and love.

I guess that eroded his sense of self-worth and value. Bound to, isn't it?'

'I guess so,' Jude nodded.

'But he's a grown-up now, Jude,' Chrissie replied more firmly this time. 'And that means you have to take responsibility for yourself, doesn't it?'

'I think he's trying.' Jude topped up her glass.

'How? Look at what happened the other night. He turned up again, like he'd just popped out for a takeaway ten minutes earlier. Months and months he's been gone, without so much as a fortnight off to see me, or Holly – he knew how I felt, what I'd said, how high the stakes were, but still he didn't come home. Then thinking he can make it all right with a bunch of blooming flowers when he does deign to come back. Pink lilies delivered today ... I ask you!' Chrissie shook her head, her eyes glowing and fiery now. 'He knows they're my favourites, but still, you'd think after everything it would warrant more than a bunch of flowers.'

'He wanted you and Holly to come and live with him in Singapore, didn't he?' Jude intervened delicately, not wanting to antagonise Chrissie further, as she could see she was getting wound up and that was the last thing Jude had wanted this evening to be. Lykke was all about happiness and calm. Not frustration and angst.

'That was never going to be practical – it was too disruptive for Holly and she'd just been diagnosed,' Chrissie snapped. Jude stared at the fluffy rug underneath the coffee table. She'd never seen Chrissie this upset before. 'And then, to cap it all, I'm still so worried about Holly. She's been having all these tests. She keeps going low, and the hospital and Dr Ben have all mentioned the pressure it's putting her kidneys under. I can't bear to think about what could happen if they can't sort things out ... she's been through so much already. I feel wretched about it. Utterly helpless and miserable and a failure that I can't do anything for my child. Then Sam turns up muddling things up in my mind when I just need to be focusing on her—'

'Oh come on, Chrissie,' Jude jumped in, keen to pull things back and salvage something of the evening for her friend, 'Sam's here to help. He wants to make things right, I'm convinced of it. And he loves you both. I don't know the real reasons why he has been avoiding facing up to things before now, but you need to listen to him at least. To let him try. If not for you, then for Holly.' Jude knew it was a horrible situation: a daughter they adored who had this awful condition. 'You're taking on too much by yourself – let Sam in.'

'To save the day – be the hero in Holly's eyes like he always is?' Chrissie let out a long, shuddery sigh.

'You know that's not what I'm saying, but maybe he has felt like he isn't good enough for a reason?'

'Hang on, are you saying that it's my fault he stayed

away?' Chrissie looked accusingly at her, as if tensely primed for any sign of betrayal.

'Hey, hold your horses! I never said anything of the sort ... but ...' Jude gulped down a mouthful of the Prosecco, instantly wishing she'd been more tactful. She really didn't want to upset Chrissie.

'But what?'

'Look, you're a hard taskmaster, not ever really trusting anyone to know what is right for Holly except yourself. And I get that. You're her mum. But it's OK to share it, let go a bit more and ask for help. Sam's here, let him in. Let him help.' Jude figured it best to come out with it. If there was to be any kind of reconciliation between the two people she cared about and loved very much, then they both needed to reflect. Chrissie could be very stubborn and controlling. And Jude knew there were valid reasons for this, given her upbringing, but she couldn't just stand by and see Chrissie and Sam's marriage break beyond repair.

'Someone has to be in charge, Jude. Tonight shows I can't trust Sam ... oh, I know Holly is up to something – I'm not daft. But she knew Sam was supposed to wait with her until I got home. He could have called. He could have checked what the arrangements were at least, to show he's thinking things through.'

'Hmm,' Jude pondered, picking up a few Twiglets. 'Holly always could run rings around him ...' Silence hung in the air. 'Oh, Chrissie,' Jude then added, stroking her friend's arm again. 'It's not too late … He's come back now, and that has to mean something. Sam isn't a nasty, thoughtless guy. I'm sure he didn't deliberately set out to not call you to check on the arrangements. Or to hurt you by being away for so long; to destroy your marriage … you know that—'

'Maybe,' Chrissie cut in, 'maybe not.' And they both stared straight ahead at the screen on the monitor. Holly looked as if she was asleep now, the book still open on top of the duvet.

Jude inhaled, at a loss as to what to say for the best. She knew Chrissie inside out, they had grown up together, and one thing she did know about her friend was that she always went into bunker mentality when she was scared. It was as if she was so entrenched in keeping it all together, for her and Holly, being in control, that she had lost sight of everything else. Chrissie had spoken a lot over the years to Jude about how she didn't ever want to be like her own mother. Unreliable and erratic on account of her alcohol dependency. And, given the strain Chrissie was under, it seemed to Jude that Chrissie's determination to be different, a better mum than her own one had been, coupled with the breakdown of her marriage and Holly's illness, had turned her into an exaggerated version of herself. But then, she'd been coping on her own – without her husband, or indeed her best friend, to help her put things into perspective – so it was little wonder that her need for control and order, so lacking in her own childhood, had now magnified.

Jude suddenly felt helpless too, at a complete loss as to what to do for the best for her friend. And figuring that life could be just so rubbish sometimes.

'Anyway,' said Chrissie, standing up. 'That's enough about me. I'm going to check on Holly and then I want to hear all about Tindledale's famous new resident, Myles King, before you leave this evening ...'

*

In the Duck & Puddle, Sam pressed to end the call on his mobile, and then picked up his pint glass, intending to finish his beer before the pub landlady, Cher, rang the Last Orders bell. But he didn't fancy it now. His heart sank. It was late, and Chrissie had just called saying she was going to bed but needed to get something off her chest first. He had managed to upset her again, the exact opposite of what he'd been trying to achieve. And he could hardly have said that Holly had told him she was allowed to be at home alone ... No, that would have just got her into trouble, and potentially damaged his relationship with her, too, as she was bound to blame him for 'grassing her up', or whatever the correct terminology was these days for a thirteen year old to use. But thank

God she was OK. Not for the first time, he cursed himself for not listening to his instincts and calling Chrissie to agree the arrangements for their daughter – that was what the distance between them all had done; made him doubt himself. Anyway, he certainly wouldn't make the mistake again of leaving her at home alone.

He puffed out a long breath and shoved his phone into his jeans pocket. So much for the upbeat feeling he'd had less than half an hour ago. And what did she mean about flowers? What flowers? He hadn't sent her flowers. Sam took a moment to try to figure it all out in his head, but all he could come up with was … if he hadn't sent her flowers, then who had? Perhaps he'd been right the first time. There was another man. Must be. And Chrissie must have been seeing him for a while. Pink lilies were her favourite flowers, and that isn't something a bloke would know after just one or two dates. No way, surely not?

Sam pushed the pint glass away, stood up, and went to leave the warmth of the village pub's log fire, which was crackling and flickering away in the inglenook fireplace as the inclement weather had gone for a chillier feel today. He'd just reached the door when his friend Matt, the village farrier, walked in with his wife, April. Sam hadn't met April before, not having been able to make it to their wedding last summer. The date had clashed with the grand opening of a new waterfront hotel in the exclusive Sentosa Cove district of Singapore, and there was no way his boss would have entertained the idea of him not being there to shake the hands of the wealthy Chinese investors in person. Sam had also missed the celebration party after the birth of Matt and April's baby ... a gorgeous little girl they named Winnie in memory of April's great aunt who disappeared during the Second World War.

'Sam, good to see you, mate. April, this is my old pal, Sam. Sam, this is my gorgeous wife, April.' Matt did the introductions with a massive grin on his face. 'So, you're back in the village now, I hear?' and Matt gave him a handshake followed by a hearty man-hug, once Sam and April had said hello to each other.

'Yep, that's right,' Sam said, trying to muster some enthusiasm on seeing one of his oldest friends. But he felt dejected, useless, mixed with a twinge of self-loathing that he'd not made more of an effort to make damn sure he had attended Matt and April's wedding. Instead, he'd been so anxious to get the recognition, the public accolade of designing such a 'wondrous palace' – as the Chinese investors had called it. And they had been so pleased ... Sam had to wonder why that had been so important to him. More important than being here for his mate.

'What is it?' Matt looked at him, concern etched on

his face. Then he turned to April and added, 'Would you mind giving us a minute, my love?'

'Sure,' April smiled and made her way over to a table where her friend, Molly, Cooper's wife, was waving to her.

'So what's up?' Matt asked. Sam opened his mouth. Hesitated. Closed it. He could hardly offload all his baggage onto Matt. No, not when they had hardly seen each other over the last few years. Plus, he wasn't good at talking about stuff like this.

'Sorry, mate. Good to see you. But I ... um ... need to go. Another time, yeah?' And with his head bowed, Sam ducked out of the pub, keen to get away and calm down. The scratchiness in his throat was back with a vengeance now, too, making his tonsils feel as if they were being wrapped, and then squeezed, in sandpaper, and in his heart he began to wonder if coming back to Tindledale had been the right thing to do after all. It seemed Chrissie and Holly had been doing very well without him around ... they didn't need him any more, and Holly was quite happy having a virtual relationship. Maybe she was better off without him in any case ... he'd put her at risk by leaving her home alone. Chrissie knew how to keep her safe, which was more than he seemed capable of doing. Perhaps he should do them all a favour and try to move on, especially as it seemed that Chrissie had already done just that.

'Hold on, mate.' Sam felt Matt's hand on his shoulder as he went to put the key in the door of the Land Rover. He turned around. 'What's the rush? Surely you've got time for a quick catch-up?'

'You don't want to hear it. Trust me—' Sam started.

'Try me.' Matt stared him right in the eye. They'd been friends for years and Sam knew that Matt could be a persistent bugger when he wanted to be.

'I dunno. Just got a load on my mind.' Sam shrugged, feeling cornered.

'Like what?' Matt wasn't giving up, so Sam pushed his keys back into his jeans pocket and leant against the car instead.

'Just stuff. Family stuff.' Sam looked down and kicked a piece of gravel away.

'Is it Holly? Is she all right?' Matt asked, standing alongside Sam now with his hands in his pockets.

'I'm worried about the diabetes. It's getting worse. We have to keep an eye on her, the doctor said.'

'Sorry, mate.' Matt shook his head. 'It's tough when they aren't well.'

'Yeah. It is. But it's more than that. I've messed up, Matt. Really messed up ...' Sam's voice drifted.

'What do you mean, messed up? Is there someone else?' Matt gave him a sideways look.

'No, nothing like that. I haven't had an affair. I wouldn't

do that. But I stayed away for far too long. Took Chrissie for granted ...'

A silence hung in the air as the two men gathered their thoughts.

'So is that why you're back?' It was Matt who spoke first.

'Yeah. I've come home to sort out my marriage ...' Sam stared into the starry night sky, stretching out across the pub car park and over the duck pond on the village green as he contemplated. This was his home ... everything he loved was here. People. The place. Tindledale really was idyllic, with the cobbled High Street and tiny Tudor shops. He loved the familiarity of it all. The place where he had grown up. Fallen in love with Chrissie. Holly was born here. So why had he stayed away for so long?

'I see,' Matt cut into the reverie. 'But that's good though ... that you're back now. Can't imagine it's easy keeping all the relationship stuff going when you're thousands of miles away.'

'No, it's not,' Sam muttered. 'But I'm making a mess of it even now I'm back.'

'Go on.'

'I left Holly on her own when I dropped her home tonight and she had an accident. Chrissie went into one. Blamed me. Said she can't trust me. I should have known that Holly mustn't be left on her own with the diabetes the way it is—'

'And I bet Holly told you it was perfectly all right,' Matt cut in, smiling and shaking his head. 'That Chrissie leaves her on her own all the time.'

'How did you guess?' Sam turned to look at his mate.

'Been there, done that, and got the T-shirt, Sam. I know all the tricks, remember.'

'Ahh, yes.' Sam nodded, remembering Matt had been a single dad to his daughter Bella before he met and married April. 'Of course you do. The other thing is, Holly and Chrissie are at loggerheads all the time. They've always had a fiery relationship, but I hadn't realised how bad it had got. The other night Holly was shouting that she hated Chrissie ...'

'Yep. Sounds about right.' Matt moved forward to stand squarely in front of him. 'Typical teenage stuff, Sam. I wouldn't get too hung up over that.'

'Do you reckon? I blame myself. If I hadn't gone away. Left it so long to come back—'

'Holly would still be yelling at her mum,' Matt interjected. 'Trust me. Bella used to shout at me all the time. Reckoned she hated me a million times a day. It's just teenagers. They all do it. Give her a few more years to get through the tricky stage and she'll be a lovely young woman. Guarantee it.'

'I hope so,' Sam nodded, mulling it all over. 'How is Bella by the way?'

'She's good, Sam. Really great. She's doing a textiles

course at the college in Market Briar. Loves it. She's turned out OK ... even if I do say so myself.'

'Nice one,' Sam put his hand out to Matt. 'And thanks for the chat, mate.'

'Any time. You know where to find me,' Matt replied, shaking Sam's hand. 'And good luck, Sam. I really hope you and Chrissie sort it out. You were always good together ...'

Chapter Ten

'So you're back in Tindledale then, are you?' Sam should have known that his mother, Linda, would carry on like this. 'I bet you're the talking point of the whole village now your marriage has fallen apart ... There's nothing they like better than a bit of scandal.' She sounded positively gleeful. Sam felt the hairs on the back of his neck bristling with irritation.

After leaving the Duck & Puddle pub last night, and then having a stern word with himself – sitting up till the early hours watching boxsets on Netflix with a bottle of brandy – he had tried to figure it all out, mulling over Matt's words of wisdom and trying to work out what to do for the best. At one point he even wondered if he was having some kind of breakdown, a mid-life crisis perhaps, as it seemed he couldn't even trust his own decision-making capabilities these days, given the massive error of judgement he'd made when dropping Holly home. So he had literally stood up and stared in the mirror that hung on Dolly's sitting-room wall above the fireplace and asked himself the question ... what matters most to you, Samuel Anthony Morgan?

Family.

That was his answer.

Chrissie and Holly. He wasn't going to lose either of them. He needed to prove that he had the commitment that Chrissie needed so that she would seriously consider giving their marriage another go. Which reminded him ... at his lowest point last night, he had wondered again if she was seeing someone else. And if she really was, then who could the other man be? It couldn't be someone in the village, surely not ... Tindledale was a very small place, incestuously so at times, where everyone knew everyone, had grown up together, and most often families were related in some way, so he was bound to have heard something; Matt or one of his mates would have told him in the pub. Sam ran through all the possibilities, like a Rolodex of potential suitors, in his head, but unless the man was a newcomer, someone he didn't know, then he had no idea who he might be. All the men in Tindledale were either too young for Chrissie to give them a second glance, were happily hooked up, or gay. But whichever way he sliced it up, the state of his marriage was destroying him. It was all well and good for him to come home now with the best of intentions, but he knew deep down it was going to take more than that to fix everything. But it was a start, at least.

Sam had eventually managed to get hold of his mum, Linda, on the mobile number that he had called last time. Which was a novelty given that, the time before that, he'd had to call his brother Patrick in Australia first to see if he had up-to-date contact details for her when he got the 'number you are calling is no longer available' message. So, having tracked his mother down and gone through the polite customary catch-up questions, Linda had then spent the first twenty minutes of the phone call complaining about the food, the heat, the foreigners ... which was quite ironic given that she was on a day tour in Istanbul. So, technically, she was the foreigner at that particular stop on the three-week cruise she had treated herself to after retiring just a few months ago, as she had informed him. Sam used the word 'retired' loosely, given that she hadn't actually had a proper, paid job since the late Eighties, when she had been a dental nurse for a while at the practice in Market Briar. But after deciding that she didn't really like other people's mouths, Linda had packed the job in and become a full-time lady of leisure. That is, until she had met Nigel, the first of many men who seemed perfectly happy to finance her luxurious lifestyle whilst flitting around the Mediterranean in between pit-stops at her flat somewhere in London.

Sam was never quite sure where she lived exactly now, not having once been invited to visit her, ever; well, certainly not since she had left Tindledale. It was as if she had left the village and not looked back since, practically cutting all ties with her previous life and those that should have played a significant part. In fact, Sam was quite sure that, if he just stopped calling his mother, it would be very likely indeed that he'd never speak to her again. He held the thought momentarily ... and then for some bizarre reason he wondered if that would be such a bad thing. But she was still his mother and, to be honest, it hurt him that she behaved in this way. He'd tried so many times to see her, to forge a 'normal' relationship with her, but whenever he suggested visiting for a birthday or Christmas she'd invariably respond with a terse, 'Whatever for?' followed by, 'The shop will post on little Holly's present', which would then arrive a few days later directly from Harrods or John Lewis with the innocuous, but quite obligatory, typed gift message.

Sam checked his watch; twenty-three minutes now they had been engaged in the call and Linda still hadn't drawn breath.

'Mum!' He could bear it no longer. 'Look. This is important. I've been trying to tell you about Holly, how she's getting on ...'

'And I'm telling you my news, it's not your turn yet.' And she actually laughed.

'Mum, this is not funny,' he attempted. Jesus, was she trollied? Sam realised then that she probably was, and pulled the phone away from his ear to stare at it as she cackled some more. Well, it would explain her attitude. She always got like this when she'd had too much to drink. But it was only ten a.m. in Istanbul. And wasn't Turkey one of those countries where alcohol was restricted? And she was sitting outside a café, she had told him so. He shook his head and tried again.

'Mum, this is your granddaughter we are talking about, the one with diabetes,' he attempted, 'unless you had forgotten.'

'Of course I haven't. There's no need for sarcasm, Samuel.' His mother's voice was like ice.

'Sorry,' he said instinctively. Then immediately hating that he sounded as if he'd reverted back to being a young boy, as was often the way when dealing with his mother. 'Look, I'm calling to keep in touch, let you know how Holly is. And I just thought you should know that I was back in Tindledale. In case you wanted to get hold of me.'

'Poor old Sam, still messing everything up. Well, good luck trying to patch your marriage back together again.' Her voice dripped with poison. 'But, you might find that ship has sailed, my boy. The last time I saw that wife of yours, she couldn't even marshal a smile onto her own face. Nothing gets past me, you know. I saw the way she was. Miserable.'

Sam flinched.

'When was that?' he asked, and then, not waiting for

a reply, he told her, 'When Holly was about five years old and had a tummy bug. Chrissie had been up all night with her and was exhausted, was that it?' Given that seeing his mother was such a rarity, Sam remembered the occasion with perfect clarity. Linda had turned up out of the blue one Sunday morning, insisting they all go to the Duck & Puddle for a nice pub lunch. But had then sulked when she didn't get her own way, before disappearing back to wherever she had come from.

'Oh, there's no need to be like that,' she dismissed, as if he was the one who was out of order. 'I don't remember when it was exactly.'

'Anyway, I didn't call to have an argument.' Sam decided to change tack. What was the point? His mother had never liked Chrissie, and he knew the feeling was mutual, and for good reason on Chrissie's part. He would never forget the scene in the hospital when Holly had been born. The three of them on the bed, having a lovely cuddle, him with Holly in his arms, marvelling at how tiny and gorgeous she was. Chrissie had leaned into him, touching her finger to Holly's little rosebud mouth and saying she was perfect. Linda had turned up in a flurry and, after peering at the baby that he and Chrissie adored with all their hearts, had said she wondered why all newborn babies were so ugly. Followed by a supercilious laugh. He had told Linda she was out of order, only for her to retaliate with, 'You always were so oversensitive.'

'Good,' Linda snapped, followed by a more bountiful, 'so how is my dear little Holly?'

'She's OK,' Sam replied, pleased to have moved the conversation on at last. 'But there have been a few problems with keeping her diabetes under control. We're all a bit worried, to be honest. She's been having more tests.'

'Oh, you're probably worrying way too much. Bet she's been sneaking the odd Mars bar or two. Not that I blame her. Can't be much fun having a ban on sweet treats. I'd never survive diabetes, having to be deprived of life's pleasures like that. Definitely not.' Linda said, her voice all breathy and airy as she turned the conversation, yet again, back on to herself. 'Besides, you always were a worrier. Now, I must dash, but I'll tell you what ... I'll get a nice present posted out to little Holly. That will cheer her up.' Sam prickled. *Like a present is going to make up for a defective grandparent like you.*

'She's thirteen, Mum. Not so little now ... Maybe if you came to see her ...' He couldn't help himself. It irked him that his mother always referred to Holly as 'little'. Besides, if she actually saw Holly, in person, then maybe, just maybe, it would galvanise her into action and spur her on to show a bit more interest in her only grandchild.

'Is she *really*?' Linda gasped. 'But she can't be. I'm not old enough to have a teenage grandchild.' And Sam could just see her now, clutching her pearl necklace in horror, making it all about her, as ever.

'Well she is.' He let his voice fade. His own mother clearly wasn't interested in Holly. In fact, he felt shocked and quite crushed by how dismissive she was being. But what hurt the most was the little-boy part inside him that still yearned for a mother that Linda wouldn't, or couldn't ever be. And it was that feeling of rejection that always got to him. He absolutely treasured Holly. Chrissie did too – no matter how much mum and daughter clashed, he knew with certainty that Chrissie cared for and loved Holly with all her heart. So how come his mother could be so cold and unfeeling?

'I don't see what a visit from me would do to help the situation ...' Linda gave a trite little chuckle, as if to make light of the situation, thereby exonerating her of any real obligation. 'Don't forget, I had all this with your father, Samuel, when they thought he might need a new kidney.' Sam blanched; this was the last thing he wanted to hear. Holly didn't need a new kidney ... and he hoped she never would. 'Yes, all those blood tests. I refused to go through with it, you know.'

'Refused to go through with what?' Sam asked, wishing he'd never called her now.

'Blood tests! To see if I was a match for a kidney donation.' He heard her take a swig from whatever she was drinking, and then swallow. 'I told them no. They weren't taking one of my kidneys and that was that! You have to be firm about these things.'

'Mum, are you serious?' Sam said, aghast.

'Of course. I had my own future to consider, plus your father died in the end anyway. So it would have been a waste!'

He was momentarily speechless.

'And if Holly did ever need a kidney?' he eventually managed, not even wanting to contemplate the thought of this for his daughter. But something inside him needed to know how his own mother would respond in this scenario. 'I hope she never does. But what would you do then?'

'Oh, little Holly wouldn't want one of my poor Prosecco-pickled kidneys,' Linda answered evasively, and he could hear her mirthless laugh from the other end of the line.

'But surely you'd have a blood test? For your grand-daughter. If only to rule you out. Or, you know, to see if you were a match ... we all would, wouldn't we? The whole family ...'

Sam found he was holding his breath as he waited for her answer. He'd always known his mother was selfish. But would she seriously refuse Holly?

Silence followed.

Sam gave up waiting for her answer.

'Well, I wouldn't hesitate!' he said, glancing at his

watch. He needed to end this call. Yet again, she had managed to drag him down. What was he thinking in even phoning her when she had a knack of pushing all his buttons and making him feel so crap about everything.

'Hmm, well you should!' Linda suddenly piped up. 'You'd do well to think seriously about whether you could go through all that. You're not getting any younger, Samuel Anthony Morgan.'

He groaned, hating how she always used his full name when imparting some kind of authoritarian words of perceived wisdom. As if it was her right as his mother. But she had no right to, as far as he was concerned, not when she had neglected to do all the other parenting things that a child could reasonably expect ... like providing food, for example. And affection, not to mention love and care, and interest. Yes, an interest in his life would have been nice. Instead of gallivanting off into the sunset as soon as his father had died. And then frequently dumping him and Patrick at Dolly's door for weeks on end, with no word of when she'd return for them. He had hated it. Hated feeling rejected. Dolly had done her best, but it wasn't the same as being wanted by your own mum.

'And with all that stress you put yourself through ... well, it can't be good for your heart,' she carried on. 'Are you sure you could cope with blood tests? Let alone giving a kidney away? It's a major operation. Just the anaesthetic alone could kill you, you know! And the way things are going with the NHS, it'll all be privatised soon in any case. So they won't do it for free, I wouldn't expect. You mark my words. And you would be no use to little Holly if you were dead.'

Sam gawped at the phone. *Is she for real?* He had thought he'd heard it all as far as his mother was concerned. Stupidly assuming she couldn't shock him any more than she already had over the years. But this! This was plain nasty. Not only was she coming up with excuses for herself not to help should it ever be necessary – and he truly hoped to God it never would be, especially if his mother was their only option for a family donor – but she was now also trying to persuade him not to help his own daughter. Staggering.

Sam looked at the ceiling before closing his eyes and letting out a long breath. He really should have known better. It was ridiculous that he'd been drawn into this hypothetical conversation in the first place. Holly didn't even need a kidney. But what did he expect? Linda to miraculously turn into a loving mother and grandmother who would do anything for her family? His mother had always been one for grand gestures, and presents from Harrods were all well and good, but when it came down to what really mattered, she was always woefully lacking. And, in that moment, a horrible, sickening realisation seeped into Sam's field of thought. *Grand gestures. What really mattered. Who does that sound like? That's what*

Chrissie said about me. Oh Christ, please don't let me turn into my mother. Or maybe I've always been like her.

When he had been mulling everything over last night, he had gone online and ordered a whole load of those products that Holly had been telling him about, even managing to get a box full of the dry shampoo with the pink flamingos on. He'd had to pay over the odds to get it shipped from America, but he hadn't even given it a second thought. He wanted to spoil Holly on her upcoming birthday. And then he'd bought her a new mobile, an upgrade on the one she already had. Plus a load of other stuff. Chrissie too. He'd ordered her a Tiffany bangle. The exact one she had oohed and ahhed over that time they had gone up to London to see the Christmas lights. Holly must have been about three, as she was wrapped up all warm in a snowsuit on his shoulders and kept blowing raspberries on the side of his face. Chrissie had laughed. They all had laughed. It had been a brilliant day. And he had promised Chrissie he would buy her the bangle, when he won the lottery or landed a decent job ... But was he just being overindulgent? Or over-compensating?

Shaking his head, as if to eradicate himself of any resemblance to his mother, Sam stood up and paced around the room. With nothing else to say, he managed a short goodbye and then pressed a shaky index finger on the phone to end the call. Sinking into the sofa, he tapped the top of the phone against his stubbly chin as he digested the call and picked over everything that had been said ... or not said, to be more accurate. Shoving his mother's selfishness aside, something still definitely didn't add up. Linda's evasiveness over a hypothetical simple blood test for Holly was even more acute than it usually was. She could have just lied and said, 'Of course I'd do a test for Holly.' It wasn't as if she was actually being asked to commit to anything right now. No, he knew her well enough to know that there was more to it. Why was she being so defensive about it? And then deflecting the spotlight from her by attacking him instead. Why on earth would she try to talk him out of getting tested too? He figured his mother must have something to hide. Well, he wasn't letting her off the hook this time. He resolved to find out what her real issue was and challenge her.

He sat in silence for a while longer, still going over and over it all inside his head as he tried to work out what was going on.

What was she hiding?

Why was she acting as though she didn't really care?

Why would she do that?

And then it struck him. It was the only reason. It had to be. She was ill! Seriously ill with cancer, or something. And it would explain her attempt to make light of the situation ... if she knew there was no possible way that she could ever give a kidney, even in the unlikely event that her granddaughter needed one. And, despite all her faults, Sam knew that Linda loved Holly, or at least cared for her; she'd never missed a birthday or Christmas present so it didn't really add up.

After inhaling and puffing out his cheeks as he let out a long breath, Sam made another call. To Dr Ben this time. After talking to his mother and hearing what she had said about his father's health and how he might have needed a donor kidney, Sam knew that he needed to find out what the longer-term prognosis might be for Holly. Sam also knew that he needed to face up to the fear. He'd been running away for too long, fearful of more bad news, of the future. Burying his head in his work had been one way to deal with his daughter's health issues, but that clearly hadn't worked either for him or his family.

The GP might not be able to shed any light on his mother's reluctance to help Holly, or indeed her current health status, but he could fill in the gaps that Sam had missed by not being at Holly's check-ups, that was for sure. Chrissie had told him how the appointments had gone, of course, when they had been talking regularly, but that hadn't been the case for far too long now. And Dr Ben might be able to help fix his head too. Sleeping tablets would be a good start, because he hadn't had a decent night's sleep in weeks. He couldn't carry on feeling this way ... he was no good to anyone. He'd made that mistake before – apathy, followed by running away and doing nothing. Denial. This time he needed to deal with it all head on and take care of what really mattered.

Chapter Eleven

'Who is she?' Myles came bounding across the main lawn towards Jude and Holly, with his messy blond hair stuffed underneath a tartan deerstalker hat and his body clad in what Jude could only describe as ridiculous hunting wear. Or maybe it was his lord-of-the-manor fancy-dress costume, on account of him thinking it was what the villagers expected. It was hard to be sure. But either way he looked utterly bonkers. And was that a real shotgun hanging on a leather strap over his shoulder?

'Hi Myles,' Jude started cheerfully, hoping to bypass another one of his deeply suspicious welcomes. She had been here at the Blackwood Farm Estate several times now, and had seen multitudes of people arrive for a variety of genuine reasons ... and some not so, admittedly. Molly, the butcher's wife, for example, turned up the other day with one of her legendary steak and ale pies as a 'welcome to Tindledale' gift for Myles and Sylvia. Only to be quizzed ridiculously about all sorts of things, before Sam had had to come over from the new stable-block construction that he was overseeing, just to vouch for her. It was same with everyone, regardless of whether they were 'on the list' or not, and Holly most certainly was. But it seemed that Myles lived in a bubble of faded grandiosity, convinced that he was continuously at risk from some kind of security threat: Jude had spotted a couple of plain-clothes security guys foraging around in a hedgerow only yesterday afternoon when she'd been here to take delivery of some curtain sample sets. It was ridiculous; like something out of a spoof spy caper, *The Pink Panther* even, seeing as one of the guys had a bushy black moustache and was wearing a beige raincoat. Very Inspector Clouseau.

'Her name is Holly. She's my goddaughter ... and Sam's actual daughter,' Jude continued, desperately trying not to stare or laugh at Myles's knee-high wool socks and corduroy breeches, or whatever they were. She certainly hadn't seen shorts like it before, though maybe in that history book the parish council had put together for tourists, called 'Tindledale through the Ages', which had lots of pictures of gamekeepers and the like dressed up in this gear. Maybe she should delicately persuade him to let her design a suitable country living wardrobe for him too! Jeans and wellies would do for sure. There really was no need for him to scour the internet looking for what he thought country gents wore. Or was this just another aspect of his need for camouflage? To hide the real Myles King ...

'Hmm. Does Sylvia know about it?' he eyed Holly suspiciously.

'Yes, Myles, she does,' Jude said slowly, as if explaining it all to a toddler. 'And remember, I mentioned it the other day and you said that it was fine for me to bring Holly to the estate to see your prize pigs.'

She knew this would appeal to his ego, as he was extremely keen to show off the micro-pigs. Yes, that's right … Jude hadn't had the heart to tell him that the ten little pigs he'd bought weren't Large Blacks at all. He'd been so impressed with himself the first time she had come here, when he'd taken her to see the arrival of the pigs, but Jude had known as soon as she saw them that they were far too small to be anything other than micro-pigs. And, after feeling anxious about Holly after the fall, she had arranged with Chrissie to spend the day with her goddaughter to see if she could cheer her up and perhaps get to the bottom of why Holly thought her mum hated her. Jude was very concerned, but didn't want to add to the pressure that Chrissie was under by talking to her about this … not when she had enough to worry about. Chrissie would be devastated if she knew that Holly thought she hated her. And Holly loved animals, so the micro-pigs were sure to appeal to her.

'That's right! A fantastic idea.' Myles waved an exuberant pointed index finger in the air, as if it had been his idea all along, and then stepped forward towards Holly and added, 'Welcome to the Blackwood Farm Estate. I'm Myles King,' he finished with a flourish, holding his palm up for a high five, and Jude willed him not to tag on the cringy intro that he had first given her on the phone – his 'you may have heard of me' line. Because she knew beyond a shadow of a doubt that Holly would have no idea who he was. She hadn't even been born by the time his fame had faded.

'Hi Mr King,' Holly smiled politely, lifting a hand up to reciprocate the high five, which she did with much enthusiasm, making Myles drop his hand down by his side to do an exaggerated groan, as if he was in real pain. Holly giggled and Jude saw a look of admiration pass over her goddaughter's face ... ahh, so she thought Myles was cool! *Well, I guess he would be to a thirteen-year-old girl, seeing as he acts like a big kid himself.*

'Hey babe, it's Myles to you,' he winked, and clicked his tongue on the roof of his mouth. Jude let out a long sigh and rolled her eyes upwards, thinking that maybe this wasn't such a good idea after all. And Chrissie and Sam would go mad if they knew a faded rock star in his forties was flirting with their thirteen-year-old daughter. But Jude soon realised that she didn't need to worry. Her boss had just pulled a Sherbet Dip Dab from his pocket and offered it to Holly, like a friendship token.

'No thanks. I'd better not ... I'm ... err ... ' Holly glanced away and fiddled with the zip on her hoody before adding 'diabetic' in a softer voice. And Jude was surprised at how shy Holly had become all of a sudden. It was unlike her. But more surprising was the way Myles reacted to this information. It was as if he got Holly right away, was on her wavelength, and instinctively knew how to put her at her ease.

'Wow. What type?' he asked, not missing a beat, as if it were a perfectly typical thing to chat to a stranger about. Holly appeared to relax, her shoulders lowered and she stopped fidgeting. 'Are you the shot-in-the-arm proper hard-core type – ' he stopped talking to make a clicking sound as he did a syringe-going-into-the-crook-of-his-elbow action – 'or the boring, live-on-lettuce-while-not-being-allowed-to-ever-have-chocolate type?' Myles pretended to sulk by folding his arms across his chest and pushing his bottom lip out. Holly looked up at him and did a half-smirk.

'The hard-core one,' Holly said, her voice only wavering momentarily, but Jude still stepped closer, feeling protective of her goddaughter and wondering if she should move the conversation on to something more comfortable for her.

'No way!' Myles said, nodding his head impressively. 'Well, put it there.' He laid his palm out flat for Holly to slide her hand across. And she did, her eyes lighting up at this unexpected praise and acceptance. 'Oh that's too bad. But I guess that means *laters* for the Sherbet

Dip Dab. You has to go,' he added in a silly voice as he talked to the packet directly before tossing it into a nearby dustbin. Then, after offloading his shotgun onto one of the security blokes, who appeared right on cue from behind a bush, he took three giant strides to stand in front of Holly and turned around so he had his back towards her. 'Piggyback to the pig pen?' Myles grinned as he bent his knees and braced his body ready for Holly to jump onto his back. She giggled, glanced at Jude, and then, without any hesitation whatsoever, Holly pushed her pink satchel out of the way and hopped aboard, before clasping her hands around his shoulders.

Moments later, Myles was galloping across the lawn towards the pig pen, with his arms looped around Holly's calves, and whooping like a kid arriving at Disney World for the first time, having the most fun ever. Jude stared after them, gobsmacked, before following on behind. He really is a looper – eccentric, even – she thought as he let out a big whinnying noise. But somehow, only he could get away with doing something bonkers like this. And Jude found herself smiling on hearing Holly's laughter, her fair hair flaring all around as Myles darted here, there and everywhere until he reached the pig pen and pretended to offload Holly inside it, and right onto a big pile of pig poo.

'Noooo. Don't you dare,' Holly yelped, pushing Myles's silly deerstalker hat forward, making it fall down over his eyes, so he then staggered around as if blind, stumbling into things and making her laugh so much that tears tumbled over her cheeks. And, suddenly, Jude saw Myles King in a completely different light. Fun and funny, he was energetic and actually quite sweet as he eventually put Holly down, very carefully, on top of a nearby stack of hay bales. She wondered if perhaps this was the real Myles? Fun and frolicky, and not the cocky, guarded persona from earlier. She found the possibility intriguing.

'There you go, Holls. Now, come and see the pigs,' he said, as if the thirteen-year-old girl was his new best friend. Holly jumped up and darted over to the pen, keen to get inside.

'Thanks, Myles,' Holly beamed, her worries from the other day, when she'd ended up on the floor by the fuse box, seeming to have disappeared. And that pleased Jude no end. It can't be easy being stuck in the middle of two estranged parents. Plus managing the diabetes had been difficult for her – it had taken her a long time to accept it, and then learn how to manage the checking and administering of the insulin. Holly had gone through a period of resentment and anger at being different from her friends. Chrissie had told Jude all about it in their long phone chats. Soon after the diagnosis, Holly had come home after a day out shopping with her friends, and had been bereft because she hadn't been able to join in when they all went for milkshakes – the enormous Galaxy bar blended ones, which had mountains of whipped cream on top and were smothered in sprinkles. It had been Holly's favourite indulgence. A big part of her social life, too, going to the shopping centre in Market Briar with the girls, and into the café, where they all sat in a booth giggling and flirting with the boys from behind their tall milkshakes with big bendy straws. Holly had taken it out on Chrissie, screaming at her for daring to suggest that a bottle of water or a glass of plain milk were good alternatives, before stomping up to her bedroom. It had stuck in Jude's mind, as Chrissie had actually cried when telling Jude what had happened, which was unlike her. She was particularly upset and fed up as it had happened a few days after the first weekend Sam hadn't come home as promised. Jude had even offered to call Sam to see if she could subtly suggest he talk to Holly about it, figuring that might make things easier for her friend. But Chrissie wouldn't hear of it. She had clammed up and apologised for complaining, saying she didn't want anyone thinking she couldn't cope.

'Can I cuddle one of them please?' Holly asked Myles.

'Sure. Which one do you want, Holls?' he replied easily, opening the gate to the pen and jumping inside before quickly closing the gate again behind him.

Holly leaned over the side and pointed to a tiny runt of a pig with pretty, tiger-like stripes crisscrossing its little back. It was in the corner all by itself, like the odd one out. And she felt really sorry for it.

'Good choice. He's my favourite too.' And, after darting his way all around the pen trying to catch him, Myles soon succeeded and scooped the piglet up into his arms before handing him to Holly.

'That's it. Hold him firmly in your arms, as if you're rocking a baby. But not too tightly, as he'll wriggle and you might drop him.' Jude watched on in awe as Myles helped Holly hold the piglet the correct way. Fondly, he touched the tip of his fingers to the pig's little head and said, 'So, what shall we call him?' Holly looked up at Myles as he continued, 'I bet you can come up with a really good name for him ...'

'Really? Can I choose his name?' Holly beamed, and gave Jude a look of pure delight, making her heart melt.

'Sure you can,' Myles nodded.

'How about Tiger?' Holly quickly decided.

'Awesome!' He gave Holly a playful nudge on the arm, and Jude grinned, chuffed to bits to see her goddaughter with an enormous smile on her face, the anxiety from before floating away. 'Right, I'll see if Sylvia can rustle up some lunch. Fish and chips be OK for you?'

'Yum. Yes please,' Holly said, giving Tiger another stroke before handing him to Myles to put back in the pen.

After washing their hands in the newly installed little

basin in the barn a few metres away, Jude and Holly had a chance to chat while Myles strode over to the manor house to find Sylvia.

'So, how are you feeling after your fall the other day? No bruises I hope,' Jude asked brightly.

'OK, thanks. No bruises.' Holly confirmed quietly, not really wanting to talk about it now.

'Good. I'm pleased.' Jude looped her arm through Holly's as they started making their way over to the manor house.

'And your mum? Everything OK now between you two?' Jude continued, treading carefully. The last thing she wanted was for Holly to clam up, or – worse still – think Chrissie had asked her to have a chat with her daughter.

'Dunno,' Holly shrugged. 'She still hates me.'

'What do you mean? I thought you two got on really well … I know you clash a bit sometimes, you always have, and that's the way it is sometimes with family. But what's changed, love?'

'She has,' Holly replied, wondering if it was all right to talk to Aunty Jude. What if she told Mum? She might go even more ballistic. Holly looked sideways at Jude as she tried to work it all out.

'How's that then?' Jude asked.

'Um.' Holly bit her lip, figuring if she trusted Aunty Jude then she might help sort everything out. She might even get Mum and Dad back together again – Mum would be happy and get off her back then, and Dad wouldn't be sad any more. Aunty Jude could talk to them both and help make the wish come true. Or, at the very least, she might have some better ideas for her Get Mum and Dad Back Together in Time for My Birthday plan than just sending them flowers and chocolates, which hadn't worked anyway. Mum hadn't been at all happy with her surprise flowers ... and had even moaned to Dad about the lilies. Holly had heard her shouting at him on the phone and knew that she needed to do something fast. Before Mum actually hated Dad or, worse still, Dad had enough of her and gave up. So she decided to go for it and tell Aunty Jude.

'Well, she's always angry and moaning. Everything I do is wrong. I can't do anything right. She's always been bossy, but it's really bad now. I can hardly breathe without her telling me off!' Holly pushed her chin down into the collar of her hoodie and puffed out a long breath. She had to admit that she did actually feel a bit better for letting it all out.

'Ahh, I'm quite certain your mum doesn't hate you, darling.'

'Why is she always annoyed with me then?' Holly asked. It was so unfair. She had tried not to wind Mum up, but it was like she wanted to be angry with her.

'I'm sorry if it seems that way. But she does care about you very much. Adores you, you know that,' Jude offered, making a mental note to have a proper conversation with Chrissie. Someone had to. It seemed the whole family – Holly, Sam and Chrissie – were each coping in isolation. None of them talking to each other properly; it was heartbreaking to see such a happy family unit so fractured and broken.

'Well, she has a funny way of showing it.' Holly couldn't remember the last time Mum was nice to her. 'All she cares about is homework and panicking about the diabetes and going to her stupid choir practice. It was never like this when Dad was at home. He always made everything good.'

'Did he?'

'Yes, he's so funny and chilled out. I wish Mum was like him.'

'She's funny too sometimes, though, isn't she?' Jude said. 'Do you remember when you were little and she went to lift that bag of flour off the shelf and it fell and puffed all over her head?'

'Yes! It was in her hair and all over her face. And she gave Dad loads of floury kisses so he got covered in it too. It was really funny.'

'And you couldn't stop giggling as she chased you around the house—'

'The flour monster!' Thinking about it made Holly feel happy and she wanted it to be like that again.

'Yes that's right.' Jude liked remembering the good

times. And she was going to remind Chrissie of them. Sam as well, if she had to. She was going to get them talking and sorting it all out, one way or another.

'I wish it was still like that.'

'Me too,' Jude grinned. 'And, you know, I think all teenagers feel the way you do. I know I did. I used to argue with my dad all the time when I was your age, and the thing is, the more you rebel, the more your mum will want to lay down the law. It's what parents do. It's their job to be the boss of you,' she offered, trying to lighten things but feeling a bit out of her depth. She didn't want Holly to think she was siding with Chrissie, or she would never talk to her, and Holly clearly needed someone to talk to right now. But at the same time ... Holly did have a point. Jude knew her friend so well, how she needed to be in control – too much so sometimes. Of course, she knew why; Chrissie felt under enormous strain with her marriage problems and Holly's health, and without enough support from Sam for far too long. But caught in the middle of it all was a vulnerable young girl who quite clearly needed both her parents. Who would benefit from the complementary elements of her parents' styles. Sam's easy-going nature to Chrissie's steadiness – if she could ease off with the need for control a bit and accept some help, and Sam could grow up and commit a bit more, then from where Jude was standing, things might be a whole lot better.

'But she's like it to Dad too.'

'Is she?' Jude creased her forehead.

'Yes, Mum is so evil to him and he hasn't even done anything wrong. And she gets cross with me because I want him to stay at our house and not at Granny Dolly's – if he came home everything would be all right again.'

Jude inhaled and kept quiet, mindful of interfering in her best friend's marriage. As far as Chrissie was concerned, Sam *had* done things wrong, but it wasn't her place to talk about any of that with Holly, so she settled on:

'Maybe your mum missed your dad when he was away. Sometimes people can get cross if they feel like they've been left to look after everything.' A short silence followed. 'Like the house and stuff,' Jude then quickly added, as the last thing she wanted was for Holly to interpret this as Chrissie being cross for looking after her without Sam around. That wasn't what Jude meant at all. It was such a minefield.

'But Dad was working to look after everything too. Pay the mortgage and all that.'

'True, and now that he's back, perhaps we can help your mum and dad get things back to how they used to be. Would you like that?'

'Yes. Definitely. I don't mind Mum being the boss of me –' Holly stopped and giggled – 'if she's funny too … like the flour monster. I want Mum to be happy again. But can I ask you something, Aunty Jude?'

'Sure. Ask away, darling,' Jude said warmly, and then waited for what felt like ages for Holly to speak.

'Will you help me please?'

'Help you?' Jude stopped walking and looked sideways at Holly, who stopped walking too, but then bowed her head and started fiddling again. 'Hey, what is it?' Jude was alarmed now as her brain immediately went into overdrive trying to work out what on earth her thirteen-year-old goddaughter could possibly want her help with. *Jesus, please don't let her be pregnant, or in trouble with the police. Or … drugs!*

'Yes, Mum's got a boyfriend you see, and—'

'*Has she?*' Jude interjected. She felt astounded, surprised and relieved all at the same time, followed by a rush of shame that she had let her head run away with such wild thoughts. She wasn't in LA any more. No, this was the sleepy little village of Tindledale, where it would be far more unlikely for young girls like Holly to be dabbling in drugs. Where would she get them, for starters? There were no nightclubs or pubs in the village that tolerated that kind of thing, and there certainly weren't any dubious characters cruising around the High Street, or not that she had noticed …

'Yeah, he's called Gavin,' Holly continued. 'And I reckon that's why she hates me. I've been thinking … it explains why she's always so moody with me. I thought at first it was because she missed Dad or was still cross with him for not coming home when he promised he would. But he's back for good now and she's still angry all the time. If it wasn't for me, then she wouldn't even have to ever see Dad again, she could be with Gavin all the time. She could let him live with her and everything.'

'Oh, I see,' Jude said casually, making a mental note to ask Chrissie about this surprising revelation, and wondering why her best friend hadn't mentioned it. They usually confided in each other, always had done over the years, and a boyfriend was definitely something that would have been discussed. Unless Chrissie had something to hide … maybe she felt ashamed, guilty, or embarrassed of course. Or perhaps a mixture of all those emotions, which was entirely possible given that Chrissie was married. To Sam Morgan. The guy they had both been friends with since primary school. Or what if the boyfriend, Gavin, was married? Perhaps that's why Chrissie hadn't said anything to her? But Chrissie wouldn't do that, would she? She just wasn't the type, was she? Jude pondered momentarily and then forced the bundle of confusing thoughts away.

'And Gavin is such a dickhead.'

Jude stifled a laugh by placing the back of her hand over her mouth and turning away. She could hardly tell Holly off for saying 'dickhead' … no, that would just make her a hypocrite, as Jude was rather fond of using that word, if the person was behaving in such a way as to warrant it. Scott, for example, her cocky American ex-boyfriend, had definitely been one. And Myles too – Jude had thought he was a giant dickhead until today, but now she wasn't so sure.... The way he had been with Holly earlier was touching, kind and absolutely not remotely dickheadish behaviour whatsoever. In fact, she felt it was fair to say that she was starting to thaw towards Myles King.

'Oh, why's that then?' Jude asked, still keeping things light. But she was intrigued to know more about the elusive Gavin.

'I dunno.' Holly shrugged. 'He just is. The daft-looking grin on his face for starters.'

'Oh dear,' Jude stifled another snort of laughter. 'So where did your mum meet Gavin?'

'At choir practice. He takes her in his car. She gets all dressed up for him. And I overheard her flirting on the phone with him ... laughing and saying "shush" in a weird way. They've been out for dinner too!'

'Right.' Jude logged this information for discussion with Chrissie later. It was hardly evidence of a new sexual relationship for Holly's mum, at the exclusion of the dad she adored, but Holly was obviously anxious about it.

Holly fell silent for a second or two, and then added in a more earnest tone, 'So will you help me, please?'

'Sure, if I can; what is it you want me to do?' Jude was never one to shy away from a little bit of subterfuge.

'Help me get Mum and Dad back together in time for my birthday. I know they still love each other. And I'm sure Mum would stop being angry and blaming me if she was happy. They could both be happy again. We all would. It would be like a wish come true. And that would be the best birthday present of all, don't you think?'

They walked on some more, and Jude mulled it all over, wondering what to do for the best. She needed to talk to Chrissie. Have a proper, sit-down, heart-to-heart, and really get to the bottom of what was going on. It was awful seeing Holly so upset, not to mention Chrissie and Sam's marriage falling apart like this when they had been so very happy. Jude remembered when they had first started dating – Chrissie had been besotted. Cautious, given her previous relationship, but still ... she couldn't get enough of Sam. And then, when they had started living together, the fun pizza and beer nights they had hosted with all their friends piled into the tiny studio flat, always with Chrissie and Sam loved up on the sofa, or messing around whacking each other with cushions, typically with one of the gang begging them to 'get a room ... for crying out loud'. And their mutual love of homemaking – Sam with his DIY building skills making their farmhouse just right; Chrissie filling it with cosy, comfortable soft furnishings and fabrics. They made a great team. Not to mention their love of music, Sam with his guitar and Chrissie's singing. And, in the days before Holly, they had travelled all over to music festivals and concerts. Jude went along too sometimes, before she moved away, with whichever boyfriend she happened to be hooked up with at the time. Remembering the fun they had seeing David Bowie perform in Madison Square Gardens in New York City – Chrissie had arranged it all as a brilliant surprise for Sam's birthday. Then to Reggio in Italy for a U2 concert, and Wembley Arena in London to see Chrissie's favourite, Robbie Williams. They had the best of times. And then the wedding. It had been like something out of a magical fairy tale. Not extravagant, but beautifully simple and low budget. Chrissie had worn a floaty white sundress with a band of wild flowers in her hair. Barefoot, she had walked with Jude through the fields of Tindledale up to the little church in the village, where Tony had escorted her to the altar to meet Sam. Chrissie's choir had sung 'Love Is in the Air' for her. And then, after the short ceremony, they had partied in the Duck & Puddle pub garden, dancing and feasting on a hog roast with all their friends. Everyone had been so happy. The image of Sam sweeping Chrissie off her feet and twirling her around and around in his arms as the sun set on the horizon, shimmering in her hair and framing the giant smile on her face, would always be in Jude's mind. It had been emotional, seeing her friends so happy, and even more reason why she had to do something now.

Jude knew her friend wouldn't thank her for it, though. She had always been stubborn like that. She remembered a time at college when Chrissie had recently dumped the guy she had been seeing and he'd pleaded with Jude to have a word with her friend, which she had, only to get her ear chewed off about minding her own business. They had even stopped talking for a week or so. Until Chrissie had apologised, and presented Jude with a lovely set of pearly eye shadows from Boots. The very palette that they had both been coveting for weeks whenever they went shopping together to Market Briar.

But Jude couldn't bear seeing Holly so down, especially with her health the way it was. And Holly thinking that Chrissie hated her was a dreadful thing. Jude bit down hard on her bottom lip, pushed a smile onto her face and resolved to help her goddaughter in whatever way she could. She wished she could come up with something. A plan to make Holly's wish come true and give her the gift she needed this birthday, in more ways than one ...

Chapter Twelve

'Come in. Please, take a seat,' Dr Ben greeted Sam in his Dublin accent. He pushed his glasses further up his nose and then gestured for Sam to sit down. Swiftly realising that the only chair in his consulting room was covered in paperwork, Dr Ben gathered the files up and promptly dumped them on the floor.

'Sorry. I hate filing,' he explained, before sitting on the corner of the desk and pushing his curly black hair away from his face. After disentangling himself from a stethoscope that was wrapped around his neck, he turned his attentions fully to Sam. 'So, how are you? I've not seen you here in a while.'

'No, I've been away working ... And I've been better, to be honest,' Sam started, and then let his voice fade to silence. There was so much he wanted to say, to ask, but he'd never been any good at 'opening up' to doctors and the like; in fact, he couldn't even remember the last time he had been to see a doctor for himself, preferring to battle on whenever he'd had a cold, or the flu. And his head was still crammed with so much stuff, it was tricky to know where to begin. His marriage. His mother. Holly.

Chrissie. His whole life. And he was messing it all up to the point where he couldn't sleep for stressing about it all.

'It's my daughter, Doctor. Holly. I know she hasn't been that well recently. Not seriously ill or anything ... but it's her diabetes, it's all gone a bit haywire ... I wanted to try and find out a bit more about what might be happening ...' Sam paused; it was all coming out in a jumble. He wanted to sound sorted, and rational, in control, like Chrissie was in these situations. But whenever he thought about Holly, and about her being ill and all the things that could go wrong, it just became a big, scary mess. 'I want to be more involved with everything, hospital appointments, that sort of thing, so I'll need to know when Holly's next appointment is too.' Sam had already mentally kicked himself for not asking Chrissie, or indeed Holly, when this was. He had decided to make sure he would be right there with Holly and Chrissie for the next appointment at the diabetes clinic. He'd taken a back seat for far too long, and that was going to stop now.

'OK, first things first—'

'And I've been doing some research, you know, on Google, to see what the problems could be.' Sam reached inside his breast pocket and pulled out the wedge of papers that he had printed off, handing them to the GP.

Dr Ben took them and, after politely glancing through, he placed them on the desk beside him. 'Ah, Google.'

'Yes, it could affect her kidneys. Chrissie, my wife, said that there was pressure on her kidneys. I've looked into it, and if she needs a transplant, I need to be sure I'm the right blood group because my mother won't even consider it and my brother Patrick – he lives in Australia – so probably too far away. And my grandmother, Dolly Morgan, you might know her, but she's getting on, and it says on the internet that eighty year olds can donate but it might be too risky for her. So you see it's vital that I'm a match ...'

'OK, Sam,' Dr Ben replied slowly, in that soothing voice that doctors use, before leaning forward and placing a steadying hand on Sam's shoulder. 'How about we slow things down and—'

'But don't you think we should be prepared, I mean, for any eventuality. Holly needs to have a kidney lined up, surely, just in case?'

'I'm not sure she does.' Dr Ben turned to the computer on his desk and tapped the keyboard, seemingly to access Holly's records.

'But we can't just leave things to chance. If her blood sugars aren't stable and her kidneys are under pressure then it makes sense to be prepared.' Sam leant forward.

'Sam, please ... I'm not sure where you've got your information from, but the tests that Holly has been having are just exploratory at this stage. There are all sorts of reasons why Holly's blood sugar isn't stabilised, and lots of ways of dealing with the problem.'

'Ah, so ... you're not worried about her kidneys?' Sam felt relieved. Dr Ben looked away from the screen and steadily at Sam.

'Holly is not in any imminent danger, Sam, I promise. However ...'

'However?' Sam felt that familiar lurch in the pit of his stomach and then the dragging sensation as if he was being cast adrift again, out into the ocean with no way of getting back to the shore. He willed himself to keep steady and concentrated on his breathing. Telling himself it would be fine. He was here. Close to his family. And whatever the prognosis was for Holly, they would face it head on and deal with it. There was no need for him to panic and run.

'We are keeping a close eye on Holly generally. Kidney disease is a danger for patients with diabetes and it can develop over a long time. The most important thing for us is to stabilise Holly's blood glucose levels and take some sensible precautions. If it makes you feel better, we can definitely make a note of your blood group now, it's all very useful to have on file at this stage. And those of your immediate family. I believe that we already have your wife's details. But there's no urgency. I promise you. So please, you really must try to relax, Sam.' Dr Ben nodded reassuringly.

'Well, it would be good to know my blood group. And my daughter's too. Best to be prepared.' Sam fiddled with his cuffs, still feeling unnerved by the conversation with his mother.

'I might have that information here, on your records, if you've ever been tested in the past for an operation perhaps, but it's not something that is done as a routine thing.' Dr Ben turned and tapped the keyboard to bring the computer screen to life, and then started searching through Sam's medical details. Silence followed. And Sam felt slightly reassured that he was getting somewhere at last. 'Ahh, no! Sorry, seems it isn't here.' Dr Ben turned back to face him.

'Oh,' Sam said, instantly deflated. 'But you can do a blood test though, can't you?'

'Well, yes, I can.'

'Great. I need to do something, you see. I've been away, for too long, I feel like I've not been doing enough for my family ...' Sam's voice wavered.

'Well, coming here is a good start. We've all got Holly's best interests at heart and I'll do whatever I can,' Dr Ben nodded, talking more softly this time.

'Thank you.' Sam nodded.

'Is there anything else that's worrying you, Sam?'

'Well, perhaps, while you're at it, some sleeping tablets would be good, please. I'm feeling exhausted and haven't been sleeping well.'

'OK, we can certainly have a chat about how you're sleeping. Pills are not always the answer ... you might find you feel calmer once we know if your blood type is a match, if that's what has been keeping you awake night after night – and it's highly likely given that you're Holly's father.'

Sam smiled, feeling less anxious already.

'Now, have you ever donated blood?' Dr Ben asked.

'Yes. Several times over the years. But not recently, as I've been living abroad for work. Why do you ask?'

'Well, your blood group will be on the donor card. So if you have the card somewhere, then you'll know right away. It's just another way to find out.'

'I see,' Sam said. *So if it's on my donor card, then it'll be on my mother's card too, and I definitely remember her giving blood some years ago when I was at school because she had to lie on the sofa all day long to recuperate. Dad had made the dinner that evening and got told off for boiling the spinach for far too long, so Mum hadn't been able to eat it, even though she had said that she desperately needed the iron to make up for the huge amount that she had given away. She said she wouldn't want to be a donor for Holly, but if she has the card, then at least I'll know if she could be. She'd feel differently, surely, if it ever came to that. Especially if she was the only one who could save Holly. My mother might be the most selfish woman I know, but one thing she loves is playing Lady Bountiful whenever the opportunity arises.*

The thoughts whizzed around, and Sam felt very much more optimistic now, thoroughly pleased that he had come to see Dr Ben. 'In case I can't find the card ... could you do a test now, Doctor? It'll save time in the long run,' Sam suggested.

'Sure. Now, if you could take off your coat and roll up your shirt sleeve, please?' Dr Ben busied himself with getting the syringe and pathology paperwork together while Sam eagerly did as he was asked. As soon as he was finished here at the surgery, he was going to call into The Forstal Farmhouse and ask Chrissie if he could go through his personal paperwork. It was all there in the old bureau in the spare bedroom – school reports, exam certificates, expired passports, etc. His blood donor card was bound to be in amongst all that and then he'd know right away. Plus going through the papers would give him something to focus on. A displacement activity to take his mind off everything, if only for a short while ... he realised that.

'OK, a quick scratch.' Sam looked away; he'd always hated the sight of needles going into flesh. 'All done. If you call the surgery in about five days' time, we should have the results.'

'Thanks, Dr Ben,' Sam said, rolling his sleeve down. 'Fingers crossed that I'm a match.'

'Yes, it's hugely helpful if one of you is—'

'Isn't my wife?' Sam interjected, buttoning his cuff.

'I can't tell you that, it's confidential, but surely you and your wife will talk about this, though I do absolutely want to stress that there is no reason to panic or over-dramatise things.' Dr Ben paused. 'Do you understand, Sam?'

'Yes, I think so.'

'Have a chat to Chrissie, so you are all on the same page, OK?' Dr Ben hurriedly pushed the blood-filled syringe into the plastic envelope for the pathology lab, and turned to add, 'How is Chrissie? Glad to have you back?'

'We're not ... um, we're separated and have been for a while. Since I've been away for so long ...' Sam attempted a shrug as he let his voice drift away, hating saying the words out loud. It made it more real, somehow, by putting a spotlight on his inadequacy, his failure to make his marriage work.

'I see ...' Dr Ben let the statement settle for a moment, before adding, 'And now?'

'I've come home.'

'And why is that?'

'Err ...' Sam hesitated, 'I need to make sure my family is OK.' Dr Ben kept quiet. Waiting to let Sam go on. 'I missed them. Chrissie and Holly. And I guess I'm ...' He stopped abruptly.

'Go on.'

'I guess I'm scared.' Sam coughed to clear his throat.

'Scared?'

'That it might be too late. You see, I ... well, I sort of

abandoned them.' He hated how it sounded. How it made him seem. Spineless and immature. 'Things weren't going too well with my wife; we had drifted a bit, because of my job, though we both agreed on it and she didn't want to come to Singapore ... And then ... when we first found out that Holly had diabetes, I ...' Sam paused, pushed a hand through his hair. 'I guess I didn't handle it very well. So I stayed away a lot, felt she managed it all better without me.'

'And you wished you hadn't?'

'Yes. I should have stayed here. Or at least made more of an effort to come home from time to time.'

'So why didn't you?' Dr Ben was looking at the computer screen, seemingly to appear pragmatic, but Sam still felt as if he was being analysed.

'Are you asking about this because of the sleeping tablets?' Perhaps that was why. 'Anyway, Chrissie reckons it's a commitment thing,' he offered, starting to wish he hadn't come to see Dr Ben after all. This was awkward. It was like being under a microscope.

'And what do you think?' Dr Ben asked, bringing Sam back on track.

'She's probably right. I've always been like it. Chrissie says I have a wall.'

'A wall?' Dr Ben turned to look at Sam head on.

'Yeah, you know. A distance. She says it's like I keep her at arm's length.'

'Ahh, I understand. So, if she's right, why do you think that is?'

'For obvious reasons,' Sam shrugged.

'Obvious?'

'Yes. Look, I really need to get going.' Sam stood up, feeling very uncomfortable now.

'Yes, of course. Sam, I know it's a difficult time for you. Do you mind if I give you my opinion? For what it's worth ...'

'Go on.'

'Maybe if you were able to concentrate on repairing your marriage instead of focusing on Holly's health – she really isn't in any immediate need of a new kidney, I promise you – then you might find that you're better able to sleep.'

'Sure.'

'How about I see you again in a few days' time and we can see how things are progr—'

'Thanks, Doctor.' And Sam left rapidly, and was striding towards his Land Rover, keen to go and see Chrissie right away. To talk about whether she was a match or not. And Sam knew exactly what Dr Ben was getting at. His fear of rejection. He had felt it that day in the hospital. The look on Chrissie's face when he had piped up about his dad having had diabetes. The silence in the room when it became apparent that he should have considered it and said something sooner. It was similar to how he had often felt as a child. Inadequate. Not good enough – he couldn't have been if his own mother couldn't really be bothered with him. Speaking to his mother had been a reminder of all the reasons why he had built that wall around himself. Protection. He'd let his anxieties from childhood spill over into his relationship with Chrissie.

He had felt happy and secure with Chrissie. He loved her to bits. Adored her. Fancied her. But then their differences had started to emerge, especially when they became parents ... He had often felt as if he was muddling through, figuring it all out as he went along, both in trying to be a good parent, and a decent husband. At times he had been like a big kid himself, making the mistake of trying to be Holly's friend, have a laugh with her, instead of being a proper father figure, solid and sensible, like his own dad had been before he died. Sam had never had that with his mother. But then Chrissie wasn't Linda. She was his wife, and he loved her with all his heart, but his insecurities had reared up and got in the way. He knew he had to find a way back to her. Be the husband he'd always intended on being, but had lost sight of along the way ...

Chapter Thirteen

Jude loved this time of year in the Duck & Puddle pub, tucked away next to the village green. The pub garden was giddy with the glorious scent from the abundance of bluebells in the wood beyond. The sun sat plump on the horizon, chalking the powder-blue sky in streaks of red and gold and orange. Birdsong mingled with the sound of goats bleating as they nudged their heads through the hedge, hoping for a titbit of bread or crisps from the children playing underneath an enormous old oak tree nearby. She thought it was one of the most idyllic places in the whole world. Which is why she had persuaded Chrissie to come out with her this evening for a drink, and hopefully a lovely long chat over a nice pub dinner of ploughman's with crusty bread followed by homemade lemon meringue pie – the 'Special of the Day', it had said on the chalkboard behind the bar when she'd popped in earlier to book a table. An absolute must at this time of year, as every villager and their dog – or pet ferret, in Molly's case – gravitated to the Duck & Puddle pub of an evening for a refreshing pitcher of Pimm's and some pub grub with good friends.

Ahh, Jude looked around the pub, preserved in time. It hadn't changed at all over the years, with its cosy snug and the little shop through the hatch selling all the essentials – sweets, crisps, milk, magazines, eggs, bread, firelighters, logs, lighter fuel . . . that kind of thing. Even the honesty box was still in place, so you could take what you liked and leave the money in the bowl. It brought back a trillion memories for her, as she'd been coming to the Duck & Puddle pub for years, and ever since she was knee-high to a grasshopper, as her dad would say. Talking of whom, Tony was standing at the bar with his best friend, Barry, each with his own silver tankard in hand.

'Hello, love.' Tony put down his drink and turned to give Jude a big bear hug. 'Have you packed up for the day?'

'Sure have, Dad.'

'Been busy?' he asked cheerfully, rubbing his hands together.

'Ooh, yes. I've been rushed off my feet in the shop. So jam-packed in there, I'm seriously thinking about expanding and buying up the whole of the High Street just to cope with the demand.'

'Really?' Tony made big eyes, sounding impressed.

'No, Dad,' Jude sighed. 'But, I wish. Honestly, I'm sure it never used to be this sleepy in the village. Why doesn't anyone want my lovely artefacts?' She pulled a pretend sulky face by pushing her bottom lip out.

'That's the internet for you,' Barry piped up, leaning away from the bar to join in the conversation. 'All those factories in China churning out their cut-price tat,' he paused to puff out his cheeks. 'They'll be the death of the small retailer, you mark my words. A crying shame it is. And I'll probably end up having to pack in the shop next year.' He tutted and then sank the rest of his beer in one, seemingly resigned to the doom and gloom of his words.

'Nah, ignore him, Jude,' Tony said, flashing his mate a look. 'You're going to retire soon anyway, aren't you, Barry? Thought you'd had enough of selling hardware and cutting keys and were going to try your hand at gardening or golf. Or doing up that old banger of yours that you've had in the garage for donkeys' years.'

'I'll have you know that my beautiful coffee-coloured Ford Cortina certainly isn't an old banger! She's a rare jewel. A classic car from the Seventies,' Barry claimed.

'If you say so,' Tony teased, shaking his head, not wanting to be subjected to yet another one of Barry's long-winded soliloquies about the coffee-coloured Ford Cortina. 'So, are you retiring or not?' he said, changing the subject.

'I'm going to have to.'

'You could undercut the Chinese manufacturers. Flog your gear even cheaper ... you've had some of that old stuff in the back of your shop for decades, so you'll not be losing out.'

'But you can't deny that less than a fiver for a multi-bit screwdriver is bloody cheap. I can't compete with those prices.'

Jude and Chrissie listened and watched, swivelling their heads to look at each man as they batted back and forth with endless quips. Jude smiled, inwardly recalling a wealth of nostalgic memories. Her dad and Barry had always been like this. A comedy double act, almost. Like Little and Large, or the Two Ronnies. She remembered watching all those funny television shows as a kid. She'd be snuggled up with her mum, Sarah, on the brown Draylon sofa, with her dad and Barry sitting on dining chairs by the patio doors so they could puff their fag smoke out into the garden so as not to make Mum's asthma bad.

'Guess not,' Tony agreed, breaking Jude's reverie and patting his pal on the back in sympathy.

'Now, back in the Seventies,' Barry started regaling them with his memories, 'when I took over the shop from my old man—'

'Ahh, yes, yes ... we know, Barry ... you've told us a trillion times,' Tony joked, rolling his eyes. 'Back in the good old days when Tindledale was mere fields and dirt tracks with none of these new-build estates, and everyone lived off butterscotch Angel Delight and Findus Crispy Pancakes! Go on, say it mate, tell us how marvellous it was then and how diabolical and awful it is now.' He lifted his arms up, as if to play an imaginary violin.

'OK, no need to be like that,' Barry laughed, going to put his oldest friend in a pretend headlock. But Tony was too quick for him, and ducked out of the way just in time.

'Well, I'd like to hear all about those good old days,' Jude intervened, shooing her dad and Barry away, gesturing for them to pick up their tankards and behave themselves, instead of jesting around like a pair of overgrown schoolboys. She had known Barry her whole life; he was like an uncle really, and so she had no qualms about telling him off or teasing him.

'What would you like to know, love?' Barry asked, ignoring Tony, who was pulling a face.

'Tell me about the Seventies: was it really hippies and flower power and flares and all that?' she asked, pushing her red curls away from her face before leaning forward in anticipation. 'Did you wear one of those Afghan coats that smelt of patchouli?'

'Oh crikey, you'll never shut him up now,' Tony said, before turning to Chrissie. 'And how are you, my love? Is Holly OK after the fall?' His forehead creased in concern.

'She is, thanks Tony. And thanks for fixing the front door. And I'm really sorry for overreact—'

'Don't mention it. You've a lot on your plate at the moment, and I'm sorry, just wish there was something I could do to help.' Chrissie nodded and flicked her eyes downward. Tony smiled warmly before adding, 'Now, what can I get you to drink, love?' He gave her arm an affectionate squeeze.

'Ooh, I really fancy one of those lovely Prosecco cocktails, please, Tony. What are they called, Jude? The ones we had the other night?'

'A St Germain,' Jude answered, then, 'good idea, I'll have one too please, Dad.'

'A san what?' Tony laughed, turning towards Cher behind the bar. 'Have you ever heard the likes of it, love? Cocktails in the village pub!' he added, astounded.

'Of course, Tony. They're all the rage these days.' Smiling, Cher shook her head. 'Coming right up, ladies. Two delicious St Germain cocktails.'

'Thanks,' Chrissie replied, slipping her handbag from her shoulder and hanging it over the back of a bar stool.

*

Later, having said goodbye to Tony and Barry, who had left to go for a curry, promising to pop back in a bit after they'd devoured a delicious Balti, Jude and Chrissie were now nattering away at a table tucked in the corner. They had just polished off generous portions of the lemon meringue pie with extra-thick gooey topping, when Myles walked in wearing another one of his silly online-purchased outfits. It appeared to be a disguise this time. An ankle-length waxy raincoat teamed with a big, furry Cossack hat.

'Oh, err, hello,' Jude said, spotting him right away, and really wishing she hadn't been licking her spoon quite so enthusiastically when he glanced in her direction. Furtively, he came over to Jude and Chrissie's table.

'Is it always like this in here?' he mouthed, his eyes flitting from Jude to Chrissie and back again.

'What do you mean?' Jude asked, trying to keep a straight face.

'You know. *Rammed*.' He shrugged furtively.

'Rammed?' she couldn't resist.

'Busy, you know … rammed with loads of people.' He pushed his hands deep into the pockets of the oversized raincoat.

'Yes, pretty much so. It's the village pub, and there aren't that many places to socialise in Tindledale, with it being such a small place and all … Why, is it a problem?'

'I don't like busy places … they're usually full of paps trying to get an unflattering photo. Or groupies,' Myles muttered, glancing around again.

'I think you'll be OK in here.' Jude motioned for him to sit down; but she could already see half a dozen villagers gawping at him, most likely wondering why he was dressed up like a Cold War spy. She didn't imagine anyone in Tindledale was likely to want to get a scoop on him to sell to a red-top newspaper, or wave an autograph book in his direction like they might have done back in the day when he was still actually famous. Rather, it was all in his head, which she thought a bit sad really. Or maybe he really was just a giant dickhead after all, and she had been wrong to thaw towards him.

Myles sat down in the space on the bench next to Chrissie and pulled the silly fur hat from his head. His face all red from wearing such an inappropriate garment on a warm, early summer evening.

'Myles, this is Chrissie. Chrissie, this is Myles King,' Jude introduced, and they both shook hands.

'Ooh, nice to meet you, Myles,' Chrissie said pleasantly, as if greeting an old friend. I used to love that record of yours.'

'Which one?' Myles asked, a little too quickly, as he settled on the bench next to Chrissie.

'Um, "Baby Blue", I think it was. Do you remember, Jude? We used to sing along to it while getting ready for a night out,' she smiled, taking a sip of her drink.

'Ahh, yes. That's right, I remember it. It went ... *Baby, baby, baby, why do you make me feel bluuuuuuue,*' Jude sang, using her folded fist as a pretend microphone.

'That's the one!' Chrissie grinned.

'Cool. Sold over a mill, that song did,' Myles said, leaning back and nodding. Jude and Chrissie exchanged surreptitious looks.

'Wow,' Jude drank some of her cocktail and then

found herself wishing she could quickly move the conversation on. She didn't want Myles to come across as cocky in front of Chrissie. But before she'd had a chance to work out why this mattered to her, seeing as they were barely acquainted (it wasn't as though he was her boyfriend or anything, and meeting her best friend for the first time), or indeed say something else to change the subject, Myles surprised her, yet again, with his sensitivity.

'You're Holly's mum, aren't you?' he turned to face Chrissie.

'Yes, that's right. How do you know that?'

'Your daughter told me when she came to visit!' he stated, as if it was the most obvious thing in the whole world. 'She's a great kid. Gentle with the animals. And whip smart too. You must be very proud of her.'

'Yes. And thank you for showing her your pigs. She hasn't stopped talking about the one called Tiger.'

'Ahh, no problem. She's welcome to visit any time,' he said, kindly. But then he went and ruined it all by leaning forward and casually helping himself to an enormous swig of Jude's cocktail, and giving her a cheeky wink as he did so. She smiled to herself at his cheek, and surmised that he was quite clearly used to doing whatever he liked without question from the flunkies who had most likely surrounded him for the majority of his adult life. Well, she wasn't one of his flunkies. She swiped her glass from his hand.

'Get your own, you cheeky cheapskate.' She made a point of downing the last of her drink. And then almost spluttered the Prosecco and elderflower cordial concoction all over herself on seeing the look on Myles's face. He definitely wasn't used to anyone questioning his actions or putting him in his place.

'Is she always like this?' Myles gave Chrissie a conspiratorial nudge. 'You know, bossy in a scary way?' and he pulled a pretend petrified face.

'Well, you did take her drink without asking, so I'd say she's well within her rights to call you out on it.' Chrissie didn't miss a beat, and Jude laughed, pleased to see her friend hadn't lost her loyalty or spirit, despite all that she was currently going through.

'Fair enough!' Myles at least had the decency to look slightly abashed. His cheeks were tinged pink when he turned to look at Jude, his face just a few inches from hers. His sapphire eyes staring straight into hers. 'Please forgive me.' And he actually took her hand and planted a lingering kiss on the back of it. To her utter dismay, Jude felt her own cheeks flush and her pulse quicken as his warm lips touched her skin.

She quickly pulled her hand back and pretended to bat his arm away in jest. Jesus, he really was the most obnoxious, cocky and quite infuriating person that she had ever met. Why couldn't he just behave normally like everyone else? Why did everything have to be so over the top with him? It was as if he actually delighted in winding her up. Teasing her. Getting her flustered. Just like he had in that first phone call when he'd made fun of her surname. And he'd been doing it ever since.

She had tried to have a sensible conversation with him just a few days ago about the curtain sample packs, but it was hopeless … he had suggested she join him in a game of Twister instead. Said curtains were boring and getting tangled up on a plastic mat was much more 'his thing'. Jude had declined, of course, but still … did he really have to behave like such an overgrown teenager? If she hadn't needed the work at the Blackwood Farm Estate to launch the interior design part of her new business, then, well … she would have told him where to go long before now. But it was intriguing the way he could come across as genuinely sensitive and kind one minute, and then cocky and crass the next … The thought lingered.

Finding herself keen to pull back some control of the situation, Jude took a deep breath and asked,

'So, Myles, how come you're in here, the "too rammed" pub, if you don't like crowds?' She tilted her head to one side. *Ha, two can play your game.*

'Sylvia said I needed to make an effort to fit in.' He said the words like an errant schoolboy having been chastised by a teacher, before doing a big shrug.

'Oh, so you thought you'd do that by coming into the village pub, in disguise.' It was Chrissie who said this, and it made Jude laugh.

'Sorry,' she hastily said, slapping a hand over her mouth on seeing his face. He genuinely looked like a crestfallen little boy as he pulled the hat from his head and stuffed it into a pocket before running a hand over his hair in an attempt at tidying it.

'What's wrong with the coat? Isn't this what everyone wears in the countryside?' Myles tugged at the front of the ridiculously oversized, waxy raincoat.

'Well, no, not really. Particularly not in springtime. And is that why you were wearing the deerstalker and breeches get-up the other day?' Jude asked, unforgivingly.

'I guess so,' he shrugged. 'Thought I'd make an effort to fit in. But in that case …' And before either Jude or Chrissie could utter another word, Myles stood up, unbuttoned the coat, took it off, bundled it into a ball and slung it underneath the bench. 'Is that better?' he asked, folding his arms across a navy blue T-shirt. 'I was roasting hot in the coat in any case.'

'Much better.' Jude nodded in approval. He looked great. And smelt great too, as a giant waft of that intoxicating Chanel aftershave permeated the air all around her.

'Good. Now, how about you go to the bar and get a bottle of Prosecco for us all?' Myles turned to Jude. 'Here,' and he pulled a credit card from his jeans pocket. 'Put it behind the bar to start a tab.'

'Err, why don't you go to the bar and buy the Prosecco yourself?' She was conscious of Chrissie smirking at his audacity too. 'And you can start your own tab while you're at it!'

'I can't do that!' Myles said, aghast, and looked genuinely shocked at the suggestion.

'Of course you can. Go on. You'll be fine. Nobody will try to take your picture or get an autograph ... honestly, you're safe enough,' Jude nodded by way of encouragement. But she was intrigued to know if he genuinely was an introvert – she'd met plenty of hugely successful star performers over the years in LA who were incredibly shy offstage – or was Myles actually deluded, assuming he was still a big name and really here to court attention? Was he secretly hoping for a bit of free publicity in a red-top newspaper tomorrow morning to boost his ego? Fame was a funny thing – she had seen how those who had it in the past still craved the limelight long after their moment had passed. Or was she being far too cynical? Perhaps she should just give him the benefit of the doubt instead?

'And if you really do want to fit in ...' Chrissie added, lifting her eyebrows, and Myles looked at the two women. His piercing blue eyes darted first to Jude, then Chrissie, and then Jude again, where they lingered as if he was trying to work out what to do. What would please her most, Jude thought ... He eventually stood up.

'OK. I'll do it.' He made going to the bar in a village pub sound as if he'd just agreed to eat a live cockroach on TV as part of a bushtucker trial in that jungle programme. Jude and Chrissie clapped in unison to spur him on.

The minute Myles was out of earshot, Chrissie shuffled along the bench so she was sitting up close to Jude.

'Well, you're a dark horse,' she started, nudging Jude in the side.

'What do you mean?'

'*What do I mean?*' Chrissie made big eyes, and then lowered her voice. 'You and him. Don't be coy, it's so obvious.'

'Obvious. What is?'

'The way he looks at you. He can't take his eyes off you. And that pretend cocky thing he has going on. Trying to seem all laddish and indifferent towards you. He fancies the knickers off you, that's what,' she said in a stage-whisper voice, referring to the phrase they used to use as young girls at school when the boy they were crushing on at the time showed an interest.

'No he doesn't.' Jude bowed her head and busied herself with inspecting the trim of her cardigan.

'Oh come on, Jude. It's so obvious there's a spark between the pair of you. And I'm not buying that, "Sylvia said I must make an effort" line. Would his housekeeper, or whoever she is, really say that to the man she works for?'

'Hmm, she might. Sylvia is very forthright.'

'No, he came in here to see you. Did you tell him you'd be here?'

'I might have mentioned it,' Jude said, remembering very well that Myles had asked what she was up to this evening and she had said she was meeting Chrissie, Holly's mum, in the village pub. So he had remembered, and made a point of complimenting Chrissie on her daughter too. Jude thought that was sweet of him.

'Well, there you go. He hates public places but he wanted to see you away from a work situation. And he's in awe of you – probably explains the brashness – the taking your drink without asking; it's all bluster. A front, if you like. What's the betting he's never had to make a proper effort with a woman before.'

'Why do you say that?'

'Well, he was a big star back in the day ... most likely used to having women do all the running while he sat back and let them. But there's no way you're like that, Jude Darling. And he knows it,' Chrissie laughed.

'Hmm,' Jude muttered.

'So, how *do* you feel about him?' Chrissie glanced over Jude's shoulder towards the bar. 'It's OK, it's heaving over there, so he's going to be a while getting served and getting back to us.' Jude looked over towards the bar too, and was pleasantly surprised to see Myles standing in the crowd, quite normally. Nobody was bothering him, hassling him, as he had feared. Although, she could see a few of the school mums nudging each other and making silly faces, as if goading one another to go and talk to him. But it was Mack, the ex-soldier, and Kitty's boyfriend, who actually spoke directly to Myles. Jude watched as Mack put out his hand, which Myles shook before saying something that made Mack do a big belly laugh. A few seconds later, the two men were chatting and nodding like a pair of old friends. 'Do you fancy him?' Chrissie nudged her, quite insistently.

'No I don't,' Jude said, far too quickly.

'Why not? He's nice. And pretty fit, and did you see those abs when he pulled the coat off and his T-shirt rose up? He must work out every day to have an impressive six-pack like that.'

'Not really, I wasn't looking. Besides, he's way too immature for me. And that silly man bun is ... well, it's ridiculously silly!' And Jude lifted an empty glass to her lips.

'It's ... um ... your drink, it's empty,' Chrissie grinned and pointed at the glass.

'I know that.' Jude placed the glass back on the table and did her best to avoid Chrissie's gaze. They'd been best friends for nearly forty years and it was clear that, even though she had been living in LA for the last however-many years, Chrissie hadn't lost the knack that best friends have of asking all the awkward questions and getting right under your skin when you least want them to. And she really wished her cheeks weren't flushing quite so much; she must lay off the Prosecco, it was no good for her. Plus she had brought Chrissie out to the pub in the hope of having a proper heart-to-heart with her about Sam. Not to talk about Myles and whether he did or didn't fancy her.

Chapter Fourteen

Half a hour later, and it seemed that Myles had forgotten all about bringing back the bottle of Prosecco; he was now having a game of darts with Mack and all his army mates over from the base in Market Briar.

'So, how are things with you and Sam now?' Jude asked.

'Pretty bad, to be honest, Jude. He just seems incapable of getting it.' Chrissie shook her head.

'Getting what?'

'The whole thing. You saw how he was the other night. Leaving Holly on her own and then going to the pub. It's immature. Why can't he just take some proper responsibility? Why is it always down to me?'

'I don't know, Chrissie. But you know he won't have done it on purpose, just to annoy you.'

'Hmm, maybe. But I'm the one who has to deal with the fallout. She begged me and then shouted and then sulked for at least an hour this evening to force me to cancel the babysitter that I had booked. Telling me she's, "not a baby and Dad trusts me so why don't you?" Until I caved in and thought, maybe she has a point. But it's hard, bloody hard ... I lost count of the times I was left at home on my own as a kid, and sometimes for a whole night. Mum would go out at teatime for "just a few" and still not be home by breakfast time the following morning. So I would just come to school and try to forget about it.'

'Oh, Chrissie. I never knew,' Jude said, shaking her head. 'Of course, I knew that your mum was an alcoholic, but not back then, not when we were kids.'

'That's because I didn't want you to know. Being friends with you at school was a good thing in my life, and I never wanted that spoilt. Ever wonder why we never went to my house to hang out? I didn't know if Mum would be slurring her words and I'd feel embarrassed. And your dad is so lovely, it was better at your house.' Jude squeezed her friend's hand. 'But, Holly isn't me, she's right ... she isn't a baby. So I cancelled the babysitter and left Holly instructions to call me immediately if she needed to.'

'Well done. I'm sure Holly will be fine, and we're not going to be out for very long. And she'll call if she isn't and you can keep in contact by text. She's going to push the boundaries. I guess that's teenagers for you,' Jude said, pleased to see a chink of a change. She was sure that if Chrissie could relax a little and ease up on Holly, then Holly would soon feel a lot happier.

'Is it though? You know, Holly and I have always clashed, but now that Sam is back it's like she blames me for everything. It's all my fault he's living at Dolly's cottage. I must have driven him away. He can do no wrong as far as Holly is concerned.'

'Oh, Chrissie, I know it's been tough on you. And you've done everything for her. You're a brilliant mum, and Holly has really benefited from the stability and structure you've given her. Myles is right in what he said earlier – Holly is a great girl. But maybe it wouldn't be a bad thing to let Sam do more now that he's back. There's nothing wrong in having a bit of help ... is there?' Jude knew to tread carefully. What she really wanted to say was that Holly thinks you hate her because you're so strict and won't give an inch. You've let your need for control distort your rationality. And I totally understand how it has happened, and why, but you have to rein it in or you're in danger of losing Holly.

'But I don't need any help.'

'Don't you?'

'Are you saying I can't cope?' Chrissie's face crumpled slightly.

'No. Not at all. I'm just saying that you and Sam and Holly were always so happy, and now you aren't. I wonder if Sam behaved the way he did in the past ... because he could. Because he didn't need to step up. Because you had it all under control so he could goof about and be the fun one.'

'But Holly won't hear a bad word against him.'

'Of course she won't. He's her dad. Her hero. And in

her eyes he has only ever loved her. I don't think you can blame him – or her – for that.'

'I'm not.'

'You sure?' Jude gently rubbed her friend's arm, keen to let her know that her intention wasn't to criticise her.

'What are you getting at?'

'OK, can I be straight with you?' Jude swallowed, and then braced herself.

'Go ahead. Seems like you already are,' Chrissie said, sounding frosty now.

'Do you want Sam back?' Jude decided to ditch her plan of asking Chrissie about the choir man, Gavin. Chrissie was bound to wonder why she was asking, especially when she hadn't mentioned him at all. She would know that something had been said, and Jude couldn't risk putting Holly in the frame. Not when things were already so strained between them. This felt like a much better place to start from, because she knew Chrissie well enough to know that if she had met another man and was seriously moving on with him, then her reaction would show it. Chrissie dipped her head and said,

'People don't just switch off their feelings.' And in that moment, as Chrissie lifted her head back up, Jude knew. She could see it in her eyes.

'You do, don't you?' Her friend was in so much pain. Her heartache was palpable. Chrissie wanted more than anything to get back with Sam – was still so in love with her husband. Jude put her arms around her lifelong best friend and spoke softly as she held her tight. 'It's going to be all right, Chrissie. I promise you. You will get through this. I know that you and Sam can work this out. And Holly is going to be absolutely fine.' And in that moment, Jude felt her best friend's body change. The concrete-like shoulders from before now surrendered and softened. Free from the proverbial weight that they had been burdened with.

'Thank you for coming home.' Chrissie sat back. 'A problem shared is a problem halved, and all that. I guess I have been trying too hard to keep it all together ... no wonder Holly hates me. I spend most of my life barking orders at her like a drill sergeant. But I want her to have the best start, to grow up having the security I never had. And I can't even do that for her ... not with Sam and me separated.'

'But it's not too late to fix that. And she doesn't hate you!' Jude reassured, recalling Holly's exact sentiment. Chrissie surreptitiously dabbed her index fingers at the corners of her eyes.

Jude saw Chrissy was now struggling to keep her emotions under control. 'I can't believe I'm welling up. Here in the pub.'

'It's fine, Chrissie. Nobody can see you. Not that they would blame you, in any case, with the strain that you've been under.'

'But it's more than that: I feel so conflicted. It's like one part of me feels so damn angry and abandoned by Sam ... yet the other half still craves him physically and emotionally.'

Silence followed.

'You know, I even had a T-shirt of his pressed up to my nose the other day. Just to feel close to him. How ridiculous is that?'

'It's not ridiculous.'

'If it isn't, then why am I so hostile towards him? It's like I want to punish him. Maybe I want to make him hate me too ...' Chrissie closed her eyes and turned her head slowly from side to side.

'Well, that's understandable. You have every right to feel angry with him. You said yourself that you feel conflicted.'

'Tell me what to do, Jude.'

'Talk to him. Let him in ...'

'Maybe you're right ... perhaps I'll call him when I get home. I'll text Holly and let her know I won't be long.' And Chrissie gave Jude a watery smile before looking in her bag to locate her phone.

*

Sam pulled up in the Land Rover and his heart warmed to see the lights on inside. Holly and Chrissie probably had their feet up watching *The Great British Bake Off*. Perhaps he should have called Chrissie to tell her he was coming over, but he didn't want to risk her putting him off or saying no. He really wanted to tell her how he felt, that they could work things through if she could just give him one more chance. That he could be there for both of them, when they needed him, all of the time.

He got out of the car, headed to the front door and pressed the bell. No answer. He tapped again. But when there was still no sign of anyone, he looked in through the front living-room window. He couldn't see Chrissie, but Holly had her back to the window and appeared to be dancing to herself with her earbuds on, completely oblivious to being watched. He grinned; she was a good mover. Eventually she turned around and nearly jumped out of her skin when she saw him, before running to the hall to let him in.

'Dad!' She threw her arms around him and removed her earbuds.

'Hey sweetheart, where's your mum? Upstairs?' Sam glanced up the staircase.

'No, she's gone out. To the pub with Aunty Jude.'

Sam felt as if he'd been punched in the stomach. Chrissie had given him a huge bollocking for leaving Holly on her own the other night and now here she was, home alone, because her mum had gone out to the pub! Sam was struggling, trying to work out how he fitted in now, in this world that had moved on without him. But how was he supposed to make any sense of it when Chrissie kept moving the goalposts? And was she really out with Jude? Or was she with this other bloke, the one who kept gnawing away in a corner of his brain like a rat, giving him a nasty headache? But he couldn't think any more about all that right now, he had to make sure Holly was OK.

'Oh,' he started, looking at his daughter, who did seem absolutely fine. 'And are you all right?' he checked nonetheless. 'Your levels are OK?'

'Yes, Dad. Of course I am.' She hopped from one foot to the other.

'Sure? Not been climbing on any more chairs, have you Holly?' Sam felt it best to at least mention what had happened the other night.

'Um,' Holly reddened. 'No. I haven't. And I'm sorry I fibbed, Dad. You know … About being home alone. And I'm sorry I got you into trouble with Mum.'

'Why did you fib, love?' Sam could feel his frustration crumbling already.

'Because …' Holly hesitated. She could hardly tell him the real reason, that Mum hadn't sent him the chocolates at all and he'd find out right away. That would ruin her Get Mum and Dad Back Together in Time for My Birthday plan. And the wish would never come true then. So she settled on, 'I didn't want you and Mum to argue again.'

'Oh, sweetheart, we weren't arguing,' Sam said, stepping forward to give her a hug. 'Mum and I just need to sort some stuff out ... In fact, that's why I'm here, to see Mum. And you of course.' He smiled, and pushed all thoughts of feeling wronged by Chrissie for having a go at him from his mind. Recognising that he needed to reassure Holly and put things right for her.

'Brilliant,' Holly said, feeling happy, but a bit worried that he still might find out the truth about the chocolates. She'd just have to hope he didn't mention them.

'So what time will Mum be back?'

'Soon – she won't leave me alone for long. She still thinks I'm a baby. But I'm a teenager and can totally look after myself. I get on a bus and go to and from school and Katie's mum lets us stay at her house on our own. Plus we already went on Survival Island with the Guides so I don't know what Mum's problem is.'

'Mum just wants to make sure you are OK. Katie doesn't have diabetes like you do,' Sam said sensibly, and he followed his daughter into the house, absent-mindedly kicking off his shoes in the hallway, just as Chrissie had drummed into him a thousand times before. Muscle memory, he mused.

'Did you bring your guitar, Dad?' Holly asked,

ignoring his comment about the diabetes being a factor for Chrissie's protectiveness.

'Of course. It's in the back of the car.'

'Cool, will you it get, please? We can play some songs together like we always used to.'

When Chrissie put her key in the door an hour later, Sam and Holly were strumming their guitars along to a rudimentary version of Ed Sheeran's 'Shape of You', laughing together as they tried to remember the words.

'Sam, what are you doing here?' Chrissie said, looking flustered and surprised.

'I came to see you. But you weren't in. Holly was here on her own.' As soon as the words came out of his mouth he regretted how accusatory they sounded.

'Holly and I agreed that it would be OK for her to stay here on her own. It was only for a short while,' Chrissie said crisply.

'And you didn't think to discuss it with me? This change of plan … especially after the grief you gave me about dropping her off the other night. And don't I get a say any more in the choices we make for our daughter?' He stopped playing and shook his head.

'Sam, it was only for a short time. And it's not exactly late. I didn't mean to exclude you, I—'

'Mum! Dad! No more arguments, please,' Holly jumped in, looking at them both. 'Come on Mum, why don't you join in? Me and Dad are having fun.'

'I'm not sure?' Chrissie hesitated. Sam willed her to give it a go. If only for Holly's sake. 'What is it you're doing?'

'I'm practising for the Summer Show at school,' Holly said, thinking of her Get Mum and Dad Back Together in Time for My Birthday plan, and mentally crossing her fingers that Mum would let Dad stay. And that Mum would join in the singing, too. They always had a laugh when she did her 'shows', so what better way to try to make the wish come true. 'Katie wants to do Ariana Grande, but I want to do Ed Sheeran. Please Mum,' Holly beamed, hoping her smile would win Mum round. Chrissie sighed, the battle evident on her face, but then relented and sank down on the sofa next to Sam.

For the next half-hour, Sam and Chrissie indulged Holly while she sat in the comfy armchair opposite them and played out the various versions of her performance. 'Refining' was the best word that Sam could come up with for Holly's show. Sam loved playing his guitar, but always knew he'd never be lead-singer material. Their daughter seemed to have inherited his virtually tone-deaf ear. It was mostly enthusiasm that was propping up her routine. Chrissie ended up taking over the singing duties while Holly focused on the dancing. Sam thought that Chrissie's crystal-clear tones gave the song an added soulfulness, but then he was biased. Eventually Holly started yawning and Chrissie insisted she go upstairs to put her pyjamas on and snuggle up in bed with a book before lights out.

'That was fun. We felt like a proper family then for a moment,' Chrissie said, closing the door behind Holly.

'We are a proper family,' Sam smiled. 'When we're together ...'

'Exactly! When we're together.' But there was no accusation in her words this time. They looked at each other and Sam could feel something had shifted slightly in his wife this evening. Not as defensive, maybe. 'And it was nice to see Holly so happy,' she added.

'That's because we're not fighting.' Sam turned slightly to look at Chrissie, slinging his arm along the back of the sofa.

'Or more accurately, she and I aren't fighting either.' Chrissie's eyes met his momentarily before she glanced away again. 'That's what is really hard. She's always better when you are around, Sam. You've always had the knack with her.'

'You're her mum, Chrissie, she loves you,' Sam told her, desperately wanting to take his wife in his arms. But how would she react?

'I'm not disputing that. And I guess I have been trying too hard to keep it all together ...' Chrissie hesitated, as if searching for the right words to say to him.

'And you've done it all so well, Chrissie.'

'I've had to.'

'I know. And I didn't mean it in a patronising way. Just that you're a great mum. A lovely one—'

'But she rarely gets the lovely mum these days. Just the grumpy and fretful one. It's no wonder she hates me sometimes.'

Sam slipped his arm from the sofa to settle around her shoulders, gently pulling her in for a hug and she didn't stop him.

'Let me stay with you tonight, Chrissie. Let me make love to you and close the distance I put between us.' Sam braced himself for rejection, but Chrissie did the last thing he expected. She leant into him and buried her face in the groove above his collarbone. For a moment the two of them sat in silence. Close. Just savouring the feeling of togetherness. With Sam anxious not to break the spell as he inhaled her familiar scent. Yearning as he felt her body mould into his.

But then the moment vanished when Chrissie pulled away and stood up.

'Sam, look, I'm glad you've come back and ... maybe I'm starting to realise that perhaps I do need help.' She paused and placed a hand at her neck. He stood up in front of her. 'That I can't do all this on my own any more, that Holly needs us both. But I have to believe that you are really here to stay. That you won't change your mind and tell me you've booked flights to Dubai or Barcelona or wherever ... to look at another exciting new project.'

Wrapping her arms around herself, she turned her face away from him. Sam opened his mouth to speak. To protest. To say that he wasn't going to do any such thing. But then swiftly remembered that he'd done precisely this before. And at least half a dozen times over the last few years. So he closed his mouth and studied the contents on top of the coffee table instead. 'I'm sorry, Sam. I'm just not ready to try again yet. It's actions not words that we need right now.'

'I know,' he said softly as he moved closer. 'I get it. Really I do. Can I at least give you another hug?' And he wrapped his arms around her, holding her tight as he closed his eyes and made a silent wish. That he'd get to do this every day. Hold her. Until they were both old and grey. That was his wish.

'Come on,' Chrissie untangled his arms from around her body and stepped back. 'Let's both go and say good-night to Holly. She'll be deliriously tired by now.'

And so they did.

Holly smiled contentedly as Sam leaned across the pink flamingo-patterned duvet cover and kissed her forehead.

And for the first time in simply ages, he felt like a normal dad again.

Chapter Fifteen

On Saturday, in the tiny boxroom of Dolly's cottage, Sam opened the old brown leather utility suitcase that he'd brought back with him from his visit to The Forstal Farmhouse. After lifting out a pile of yellowing papers – mainly school reports, letters and bank statements – from the suitcase, he found a clear plastic wallet with an expired driving licence inside and what looked like his NHS medical card. He reached inside the wallet, hoping that he'd had the initiative to store his blood donor card alongside it. That would have been sensible – to have medical information all together. But then Sam had never been one for doing things that made sense.

Sam inhaled through his nostrils and then puffed out a long breath as he resolved to try again to sort things out. Properly this time. Holly was coming over tomorrow to help make fruit scones for the Tindledale WI afternoon spring tea that Dolly was hosting on Monday. And Sam had decided that he was going to talk to Chrissie, to find out what had happened with her blood tests and to suggest he should go along to the hospital with them for the next appointment. He was determined to demonstrate his intentions – actions spoke louder than words, after all, like Chrissie had said. It would show her that he was trying.

Ahh, he unfolded a crumpled piece of lined A4 paper. It was one of Holly's animal stories that she had written when she was much younger. This time about a unicorn. After smoothing out the paper, he read her words written in joined-up, but childlike handwriting, and smiled at the memory of that blissfully happy, hot summer not so long ago. Only six years. Time sure does fly when you're having fun, he thought, then quickly berated himself for feeling cynical and sorry for himself. But somehow the past six years felt like an eternity, given how everything had changed so much. If only he had known then what he had to lose now, less than a decade later … perhaps he would have cherished it all so much more, and made better, wiser decisions. Instead of hiding behind the premise of providing for his family, making sure they had enough money and material things, when all the while he had been running. Running away from his other responsibility, which was to be there for them and face up to what his daughter was going through. To be present. He looked again at the words on the piece of paper in his hands.

To Daddy.

The Magic Unicorn by Holly Morgan.

Age 7 years old and 11 months (nearly 8 years)

The Wish

Sam felt his chest tighten as he remembered Holly sitting on his lap outside in the garden, reading the story aloud to him and Chrissie, and being delighted by their enthusiastic oohs and ahhs in all the right places. They had clapped afterwards, and Chrissie had produced a pile of profiteroles with extra squirty cream that they'd devoured after their barbecue. The day had also stuck in his mind because, later, when Holly was in bed, he had got hold of the can of cream and squirted it down Chrissie's top, prompting a lovely romp on the old sofa in the summerhouse. He remembered feeling so content on that sofa as they had lain in each other's arms, watching through the open doors as the sun set on the horizon over the top of their happy home.

Bringing his thoughts back into Dolly's boxroom, he carried on reading, and had just got to the bit where the magic element of the story finally kicked in, when he heard a soft tap on the bedroom door.

'Only me, love.' It was Dolly, with a mug of tea in one hand and a plate piled high with a clotted cream and strawberry jam-topped scone in the other. 'Thought you might like a mid-morning snack,' she said, popping her head around the doorframe and placing the plate down on a nearby cabinet. 'Still warm from the Aga, the scone is,' she chuckled, quickly swiping her hands together to wipe a speck of cream from her fingers. 'Holly is going to love them.' Sam turned quickly to look at his gran, feeling concerned. 'Don't worry, I have a recipe for a special healthier batch for her with reduced sugar, wholemeal flour and grated apple and cinnamon. Topped with diabetic jam, they'll taste absolutely delicious. And she can take pictures and snap about them on her phone to her friend Katie. Or however it is they communicate these days. You know how she likes to get involved in all that "styling", as she calls it.' Dolly shook her head in bewilderment, making her soft grey curls jiggle around her age-lined face.

'Mmm, I'm impressed. And thank you, this tastes good,' he said, through a mouthful of fruit scone.

'Did you find what you were looking for, Sam?' Dolly asked, coming properly into the room and sitting on the bed beside the suitcase.

'Not yet, but I'm still searching,' he started, before pushing the rest of the scone into his mouth and washing it down with a big gulp of the hot, sweet tea. Dolly patted his arm gently.

'I saw Tony earlier this morning when I popped into the village to get the baking supplies,' she said. 'He mentioned Jude and Chrissie were in the Duck & Puddle the other night …' Sam took another swig of the tea and then sat down next to her.

'Oh, just the two of them?' Sam couldn't help himself.

'Um, he might have said there was a man with them

when he went back to the pub after having a curry with Barry...' Dolly looked away.

'I see,' Sam replied, his fears confirmed, and he immediately wondered who the man was. 'Did he know the bloke?' Sam wondered if this mystery man had been a factor in Chrissie turning him down the other night.

'I don't think so. He didn't say.' Silence followed. 'It was said in passing. Tony didn't mean anything by it ... only that it was nice to see Chrissie smiling. And you can't blame him for wanting her to be happy. She's been friends with his Jude since they were little girls.'

'I know,' Sam sighed.

'Now, don't be stewing on it, Sam.' She looked at his face. 'Come on. Chrissie wouldn't carry on like that. Not in the Duck & Puddle. I wish I hadn't mentioned it now. The man could very well have been with Jude ...'

Sam hoped she was right. And his gran had never been one for airing the family's dirty laundry in public. He remembered years ago when his mother, Linda, had shouted her mouth off in the busy Post Office part of the village store when someone in the queue had told her off for tutting about the wait to be served. Linda had been in a hurry, apparently, and saw no reason to have to put up with the old lady, Hettie, who owned the haberdashery shop, taking forever to find the right change to pay for a single stamp. Dolly had heard about the commotion before Linda had even made it back home. And he had a vivid memory of them then getting into another quarrel about it because his mother had no sympathy for the fact that several of the older villagers were up in arms over poor Hettie being made to feel like an inconvenience.

'Hmm,' Sam roused himself, 'you know, Chrissie had left Holly on her own when I went over there the other night.'

'Really?' Dolly looked surprised. 'Well, it won't have been for very long, I'm sure. Chrissie is a great mum, Sam.'

'Yes, I know,' he nodded. 'I wasn't trying to say otherwise. I was annoyed initially, after the ear-bashing she gave me for leaving Holly on her own. But I can see that Chris is just trying to give Holly some freedom – loosen up a bit with her. Think she realises that she's growing up and needs a bit more independence.'

'Yes. And now that you're back, it's bound to feel like everything has changed. The most important thing is for you to talk things through sensibly and calmly. You both want the same things for Holly so there is no need for arguments,' Dolly responded. But Sam knew that was easier said than done. 'Now, shall I give you a hand to find what you're looking for?' she asked, changing the subject and picking up one of his old school reports.

'Thanks, Gran. I've been looking through all this stuff, to see if there is something in here that's useful for Holly. Like my blood donor card. And I need to talk to Chrissie to find out about her blood tests. I've got a horrible feeling she isn't a match for Holly, and if she isn't then it's doubly important that I am, if anything were ever to go wrong.'

'There's no reason to think that anything will go wrong though, son. Dr Ben was very reassuring about Holly's prognosis,' Dolly said. The last thing Sam wanted to do was to worry Dolly, but he had already told her what the doctor had said. 'Didn't he say that there is no reason to worry right now? That Holly is being well looked after? And Chrissie isn't one to deliberately keep you in the dark,' Dolly reassured him.

'True. But if she already knows that she isn't a blood match then I imagine it was a terrible disappointment. I really do need to talk to her.'

'Well, she might have only found out recently and been trying to work out what it means. I'm sure she's doing her best to muddle through it, just as you are,' Dolly patted the top of his thigh affectionately.

'I guess so,' Sam said, putting his arm around his gran and feeling a rush of affection for her. Dolly could always be relied upon to see the positive in people. She was very generous like that. And he was barely 'muddling through' ... 'making a massive mess of it' would be a much more accurate description.

'Come on, stop feeling sorry for yourself. And let's find that donor card.' And she stood up and started rummaging through the suitcase. 'And, come to think of it, I probably have your father's old blood donor card knocking around somewhere – your mother didn't want to hang onto any of his old papers after he died ...' She paused, as if pondering whether to pass comment on this fact, but instead continued with, 'It might come in handy to show Dr Ben. You know, as an indicator of what your blood group is likely to be. Might make you worry less.'

'Thanks, Gran. Don't suppose you have Mum's by any chance?' Sam thought it was worth a shot. They might have been kept together or something, you never know.

'I doubt it, love.' She shook her head. 'Hang on, I'll be back in a jiffy, I think his papers are in an old hatbox in my bedroom,' and she went to leave. 'Ooh,' she popped her head back around the door, 'and I'll book an appointment first thing on Monday to see if I'm a match.'

'Gran, you don't need to do that—'

'But I want to.'

'You might be too old though.' The words were out before he had engaged his brain; he hadn't meant to offend her.

'Charming! Well, we'll see about that. I'm as fit as a fiddle, me.'

And they both laughed.

Chapter Sixteen

'Good morning, Mrs Morgan. This is your husband, Mr Morgan,' Sam ventured optimistically. Having slept well for the first time in ages, he'd woken up with a renewed resolve. Things had been great the other night. Just like the old days. Singing and playing the guitar, and then he and Chrissie having a chance to properly talk without any recriminations. And there had definitely been a sea change in Chrissie. It wasn't like she had totally cut him dead when he had wanted to make love to her – just that she needed more time. And so he was sure there was a seed of hope for their marriage now. And he fully intended on nurturing that seed.

'Well good morning to you too, Mr Morgan.' He knew that Chrissie was smiling at the other end of the phone, which was a great start to the day as far as he was concerned.

'Chrissie, I just wanted to ask you something. I didn't get a chance to the other night … it didn't seem like the right moment.'

'What's that then?' She sounded guarded now, so he knew he'd have to tread carefully.

'I was talking to Dr Ben. I went to see him about a few things ... we talked about me having some blood tests, just as a precaution in ca—'

'Is this about Holly's kidneys?' Chrissie jumped in.

'Yes. You know ... if things don't improve.'

'What did he tell you? Did he say anything about the tests she's been having? Because I've not been told yet. And I am her mother. I'd like to know too.'

'Hang on, please don't get upset. He didn't tell me anything new. But isn't it right that we both know about any developments, so that we can deal with it together?' Sam swallowed, keen to keep things upbeat and nice between them. He'd promised Holly there would be no more arguments, and fully intended to stick to that. There was a pause at the other end of the line, as if Chrissie was mulling this over.

'Yes ... I'm sorry, you're right,' she then said in a softer voice.

'I don't want you to shoulder this all by yourself any more,' Sam mirrored her voice. 'I meant what I said. Actions not words, right? I do get it. I promise ...' He paused, letting his words sink in. 'I was going to ask if you've had your blood tests done? To see if you're a match.'

Chrissie took a deep breath before speaking. 'Yes, I have. And I can't donate a kidney.' Sam's heart dropped.

'What do you mean?'

'I've got hypertension, which rules me out right now.

And before you ask me why I didn't tell you … well, there hasn't been a good moment, it's not something that you can just drop into the middle of an argument, or a squeaky rendition of "Shape of You", is it?'

Sam smiled ruefully, appreciating her attempt to make light of the situation, but Sam knew this wasn't funny.

'Oh love, I'm sorry – do they know why your blood pressure is high?'

'It's likely to be stress, Sam.' The tightness in her voice was back.

'Chrissie, stress can be beaten, and I promise that we'll work on that too. Maybe we could go for a run, or take up yoga together—'

'Sam! Enough already.' Chrissie laughed. 'I am working on it and Dr Ben has been great. But it's pretty crap about the blood results. That would have made things much easier. It will be down to you to donate a kidney, it seems. But just the thought of it ever coming to that makes me feel physically sick.'

'Me too. But this is just a precaution. Does Holly know anything about it?' he asked.

'Not specifically, but she's not stupid and she knows how she is feeling,' Chrissie lowered her voice.

'Maybe I'll check how she's coping when she comes over later,' Sam said.

'That would be nice, Sam. But please be careful. Holly is pretty sensitive at the moment.'

'I know and I will. I promise.' And after saying goodbye he ended the call.

*

Holly took another bite of the scone before positioning it on a plate next to a mug of warm milk beside the Aga, aka Beryl the Peril. After carefully dusting just the right amount of cinnamon across the top of the milk, she selected her favourite photo app filter and took a few more pictures. Perfect. It was all coming together nicely. Just like her Get Mum and Dad Back Together in Time for My Birthday plan. And she hadn't even really had to do anything much … it had sort of happened anyway, with Dad coming over and Mum joining in the singing. It had been a fab night. Just like before … She just hoped Mum didn't go and ruin it all by being moany again, or nasty to Dad.

'Everything OK?' Dad asked, making her jump and almost drop her cherished crystal-embellished iPhone into the milk as he came into the kitchen.

'Dad!' she scolded, deftly saving her phone from an untimely demise. 'You almost ruined it.' She waggled the phone in his face.

'Oops, sorry, sweetheart. Everything OK?' Sam asked, inwardly sighing with relief, as he knew he'd be in big trouble if he was to blame for anything whatsoever happening to her phone, which seemed to be permanently welded to her right hand these days. Maybe now was a good time to have a little chat with her, to see if she was worried about anything? She seemed pretty relaxed, so that was a good start, at least.

'Yep, and this is going to look so good on my Instagram.' Holly showed him the picture. Sam nodded, impressed with his daughter's artistic flair; the photo looked as if it had been taken by a professional photographer for one of those glossy, achingly trendy lifestyle books that you saw on coffee tables in swanky hotels and airport lounges. Sam recalled flicking through them one time in the British Airways lounge at Singapore Airport when his flight home had been delayed, yet again. It had been their wedding anniversary weekend, and Chrissie had been so disappointed when the elaborate meal she'd prepared to surprise him with had been ruined. With hindsight, he should have realised back then that their marriage was seriously falling apart, but he hadn't. Neither of them had. Instead, they had adopted a politeness with each other for that weekend, a kind of distance that papered over the proverbial cracks until it had been time for him to return to the airport.

And then the awkward pattern had set in, making it so easy to perpetuate each time he had come home.

'I'm impressed, Holly.' Sam ran his fingers through

his messy brown hair before pushing both hands into his jean pockets.

'What's up, Dad?' Holly tilted her head to one side, making her honey-coloured hair fall over one side of her face.

'Um, what do you mean?'

'It's just that you always do that ...' she gestured with her hands and slumped her shoulders, mimicking his stance, wondering what her dad wanted to talk to her about. It was so obvious something was up. And she wondered why he didn't just come out with it, instead of acting weird. He was picking at one of the scones now and making her feel as if she had done something wrong.

Holly flopped into the cosy patchwork-covered armchair and pushed out a petulant bottom lip, wondering if now was a good time to ask if she could live here with him all the time. Maybe it would be for the best. Mum might lighten up if she wasn't with her twenty-four seven. And then she might be nice to Dad too ... Or if Mum was never going to take Dad back, then she could be with Gavin whenever she wanted to. Maybe Holly should just face up to it and be one of those kids from a broken home. Mum and Dad had seemed happy last night but now Dad was back here at Granny Dolly's again – she had hoped Mum would let him stay after they had such a fun time doing the singing, and maybe she should accept that nothing was going to work. Katie Ferguson's mum and dad split up years ago, and she is still all right. In fact, she even gets extra perks, like double pocket money, because her mum gets angry when her dad transfers money into her account, so then she gives her even more. It's like a competition to see who can be the nicest parent.

'Do what?' Dad jolted into her thoughts. Holly pulled her bottom lip back in and stuck a smile on her face. He'd never agree to her living here if she was sulky. And what if he turned on her too? Like Mum had. No, she had to make an effort or she would not even be from a broken home … she would be from no home at all. Or maybe Aunty Jude would let her live with her and Lulu, and Uncle Tony and the golden retrievers … Betty, Bob and Barney. That wouldn't be so bad. Hmm, on second thoughts, no, it really wouldn't be the same at all.

But she couldn't think about that now. No, she had to be nice to Dad. It wasn't his fault Mum was so mean, she could easily have let him stay after having such a good time with him the other night. So maybe if she did live with Dad and wasn't there all the time getting on Mum's nerves, then she might chill out a bit. *Mum might even take him back then. You know, if she really misses him. And me. Like properly misses us….*

'Earth to Holly. What's the matter?' Sam interrupted her thoughts.

'Nothing,' Holly grinned and jumped up. 'Would you

like a scone?' She quickly got one from the plate and went to hand it to him.

'Oh no, love. I'm stuffed. Couldn't eat another thing,' and he patted his stomach to punctuate the point.

'But these are special ones. Granny Dolly found the recipe especially for diabetics. Not that you need to be a diabetic to eat them, though, as anyone can, but they are extra healthy. And low sugar. With carrots and stuff in them too.'

Sam looked at his daughter's little face. All eager and willing to please, and he relented. It wouldn't kill him to try one of her 'special' scones.

'Oh, go on then.' And he took the scone from her hand. As he chewed, he pondered again about asking her if she was OK, do a sense-check that she wasn't worried about the tests, or anything else for that matter. Looking at her now, beaming with happiness and keen to hear his verdict on the scone, she looked absolutely fine. But he wasn't totally insensitive and he knew she had a knack of putting on a brave face – like she had over claiming to have been cool with just speaking to him on Skype while he was away. And he knew things weren't perfect for her, and that the diabetes had taken its toll on her life. And him and Chrissie having been at loggerheads for so long can't have been any good for her either. At least that seemed to be improving a bit. 'So, what do you think then, Dad?' Holly prodded his arm and nodded at the remnants of the scone in his hand.

'Mm-mmm. Not bad,' he said, finishing the last of the scone and licking his lips. 'You're a great baker, Holly. You could go on that *Bake Off* programme, darling.'

'Don't be silly, Dad.'

'Why not?'

'I dunno,' Holly shrugged, 'not really my thing.'

'So what is your thing?'

'You know,' she grinned, 'writing stories. Watching Zoella – YouTube stuff. And playing the guitar. Singing too ... like we all did the other night.' Sam spotted the hopeful look on her face and instantly decided to do something about it. He'd loved messing about with Holly and Chrissie that night. He wondered if the old adage about the healing power of music was true; it certainly seemed to be in their case.

'Hang on then. I'll be back in a sec,' he said.

After bounding up the stairs, two at a time, to his room, Sam made it back to the kitchen in record time, with his guitar on a strap over his shoulder. He did a quick tune-up and strummed a few chords.

'OK, what is it going to be this time?' he smiled.

'Ooh, I've got my guitar here too – I was practising the other day with it after school.' Holly dashed out to the hall and grabbed the nylon case, unzipped it and pulled out her lilac-coloured guitar.

'That's nice.' Sam pointed to the crystal butterfly motif just below the bridge.

'Oh, I did that myself – customised it,' she grinned, tilting the guitar up so the butterfly twinkled underneath the kitchen light. 'So, what shall we play?' She pushed up her sleeves in preparation.

'How about that song from *Frozen*?' Sam suggested, knowing it was one of her favourite films. But, on seeing her pull a face, he offered up an alternative. 'What about that one from the *Moana* movie then? What was that song you sang to me on Skype that time?'

'"How Far I'll Go"?' Holly pondered. She used to love it. Last year. But that was like ages ago. 'Dad, that's so lame.'

'Ahh, I see.' He smiled at her fickleness ... but then realised that it was just part of being a thirteen year old.

'Why don't we do that old country one you love?' she suggested. *Yes, this is a good idea, it will make him feel happy. He loves the Dolly Parton and Kenny Rogers one. If we do it, then he'll remember the good times and let me stay with him so we can do more of his favourite songs together all the time. Just like we used to.*

'Which one, sweetheart?' Sam chuckled to himself at her 'old' reference. Anything recorded more than a year ago was ancient as far as his daughter was concerned.

'You know, the "Islands in the Stream" one ... It starts

like this ...' Holly started singing as she tried to play the opening chords, but her guitar skills weren't really good enough to get it right.

'Excellent choice,' Sam joined in. He was a much better player.

'I'm rubbish at the guitar,' Holly stopped playing and got on with singing instead. The song wasn't really her thing, but Dad loved it. Even Mum used to join in and sing the Dolly part to his Kenny. And she had really loved watching them happy together ... enjoying themselves and giggling as they really got into it and messed around, pretending to have microphones in their hands as they strutted around on an imaginary stage. Dad had even lifted Mum up in the air one time and twirled her around the lounge, nearly bumping her head on the light shade by mistake. Before they fell over and ended up having a big cuddle on the carpet.

'No, you're not, love. Come on, we'll do it together,' he laughed, getting in to the groove now as they built up to the chorus. They had just reached the 'no one in between' bit when she felt her eyes stinging. She thought of Gavin getting in between her parents and spoiling it all. She managed to carry on until the next verse in a wobbly voice before tears pooled and slid down her cheeks.

Sam immediately stopped playing, placed his guitar on the kitchen counter and enveloped his daughter in an enormous hug.

'What's the matter, darling?' he asked, gently resting his chin on the top of her head.

'Nothing. It's fine. I ...' He could feel her small shoulders trembling as she went to free herself from his embrace.

'Well, it doesn't look like it.' A short silence followed. 'Come on, let's sit down.' Sam sat and motioned for Holly to join him. She didn't want a cuddle, that was clear, as she'd pulled right away from him and was busy stroking Dolly's tabby cat, which had sidled over and was now basking on the counter in the heat from the Aga.

'What's getting you down? You know you can tell me, or Mum, anything,' Sam ventured, figuring it a good place to start.

'No I can't. Not Mum anyway. She goes mental over the slightest little thing.' She shrugged.

'That's because she stressed and a lot of that has been my fault,' Sam said, fairly. At this Holly burst into tears all over again. Sam opened his mouth. He scratched his head. Put a hand on his daughter's arm and was just about to try another tack – ask her about school. Chrissie. A boyfriend? Surely not? She wasn't old enough for all that. Was she?

'Everything is ruined. It's never going to be good again. If the love goes ....' Sam creased his forehead in concern. *The song. Oh God.* And the penny dropped. *She's petrified that it's over between me and Chrissie. That our love has gone for good.* 'Not if Mum hates me and we aren't all together. How is that even going to work? If Mum won't let you come home, then I want to live with you!' Holly couldn't keep it in any more. *Better out than in, that's what Gran always says. I've tried to be sensible about it. But I'm no good at plans or being patient. Look where the last plan got me? I fell off a chair, and Mum blamed Dad for leaving me on my own – like I'm some sort of little kid. But at least Dad doesn't think I'm just a kid. He trusts me. And talks to me like I'm a proper person. He cares what I think. I wish Mum did too.*

'Mum doesn't hate you, sweetheart.' Sam was shocked. 'Why would you think that?'

'Why else is she so strict then?'

'Because she cares, Holly. And she is trying to lighten up ... she let you stay at home by yourself, didn't she? She adores you and loves you with all her heart.'

'Well, she has a funny way of showing it.'

'Listen to me, Holly,' Sam looked his daughter in the eyes. 'Sometimes there are other reasons why people do things. Other stuff going on. It's not always about you.' As soon as he said it, Sam could have kicked himself for how his last sentence sounded. It had come out all wrong. He went to hug her. To try to explain, but Dolly appeared in the kitchen, nearly colliding with Holly as she pushed past her great gran and ran upstairs before slamming the bedroom door.

'Found them!' Dolly waved a faded old brown envelope

in the air, then paused. Registered what had just happened and then added, 'What on earth is going on?'

'Found what?' Sam blurted out in his bewilderment and concern for his daughter.

'The donor cards.' Dolly said this in an exaggerated whisper.

Your dad's. *And* Linda's!' Dolly placed the envelope on the side. 'I'll go after her.' And she turned as if to go, but Sam put a hand on her arm.

'Err ... no. Thank you. I will.'

At the door of Holly's bedroom, Sam knocked softly and waited. No answer. He knocked again.

'Holly, can I come in, sweetheart?' More silence. 'I'm sorry, that came out all wrong ... of course it's about you,' he said, suddenly remembering what Matt had said in the car park. He vowed to read some sort of manual before talking to his teenage daughter again. No wonder Chrissie was stressed. 'You mean the world to me and your mum.' Sam gave her a bit more time and then slowly opened the door. This had to be sorted out.

Sam walked over to the bed where Holly was lying curled up in the foetal position, cuddling a big teddy bear. She looked so tiny and vulnerable, just like a little girl, in contrast to her thirteen years. He sat on the side of the bed and put his hand on her shoulder.

'Fancy a cuddle?'

She moved her head. The affirmation was slight, but

it was good enough for him to know it was a yes, so he scooped his arm around her back and gently pulled her up into a big bear hug.

'It's going to be OK, Holly, I promise you.'

'But how can it be?' She sat back against the crimson velvet headboard and pulled her knees up under her chin and wrapped her arms around herself. 'My birthday is going to be rubbish if you and Mum are not together …'

'We will find a way to make it good. I love your mum very much and, well … what I meant when I said that it isn't about you, is … that …' He paused, wondering how much to tell her. 'You see, there are things I've done that I shouldn't have,' he settled on.

'Like what?' Holly jumped in.

'Well … not being around for starters … Not being here for Christmas. Mum was very upset about that,' he said, dipping his head.

'But that wasn't your fault. And I was OK with it, so why wouldn't she be?'

'It's a bit more complicated than that, love. Things haven't been how they should be for me and your mum for a long time. And none of that is your fault. But the love isn't gone, darling. I still love your mum, and I think she might still love me too.' Silence followed. 'Do you hear me?' Sam reiterated, keen to make sure she understood. Holly nodded. 'But I am going to do everything I can to make things right again. To make Mum happy again. And you. And me … so that you can have a lovely birthday, just like we always have.'

Chapter Seventeen

Jude unclipped Lulu's lead and let her run into the little play area that Sylvia had set up in the boot room by the back door of the Blackwood Farm Estate manor house. It was a sensible option, seeing as Jude was spending more and more time here, having taken on some part-time help to run the shop while she was away.

In one corner by the radiator was a plush, plum-coloured velvet day bed for Lulu to lounge on, which she invariably did – complete with supersonic loud snores that made the kitchen staff next door chuckle as they prepared gourmet meals for the properly pampered pooch. And in the other corner was a selection of dog toys for Lulu to play with or, if that was too much exertion for her, then she had her own TV on the wall, especially fitted low down at her eye level, so that she could watch an assortment of dog-friendly programmes. Her current favourite, according to Pat, one of the cleaners, was that *Secret Life of Dogs* series.

Not that Jude had initiated any of this. Absolutely not. It was Myles who had insisted, by saying, 'You can't concentrate on getting the house right with Lulu running

Alex Brown

all over the joint.' This was shortly after Jude had been hanging a pair of exquisite silk curtains and Lulu had slipped her collar from where she had been secured with her lead tied to a banister, and clawed the corner of one. So Myles had then insisted that Sylvia should get the boot room fitted out forthwith. And they had all sighed in relief.

After popping her head around the kitchen door and waving at April from Orchard Cottage, who was delivering a crate of her award-winning ciders, which Myles had asked to sample, Jude helped herself to a cup of coffee from the machine by the giant range cooker, and pressed on the intercom for Sylvia to come and collect her. This had become her usual routine now, whenever she was spending the day at the manor house, and it suited Jude just fine. No more traipsing around the grounds looking for someone to let her in. Sometimes she came across Sam overseeing whatever delivery or construction was scheduled for that day. But it was all a bit frenetic, to be fair, with Myles mostly running around the pig pen, or hurtling all over the estate on his new quad bike, bellowing instructions to whoever was within earshot.

'Hi Jude,' Sylvia greeted her pleasantly as she arrived in the kitchen, followed by, 'don't rush, you finish up your coffee first, my dear.'

'Oh, thanks.' Jude drained the last of the latte and gathered up her sample books, mood boards and swatches.

'How are you today? Has his lordship been treating you well?'

'He has,' Sylvia laughed. 'It's always a pleasure when you're scheduled to visit – it puts him in a good mood, that's for sure. And that makes my job a whole lot easier, I have to say. I might even manage a bit of time off this afternoon. I thought I might venture in to Market Briar and have a look around the shops. In peace. Without the walkie-talkie.' She waved it in the air for good measure.

'I'm pleased to hear it. You deserve a bit of downtime,' Jude said kindly. She had come to see that Myles relied far too much on Sylvia, treating her like his beck-and-call woman, with little regard for her own personal requirements, such as a bit of time off for herself now and again.

'Indeed. And if you wouldn't mind taking your time over whatever he gets you involved in, it would be much appreciated.' A mischievous smile flitted across Sylvia's face.

'I'm sure I can manage that,' Jude winked, relishing in the subterfuge. After the shaky start when they had first met, she was really warming to Sylvia these days, and the pair of them had settled into an unlikely friendship. A mutual understanding of each other brought about by their sometimes insufferable, but always entertaining boss. 'Now, where is he? Or, to be more precise ... where does he want me today?' It was always a lottery – Jude had given up trying to work with Myles in an orderly way, working through the house in a logical order, tackling reception rooms, followed by bedrooms, bathrooms, etc., as she had with her many previous clients. She knew Myles had given her free rein, but still, she had to have some idea of his preferences. And he had kind of gone back on his word with that, in any case, and had taken to springing ideas on her. Last time he'd been adamant about wanting a Pokémon-themed dining room. Nothing wrong with that, Jude had thought, but this particular dining room was actually a vast space. The old banqueting hall, which had always been made available to the villagers by the previous owners, Lord Lucan and his wife, Marigold, for things like the WI summer party or the May Fair, when the weather had turned. And Jude had been made aware that the Tindledale Parish Council were hoping that Myles would consider continuing with this tradition. So a hundred-foot Pokémon hall wasn't really appropriate. It had taken her a whole day to convince him to consider something more 'in keeping with the tradition of the house'.

'He's asked me to bring you to the basement today.'

'The basement?' Jude lifted an eyebrow, feeling intrigued. 'But what about the rest of the bedrooms? We've only agreed the design specifications on three of them ...'

'I know,' Sylvia momentarily closed her eyes and shook her head in exasperation. 'But he was quite specific.

Apparently, he has a surprise for you. Another one!' And the two women exchanged knowing looks.

'Oh dear.' Over her time designing the interior for Myles, Jude had come to realise that her client was extremely fond of springing surprises on her. Last time she'd been here, he had greeted her with a pair of ginger woolly llamas in tow, Clarissa and Clive, who were being set up in an area over behind the old lavender field, which had been ploughed recently, ready for replanting.

'Guess we had better get on with it then ... we know how he hates having to wait for his big reveals,' Jude laughed, inwardly thinking what a boy Myles was, and she still couldn't work out if this youthful exuberance was endearing, or just a right pain in the arse. Scott, her boyfriend back in America, had been juvenile, and that had grated on her. But, somehow, Myles seemed to be growing on her. She had thought a lot about the way he had been with Holly when she had visited – really thoughtful and generous with his time. And then that night in the Duck & Puddle when he had been charming and kind to Chrissie. And she had looked over and seen Myles – global rock superstar (albeit faded now) – playing darts with Mack and his army pals, plus Cooper the village butcher, Matt the farrier, and Lawrence, who owned the B&B and ran the Tindledale Players am-dram society ... so an eclectic group. But they were all laughing and joking around as if they had known each other all their lives. It had been fascinating seeing Myles seemingly out of his comfort zone, because that was just it, he hadn't looked uncomfortable at all. He had looked happy, relaxed, and as if he belonged here in Tindledale. The silly persona – bizarre costumes and exaggerated behaviour – had vanished, and he was just one of the blokes. Somehow, seeing him in a normal setting, in a T-shirt and jeans, a pint glass in one hand and a dart in the other, had a certain appeal. And Jude had been thinking a lot about what Chrissie had said that night in the pub about Myles fancying her …

'Lead the way then, please Sylvia,' Jude grinned, having never been down to the manor house's basement before. She was looking forward to it and intrigued to hear what Myles had planned for what she imagined would be an absolutely enormous space, or a series of smaller ones. Surely it couldn't be one huge room underground, she thought, purely from a structural point of view.

*

Fifteen minutes later, and Jude was standing in a room the size of a football pitch, with eight tall, fluted columns dotted around to support the ceiling. Lit only with tea lights positioned inside the old-fashioned gas lamps that still hung on the walls, it gave the space a cosy, flickering orange glow. Like an animated sepia photo taken in the olden days. Faded but totally atmospheric.

'*Swimming pool!*' she echoed, practically dumb-founded. But that's what Myles had said. And it might be the kind of thing they have in the basements of the big houses in Primrose Hill in London where he's from. But she'd never seen the likes of it here in the sleepy little idyll of Tindledale.

'So, what do you reckon?' He was bouncing around like an over-excited Golden Retriever puppy. Darting towards the centre of the room and back to her, flinging his arms around, his eyes twinkling with excitement in the candlelight. And his hair was different. The silly man bun had gone, replaced with a cool cut that Jude thought really suited him. He no longer looked like an overgrown teenage hipster, but more like a proper forty-something man. A good-looking one, at that. She was impressed. And, dared she say it … attracted to him. But she was here to work, she swiftly reminded herself.

'Err … um, well … yes. I can see your vision.' She stalled for time to formulate a sensible response, all the while thinking, is he actually *insane?* She had worked on some huge, spectacular projects in her time, but this … well, it was crazy.

'It's going to be awesome. And look …' He grabbed the pile of mood boards, sample books and swatches from her arms and dumped them on the dusty floor before taking her hand and literally running her to the side of the vast room. 'See here,' after dropping her hand, he shoved his shoulder against a small, arched door. 'It always does that,' he laughed, and Jude guessed that he had been here in the basement working on this idea for quite some time. He gave the door another shove, and this time it opened, scraping across concrete; the noise set her teeth on edge. But then there was daylight. 'Perfect, yes?'

'What for?'

'For the villagers to get in of course.' Myles said it as though it was the most obvious answer ever.

'The villagers?'

'Yes, the villagers. For the May Fair.' Myles was standing outside on the grass now, with one hand sweeping his blond fringe away from his face, the other gesturing behind her. 'You didn't think I was planning on keeping the swimming pool all to myself, did you?'

'Well …' Jude couldn't help herself from smiling, and then laughing. How could she not? His enthusiasm was irresistible, and she knew he had the funds to finance such a big project. He had told her so, when she had baulked at his request to buy a rare nineteenth-century Meiji period Japanese silk painting for £35,000, thank you very much! Just to hang on the wall in one of the guest bedrooms that most likely would never get used. 'Of course not, but are you sure? I mean, nobody in Tindledale expects you to provide a public swimming pool. Not to mention, in time for the May Fair … which is only – ' she pulled her iPhone from her pocket to check the date – 'eighteen days away now.'

'Yeah, I know that. But it would be so good though, wouldn't it? And it won't be just a swimming pool. It would be a proper tropical island and traditional beach mash-up too.' His eyes sparkled with enthusiasm. 'Yeah, in here we'll have the tropical island theme around the swimming pool – with an authentic swim-up bar! Cabanas dotted around selling smoothies for the children. And pineapple lollies – I love them; you get a chunk of pineapple and stick it on a stick. Literally. That's all there is to it.' He really was a big kid. 'And we can have real coconuts with holes drilled in for a straw! And fountains. You know, those ones they have in parks in London that spray jets of water up in the air – I'll source a company to supply them. And we'll have sand. With deckchairs dotted around. And someone said the village has a mobile fish-and-chip van that parks up in the High Street every Thursday. Well, we'll get it here. And an ice-cream van! It'll be brilliant. Just like a proper British seaside. You said yourself that the parish council want to carry on using the house for their WI gigs and stuff … and they can in the winter. The beach theme will be for the May Fair and then the swimming pool can be used for the rest of the summer. So they're going to love it.

Year-round access to the Blackwood Farm Estate, courtesy of yours truly.' Myles did a theatrical bow.

And then Jude got it. She realised what was going on here. This, in addition to all the numerous different outfits, costume changes on a near daily basis. He was playing a part. Trying to find out which character he needed to be in order to fit in. Be an integral part of the community. And that was fair enough. But what baffled her most, was why? He had no ties with Tindledale – Sylvia had said he had grown up in London and had picked Tindledale as the place he wanted to 'retire' to, now that his rock career was over, by simply sticking a pin in a map. Literally, that's what he had done. Sylvia had told Jude, and she didn't doubt it for a second. It was just the kind of thing Myles would do. Choose where to live his life on a whim. And it actually made her feel a bit sad for him, that he didn't have those ties anywhere else. What about his family? His parents? Where were they? Where was his real home?

Jude had 'retired' in a way as well, had come to Tindledale for another way of life too, but it was different for her. She had roots here. Her dad, her best friend, she had grown up in Tindledale. Her whole life was here. Apart from Maggie. If she could just teleport her here from LA, then life would be perfect. She'd be surrounded by the people she loved, and who loved her.

'So, will you help me do it?' Myles looked at her, his

sapphire blue eyes locked onto hers in earnest. And she didn't have the heart to crush his enthusiasm with talk of timescales, financials, risk assessments and the like ... not to mention planning permission, public event licences, and amenities like toilets and parking and first-aid provision. All of that took time. And there was simply no way it could all be achieved in a matter of weeks. But the words were out of Jude's mouth in an instance. She seemed compelled to be complicit in his adventure.

'Of course I will.'

The words sank in.

Oh dear, now I'm going to have to pull off a flaming miracle. And since when did I become an events organiser? Oh well, it might be fun ... and it's not like I'm rushed off my feet at the shop in the High Street. Which reminds me, I might have to have a rethink about the viability of having an actual shop that sells only a few candles and home comforts each week. Maybe I'm just not cut out to sit behind a counter all day long. My long-cherished dream seems to have lost its shine now. Perhaps a home office would suit me better for managing the interiors and events side of the business, and I could supply the overseas stuff from there too. And I wouldn't need to pay someone to sit in the shop when I can't be there, not to mention all the commercial overheads that come with having a retail shop ... hmmm.

'Brilliant!' Myles boomed, breaking Jude's reverie. 'Knew you'd go for it and think it was a fantastic idea.

I've already got a company lined up to bring the swimming pool. They can install it in two to three days and they'll even run it too ... provide a lifeguard to make sure it's safe and all that. Did you even know that you could hire a swimming pool?' Jude shook her head, bamboozled. 'No, nor did I till yesterday, when two seconds on Google told me that you most definitely can. It won't be a sunken one. There isn't enough time for all that digging, but it'll still be good.' And he placed his hands either side of her face and exuberantly kissed her left cheek, before pulling her in for an enormous hug. Jude felt her arms instinctively wrap around his back as she breathed in that deliciously, dangerously intoxicating Chanel scent. If any other man had been this presumptuous, then she would have batted them away in an instance, but it felt different. Myles was just the kind of guy who could do this ... And she liked it. Quite a lot.

Dropping his arms, but keeping hold of her hand, he started walking her towards the gate at the far end of the grounds.

'Where are we going now?' she asked, feeling breathless, his spontaneity was exhilarating.

'You'll see. But we'd better hurry up or we'll miss it.'

'Miss what?' Jude squeezed his hand to get his attention as they were running now. Fast across the grounds, with the warm air fluttering around their faces.

'The six donkeys I've got turning up in about – ' he paused to check his watch – 'two minutes!'

'Oh. Right. I see,' Jude managed, incredulous all over again as she surreptitiously brushed beads of sweat from her top lip.

'They're going to look insane mooching around the garden. And kids love donkey rides! Talking of that, how about some beach huts too, just in case it starts raining on the day? That would be totally rubbish. And steel drums for an authentic calypso vibe.' Myles grinned, squeezing her hand tighter. 'It's going to be awesome – like a real beach right here in the rural village of Tindledale.' And Jude couldn't help herself from thinking that, actually, he had a very good point. If they could pull it off, then it would be truly spectacular.

Holly for one would absolutely love it. And Jude was sure Myles would let Holly, aka his new best friend, have an exclusive, private first go in the swimming pool as a fabulous present, which was all the extra incentive Jude needed to try to make it all happen in time for her birthday. Especially as it was looking a bit unlikely that Holly was going to get her wish for her parents to get properly back together in time for her birthday, with the way things were between them. Chrissie had told Jude as much last night when she had phoned to see how her friend was. 'I feel like Sam could be getting it finally, but I need more time, if I'm going to trust him again,'

Chrissie had said, followed by a huge sigh of resolve. So Jude reckoned there was every reason to try to put a smile on her goddaughter's face for her fourteenth birthday ... she had promised to help Holly if she could. And she never went back on a promise. So she had a good mind to get Chrissie and Sam along to the swimming pool too for a private session, and make them find a way to work things out more quickly. Jude knew Chrissie and Sam were meant to be together ... it was just a matter of time. Time that Holly truly wished would hurry up.

Chapter Eighteen

In the doctor's surgery waiting room, Sam checked his inside coat pocket again to be sure. Yes, the donor cards were still there. He hadn't managed to find his, but was over the moon that Dolly had been right – his dad's card, *and* his mum, Linda's, were inside the hatbox. And he had been thinking a lot about what Dolly had said regarding hope, so that's exactly what he was doing from now on. Hope and positive thinking, that's what it was all about. Look where negativity, blaming himself and feeling inadequate had got him? As soon as Dr Ben had confirmed his blood group was a match with Holly's, and that Linda was a potential match too, then Sam was going to see Chrissie to give her the good news. He hoped this would show that he was thinking logically and planning ahead. That he was here for the long haul and not about to chase another overseas project. And he wasn't just doing this to prove something to Chrissie. It was also because he wanted to do everything he could to make sure that Holly was kept well. He wanted to make sure all her records were up-to-date and the information was correct. That had to be a good thing – even if, as he wanted to believe, it would never be needed. He patted his coat; the cards were in the inside pocket, like lucky charms, he hoped, to help him and his family through.

His thoughts turned to a letter that Dolly had found in amongst his dad's old paperwork. It was addressed to him and Patrick.

It's time for me to say goodbye to you, Samuel and Patrick. My two wonderful boys. I want you both to know that I will always love you. I leave feeling incredibly blessed to have been a part of your lives and I know that you will grow into fine young men that any man would be proud to call his sons. Please look after your mum, and see if you can cut her some roses from the garden from time to time. I know one day you will have your own families who will bring you as much happiness and joy as you two have me, so keep those loved ones close always, because love is all you have at the end of the day …

Sam had cried on reading that part of the letter as he reflected on how his dad's words and wishes contrasted with his own actions. He hadn't kept his loved ones close at all. What a fool he had been! And he doubted that his dad would be feeling proud of him right now. Rob had then explained how he had been having treatment in hospital for cancer, exacerbated by his Type 2 diabetes.

And Sam had taken a bittersweet moment of comfort in this knowledge, that maybe he hadn't somehow passed the diabetes on to Holly through his genes after all. He had assumed his dad had the same type of diabetes as Holly, but now it seemed this wasn't the case.

Sam had then cried in sorrow and sadness as he had tucked the letter back inside the envelope. His lovely, thoughtful, kind dad had wanted him, and Patrick, to know what was happening. He hadn't wanted them kept in the dark at all. That had been Linda's doing, because Rob had written on the back of the envelope: *I've asked your mum to pass this letter on to you.*

And, strange as it might be, Sam didn't feel angry about that any more, because it really didn't come as any surprise that she had withheld the letter, or perhaps she had simply forgotten about it, not considered the importance of it. His mother would always be the way she was, self-centred and narcissistic, and there wasn't anything he could do to change that. And something he was starkly aware of now was that not all people made perfect, or even adequate, parents.

Another positive was that Holly had told him her next appointment with the consultant at the hospital would be on Thursday next week, and he had already squared it with Myles to take the day off – well, with Sylvia to be exact, as she was the real one in charge down at the Blackwood Farm Estate. She was the one who had placed the advert on the architects and planning recruitment website that he had responded to. He had also had a conversation with the endocrinologist's secretary at the hospital, ahead of Holly's next appointment, and asked for some time to speak with him on a one-to-one basis so he could really understand exactly what was happening with Holly, about the tests she'd been having, what the problems might be and what they could do to help at this stage. Sam felt so much better for taking control of the situation. Having a plan.

He was just about to take another look at the donor cards, even though he knew all the details, he had looked at them so many times, when the red light buzzed on the wall to tell him it was time to see Dr Ben. So, with a bit of a spring in his step, and a smile on his face, Sam made his way into the consulting room.

'Good afternoon, Sam, how are you today?'

'Much better, Doctor Ben. Really great. I found my parents' donor cards.' He could hardly wait to show them to him. 'Well, I didn't actually find them myself, I have my gran to thank for that.' He grinned. 'I didn't find mine, though, but that's OK now that you have the blood test results.' Sam's smile widened as he took a seat after placing the cards on Dr Ben's desk. 'It was a bit of a result that Dolly had my mother's card. She hasn't exactly been forthcoming in wanting to get tested,' he admitted. 'But I'm sure if she is the right blood group, then she might be more open to the idea ...' He paused to shake his head, knowing that this was mostly wishful thinking on his part, but if it ever came down to it ... well, there was no point speculating but it was important to know and he remembered his pledge to stay hopeful. 'And I've been doing a bit more research. I Googled blood groups and how they are inherited and all that. And both my mum and dad are blood group B, so that's easy enough.' He pointed to their cards on the table. 'I'm going to be a B or an O, most likely an O as that's the most common blood group. And that means Holly has to be an O, if Chrissie and I both are.' Sam seemed to remember Chrissie telling him she was an O. 'So that's really good news isn't it, Doctor? If I'm an O then I can donate to Holly.' Sam knew that he was talking too much, so he shut up and waited for Dr Ben to find his results.

Silence followed.

Sam could hear the happy sound of children laughing outside the surgery window so he focused on that while he waited. He smiled and vowed to take Holly over to the village green later. She'd like that; they could take her bike down on the far side where it sloped right down, just like he had as a kid with his brother Patrick. Which reminded him, he needed to give Patrick a call, they hadn't spoken for ages. Perhaps if he could sort everything out properly with Chrissie, the three of them could go to Australia for Christmas – Holly would love that. He would scan the letter from their dad so that Patrick could have a copy too. It's what their dad would have wanted ...

'I shan't keep you waiting much longer, Sam.' Dr Ben picked up the donor cards and opened them again, and then consulted something on the screen.

'Everything OK?' Sam asked. 'Sorry the cards are a bit faded, my dad died years ago, and they've been in an old hatbox ...'

'Yes, yes it's fine,' Dr Ben said. And a little awkwardly, Sam thought. He inhaled and swallowed hard, a creeping feeling of unease coming over him. A little while later, and he could bear it no longer.

'It isn't, is it?' Sam leant forward as if to see the screen, fully expecting Dr Ben to shield it from him as doctors usually did. But he didn't. Instead he leant back and let Sam see what was written. His blood group information was right in front of him. And it wasn't right. It couldn't be. His eyes raced over the screen. Again and again. Each time his brain trying to process what they saw.

Samuel Anthony Morgan.

Blood group A.

Sam's mouth went dry.

It was a few seconds, but felt like an eternity, before he was able to articulate his thoughts in order to talk.

'But that can't be right. I'm an O or a B if both my parents are a B. I looked it up. Two Bs can't have an A child. So I have to be either O or B. How can I not be? And Holly? What blood group is she?'

'I'm not sure I have that—'

'If it isn't on the computer then the hospital will know.'

Sam felt panicky now. But there was still a glimmer of hope. If he had understood the charts on the internet correctly, then Holly could have inherited his A blood group and then he'd still be able to donate to her. Dr Ben turned to face Sam and paused, as if in thought, deliberating what to do for the best. Then he picked up the phone and told the person on the other end of the line who he was and why he was calling.

'Yes. Yes that's right.' There was a short silence then, 'My patient's name is Holly Morgan. I need to know her blood group. I can't find it on the system.' And he gave her date of birth. A few seconds later, he got the reply. Wrote it on a piece of paper and moved it across the desk towards Sam.

O.

Sam's heart plummeted.

His research said that people with blood group O could only receive a kidney from a person with the same O blood group.

Not A.

Definitely not A.

A was no good at all to his daughter.

Beads of sweat formed on his forehead. He tugged at

the collar of his coat, desperate for air. His lungs felt as if they were being trampled on, squeezed by a slab of concrete. And then a hideously bizarre thought rushed into his head – this would suit his mother no end. Her 'poor Prosecco-pickled kidneys' could remain in place, with her being a B and therefore unable to donate to her granddaughter, should the need ever arise. She was off the hook, exempt from any kind of responsibility to her family. Yet again. Whereas, Sam, so keen to take responsibility, couldn't do anything to help.

'Your blood test result is absolutely conclusive, Sam. I'm very sorry it isn't the news you were hoping for. Are you sure these donor cards are correct? They haven't been tampered with? As you said, they are quite faded.' Dr Ben picked up the cards and scrutinised them again. But Sam knew that the doctor was just stalling for time, clearly keen to try to soften the blow somehow.

'I'm sure. That's exactly how they were given to me and I can't imagine my gran would have altered them.'

'I really am sorry, Sam.' Dr Ben handed the cards back to him.

'So what now?' Sam didn't know what else to say as he still tried to take it all in. He couldn't even contemplate yet why his blood group didn't match that of his parents. Or was it fear that he was feeling right now? Fear of what this devastating revelation implied. But before he could go anywhere near that train of thought, he first needed to know about his daughter. Where did this leave her? 'What about Holly?'

'Well,' Dr Ben coughed to clear his throat and pushed his glasses further onto his nose. 'Holly's consultant will be able to talk to you more, but please remember that we don't know for certain that she will ever need a transplant, and even if she did then she'd be placed on the register ...'

'But what if she needs the kidney right away and there just isn't one?' Sam, shoulders hunched, felt as if he was going mad. The kind of madness that comes from not being able to do anything whatsoever. He wasn't stupid. As the realisation sank in, Sam knew that Linda was behind this. He knew it in his heart, and he felt like a complete and utter fool for thinking she couldn't surprise him any more. When, here he was ... relying on her in the most critical way possible, with his daughter so dependent on the result, and she had let him down yet again. He knew what this devastating information meant. His dad, Rob. That lovely, caring, kind man, wasn't his biological father. It was the only explanation. And, given what he knew of his mother, it was the most plausible. And no wonder she had been coy about getting tested, and had tried to persuade him not to. She didn't want her secret discovered. A nasty, big can of worms to be crowbarred open after all these years.

How could she?

How could she let him live a lie for his entire life?

And what about Dad? Did he even know that he wasn't my biological father? Did he die never knowing the truth? He must have done, because if he did know then he absolutely never let it show. He was a brilliant dad. The best. And Patrick? Does this mean he isn't my biological brother?

Sam felt as if his head was going to explode, the pressure was that intense. And he knew his first thought, when it came to Patrick, was how to break the news to him, thinking about how it may affect him that they might not be brothers after all.

He stood up, in need of some fresh air.

'Err ... um, I ... err ... have to go,' he said, his voice quavering, barely able to formulate how he was feeling right now into comprehensible words.

'Please, Sam,' Dr Ben stood up too, 'there's no need to rush away. You're my last appointment of the day. Stay, and let's talk. I realise this has come as a huge shock, but we don't know for sure that the donor cards are wholly accurate ... perhaps talk to your mother? Maybe she can reassure you, put your mind at rest. Please don't jump to any hasty conclusions that may bear no resemblance whatsoever to the truth.'

But Sam knew that was never going to happen. His mother cared only for herself. Always had done. And always would. She had never really been there for him ... so perhaps it was time to end their toxic relationship once and for all.

Chapter Nineteen

Holly couldn't believe it. She had just arrived at the hospital with Mum for her appointment with the consultant.

'Dad! You came,' she beamed, hurtling over to where he was sitting with a Costa cup in one hand and mobile in the other. He placed the cup on the little coffee table, put his phone in his jeans pocket and stood up. Holly gave him a hug and then looked back over one shoulder at her mum, praying that she wouldn't be in a mood and get cross that Dad had come. *What if she makes him leave? Well, I won't let her. She has no right. Dad said he'd make it all right but he can't if she won't let him.*

'Of course,' Sam grinned. 'I wasn't going to miss your appointment. I thought I would surprise you,' he said. Chrissie had only waved at him from the door when he had dropped Holly home last time, so Sam hadn't got the chance to ask if he could drive them to the hospital. But a surprise was nice, wasn't it? 'And, I was thinking … how about we go for pizza afterwards. What do you reckon?' Sam glanced at Chrissie, willing her to be OK with this plan. For Holly's sake. And, if he was totally honest, for his sake too. He hadn't been able to tell Chrissie yet that he wasn't a blood match. Although he was struggling to trust his own judgement now. And was it any wonder, after discovering that his whole life was one enormous lie … thanks to his mother. He might not be able to be a blood match for Holly, but he could absolutely be a good dad. And a better person than his mother was. He hated the thought that he might be like his mother, the woman who clearly had absolutely no respect for Rob, the man who Sam had thought was his father. Let alone the man who really was his biological parent … the mystery man who he suspected probably knew nothing of his existence. Because if he did know, then surely he would have tried to contact him, if only out of curiosity. So how was that fair? A lifetime of not knowing you had a son? Sam couldn't get his head around that. He just couldn't. And it wasn't bloody right. As far as he was concerned, a child had a right to know who their own father was. But he needed to focus on this now, on Holly, that was the most important thing today.

Sam smiled cautiously at Chrissie, who returned it. He could see that she was anxious, the tightness around her smile belying her calm and controlled exterior. But then he was pretty anxious himself. They had no idea what the consultant would say. Please God, he really hoped it was going to be good news …

'Mum, can we? Pleeeeease,' Holly pleaded, thinking

of her 'Get Mum and Dad Back Together in Time for My Birthday' plan. This was the perfect chance to make the plan actually work. And she was over the moon to see that Dad was keeping his promise to fix it all in time for her birthday. Today was going to be just like it always used to be before Dad went away to work.

'You like pizza,' she quickly added in an attempt to persuade her mum, and thinking how good it would be to have a brilliant time with both her parents. Especially if she could find a romantic pizza place with candles and all that stuff. Like a proper Italian restaurant. She would make sure they sat opposite each other and then she would go to the loo and spend ages in there on her phone so they could be alone. Oh yes, it was going to be so awesome. And with a bit of luck she could have a ham and pineapple pizza – her favourite! Chrissie nodded. Took off her gloves and sat down opposite where Sam had been sitting.

'Purlease, Mum. Pretty pleeeeease,' Holly tried again, impatient to know right away. *Why isn't Mum saying anything? Why is she just giving Dad the evils and being horrible about his brilliant idea. Poor Dad. He's come all this way to surprise us and treat us to a fantastic time afterwards and she obviously just wants to ruin it all. Why can't she just be pleased for once?*

'What do you say, Chrissie?' Sam asked gently, knowing not to pressure her and grateful that they were the only ones in the waiting room. He really didn't want an audience if his plan went horribly wrong. Chrissie looked him right in the eyes, before glancing away ... and for a moment, Sam thought she was going to cry. She sniffed and chewed the inside of her left cheek.

'Please Sam, I can't think beyond the appointment right now,' she said, quietly. He saw her look at Holly before turning her face towards his. 'Let's see how things go, and then we can decide what we're going to do afterwards,' she finished, and then busied herself by unravelling her long silky scarf and trying to stuff it into her bag.

'Oh, Mum!' Holly leapt forward and threw her arms around Chrissie's shoulders. 'Thank you. Thank you, thank you, thank you.'

'OK, sweetheart. Like I said, let's decide after we've heard what the doctor has to say ...' Chrissie reciprocated the hug before untangling her daughter's arms from around her neck and indicating for her to sit down beside her.

But Holly didn't sit next to her mum. She sat down next to her dad instead and grinned from ear to ear like a looper. So hard, her cheeks were properly aching. Mum had practically agreed to going for pizza – all that about deciding later really meant yes; she just wants to keep Dad keen. Holly had read all about that 'treat them mean, keep them keen' stuff. Mum definitely had been mean to Dad, and now she had worked out why. If only

Gavin would do one! And then there would be no reason why the wish wouldn't come true and Mum could take Dad back. She found her phone inside her jacket pocket, flicked it to silent, and keeping it within the denim fabric so as to not get caught, she surreptitiously Snapchatted her best friend, Katie. All the while trying not to look at the Please Switch Off Mobile Phones sign on the wall opposite her. *But this is an emergency. Well, not an actual emergency, emergency, like a car crash or whatever. But it's still extremely important. And it's not like the Intensive Care bit is next door, or there are vital heart monitors or anything in this part of the hospital. This is just a waiting room. And it's not even a proper hospital room … only a Portakabin.*

Holly finished tapping the keyboard on the screen and pressed to send.

Mum and Dad are getting back together!

Moments later, Katie replied.

For real? Followed by three love eyes emoticons.

Holly was just about to reply when a nurse appeared in the doorway and beckoned them all to follow her in to see the doctor.

*

The consultant seemed to know Holly really well, Sam thought, noting her kindly eyes with a sparkle in them.

The picture on her desk was of her with two girls, obviously her daughters, one of whom looked as if she was the same age as Holly. She was asking Holly about school and listening enthusiastically about her upcoming performance.

'So, let's have a look at what we have here, then.' The doctor looked at her computer, referring to some paperwork she had in front of her too. 'Your blood sugars have been erratic for a while and, looking at the notes, it doesn't seem that there is a clear indicator as to why, Holly. Your diet looks quite well controlled, if you take your mum's good advice, that is.' She smiled at Chrissie, who still looked tense, twiddling a tissue in between her fingers, but she smiled back.

'That's good then, isn't it?' Holly grinned.

'Well,' the doctor nodded, 'it is good that you're being sensible. But the key to managing diabetes successfully is about getting the balance right – between insulin, food and activity. And it can take a bit of practice, and sometimes you need a bit of help.'

'What about Holly's kidneys, Doctor? There were some concerns over her readings.' Chrissie's voice wobbled slightly as she asked the question. The doctor referred to the screen again.

'Ahh, yes. But things seem to have stabilised now,' the doctor said, looking at Holly. 'We'll have to monitor things, of course, but I'm not concerned at this time.'

Sam and Chrissie immediately looked at each other on hearing this news, the relief palpable. Sam could see tears welling up in his wife's eyes and he reached his hand out to her, which she gripped tightly, before composing herself.

'What about her blood sugar levels?' Chrissie asked. 'Is there anything I ...' She stopped and looked at Sam before adding, 'We ... can do?'

'Well, as a matter of fact, I've been putting some thought into that,' the doctor started. 'There are tools available to help Holly's body find the right balance. I think a pump might work; they are quite expensive but we should be able to get the funding from your local authority.'

'I'll pay for it. No prob—' Sam jumped in, but then fell silent on seeing the look on Chrissie's face, indicating for him to calm down.

'That shouldn't be necessary,' the doctor said discreetly before turning her attention back to Holly.

'What's a pump? Can I wear it while I'm dancing – it won't get in the way, will it?' Holly frowned.

'Well,' the doctor laughed and nodded. 'You'll still be able to dance, Holly. There are some really small and compact pumps out there which fit in your back pocket, a bit like a mobile phone.'

'Ooh,' Holly beamed on hearing this.

'The pump will take your reading and then administer

the insulin; it manages things for you. It can be a bit inconvenient, but many people love the pump and find it makes their lives much easier.'

'It sounds amazing. When can we get the pump?' Sam asked.

'It won't happen immediately. You'll need two letters, one from me and one from your GP – he'll sort it out with your local NHS trust and put a good case forward on Holly's behalf. She will need to be fitted, but hopefully it won't take too long. In the meantime, we'll keep a good eye on things.'

*

Outside the consulting room, Sam couldn't resist pulling Holly and Chrissie in for a big cuddle. He felt as if they'd had a huge reprieve. Like a big weight had been lifted from his shoulders, and he could see from Chrissie's sparkling blue eyes and wide smile that she felt the same way too. Sam ruffled Holly's hair, which earned him a frown and a, '*Dad* – it took me *ages* to straighten it!'

'I think it's time we went for that pizza, don't you?' Chrissie said, linking arms with them both.

*

After Sam had got over the initial relief at Holly's good

news, he found that it was hard for him to truly enjoy the rest of the afternoon in the pizza restaurant. The question mark over his blood type was nagging away at him. If Rob wasn't his father, then who was? Knowing his mother, it could literally be anyone. The thoughts kept going over and over inside his head as he listened to Holly chatting away, barely managing to draw breath. And she was especially happy in being allowed her favourite pizza. And getting to share a dark chocolate mousse with Chrissie.

'What's up, Sam, you seem a bit distracted?' Chrissie asked, when Holly went to the loo, leaving the two of them alone.

'Oh, nothing, I … it's just been a long day, that's all.' Sam pushed a smile onto his face. He desperately wanted to unburden himself, but now that Chrissie was here in front of him, he just felt that he couldn't bring himself to tell her. Sharing the news that Rob wasn't his biological father … the awful reality was too terrible to share. Even the realisation that Holly's diabetes hadn't been passed down by him was little consolation. Sam's father had been the epitome of what a good father should be, and now he'd had time to absorb the information, Sam felt that his own inadequacies were making sense. Of course, he could never be like Rob, because he wasn't his son. He remembered all the acts of love and kindness that Rob had shown him – showing him how to ride a bike for the first time, helping him with his homework. Always cheering him on. He was taken far too young. Sam had only been a boy when Rob had died, but he still missed him every day. Sam felt his throat constrict.

'By the way, did you ever get the results of your blood tests?' Chrissie looked at him quizzically, and touched his arm gently. 'Sam?'

'Oh, yes, the blood tests. Sorry, I was miles away,' he started. 'They said ...' Sam stopped. He couldn't say the words. He had an overwhelming urge to run again, to get outside and take big gulps of air. 'Sorry ... I just need to get away ... it's too much.'

Chrissie pulled back suddenly and touched his arm, as if to stop him from going.

'Is that what this is about? Now that Holly isn't in danger, you're going to ship out? Just like you usually do?' she sighed, shaking her head.

Sam swallowed hard. Trying to sort out the jumble of emotions crowding his head – his mother, Rob, Holly, Chrissie.

'No, that's not what I meant—'

'I knew I shouldn't have trusted you,' Chrissie snapped. 'You were bound to go chasing after the next exciting project again sooner or later.'

Her accusation cut through him like a sharp knife of anger. 'You make it sound like I made the decision to work away on my own. But we agreed that I would go, that it was the best thing to do. I would pay and you would stay, isn't that what you said?'

'But I didn't mean for ever!' Chrissie admonished.

'And I asked you both to come too. Join me in Singapore. And Dubai before that. But you wouldn't.' Sam puffed out a long breath of air and glanced towards the other end of the restaurant. Holly had been a while, so she'd be back soon, and the last thing he wanted was for her to see them arguing again.

'It wasn't right for Holly,' Chrissie said, quietly.

'Right for Holly? Or right for you?' Sam felt the heat of his own anger rise up inside him now. Yes he'd played his part in all of this. But what about Chrissie? The stubbornness; her unwillingness to bend.

At that moment, Holly came back to the table, her smiles now disappeared as she picked up on the tension between them, the accusations that hung in the air. All of the frustration and anger was crowding in on Sam now.

Linda and her lies and cold-heartedness.

Chrissie with her obstinacy.

Holly's diabetes.

All of it drowning him.

And he snapped.

'Just because I was working thousands of miles away doesn't mean I don't care? It doesn't mean that you're a better parent than me, you know. And I didn't see you complaining when you wanted for nothing,' he glowered at Chrissie.

'Sam!' Chrissie's eyes flicked to Holly.

'I'm not a child,' Holly said, 'So you can both stop treating me like one.' Sam and Chrissie fell silent.

A few seconds later, Sam stood up.

'I think I'd better go.'

Chrissie turned to Holly.

'Darling, I'm sorry. Dad and I need to sort some things out; it's just a silly argument ...'

'Stop it! I *hate* you!' She looked at her mum first, and then her dad. 'I hate you *both*.' Dad had promised he would sort it out. But now it was all going wrong. Holly wished they would just stop it. Shut up. This was her life too they were fighting and yelling about and ruining. Dad had said none of it was her fault, but she wasn't so sure now. She knew they were stressed out about the diabetes. Everything was ruined. The wish was never going to come true.

Chapter Twenty

Tony Darling puffed out a long breath of air, shook his head as he stared at the tins of paint piled up on the old stone floor and thought Myles King must have more money than blooming sense.

'You don't like it. Do you?' Jude asked, waving the colour chart in front of him. She knew her dad wasn't a fan of expensive paint that couldn't be bought straight from the builders' merchants down on the industrial estate, but Myles was insistent that the walls surrounding the swimming pool were painted in Farrow & Ball's Manor House Gray. She probably shouldn't have shown him the chart at all, but he had been so enthusiastic and, well ... it was nice that he was taking some responsibility. And far better than him not caring at all, even if he had chosen purely on the name. Manor House Gray, 'sounds countryside-ish, yeah?' had been his reasoning, and therefore in keeping with his country pile on the outskirts of the rural village of Tindledale. 'You know, wisteria-clad old manor houses with in-and-out driveways and an ancient Labrador lolling about on the lawn. Afternoon tea and all that chintzy shizz. Yep, this is deffo the one,' he had finished making his choice by tapping the chart with a flourish. Then, hopping back on his quad bike and zooming off to check on the micro-pigs, sorry ... Large Blacks! Myles still wasn't convinced that his beloved, but very tiny, sweet little pigs weren't going to grow any bigger, despite Jude and Sam both having told him umpteen times by now. Even the man from DEFRA, who had come to inspect the Blackwood Farm Estate and check that everything was set up as it should be, had pointed out this fact to him. But no, Myles was having none of it.

'*Chintzy shizz?*' Jude had exclaimed, dumbfounded. Did he really decide on a few grands' worth of paint because it was like chintzy shizz? But he was the client, after all, and her work mantra had always been ... the client is right. Except for that time in Dubai when the son of an Arabian royal prince had wanted her to source a flock of seagulls and have them circle above the infinity pool to create an authentic British seaside sound. Jude had drawn the line at that nonsense.

'Nothing to do with me, love. I haven't got to gawp at it all day long.' Tony rummaged in his tool bag for a bit before finding an old paint-splattered screwdriver and set about opening the first tin. He did a comedy double take as the lid came off. 'Blimey! He paid how much for this, did you say?' he joked, and then, 'last time I saw this colour it was on a dreary documentary about a battleship.'

'Oh, Dad, it's not that bad. At least it's a neutral tone … you should have seen his first choice. You'd have really hated that.'

'Spose so.' Tony started mixing and then dolloping out the paint into a tray, ready to roll onto the prepared walls. 'Right. Best be getting on with it then, if I'm to have this lot done in three days. Barry has said he'll give me a hand, but still, we're going to be hard pushed …' He paused to suck in a big breath and shake his head again in that way painter and decorators do. 'Are you sure I can't have an extra day or two?'

'Quite sure, Dad. And I know it's tight—'

'*Tight?* I'll say … it's tighter than old Mrs Pocket's purse when she's sorting out the parish council budget.'

'Ha-ha, how very funny you are with your made-up analogy,' Jude laughed, patting her dad on the arm. Tony pulled a face. 'But it is for a good cause, for the villagers,' she reminded him. 'And Holly is going to love it too.'

'Hmm, if your boss manages to pull all this off in time for the May Fair.'

'He's not my boss. He's a client, Dad … well, more like a friend now, really.' Jude lifted one shoulder and pushed her red curls back over the other. 'And he's actually not such an idiot as I first thought he was. He's got a sensible side too, you know … once you get to know him a bit. And he was really lovely with Holly when I brought her over to visit the estate.'

'If you say so,' Tony stated, and then quickly changed the subject with, 'what's happening with the licences and planning permission and all that?' on seeing his daughter's disgruntled face. It was as obvious as a flashing Belisha beacon that she had a bit of a thing for this Myles. And something Tony had learnt over the years of being a single dad to a daughter was that it was best to never, ever, *ever* pass comment on stuff like that. It would only backfire. And he much preferred having an easy life.

'Well, Myles has got his lawyers on it and they're getting the council to fast-track it all. They already have the parish council onboard.' Jude picked up a roller and went to submerge it into the paint.

'Err, best leave that to me, love.' Tony took the roller from her.

'Sorry, just trying to help, thought you were tight for time.'

'I am. But I've seen your decorating skills ... and it's important it looks professional, even if it does have to be a rush job.' Tony shook his head, and Jude nudged him in the ribs. He then added, 'The parish council are bound to be onboard if they haven't got to cough up for it ... and I reckon if Myles chucks enough money at this, he'll get the result he wants,' as he started rollering the nearest wall.

'I guess so.'

'And I'm not usually one for all that cronyism and

backhanders to jump the queue, but in this case it's warranted, especially if it puts a smile on little Holly's face. We don't want her disappointed ... not after everything she is going through. How is she getting on, love?'

'Better, we think. Chrissie said they were at the hospital and the doctor is talking about a special pump which will help her manage things,' Jude told him, leaving out what had happened afterwards. Chrissie had told her last night over a large glass of Prosecco in the Duck & Puddle pub. And Jude had wondered what could possibly be going on with Sam. It had all been heading in the right direction, but it seemed there was still so much they needed to get off their chests. And Holly wasn't even talking to either of her parents now after she'd witnessed them going for each other. She was even staying at Dolly's house now. So it was such a terribly sad mess of a situation for the whole family to be in, and Jude really wished there was something more that she could do for them all.

'Well that's good news at least.' Tony stopped rollering and shook his head. 'And Chrissie and Sam, has that helped them sort out their differences?'

'Not exactly. I think they still need to do a bit more listening to each other.'

'That's the way it goes sometimes though, love. Stuff like this – when a marriage is already on rocky ground and then something major happens, like a child having health problems – it can break families apart. People talk about it making them stronger, bringing them together ... and they're the lucky ones. But ... take your nan and granddad, your dear mum's parents ... nearly destroyed their marriage when Sarah died.'

'Did it?' Jude asked, not having heard about this before.

'Yep. Terrible bust-ups they had for a few years afterwards. And they had a rock-solid marriage up to that point. They eventually muddled a way through, but it was never the same for them again.'

'That's really sad, Dad. I never knew.'

'Course you didn't, darling. You were just a little girl at the time, and one whose Mummy had died. I wasn't letting any of that other stuff upset you too.'

'Dad, you really are amazing.' Filled with a sudden rush of affection, Jude wrapped her arms around her dad's back and squeezed him tight.

'Hey, what's all this for?' Tony asked, his voice tender and kind.

'Because I love you.'

'And I love you too, my girl.'

'It must have been really hard for you when Mum died ... and you were only young yourself, weren't you?' Jude said softly, burying her face into her dad's white overall and inhaling the evocative scent of her childhood ... emulsion mingled with Golden Virginia rolling tobacco.

'Yes, nineteen eighty-six it was, and I was still quite a young man. And I won't lie,' Tony turned around and faced his daughter. Patting the side of her arm, he told her, 'it was tough, love. The hardest thing I've ever had to get through. But having you made it possible. You kept me going, sweetheart.'

'Oh, Dad,' Jude managed, worried her emotions would spill out onto her face if she said anything more. But, after pulling her top lip down and pressing her teeth hard into it, she then added, 'I'm so pleased you did keep on,' and kissed his cheek.

'Well, someone had to keep you on the straight and narrow. You might very well have ended up in prison or something otherwise ... a little firecracker you were when you were growing up.'

'Oi! I wasn't that bad, Dad.' She play-punched him on the arm.

'Well, you had your moments, love, to be fair.' Tony went to duck when Jude pretended to swipe him one. 'But, seriously, I'm ever so proud of you, darling. You've turned out pretty good, even if I do say so myself. You're a smart, independent lady with her head screwed on the right way ... and your mum would have thought so too.'

'Ahh, thank you, Dad.' Jude put her arms around him again and took another whiff of her dear dad's signature scent, nostalgic and comforting and heart-warming all rolled into one. She was so pleased that she had come home. Even if the shop wasn't panning out the way she had hoped, it had still been worth giving up her life in

LA just to be back where she belonged. And with all that was going on with her best friend Chrissie, and goddaughter Holly, it had made her realise that her own family, her dad, was now even more important to her than ever. While he wasn't that old, he wasn't getting any younger ... and she wanted to make the most of every moment she had left with him, whether that be twenty or, with a bit of luck, even thirty more years.

'Now. Enough of all this. Work to be done,' Tony chuckled and turned to get on with some more rollering. And then, on remembering something else important, her put the roller down and looked again at Jude. 'What about the testing? Does that matter now? You said Chrissie couldn't donate, but what about Sam? And what about us? Dolly, and everyone else in the village? When can we get tested? Cos I'm absolutely sure we'd all be up for it – and you never know ... someone is bound to have the right blood match. Pretty much the whole of Tindledale is related in one way or another ...' He shook his head.

'Dad, it's not that bad. You make it sound like Tindledale is some kind of weird cult where brothers and sisters get married as a norm.'

'Don't be daft! I'm just saying that most of us have grown up together and we all look out for each other. And everyone in the village is talking about it,' Tony paused, 'and not in a gossipy way.'

'Well, that makes a change. I had forgotten how it's impossible to have a private life in Tindledale, but it's all coming back to me now,' she rolled her eyes, recalling countless times over the years growing up here, when Tony would know that she'd bunked off school and gone on the bus to Market Briar with Chrissie before she had even opened the garden gate on getting back home. Or what about the time she had tried to pinch a bottle of Lambrini from the little off-licence section at the back of the village store, for her and Chrissie to drink before the end-of-school disco? The shop owner, Tommy Prendergast, had phoned her dad before she'd even realised she'd been caught. Tony had then turned up in the village square, jumped out of his white van and given her what-for in front of all the Territorial Army cadets who were practising for some sort of ceremonial thing by the war memorial. She had been mortified.

'People just care, love. So you can't blame them for wondering what's going on and, more importantly, if they can help out.'

'Hmm, well, it looks like Holly is going to be fine, especially once they get this pump for her. But Chrissie did say that she thinks Sam has had the blood test ... well, he didn't come right out and say so, but she thinks he isn't a blood match for his own daughter. He would have said if he was, wouldn't he?' Jude said, remembering how upset her best friend had been.

'Err, I guess so.'

'But he didn't give her a straight answer when she asked him ... before it descended into a row, that is.'

Tony looked thoughtful. 'Now, that's a real shame.'

'Yes, yes it is,' Jude said quietly.

'Well, the pair of them need their heads banging together, if you ask me. It's not right that they're tearing themselves apart like this, when there's one thing that might actually help them ... and they aren't doing it!'

'What's that then, Dad?' she asked, keen to find out so she could pass it on to Chrissie.

'Talking! That's what they must do. They need to bleeding well talk to each other,' Tony stated, dabbing his roller hard onto the wall to punctuate his point. 'It's vital, especially when there's a little girl at the heart of all this. If they can't talk properly to each other then there's no hope for them,' he finished, pragmatically.

'But sometimes that's the hardest thing of all to do.'

'I know, love,' Tony softened. 'Perhaps I should pop over and see Dolly. I might be able to have a chat with Sam if he's there ... see if I can get through to him. Help him see a way forward. I've always tried to do that since Rob passed away. And if you talk to Chrissie ... Well, you never know, between the pair of us we might actually make a difference, and get them actually speaking to each other some time this side of Christmas.'

'Good idea, Dad. Give Sam a bit of fatherly advice, you're good at that. And I thought I might go over to Dolly's on Saturday to see how Holly is coping given that she's not even talking to Sam and Chrissie ...'

'And that's another thing Chrissie and Sam need to be thinking about – talking to Holly, properly. She's growing up and they have to give her a bit of credit. All the while they're taking it out on each other, they aren't putting her first.'

'All right, Dad. Calm down,' Jude shook her head and smiled, suddenly feeling protective of her best friend, and Sam too. 'I'm sure they realise that.'

'Yeah, I know,' Tony puffed out a weary sigh. 'They're a lovely family ... and they are part of our family ... it's not just blood that ties people together. You and Chrissie have a shared history, you've grown up together, and that binds people too. And Sam's dad, Rob, I miss him every day – he was my oldest and closest friend. He had diabetes as well, you know? Not like Holly has it, bad, and it wasn't what killed him. It was the cancer, and that has a lot to flaming answer for too. He was a top bloke, Rob, and he died far too young. Like your mum. Life can be so bleeding cruel sometimes.'

'I know, Dad. And it will be OK. We'll all get through this. And we will make sure Chrissie and Sam, and Holly are all right,' Jude soothed, hating seeing her dad upset. He was such a kind man … he really cared about everyone. And it was so the right thing for her to come home. She couldn't bear to think of him having to worry about all this on his own. Not after everything he had done for her over the years … it was the least she could do to be back here with him.

'Let's try to be positive. You have a chat to Sam on Saturday. And I'll tell Holly about all this …' she waved a hand around the basement. 'It might help cheer her up a bit if she has something nice to look forward to. And I'll talk to Chrissie as well. I might even be able to come up with a plan to get her and Sam in the same room at least … lock them in if I have to. Perhaps a little get-together at Dolly's on Saturday evening, I'm sure she'd be up for having Chrissie over to hers to see Holly. I'll ask her. And I'll tell Chrissie that you're taking Sam to the pub so she doesn't have to worry about him being there and getting into another argument … and then they can "bump" into each other or something,' Jude said, thinking out loud. 'Will you help me shove them both into Dolly's sitting room or whatever?' she added, getting into her stride now.

'That's my girl. Of course I will. You've always been good at coming up with inventive plans. Glad to see all that mischief in your teenage years hasn't gone to waste.' They both laughed.

'And while Chrissie and Sam are "sorting out their

differences", aka actually talking to each other, I can have a chat to Holly ...'

'Good idea,' Tony nodded. 'You've always been good with her too so at least she'll have you to talk to while her mum and dad get their act together. I'll drive us over if you like ... that's if I've got all this lot done by then.' He groaned, eyeing all the wall space that was yet to be painted.

'Brilliant! You'd better get on with it then!' she said cheekily, before scarpering. Blowing her dad a kiss over her shoulder as she went.

Chapter Twenty-One

Jude had just finished explaining to the guy from the tropical cabana supply company where the swimming pool was going to be, when Myles came galloping across the lawn on the back of a beautiful brown and white stallion.

'Eaaaaasy does it, Bullseye. That's my boy,' Myles said, patting the side of the horse's neck to calm him as he came to a halt. After swinging himself off and down on to the newly mown grass, Myles tethered the horse to a nearby fence, fed it a carrot from his pocket and then stood squarely in front of Jude, looking ridiculous in leather chaps over jeans, a yellow checked shirt, jaunty neck tie and a cowboy hat. On his feet were black leather cowboy boots complete with shiny silver spurs at the ankle. 'Howdy partner!' he said in a comical Deputy Dawg accent, as he doffed the hat.

Jude stared, goggled-eyed and speechless. Her jaw dropped. Myles laughed, and then actually had the temerity to put the tip of his index finger to her chin so as to reunite it with the rest of her face.

'Get off me, you loon,' she smiled, shimmying her face

away from his touch, but only pretending to be put out, because it was really hard to be serious whenever he was around. His carefree, effervescent approach to life was highly seductive. Plus he'd just treated her to a delicious whiff of his intoxicating scent, making her stomach do a tiny flip.

'So, what do you think?' Myles asked, taking a step back and flinging his arms out wide as if he was about to burst into a rousing rendition of 'Oklahoma', clearly impressed with his new costume.

'Um,' Jude tried to stifle a giggle. 'It's different,' she ventured, 'but what have you come as ... Sheriff Woody?'

'Ha-ha! You're so funny, Jude.' He winked. 'I think it's cool. And so the right look for a horseman, don't ya think?' he grinned and nodded, assured as ever.

'I guess so. But since when did you own a horse?' she asked. He hadn't said a word about it before now, and she had been here at the estate nearly every day this last week.

'Since earlier this morning when he arrived.'

'And you named him Bullseye ... are you trying to star in your very own version of *Toy Story*? You really are just a giant man-child, aren't you?' she laughed.

'Nooo, of course not,' and for a moment, Jude could have sworn that Myles looked crestfallen, taken aback by her jokes. Hurt even. And it bothered her. After the way she had seen him be with Holly, and then Chrissie in the pub, and the time they had spent together recently, she knew that he wasn't just the jovial and cocky Flash Harry that he made himself out to be. So she didn't want to hurt him by seemingly having a joke at his expense.

'Sorry,' she quickly added. 'I didn't mean anything by it.'

'I know,' he shrugged, 'it's fine.'

They both fell silent. And she wondered if it really was fine ... or if he was just saying so to avoid friction between them.

Jude moved towards the stallion's face and gently stroked his nose, unsure of what else to do. And why was Myles looking at her in this way? Like a little lost boy all of a sudden. He even bit his bottom lip, before looking her up and down as if pondering his options, or weighing her up, perhaps, wondering if he should say something else. But he didn't.

And more silence followed.

Then she took action, by saying, 'Bullseye is so hand-some,' as a way to move the moment on. She never had been one for awkward silences. Far better to just come out with it. But she didn't really know Myles well enough to work out how he might react if she asked him why he seemed upset with her all of a sudden. Plus, her dad had a point earlier ... Myles was her boss at the end of the day. No matter how much the lines had been blurred on that score, he was still paying her wages, even if he was getting more and more involved, to the point where he was practically taking over the whole refurbishment. In addition to turning the Blackwood Farm Estate into some kind of theme park with a petting zoo. So she kept the conversation focused on the horse. 'And a thoroughbred, by the looks of him,' she added, knowing a bit about horses, having grown up with Matt, the local farrier. He'd been horse mad and had taken her riding in the summer time when they were teenagers.

'That's right. I found him through a specialist breeder on the internet in Ireland,' Myles told her casually, his nonchalant demeanour back in place now. He handed her a carrot to feed to Bullseye. 'Fancy a ride?' And he turned to look her right in the eye.

The silence returned, apart from the chomping noises coming from Bullseye's mouth.

'Err,' Jude went to reply, willing her cheeks to stop burning.

'Shit. Sorry,' Myles laughed. 'Didn't mean it like that ... you know, as in *ride*, ride. As in a shag. Bed. And all that ...' He rolled his eyes, and then swiftly added, 'Not that I wouldn't be up for it. Course I bloody would. You're gorgeous, of course.' Jude stared, speechless. 'I should go, shouldn't I? Before you belt me one. You've got that look in your eye.' And he pulled a mock-petrified face.

'Err,' she opened her mouth again, 'um ... what do mean, look in your eye? What look?'

'That look you do. Like you want to put me across

your knee and spank the living daylights out of me for being so bloody annoying.' He pushed the cowboy hat off his head so it hung by the string down his back and shoved a hand through his short blond hair.

'Oh. Um, well, I don't, um ... you know, want to put you across my knee. And you aren't annoying. Really you aren't.'

'You sure?' he asked, keenly.

'Yes, of course ... quite sure.'

'That's a good thing then, isn't it?' Myles said, lowering his voice, and sounding uncharacteristically serious, and dare she think it, actually charming ... even if he was staring at her lips and making her feel quite unnerved. She looked away. *Now this is really awkward. Is he coming on to me? It sounded like he was, but now he thinks I'm scary. And not in a good way. But why is my stomach flipping like this? Yes, he's grown on me over the time we've worked together, but still ... He's not my type! Is he? Not after Scott. Maybe he's just playing with me. It's hard to be sure.* Jude mulled it all over, not used to feeling on the back foot like this. Unsure. She normally had a witty one-liner, or a snarky comment ready for times likes this ... but all of that was eluding her right now.

But Jude was saved from saying, or indeed thinking anything more, as Sylvia was powering her way towards them with a clipboard in one hand and a walkie-talkie in the other.

'There you are,' she said, addressing them both. Then turned to Myles with an exasperated look on her face.

'I've been looking all over for you. There are a team of people here at the back gate with two juggernauts chugging away, spluttering diesel fumes all over the place because they refuse to switch the engines off – something to do with needing to keep the generators topped up or whatever,' she tutted. 'Anyway, they are from ...' she paused to consult her clipboard, 'ahh, yes, here it is. I had to write it down because they aren't on my list so I wasn't expecting them,' she added pointedly. 'Billy Randall's Most Amazing Funfair and Theme Parks,' she coughed to clear her throat, and then finished with, 'Limited!'

'Good-oh!' Myles said.

'And the one in charge says they are here to erect a carousel. One with painted horses that go up and down! Those were his exact words, when I dared to ask what he meant ... I might add.'

'Fantastic! So they managed to get one here ... that's a relief as they said they might not have one available with it being such short notice and all that ...' Myles added, seemingly oblivious to Sylvia's disdain.

'So you *are* expecting them then?' Sylvia asked, incredulity spread all over her face.

'Sure am.' Myles caught Jude's eye and then added, 'Thank you, Sylvia. And I'm sorry I didn't mention it. I guess I just forgot in my silly excitement. The way *big kids* do!' Jude flicked her eyes to the ground – so he had been hurt by her stupid insensitive comment. And then he leant across and put his arm around Sylvia's shoulders, pulling her in for a big bear hug. 'Will you forgive me? I really am sorry.'

'Oh, be off with you. You know I can't stay cross with you for long,' she said, batting the chest part of his checked shirt with her clipboard. 'But will you please try to let me know next time?'

'I'll try. Promise,' he agreed. 'Right, I had better get over to the back gate then. We don't want to upset the neighbours by polluting the lovely clean air of Tindledale!'

Moments later, having hopped up and into position on Bullseye's saddle in one swift movement, Myles was off, galloping across the grass ahead of them. Jude was impressed … he was clearly a very adept horse rider.

'Did you know he was buying that horse?' Sylvia asked, turning sideways to talk to Jude as they walked back towards the house.

'No. He bought it on the internet, apparently … and why not? He's a fantastic rider.'

'He certainly is. But then is it any wonder?' Sylvia said, her face taking on a film of sweat in the warm spring air.

'How come?'

'He grew up on a farm! So it stands to reason that's where he learnt to ride.'

'Really? I thought he was from London,' Jude said,

surprised by this revelation which seemed in contrast to the impression Myles had presented of him being a bit clueless when it came to country ways. The image of him in the mustard-coloured breeches and knee-high socks sprang to mind.

'Ah, yes, he is from London. But he had to move around a lot. When I say that he grew up on a farm … he spent some summers on one for a bit. On and off until he left care.'

'Care?'

'Yes, that's right. Myles grew up in foster care with numerous different placements. I think he had been to twelve different schools by the time he was old enough to leave full-time education.'

'Gosh, I didn't know …' Jude pondered for a moment; this made a lot of sense … It explained why Myles seemed to be so keen to fit in. To find his place. She imagined he must have felt extremely unsettled growing up with no permanent place to call home. And her heart softened for him. There really was so much more to Myles King than she had first thought.

'Yes, of course that part of his background isn't plastered all over the internet, but it's not a secret … he won't mind me telling you,' Sylvia clarified, just in case Jude thought she was gossiping inappropriately. 'The rest is there though … I assume you've seen it all. The sensationalist newspaper articles.'

'No, I haven't. Of course, I took a look at his Wiki page, I do that with all my clients, but I tend to ignore the rest as in my experience it's never very accurate,' Jude said. But to her shame, she had just assumed that Myles was cocky and over-entitled and had got lucky with a record deal or whatever it was that had started him on the road to international fame in the first place. That was how he came across in that initial phone call, when he had been downright rude and extremely presumptuous. And not at all like her previous clients, some of whom were megastars and would never make the initial contact call themselves. That's what PAs and managers were for. Well, she wouldn't make that mistake again. Judging before she really knew.

'Well, you must be the only person who hasn't. Most people who meet Myles know all about him, they've read every single seedy thing about him ... it always becomes evident right away. The questions they ask, the intrigue, the fascinated looks on their faces ... but can you blame them? These days it is perfectly normal to know everything about famous people. You can even talk to them directly on Twitter and such like. It never used to be like that back in my day.'

'Very true.'

'But I don't know what's come over him these days ... ' Sylvia shook her head in worry, '... you know, he never used to be this impulsive. Lurching from one new idea to another. Buying animals and expensive artwork like it's going out of fashion.'

'Really?'

'Oh no, when he was singing and touring ... at the height of his career, he was very different. Totally focused and committed to the music. He spent all of his time either on the road, or in his studio composing new song lyrics and rehearsing them over and over. Until ...' Sylvia stopped talking.

'Until what?' Jude asked, squinting into the sun as she turned to look directly at Sylvia.

'Err ... until it all stopped, is what I meant,' Sylvia added vaguely.

'He stopped making music, do you mean?'

'Yes, well he had to, didn't he? Couldn't carry on after all that—'

'All what?'

'You mean you don't know?' Sylvia stopped walking to turn her head to face Jude.

'No. I've no idea what you're talking about.'

'Oh gosh, well, the papers had a field day with it all. It's why he came here in the end, to get away from all the paps camping outside day and night. They just wouldn't leave him alone.'

'But why?'

'The drugs, dear!' Sylvia told her in a hushed voice.

'Myles was on drugs?' Jude asked, her eyes widening, and her heart dropping.

'NO. Oh *no*, that isn't what I meant,' Sylvia said, as they reached the back of the house. 'He never touched them. It was his fiancée ... she kept it well hidden from him, but then she overdosed in the end and left him heartbroken. I'm surprised he hasn't told you ... Not that it's a secret or anything. And I wouldn't be talking about this either, of course, if it was. Sorry, I just assumed that you already knew.'

'Nope. Not a word,' Jude said, suddenly feeling overcome with sorrow for Myles. What a tragic thing to happen. Yet he seems so upbeat and happy, like he hasn't a care in the world.

'Really? And with you two so close. You're the first woman I've seen him even remotely happy to talk to. He was in quite the doldrums until you turned up. You make him smile, my dear, and laugh. And that is a very good thing indeed. It's about time Myles had some fun and happiness in his life.'

'And he makes me smile and laugh,' Jude nodded, even if she had found him infuriating at the start. But they had settled into a kind of groove now where he definitely did make her laugh and smile on a daily basis.

'I'm pleased to hear it. And I am sorry that we got off on the wrong foot ... Myles was so adamant that people be kept away from him. And you can't blame him after everything that happened. The newspapers hounded him for a scoop, anything to try to get some scintillating bit of detail about Genevieve.'

'Genevieve Chevalier?' Jude vaguely remembered reading something about her dating a British rock star in a glossy magazine a few years back. There was some kind of super-injunction in place to protect her privacy.

'Yes that's right. The supermodel. And the press just wouldn't let it go. Do you know that I caught a female reporter one time trying to wangle her way into his house in London? She pretended to be a cleaner sent from the agency. And was rifling through Genevieve's dressing room, taking pictures of her shoes of all things, when I caught her. Why anyone would want pictures of a person's shoes is beyond me.'

'That's awful,' Jude said, stamping the grass off her sandals onto the mat by the back door.

'Yes, it was. But he's much happier now. Thanks to you!' Sylvia tilted her head to one side.

'What did I do?' Jude asked, intrigued.

'You've given him a purpose, my dear. All of this ... letting him get involved in the refurbishment,' Sylvia waved the clipboard around the hallway. 'It's something to focus on. And please do give him a chance—'

'What do you mean?' Jude creased her forehead.

'I think you know what I mean! He isn't the crass man that he makes out to be. You see that, don't you?' And with that, she pushed her clipboard under her arm and marched off towards the kitchen, leaving Jude to think about everything that had been said.

Chapter Twenty-Two

Saturday evening, and after pulling up in the van outside Dolly's cottage, Tony and Jude – with Lulu under her arm – got out and went to push open the gate in the white picket fence. The homely scent of cinnamon from Dolly's baking permeating the dusky evening air all around them.

'What are you coming in for?' Tony looked back to his mate Barry as he went to open the driver's door. 'I thought we agreed that I would go in and persuade Sam to come out for a pint in the Duck & Puddle pub – that I would tell him you were waiting in the van because the engine is playing up and we can't switch it off in case it doesn't start again. That's what we came up with!'

'But it's boring waiting out here!' Barry piped up, plucking a rollie from behind his ear.

'So we'll tell Sam that he needs to get a move on ... that's the whole point of you being in the van! So we can get Sam out quickly.'

'That's right, Barry,' Jude said. 'Chrissie is at choir practice and I've already said that I'll see her in the pub later when it's finished. After I've had tea and a chat with

Holly. It was the only way to get her and Sam together ... I tried to get her to cancel the choir practice and come to Dolly's house instead, but she was having none of it – says it's the only thing keeping her sane right now. "Head time". That's what she calls it. And with Holly still refusing to even talk to her, Chrissie thought it best to give her some space ... and not be seen to be crowding her.'

'And we don't want to miss Chrissie in the pub!' Tony pitched in. 'As soon as she realises Jude isn't there, she might leave. I've squared it with Cher for the pair of them – Chrissie and Sam – to be locked in the little function room out the back.'

'How are you going to do that then?' Barry flicked his lighter, attempting to get it to ignite.

'I dunno. But we'll work that out when we get there. Go on, get back in the van, you big wimp. We need to get a move on.'

'But I need the loo,' Barry replied, pulling an agonised face.

'BARRY!' Tony and Jude exclaimed in unison, stopping to stare at him.

'For crying out loud. There's always one,' Tony added, shaking his head in mock despair.

But before any of them could deliberate further on how to stop their not-very-well-thought-out plan from falling apart completely, Dolly pulled open her front door and chivvied them all inside.

'Now, how about I make you two gentlemen a nice cup of tea before you head back out,' Dolly offered, looking at Barry's gleeful face.

'Oh, that would be lovely,' Barry jumped in, ignoring Tony's elbow nudge in his back. 'Mind if I borrow your bathroom please, Dolly?'

'Of course, be my guest, love. There's a cloakroom through here,' and she showed Barry where to go, then turned to Jude and Tony. 'Come in to the kitchen and get yourself comfy.' She gestured to the patchwork armchair beside the Aga.

'Thanks Dolly, but we'll not intrude, we need to get to the pub ... if you know what I mean.' Tony indicated with his head into the sitting room where he presumed Sam was. He had already run the plan by Dolly yesterday when he had called in to see her.

'Oh yes, silly me, I wasn't thinking. Just a minute,' she chuckled, tapping the side of her nose conspiratorially. Dolly had told Tony that she thought it was a great idea to try to get her grandson and his wife back on good terms. She hated seeing her family upset and broken apart. 'Go on in. And why don't you go on upstairs, dear?' she said to Jude. 'I can take your cute dog into the kitchen for a cuddle, if you like. Might cheer her up as she doesn't look too happy.'

'Ahh, thanks. But please don't be taken in by her sad face . . . she's quite the diva really,' Jude laughed, unfastening the cute little neckerchief that Sybs from the haberdashery shop had kindly made for Lulu.

'Holly is in her bedroom, she'll be really pleased to see you ... she doesn't know you're coming for the special tea – I didn't want to spoil the surprise for her,' Dolly smiled warmly, taking Lulu in her arms. 'It's the first on the left at the top of the stairs.'

'Great. See you in a bit,' Jude smiled, placing a hand on the banister.

*

Earlier, in the village square, having leapt off the bus back from Market Briar with Katie, Holly had stopped and stared. Gavin, the choir man, was going into the village hall and he had his arm around Mum's shoulders. Holly really wanted to scream at him to leave her mum alone. It was all his fault. Dad might think he was to blame, but before Gavin had become Mum's boyfriend, she had been nowhere near as bad. She was still bossy back then, but not like she had been since before Dad came home. Gavin can't be very nice to her. And aren't you supposed to be blissfully happy when you first start going out with someone? Well, Mum doesn't seem loved up like that. Maybe she really wants to dump Gavin but doesn't want to hurt his feelings, Holly wondered, thinking about Josh at school. They had dated for eight days, but then she'd got fed up with him always borrowing her phone because his had run out of credit. She had tried to text him at least three times to tell him he was dumped. Katie had to tell him in the end, and she said he was well upset. She thought he was going to cry, his feelings were that hurt. Maybe she should offer to dump Gavin on Mum's behalf. She could text him from Mum's mobile, no problem. Or maybe it was all just wishful thinking? If it wasn't for Gavin, then everything would be so much better. Mum and Dad had been getting on ... until the bust-up in the pizza place. And the Get Mum and Dad Back Together in Time for My Birthday plan would have a much better chance of working if Gavin wasn't hanging around all the time trying to ruin it. And stop the wish from coming true.

'Are you OK, Holls?' Katie asked, linking her arm through hers.

'Did you see that?' Holly said, lifting her free hand to point in the direction of the village hall.

'Yes. Where are they going?'

'To choir practice. That's Gavin.'

'Is he your mum's new boyfriend?'

'I guess so.' Holly shrugged.

'So, he's like your new stepdad then.'

'No he isn't!' Holly felt her face burn. Her heart was running fast inside her chest. She actually felt a bit of sick in her mouth. She pulled a bottle of water from her satchel and had a big swig.

'He will be if he marries your mum!'

'Stop it! He can't marry my mum, she's already married to my dad.'

'Holls, don't get upset,' Katie stopped walking and looked at her.

'What else can I can do then?'

'Get even!' Katie said, looking her right in the eye. 'That's what my mum says. "Don't get upset. Get even!"'

'But how?' Holly said, scanning her best friend's face, searching for the answer to her prayers. No matter what Dad had promised about fixing it all before her birthday ... all the time Gavin was there taking Mum away from him, it would never be fixed.

'Is that his?' Katie asked, pointing to the beige car parked opposite the village hall.

'Yes, why?'

'Come on, you'll see.' And Katie grabbed her hand and ran towards the car. Moments later, Katie had pulled something off the tyre. 'Quick, do the other one too,' she said to Holly. And so she did.

*

Jude was back downstairs now and standing in the

hallway, where Sam was gathering up his phone and wallet off the hall table ready to leave for the pub.

'Holly's not there,' she said.

'Maybe she's in the bathroom, have a look in there, Jude,' Sam indicated with his head as he pulled on a jacket.

'Barry's still in there, taking ages he is.' Tony let out a disgruntled sigh.

'Try the upstairs one, she's bound to be inspecting her teeth or spraying that lavender colour she likes onto her hair or counting her eyelashes or some such thing,' Sam smiled, constantly baffled by how long his teenage daughter's personal grooming seemed to take these days. Jude ran upstairs and knocked on the door.

'Holly? Surpriiiiiiise,' she said brightly, but there was no answer.

'Gran, do you know where Holly is?' Sam called through into the kitchen as Jude returned shaking her head and shrugging her shoulders.

'Upstairs in her bedroom, love. Why?' Dolly came into the hallway, wiping her hands on a flowery-patterned pinny.

'Jude says she isn't there. And she's not in the bathroom either,' Sam said.

'Well, she must be here somewhere. Maybe she's in my room ... I did say that she could have a spritz of my perfume. She's at that age ...' Dolly smiled fondly, looking to Tony and Jude. 'I'll go and have a look.'

'No, it's OK, Gran. Save your legs – I'll go,' Sam said, already taking the stairs two at a time as he tried to ignore the dart of unease in the pit of his stomach, which was immediately confirmed when he pushed open the bedroom door and saw his daughter wasn't there. 'She's not in here,' Sam yelled down to the others as he raced back down the stairs. He pulled his phone from his pocket. 'Right. We need to find her. I'll call Chrissie and see if she's gone there. To The Forstal Farmhouse.'

'Chrissie is at choir practice, Sam,' Jude told him.

'And Holly wouldn't just go out without saying any-thing,' Dolly added, cheerfully.

'Then where else could she be?' Sam started tapping the screen of his mobile, conscious of the panic rising in his voice.

'What's going on?' It was Barry back from the cloak-room with a bewildered look on his face.

'Holly isn't here,' Jude quickly told him.

'No answer!' Sam waved his phone in the air as Chrissie's voice came on the line reading out the voice message. 'I'm going to look for her.' He went to pull the front door open.

'Hold on, son. No need to panic,' Tony stepped in, placing a hand on Sam's arm. 'She's probably hiding somewhere, all ready to jump out and surprise us ... do you remember when you used to do that, Jude?'

'Yes, when I was about six years old. Dad, Holly is thirteen, she doesn't do that kind of thing.' Jude shook her head. 'I think Sam's right, we need to look for her. Come on, let's all search the house. Barry, you go around the garden.'

'Right-o.' And Barry darted straight out through the front door.

'I'll do upstairs. You do downstairs, Jude,' Tony instructed. 'And look everywhere ... just in case. You never know ... she might have hidden in a cupboard or in the pantry or something, and fallen asleep. Yes, yes, I know she isn't six years old ... but kids are always full of surprises.' And he was off, haring upstairs, and calling out Holly's name.

'What about her best friend, Katie?' Jude turned to Sam as they went into the sitting room, 'would she have gone to her house, perhaps?'

'Not without saying, she's usually pretty good about that sort of thing,' Sam shook his head, but then thought back to the time Holly had duped him into leaving her at home alone. 'But I should check.' And he went to leave the cottage again.

'Have you got Katie's phone number?' Jude continued. 'You could try calling her first, save racing over there. Holly might not thank you for showing up out of the blue. She might think you're checking up on her. And with things the way they are ... it won't look good.'

'That's a good idea,' Dolly stepped in, 'and why don't you try Holly's mobile number too before we jump to conclusions. I'm sure there's a simple explanation.'

Sam pressed to ring Holly's phone.

An Ed Sheeran song ringtone rang out.

And it was coming from the kitchen.

Sam dashed to find the phone, closely followed by Jude and Dolly.

'Her bag!' Sam lifted Holly's patent pink satchel from the back of a dining chair and rummaged through it. Everything was inside. Her phone. Hairbrush. Purse. Keys. A book. Make-up. Bits and bobs. He tipped it all out on the kitchen table. And ... oh God. 'Her insulin!' Sam held the kit containing everything Holly needed to check her levels and inject herself.

'She's definitely not in the garden.' Barry appeared back in the kitchen, bringing a swirl of evening air in with him. 'And I've checked in the shed and the summerhouse. Not a dicky bird, which is just as good. Don't fancy her chances if she was hiding outside somewhere ... in the woods or whatever. It might be nearly summertime but it's still a bit parky out there and the temperature drops quite sharply in the middle of the night in amongst the trees!' He drew in a sharp intake of breath so they were all definitely under no illusions as to just how cold it could get outside of an evening, in the dense woods or open fields of the countryside.

'OK, Barry, we get your drift.' Jude glared at him, conscious of Sam's stricken face in her peripheral vision. The last thing any of them needed right now was an image of Holly huddled up on her own outside somewhere in the fields or lost in the woods.

'And she's definitely not upstairs.' Tony came through the doorway and stood by the Aga.

'I should call Mark in the police house.' Sam grabbed the landline phone off the wall. 'She can't be going off on her own. Chrissie specifically said that we needed to keep an eye on her ... while we're getting her levels under control. And what's she going to think now? I should have been more responsible. I can't even be sure when I last saw Holly ... not in the last couple of hours.'

'Hang on! Let's at least ring Katie first. She might have gone to see her, meet her ... we don't know,' Jude said, trying not to panic for Sam's sake. But just how long did you wait until you called the police to tell them a child was missing? And it wasn't like Holly was a three year old – she was a teenager, after all. 'Dolly is right. There could be a simple explanation, and it's not like she knew I was coming over to see her, so she may well have popped out to visit her friend. Are we sure she hasn't left a note on the side or something? And you know what thirteen-year-old girls are like ...' Jude looked to her dad for confirmation.

Tony shrugged and nodded in agreement. 'You see! Dad thinks so too. She's probably dashed out to meet her mate and just forgotten to take her bag. I've done it so many times,' she added, to make light of the situation, in the hope of easing Sam's now very obvious anxiety.

Jude took Holly's mobile from the kitchen table, and after scrolling through her goddaughter's contacts – luckily there wasn't a lock on the keypad – she found the girl's number and rang it. Katie answered right away.

'OK, love. Right. I see. Yes. Thanks for your help. Yes, yes, we'll let you know. I promise. Yes, I'm sure she'll be fine,' Jude said to reassure young Katie, after she confirmed that Holly wasn't with her.

'That's it! I'm definitely phoning the police,' Sam stated, tearing his jacket off and slinging it on the table. 'Holly isn't like other healthy girls her age … she's vulnerable without her insulin. Anything could happen and I'm not risking it.'

'In that case, we need to get Chrissie,' Jude said, torn between looking after Sam who was panicking now – his hands were shaking as he pressed the numbers on the keypad – and making sure her best friend was all right. Jude knew that the second Chrissie was told that Holly wasn't where she was supposed to be … well, she was going to break down, and panic too, for sure. And the news that Holly was missing could very well be the last straw after all the anxiety Chrissie had gone through recently.

'I'll go,' Tony said firmly, on seeing his daughter's dilemma. 'Stay here and help Sam and Dolly. And don't worry, love. I'll look after Chrissie and get her here right away without causing her too much alarm.' He gave Jude a quick kiss on the cheek. 'Come on, Barry. You can keep a look-out in case Holly is in the village somewhere. She might be with the bunch of kids who hang out in the bus shelter.' And the two men wasted no time in heading for the door.

*

But Holly wasn't in the bus shelter.

Instead, she was running as fast as she could.

She knew that she had really done it now.

She was in serious trouble!

When Aunty Jude had knocked on her bedroom door earlier, Holly had been on her laptop in a group chat with her friends on Snapchat, when a message from Katie had popped up saying that Gavin's car had been in an accident! Her cousin, who worked for the AA, had got the call to recover it. Katie had heard him telling her mum. He'd said the call-out was to a man called Gavin in a ditch on the outskirts of Tindledale. And Holly had panicked. And then crept downstairs and silently slunk out of the back door.

What if Chrissie was in the car too?

Chapter Twenty-Three

'Have I got this right then, Sam?' Mark, the village policeman asked, 'you last saw Holly at about six p.m., that you can be sure of ...? Making it about two and a half hours ago.' He glanced at the kitchen wall clock and then double-checked the time against the screen on his handheld device where he was entering all the details.

'Yes, it was definitely then as I asked her if she wanted something to eat – she has to eat regularly, you see. She's a diabetic,' Sam said, desperately trying to keep a clear head. *What if something has happened to her? You hear about it all the time.* 'Look, I don't mean to be rude,' Sam went on, 'but I need to go out and look for her. It's no good us all standing around here talking, when she could be outside on her own. And she doesn't have her insulin with her. What if she needs it? What if she has a hypo? Passes out on her own, or even if she is with a group of friends, they won't know what to do, will they?' Sam went to leave the kitchen, determined to find Holly before Tony and Barry arrived back with Chrissie. And he dreaded to think what she was going to say. What if she blamed him for not looking after Holly properly? Not that he would be fazed if she did. He was past caring. He'd take all the blame if it meant that Holly was safe. Back here with him. Or Chrissie. Dolly. Any of them. It really didn't matter, just as long as she was all right.

'And we will find her, Sam. There's a car already on the way from police HQ in Market Briar,' Mark said calmly, politely declining the mug of tea that Dolly went to offer him. 'It's best in situations like this—'

'What do you mean? Situations like this?' Sam jumped in and started pacing up and down, his hands at the side of his head.

'He just means …' Jude started, seeing the fear in Dolly's eyes and the sheer panic on Sam's face, '… that there is a procedure to follow. That's all. Dad and Barry are already in the village, they'll probably call any second now to say that they've found her messing around with a bunch of mates in the bus shelter. Come on, Sam, she's going to be fine.' Jude placed a hand on Sam's back as he pulled a chair away from the table and slumped down into it.

'Yes, it really is best if you stay here,' Mark said. 'Holly will need you if she comes home of her own accord. She may well be upset or scared if she sees me here,' he lifted his eyebrows, 'a great, big, walloping police officer in a uniform with all this gear – baton and cuffs and all. You don't want her to think she is in trouble now, do you?' he smiled, to try to put them at ease.

'But she isn't in any trouble, though, is she?' It was Dolly who asked, with worry etched all over her lined face as she sat down next to Sam and patted the top of his arm.

'Absolutely not,' Mark assured them both, then stepped closer to Jude. 'Do you have a second to go, err ... go over some more details?' he asked her quietly, indicating with his head towards the hallway as Dolly stood up and put her arm around Sam's shoulders.

'Yes, sure. Of course, let's give them some space for a moment,' Jude said, moving out of the kitchen and pulling the door closed behind her.

'Has she ever run away before?' Mark asked, keeping his voice very low.

'Not that I know of,' Jude shook her head.

'And would you know if she was having any sort of trouble?'

'Trouble?' she lifted an eyebrow.

'Bullying. Social media targeting, trolls ... that kind of thing,' he prompted.

'No. I'm quite sure she isn't being bullied. I think Chrissie would have told me if she was ... but ...' Jude stopped talking and looked towards the kitchen.

'Go on,' Mark said. And they both moved closer to the front door and away from the kitchen so as to be definitely out of earshot of Sam and Dolly.

'Well ... it's just that she's had a tough time recently. She's not talking to either of them – her parents that is

– at the moment. Chrissie and Sam have been, um ... err ... well, they are separated. They've been having some marriage problems,' Jude dipped her head, concerned that she might be talking out of line ... betraying her best friend by speaking about her personal business. It wasn't every day that you had to talk about this sort of thing to a police officer.

'I see. But why isn't Holly talking to them?'

'They argued in front of her and ... um, well ... you see, she really just wants them back together in time for her birthday,' Jude said, remembering the chat she'd had with Holly after seeing the pigs on the Blackwood Farm Estate.

'Thank you,' Mark entered the additional information onto the screen of his handheld device. 'Is there anywhere you can think of that she might go?' he then asked, but before Jude could answer, the doorbell rang and Sam came tearing out of the kitchen to grab the door open, praying it was Holly, back home safe. Mark and Jude stood back behind him.

Sam blinked.

Gulped.

And then his jaw fell open.

'What the bloody hell are you doing here?' he just about managed to bark.

His mother was standing right in front of him with an extra-indignant look stamped on her already perpetually dissatisfied face. She had a bottle of claret in one hand and a travel bag dangling from the other.

'*Well*, this is *very* charming, I must say!' she said, striding straight on into the cottage, forcing Sam to take an immediate step backwards and almost barge right into Jude and Mark. 'I've cut my holiday short and come all this way from the airport to see how my little Holly is. After our conversation, I had a bit of a think, and well,' she paused, pushed one shoulder up and pursed her lips, '... maybe I might be able to help out after all – and this is the way you greet me. And you could have told me you were staying here ... at Dolly's little house, instead of leaving me to find out from a complete stranger in the pub ... when your own house had not one single light on. No, it was cloaked in darkness, like something out of a horror film!'

Sam bit down his disappointment at not seeing his little girl standing before him, returned home safe and sound.

His hands tingled with indignation.

How dared she?

His mother was drunk on duty-free too, if the fumes emanating from her were anything to go by!

How dared Linda turn up out of the blue without a care in the world, when she had just dropped a gigantic wrecking ball into his life. Even if she didn't know that he knew – that she had kept the truth about his dad from him for his whole life, and Rob had most likely died not even knowing – that really wasn't the point.

'Get out!' Sam yelled, absolutely seething.

'I shall do no such thing!' Linda sniffed. 'There's a taxi that needs paying for, for starters,' she motioned with her head to the lane outside, as if expecting Sam to pick up the tab. 'And … what's he doing here?' She eyed Mark up and down. 'Not done something naughty have you, Samuel?' And she fixed her shark-like eyes on her son momentarily, before looking again at Mark, and then actually simpered like some silly schoolgirl.

'What's going on?' Dolly opened the kitchen door, and then took one look at Linda and put a hand to her mouth. 'Oh no! Do you know what's happened to Holly? We've lost her you see,' she gasped, then held her breath as if in preparation for bad news. The two women exchanged looks.

'Oh please, dear God, don't tell me I'm too late,' Linda exclaimed, dramatically dropping the travel bag by her feet and looking again at Mark. 'Noooo, my poor little Holly. My angel,' she cried, then placed a hand on Mark's police-uniform jacket. 'I'm her grandmother. I loved that child with all my heart.'

'STOP IT! Holly isn't dead, you stupid woman.' Sam couldn't help himself, and stormed off into the sitting room. Anything to get away from Linda and her phoney, sickening, Lady Bountiful act.

Sam placed his hands on the mantelpiece, using it as a crutch to lean on, to think and to breathe in a desperate attempt to clear his head. This was about Holly. Not him. He had to keep his wits about him. There was no space in his brain to deal with anything else right now, other than finding out where she was. He knew she wouldn't just go out without telling him or Dolly, no way. She wasn't that kind of girl. And that meant one thing ... he knew it in his heart. That she had run away. And it was his fault. Holly hadn't spoken to him or Chrissie since that afternoon in the pizza restaurant, and who could blame her? She'd had enough of the arguing. And he had promised her he'd make things right. He had let her down. Again. He so wished he had managed to fulfil the promise ... Sam clenched his jaw, forcing himself not to cry. But it was no use, and a solitary, stinging tear slid down the side of his face.

'Sam, are you OK?' It was Jude, softly closing the sitting-room door behind her.

'Yes, yes, I'm all right.' Sam quickly composed himself and rubbed the tear away before turning around to look at her. 'I could just do without my ridiculous mother right now,' he said, pacing up and down with a thunderous look on his face.

'Hmm, I can see why ... is she always like that?' Jude

asked, tilting a thumb over her shoulder, not having seen Linda Morgan in years.

'Jude, she's horrendous. And all that pretending to care. The only person that woman cares about is herself.' He waved a hand in the direction of the hall. 'But it doesn't matter right now. We just need to concentrate on getting Holly back.'

'And we will, Sam. What would you like me to do?' Jude asked calmly, keen to be of the maximum use to her best friend's husband. This was exactly why she had come home after all ... to be here for her friends and family when they needed her the most. Just as they had been for her when her mum had died.

'Could you do me a favour and get rid of my mother, please? Tell her to go and ... I don't know, wait in the Duck & Puddle or something? I just can't deal with her right now.'

'Yep. I'll do my best.' But as Jude went to open the sitting-room door, Chrissie appeared, looking completely panicked, closely followed by Tony, Barry, Dolly, Mark and Linda ... who was still wittering on about the waiting taxi and, 'Would someone please tell me what on earth is going on?'

'Oh my God,' Chrissie dashed straight over to Sam. 'Tony has told me what's happened.'

'Well, I wish somebody would tell me!' Linda huffed,

marching over to the wing chair and plonking herself down into it. 'I come all this way an—'

'Are you still here?' Sam cut her off sharply, throwing her a look.

'Well!' Linda quipped. 'What sort of a way is that to speak to your own mothe—'

'Shut up!' Sam snapped.

'Oh dear. How about a brandy?' It was Dolly who intervened as a potential peacemaker, moving closer to Sam. 'For the shock, come on, love. And I can see that you're upset. Let's sit you down,' and she gently steered him towards the sofa. 'You too, Chrissie, darling,' she soothed, shepherding Chrissie to the sofa as well, 'that's it, there you go.' Dolly then turned to Linda and told her firmly, 'Holly is missing, so if you don't want to get in that taxi and go back to wherever it is you came from, then it's probably best if you keep quiet. Now is not the time, Linda.'

Linda pushed her bottom lip out, stared at Dolly for a second, as if mulling over whether to challenge her or not, and then said,

'Fine. In that case, I suppose I had better sort out the taxi myself then,' and she hauled herself back out of the chair and went to find her purse, huffing and muttering under her breath all the way.

'Sam. Chrissie,' Mark turned to them and they both stood up. 'I'm going to go now and see where we are at with finding Holly. A family liaison officer is on the way here—'

'Oh no, please ... not a family liaison officer ...' Chrissie wept, tears pouring down her face as her legs buckled and she wobbled into Sam. He instinctively put his arms around her body to save her. 'I know what that means, I've seen this on TV programmes,' she looked at Mark, 'you think she ...' her voice quivered and then petered out, unable to say what they all feared most.

'Chrissie, it's just a procedure. It doesn't mean any-thing,' Tony said, looking at Mark to let him know that it was OK to leave and that he would handle things this end. He motioned for Sam and Chrissie to sit back down.

'That's right, Chrissie,' Linda reappeared. 'Kids run off all the time. She'll be back when she's hungry. Sam was a nightmare for doing it at that age – hiding out in the woods. Always reappeared at dinner time though,' she finished with a supercilious smile, making Sam want to grab her by the collar and forcibly turf her out of the house. As if she would know anything much about what he did as a thirteen year old when she was rarely around to notice! Let alone provide a dinner. But he really didn't have the energy to challenge her on it right now ...

'These are different times though, Linda,' Barry jumped in, shaking his head as he went and stood in the corner close to Tony.

'They sure are,' she paused, and then did a double take,

as if seeing Barry for the first time. 'Blimey, you're Barry Lester! I didn't recognise you at first. But then you had long wavy hair down to your shoulders the last time …' Her voice trailed off.

'That's right, but that was donkeys' years ago,' Barry muttered, turning to help Tony and Dolly bring out some dining chairs for them all to sit on.

'Hmm, those were the days,' Linda sighed with a faraway look in her eyes, and then changed the subject. 'I take it I'm allowed a little drink? Seeing as I've not even been offered a beverage,' she asked to nobody in particular, waving the bottle of red wine in the air. Everyone swivelled to stare at her audacity.

'Yes, yes of course, I'll get you a glass,' Dolly politely replied, never one to make a guest feel unwelcome in her home. She walked over to the rosewood sideboard and found a goblet, which she handed to Linda.

'Corkscrew by any chance?' Linda said, not even bothering to thank Dolly for the glass.

'Here! There's one on this,' Barry passed a bunch of keys over without even looking at her.

'Cheers!' Linda wrestled the cork free and poured herself a generous measure of red wine, placed the bottle on the hearth close to her feet, lifted the glass in the air and slurred, 'Well … there's never a dull moment in sleepy old Tindledale now is there?'

Chapter Twenty-Four

'Why is it taking so long?' Chrissie turned her face sideways to look at Sam, her arms crossed and wrapped around her body in an attempt to comfort herself. 'I can't bear this. We should be out there searching for Holly.' She rocked backwards and forwards.

'I don't know,' Sam shook his head and reached a tentative hand out to rub Chrissie's back. She didn't seem to mind, so he kept it in place and assumed their differences were forgotten for now. Holly not being where she was supposed to be – upstairs in her bedroom – sure had put things into sharp perspective, and for both of them, it seemed. 'But I agree – we can't just sit here doing nothing. I feel completely useless. How is this helping Holly? I'm her dad, I should be out there with Mark scouring the woods, the fields, the lanes, the bus shelter in the village square.'

Chrissie creased her forehead and locked her eyes onto his as if really seeing him, and hearing him, for the first time in ages ... and something changed in her demeanour too.

'Sam, look, about the other day, when we took Holly for pizza ...'

'You don't have to say anything now, not while Holly is missing,' Sam said, trying not to add to their woes.

'No, I know that, but I want to. I should have let you say what you needed to, not had a go at you. But I'm stuck in old habits.' She cast her eyes downwards. 'And what if Holly has run away because of me, Sam? It could be my fault.'

'Of course it isn't your fault. You're always doing your best for her.' Sam gently lifted Chrissie's chin so he could look into her eyes.

'But I don't always get it right. I can see that now. I know that I'm stubborn and always taking charge – making decisions for everyone without asking what they want ...' She looked at Sam meaningfully. 'Holly needs us both, and I must let go a bit ... I have been listening and I can see what our problems have been doing to her. If Holly comes back ...' Chrissie was crying now.

Sam took her in his arms and gently stroked her back. 'Hey, *when* Holly comes back, not if ...'

'I know that we have to work together and I'm willing to try if you are. Just please, please let her get back safely.' Chrissie cuddled into him. It was ironic, thought Sam, that now, in this moment, they were together. United. If only Holly was here too.

*

Over on the Blackwood Farm Estate, Holly pushed open the little wooden Hobbit door that led into the garden and managed to make her way to the barn, near where she knew the pigs were kept. She'd be safe there for now. She could hide in the barn until the morning and then, when it was daylight, she would see about getting on a train. She could walk to the station from here. It wasn't that far. But she had no chance of getting there in the dark. The country lane to the station was steep and there were no street lights so it was scary with all the trees arching together to make a tunnel of darkness. And with her eyesight already feeling a bit misty where her levels were dipping from not having eaten in a while, she didn't want to risk it. Plus she couldn't leave Tindledale without saying goodbye to Tiger. Not with him being the runt of the litter. And the other pigs didn't even like him; she had spotted that the very first time she saw him in the corner of the pen.

Holly found the pig pen and lifted Tiger up to her, opening her hoodie so he could snuggle inside against her body. It was getting cold now that the sun had gone down, so she went inside the barn and sat on a big bale of hay.

'Hey, Holly!' It was Myles, with a big handheld torch in his hand. She quickly stood up, feeling scared. But he didn't look cross. 'It's OK.' He set the torch down on

the ground and jumped up onto one of the bales of hay.
'Mind if I join you?'

'Um.' She nodded, her heart hammering.

'What have you got there?' He pointed to her hoodie.

'Sorry, I just wanted to see Tiger before I leave,' she
said, willing her heart to slow down. She felt a bit light-
headed now. And then realised. Oh no. In her panic, she
had come out without her bag. Her insulin. Her phone.
And it made her panic more.

'Leave? Where are you off to, babe?' Myles asked softly.

'I'm not sure yet,' she said, leaning back against a bale
of hay. She reckoned she had about half an hour before
she'd need to get her insulin. Maybe she could go back
to Granny Dolly's house to get it. Hmm, too risky. What
if the police were there? What if someone had seen her
pulling those things off the tyres on Gavin's car. What
if her Mum was hurt? Maybe she should go home, see
if Mum was there and if she was all right. She could get
her insulin then too.

'Ahh, I get it. Are you running away?' Myles asked. She
managed a shrug. He waited a minute before carrying
on. 'You know, there was a time when I wanted to run
away ...'

'Really?'

'Yep.' Myles nodded. Come on, let's go back to the
house, it's nicer in there than in this smelly old barn,
and I'll tell you all about it.' Holly looked down at

little Tiger who was fast asleep now. 'Bring him with you. Be a shame to wake him up.' She beamed. Myles was so cool.

On a big squishy sofa beside the massive flatscreen TV, Myles told her.

'It was years ago, when I felt sad. Is that why you're running away, Holls?' he looked sideways at her.

'Yes, and ...' She nearly told him about Gavin's car, but stopped herself. She felt ashamed. 'Why did you feel sad?' she asked Myles instead.

'Mainly because I didn't have a mum and dad.'

'How come?'

'My parents didn't know how to look after kids properly, so I grew up in foster care.' He said it just like that, and it made Holly feel very grown-up. He obviously trusted her to tell her his personal stuff.

'Did you feel very lonely?'

'Yes I did.'

'So who looked after you?'

'Strangers mostly. I lived with an aunt for a bit, but that didn't work out, and then an older cousin, but then he went to prison, and so ...'

'That's so sad,' Holly said, feeling sorry for him. It was so unfair. He was a really nice man. And he was cool. She liked how he talked to her like she was an adult. Not a child.

'It is. But then I wasn't lucky like you.'

'How do you mean?'

'Well, I didn't have a mum and dad like you do, who love you and are probably wondering where you are.' Holly kept quiet. 'And your aunty Jude, she loves you a lot as well. She might miss you if you run away.' Maybe he had a point. Holly stroked the top of Tiger's little head. He snuffled against her T-shirt.

'I don't think my mum and dad will even notice I've gone,' Holly said solemnly.

'Do you reckon?' Myles asked, all casually.

'They keep having massive arguments right in front of me.'

'What about?'

'Dad being away, letting us down, the usual stuff ...'

'Sorry to hear that, Holls. You know, sometimes people get angry because they're scared or upset, and that's probably what happened then. They might be scared now too, if they don't know where you are ... Is that why you're running away? Because of the arguments?'

'It's another thing too ...' She stopped talking.

'Go on. I won't tell anyone, I promise. Unless it's really bad.' He made a silly face. 'But we can decide together what to do, if it's extra bad, OK?' And he smiled really kindly, so Holly told him about the car and the accident and that her mum and Gavin might be hurt. A few seconds later, and Myles said, 'So Katie's cousin is an AA recovery man?'

'Yes, that's right.'

'And you took the caps off the tyres?'

'Yes,' Holly said, pressing her chin on to the top of Tiger's warm little head for comfort.

'I don't think you have anything to worry about then, babe. Gavin's car won't have gone anywhere. If it's an old car then he's probably just got two flat tyres. And even if he had driven it before he realised, and then had an accident, I don't think the AA man would be the first one on the scene.'

Holly leant back against the sofa and closed her eyes.

'Do you think I could have a drink please, and a biscuit?'

'Coming right up. Are you feeling rough, Holls?' Myles asked, and Holly wondered why his voice sounded a bit muffled.

'Yes, I am a bit.' She opened her eyes again.

'Do you need your insulin?'

'I haven't got it with me.'

'Better not leave you on your own then,' he said, all calmly. Not like Mum, who would definitely panic, thought Holly. And then she felt bad all over again for messing around with Gavin's car. 'I'll call Sylvia,' and he picked up the walkie-talkie. 'How about I call your Aunty Jude as well?'

'What for?'

'To see if she wants to come over. You get on well with her, and she could get your insulin too and bring it with her. I don't think she'll make you go home. Not right away, if you want to hang out here for a bit longer. What do you reckon? Sylvia will make us some dinner too. Fish and chips – you like that, don't you?'

Holly thought Myles looked a bit worried ... so she agreed.

'OK.' She managed a smile. 'But I don't want her to bring Mum and Dad here.'

'That's fine. Have a chat to Jude ... and, you never know, things might turn out all right in the end, if you can be brave enough to stick around and give it all a go.'

*

'Son, it's going to be all right,' Tony leant forward from the dining chair where he was sitting and placed his hand on top of Sam's knee. 'It's only been five minutes or so since Mark left.'

'Is that all?' Sam asked, gulping down the single measure of brandy from the glass that Dolly had pressed into his hand.

'But it feels like an eternity,' Chrissie said, putting her palms onto her cheeks to mop her tears before leaning back into Sam's chest. He put his arm around her shoulders and pulled her close, pressing his chin into her hair to comfort her.

'I know, but Mark will find her,' Tony said, exchanging

glances with Jude who was sitting on the arm of the sofa next to Chrissie, and wondering if Sam had a point. He wasn't sure he could just have sat and waited if something like this had happened when Jude was Holly's age. He would have wanted to be out there hunting and scouring every single corner of Tindledale and the surrounding fields, woods and valleys until she was found.

'I say we give it another ten minutes and then we all go out and look; we can get the villagers out too,' Jude suggested. She hated just waiting here as well, feeling helpless. Holly had only been gone for three hours that they knew of, but every single second felt agonising to her, so she dreaded to think what Chrissie and Sam were going through.

'Yes. Please, that has to be better than sitting here,' Chrissie looked up at Jude with pleading eyes.

'I'm getting my jacket back on,' Sam stood up, resolute. 'This is a waste of time waiting here, I don't care what Mark says.' He was just about to leave the sitting room when a mobile rang out somewhere inside the cottage.

They all leapt up. Dolly. Tony. Barry. Chrissie. Only Linda stayed in her seat, having near polished off half the bottle of wine by now.

'That's my phone!' And Jude raced into the kitchen to retrieve the mobile from her bag. Seconds later, and she was back in the sitting room with tears of joy in her eyes.

Thank God, her goddaughter was safe!

355

And not lying unconscious somewhere.

'I know where Holly is!' she told them all, waving her mobile around like it was a satellite tracker with a pulsing red dot pointed directly on to Holly.

Sam instantly felt the knot of anxiety dissipate as relief flooded through his veins. He gasped and then, after removing his arm from around Chrissie's shoulders, he bent over and placed his hands on his thighs in sheer relief.

'Myles found Holly in a barn having a cuddle with Tiger!' Jude told them all.

'A *tiger!* The girl has guts, I'll give her that,' Linda piped up, nearly sloshing wine all over the place as she pointed an index finger in the air and shifted in her seat.

'SHUT UP!' Sam, Tony, Barry and Jude all bellowed in unison. Dolly took a sharp intake of breath and put her hands up to her face before saying, 'Thank heavens our Holly is safe.' She gave Sam a hug, then Chrissie, squeezing them each as tight as she could.

'Well, what are we waiting for?' Sam hollered, reaching for Chrissie's hand and giving it a triumphant squeeze. Everything was going to be OK now. He just knew it. It had to be. Holly was safe. And this was the start of their family's fortunes turning around. 'Come on, let's go and get Holly.' He looked at Jude. 'Thank you. Thank you. Thank you. Thank you.' And he planted a big kiss on her left cheek.

'What did I do?' she laughed, giving him a hug.

'Allowed me to breathe again for starters,' Chrissie said, puffing out a long breath of air before also giving Jude a big kiss of gratitude for being the bearer of the good news.

'Please can you get in touch with Mark and let him know that she's been found?' Sam said, over his shoulder, his heart having soared right up to the top of the emotional rollercoaster. He and Chrissie made a bolt for the door, but Tony blocked their exit.

'What are you doing?' he asked, and Sam's hand froze on the door handle. 'You can't drive.' Tony shook his head.

'Yes I can. I need to get Holly home.'

'Tony's right, my love,' Dolly stepped in, 'you've had a brandy. That was my fault, I shouldn't have given it to you, but I thought it might help. For the shock.'

'I'm not drunk,' Sam said, going for the door again.

'Sam ... we know you aren't,' Tony said, 'but you're still shaken up. It's not wise to drive.'

'Honestly, I'm OK.' He looked at Chrissie, and meant it, but she was still smiling. Thankfully.

'Err ... you really can't go, Sam,' Jude said awkwardly, shoving her phone into the back pocket of her jeans. She glanced first at Chrissie. Swallowed, took a big breath and then told them both, 'There's no easy way to say this so I'll just come out with it. Myles said he thinks it's best if I go. I'm sorry ... she's still upset, you see, she doesn't want either of you to—'

'What?' Chrissie slumped down on to the sofa. 'But we're her parents, and we've been out of our mind with worry,' she added, holding her head in both hands.

'It's fine.' Sam jumped in, looking at Chrissie. 'Let Jude go. The priority is to get Holly home safe and, most importantly, she has to be happy. And we have to respect her wishes ... especially as we haven't managed to do that so well lately.'

'OK.' Chrissie eventually nodded her consent. 'You're right.' And she touched Sam's arm.

'I know you need Holly home as soon as possible so that you can sort all of this out with her properly, but we know she's safe now.' And Jude went into the kitchen to get Holly's bag. 'I'll take her insulin too,' she added, keeping her voice measured. Myles had said she needed to bring the kit quickly, but Sam and Chrissie didn't need any more to panic about right now.

'Thank you,' Sam replied. The sooner they got Holly back, the sooner he and Chrissie could start making things right. So what did it matter who went to collect Holly? And he allowed himself a fleeting moment of 'what if?' What if something had happened to their daughter? It just didn't bear thinking about ... so the best thing they could do now was to make the most of this second chance.

'I'll be as quick as I can.' Jude nodded, and left the room.

'And I'll get on to Mark right away to tell him the good news,' Tony said, waving goodbye to Jude.

'Well, now that the panic is over, we can all relax,' Linda started up, filling her glass with another measure of wine. 'Do you remember when we were kids, Barry?' She looked across the room to where he was standing.

'Not really. Like I said earlier, it was a long time ago,' Barry replied, picking up a newspaper from the coffee table. He flicked through it, seemingly uninterested in anything Linda had to say. Tony came back in the room with two cups of coffee in his hands.

'I've spoken to Mark, and it's all fine; he's going to call in tomorrow when things have settled down. Just a routine thing to see that you're all OK,' he nodded. 'Here, get this down you. Holly will be home soon and you'll both be needing clear heads.' He handed a coffee cup each to Sam and Chrissie.

'And you can stay here this evening if you want to,' Dolly said to Chrissie. 'Colin is on an overnight coach trip to the tulip farm in Amsterdam, so Holly can always come in with me, and then you and Sam can have some time to talk ...' She looked at Tony.

'Yes, that's a good idea,' he said, 'after everything that has happened tonight, you won't want to be at home on your own, Chrissie love.' Tony cottoned on quickly that

Dolly was attempting to resurrect the original plan – to get Sam and Chrissie together so they might find a way to work things out. Although he had a feeling that the two of them were well on their way already. It wasn't nice that Holly had run off, but it sure had shaken the pair of them up ... better than any head-banging-together idea that he, or Jude, or Dolly could have cooked up between them.

'Uh-oh. Not sorted your domestic problems out yet?' Linda butted in, looking at Sam and then Chrissie. 'And there was me thinking you had the perfect marriage ...' She slurped another mouthful of wine down.

'Think you might have had enough of that, Linda.' Tony went to take the bottle away.

'Oh, don't you start. I remember you too, Saint Tony!' Linda grabbed the bottle and nursed it to her chest. Tony shook his head and went to stand near Barry by the coffee table.

'For crying out loud, will you please just stop!' Sam said, staring at his mother. 'Honestly, we've had the most horrendous last few hours and now we are all over the moon. Holly will be here soon. Why can't you just be happy for once?' he shook his head and let out a long sigh of frustration.

'Oh Samuel, don't be so oversensitive!' said Linda, doing a little laugh as she looked around the room to see if Chrissie, Dolly, Barry or Tony might join in her bullying of him. None of them did.

'*Oversensitive!* Are you for real?' Sam retorted, feeling the pulse at the side of his neck firing up. He really wanted to keep things civil ... at least until Holly was home and safely tucked up in bed, but his mother was pushing him like she always did. Only this time it was different. Knowing what he knew – that she had lied – felt like a game-changer now she was here in front of him. He had thought it shouldn't matter – Rob was his dad at the end of the day. And he had been a brilliant dad too, so why *did* it matter? Maybe he should just let it go. But then where did that leave Holly? And then Sam knew why it mattered so much. Linda had deceived him, and in doing so she had changed the course of everything ... even Dolly being his grandmother. Sam had come to that realisation in the middle of the night when he'd been lying awake, going over and over it all inside his head: that if Rob wasn't his biological father, then technically, Dolly wasn't his gran, or Holly's great-grandmother. They weren't related at all. So it wasn't just about him. Linda had hoodwinked them all. And it stuck in his throat to see her sitting here across the room from him now, having a laugh like she hadn't a care in the world.

'No wonder little Holly doesn't even want to talk to you,' Linda kept on. 'But then that's teenagers for you. So contrary. Sam, do you remember when you used to—'

'NO!' Sam turned on his mother. He was so close to having it out with her now. 'No I don't. And do you know why?' he flashed a look around the room and then carried on, 'because your version of the past is a fabrication. A giant lie!' He finished the last of his coffee and placed the cup on the table. An awkward silence ricocheted around the room. Chrissie looked at Sam, her forehead creased.

'I beg your pardon!' Linda said, indignantly.

'That's right. Take umbrage … like you always do—'

'I most certainly do not.' She rearranged herself in the chair, and then, ignoring Sam, turned to Barry and said, 'Do you remember when we were teenagers? We used to ride around the valleys and out into the fields?'

'No, can't say that I do,' Barry glanced up from the newspaper, flicked his eyes to Sam and then busied himself by burying his head back in the page.

'I'll make us all some more coffee and fetch in a cake, I've got a lovely Victoria sponge going spare … I always make extra, just in case. Shan't be a minute.' Dolly darted to the door, clearly desperate to defuse the awkward atmosphere. Tony shot Linda a look, then pushed back his sleeve to see the time on his watch.

'Thanks Gran,' Sam called after her, keen to rein things in and get them back to pleasant. Holly would be home soon. Now certainly wasn't the time or place to challenge his mother. But she just wouldn't give it a rest, and opened her mouth again.

'Oh, you must do, Barry. The good old days – now, how old were we?' She paused to make a show of trying to remember by tapping an index finger on the side of her mouth, her eyes closed tightly. 'I wasn't long out of school. And you fancied me!' Barry visibly groaned, shook the newspaper out and turned the page. Sam rolled his eyes and squeezed Chrissie's hand, wishing his mother would be quiet. And her version of past events were clearly figments of her imagination ... Barry had no idea what she was going on about.

'Not long now. She'll be home any minute,' Sam said, smiling at his wife, both relieved that Holly was safe and their animosity forgotten. And he hoped it would stay this way ... He wanted that more than anything. Even more so now, and for Holly's sake too.

'Don't blame you, though, I was a bit of a looker back in the day,' Linda harped on. Sam tried to block out her drunken drivel and focus on what he was going to say to Chrissie later on, when the others had all gone home and Holly was safe in bed. No more arguments. He was prepared to do whatever it took, and was going to make sure she understood that they would do it together. 'We had some fun times in the back of that car of yours.' And Linda did an exaggerated wink in Chrissie's direction. Sam bristled. He glared at his mother, not daring to even open his mouth this time as he was that close to losing his temper with her.

'Come on now, Linda,' Tony said. 'That's enough. You're embarrassing the poor girl. Sam, and Barry too.'

'It's fine, Tony. Honestly, let's just get Holly back and then we can all relax,' Chrissie said, charitably. Sam nodded, thinking how kind Chrissie had been in tolerating his mother over the years. He hadn't really appreciated this until now. Even though they had hardly seen Linda, it somehow made her behaviour even worse with it being concentrated into slots of total awfulness here and there.

'Yeah, maybe we should go, Tony, and leave them to—' Barry started, clearly keen to escape from Linda, but was interrupted when Chrissie's mobile rang.

'It's Jude!' she said, quickly answering. 'OK. Yes, that's fine. Jude please tell her I love her. Her dad too,' she smiled at Sam. 'And we'll see her soon.' Chrissie pressed to end the call and turned to him. 'Holly wants to stay there for a bit longer ... Myles is organising fish and chips, her new favourite apparently,' she smiled wryly. 'And she's checked her levels and everything is fine.' Her voice tailed off.

'That's good then, maybe she just needs some space. She's safe and we are here waiting for her, no matter what,' Sam nodded and squeezed Chrissie's hand.

'And Jude will look after her,' Tony added.

'You're too soft, that's your problem, Samuel.' Linda was up on her feet now, tottering around looking for her travel bag. 'I'm sure there was another bottle here somewhere.'

'You've had enough!' Sam told her. 'Have a coffee instead and sober yourself up.'

'Just like your father ... he was boring too,' Linda slurred, and nearly fell on top of Tony after catching the heel of her shoe on the corner of Dolly's tassel-trimmed rug.

'What did you say?' Sam snapped, impulsively. Tony turned to face him after helping Linda to steady herself. Silence. He could feel Barry, Tony and Chrissie's eyes on him. But Linda was more interested in draining the last drop of wine from the goblet. 'Come on, Mother. I'm waiting. Tell me *all* about my father. I want to know.' And as soon as the words were out of Sam's mouth, it was as if a dam within him had burst wide open to let all the frustration and disappointment flood out from him. The resentments that had been building up over the decades: Linda going away when she needed him most; the put-downs; making him feel like he wasn't good enough; her constant chipping away at his self-worth; her disregard for her granddaughter; her nasty comments about his wife; her never really giving a damn about him, or anyone else for that matter. Not ever. And he'd had enough. Had enough of trying to keep it all inside him. Enough was enough. He looked again at Chrissie ... now was his chance to wipe the slate clean and start afresh for his family, and there was no way he was going to let his mother spoil it any more.

He was done with her.

But first, he wanted the truth.

'A Cortina!' Linda shrieked, standing back up. 'That was the car.'

Sam stared at Barry. What was she going on about now? But then something else happened within him. A realisation. A hot trickle of adrenalin radiated from his chest. To his arms. Hands. Fingertips. Legs. Head.

No.

It couldn't be true.

Barry?

But hadn't she just gone on about all the fun they had in the back of his car?

Sam stepped backwards, with his mind hurtling all over the place like a ball inside a pinball machine. He inhaled through his nostrils, and shook his head, desperate to get a grip on something tangible. Something real to anchor him.

'Barry is my dad!'

Dolly appeared in the doorway, then stopped as if frozen in time, with a tray full of coffee and cake in her hands.

Nobody said a word.

Barry paled. Dropped the newspaper and then

slumped into the nearest dining chair. Sam swivelled his eyes onto him. Scrutinising him for clues.

'It's not true.' Barry shook his head vehemently. 'It can't be. She's drunk. And I never went near her. Not ever.' He looked at his mate Tony.

More silence.

Sam fixed his eyes back on his mother.

'Err ... um, no. Don't be silly,' Linda started with a nervous little laugh. 'Of course he isn't. Rob was your dad.' And she started rummaging in her travel bag. 'What's got into you all of a sudden?'

'Don't lie!'

'What on earth is going on?' Dolly asked, and after placing the tray down on the sideboard she moved into the middle of the room and stood directly opposite Linda. 'Why does Sam think that Barry is his father?'

'Gran, I'm so sorry,' Sam said softly. 'I never meant you to find out like this.'

'Find out what?' Sam took her hands in his, hating how this had all panned out. What the bloody hell was wrong with him that he couldn't have just kept his mouth shut? At least until he had a chance to get his mother on her own. But it was too late now.

'Why don't we sit down, Gran? Or go into the kitchen, perhaps; it will be easier in there to explain—'

'Oh for goodness' sake. Stop fannying around,' Linda said with sudden clarity, and leant into Dolly to tell her.

Brutally so. 'Samuel here isn't your real grandson. Happy now?' And she turned to Sam and glared at him as if he were to blame, as though it was all his fault for making Linda break an old lady's heart.

'You hateful old wit—' Sam yelled, willing the tears of anger and frustration and devastation not to spill out onto his face. It was Chrissie who steadied him, moving next to him, her calming touch giving him strength.

'Well, at least I made sure you had your real father's name,' Linda pouted, seemingly oblivious to the impact her bombshell announcement was having on everyone in the room. Dolly covered her mouth with her left hand in horror. Tony stepped forward to place an arm around her shoulders, his heart going out to the elderly woman. Finding out like this that your own deceased son wasn't the biological father of your adored grandson, after all these years, was unbelievably cruel.

'What the hell do you mean?' Sam was shouting now. Absolutely furious that his mother was being so disgustingly blasé about it all. Not to mention the hurt and anguish she had inflicted on Dolly. 'Sam? Are you saying that my biological father is called Sam?' He racked his brains in a desperate attempt to figure out if he knew anyone else called Sam. Anyone at all. Anyone in Tindledale who was around the right age to be his dad. But what if the man wasn't from Tindledale? He could be from anywhere, for all he knew.

'No,' Linda spoke, this time with at least a shred of decency as she flitted her eyes downwards to the rug beneath her shoes.

'Then tell me. Tell me right now, or I swear to God I will—'

'Come on, it's OK Sam, we'll sort this out, it's going to be—' Chrissie tried, and went to put her hand on his arm again. But Sam was so fired up that he was having none of it, and pulled away from his wife and fixed his eyes on his mother.

'I'm waiting. I want to know the name of my dad. My biological father. Right now!'

An agonising silence followed.

Barry, Tony and Chrissie all bowed their heads, none of them daring to even breathe, but all wishing they were anywhere else but here right now.

Dolly moved into the centre of the room and right up close to Linda.

'You know, I always had my suspicions about you,' she said, calmly and with dignity, pointing a finger in the other woman's face. 'I knew you weren't to be trusted. You may have hoodwinked my dear son, Robert, for all those years, but you never fooled me.'

'Oh purlease, Dolly Morgan, you aren't all that yourself, you know,' Linda sniffed. 'You always did like to look down your nose at me ... so you aren't the charitable, kind old lady that you make yourself out to be.'

'Right. That's enough,' Tony intervened. 'You need to leave right now. Come on. Get your stuff together and I'll take you to the station.' And he went to bundle Linda from the room.

'Take your hands off me.' Linda wrenched herself free.

Tony, not the kind of man to hassle a woman, lifted his hands up in the air and away from her. Chrissie helped Dolly over to the sofa to comfort her.

'She's not going until she's told me!' Sam thundered. 'And then you can get on your way.' He stood in front of his mother, fearless now the secret was out and the worst of the damage had been done. He would pick up the pieces with Dolly later, tell her how much they all loved her, no matter what.

'Yes, *all right!* But there's no need to shout in my face.' Linda scanned the room, clearly realising that she was snared like a fox in a trap. 'It's true. Robert wasn't your real dad.' A collective gasp ricocheted around the room.

And she fixed her eyes on one man.

They all turned to see.

'Tony is!' she paused for dramatic effect. 'Samuel *Anthony* Morgan ... meet your real dad, Tony Darling!' And at that exact moment Jude appeared in the sitting room with Holly by her side.

'*Dad?*' she stopped moving and stared at him. 'What's going on?'

But Tony didn't look at Jude. His eyes, full of sorrow

and hurt, were fixed on Linda. How could she? He looked at Sam. His head moved from side to side as if in slow motion. It was as though time had stood still. Frozen. *I didn't know. I never did. I was infatuated back then, but I stopped it. I stopped it all as soon as I saw that ring. The big, shiny engagement ring. Barry used to let me use the Cortina. And I was weak. It was wrong. All wrong. Rob didn't deserve it. He was my best friend.* The words were going round and round inside his head but nothing was coming out of his mouth. Tony felt as if he was sinking. The floor, like quicksand now around his legs, pulling him under. The room swayed. He put a hand to his head.

'Dad! Please. Please, someone tell me what's going on?' Jude darted forward and took hold of her dad's arm, helping him as he staggered to the nearest chair. Chrissie quickly took Holly from the room.

'I didn't know!' Tony managed to get the words out as he tugged to loosen his shirt collar. 'I'm really sorry, Sam. I honestly didn't know ...'

Chapter Twenty-Five

Two weeks later ...

The day of the May Fair, and Holly felt so happy that she thought her heart might soar so high and burst right out of her chest into a million, trillion, tiny, fluttery pieces of joy. The church bells of St Mary's were ringing out across the fields as they all walked in the glorious sunshine to the Blackwood Farm Estate. Aunty Jude ... her actual *proper* aunty now – how brilliant was that? – had sorted it for her and Katie to be the first ones in the swimming pool. And she couldn't wait. But the best bit of all was that Mum was being really nice to her now. And Dad too. Mum had said that life was much too short for recriminations and resentments, or something like that ... anyway, it didn't matter now, because Dad had just put his hand on Mum's arm. Yes, she could see them up ahead, even through the trees; she knew she hadn't missed it. Dad definitely had touched her, and Mum hadn't even moved away from him or anything. And that meant one thing. They were getting back together. In time for her birthday! The wish was actually starting to come true.

'Come on,' Holly said to Katie, who was walking alongside her, 'race you.' And, after grinning at her best friend, Holly started running as best as she could, heaving the big bag of all her swimming gear up under her arm, her long red silky scarf flaring out behind her. And she didn't feel breathless or weak or anything. She felt on top of the world. The happiest girl alive. And it was amazing.

What a surprise she'd had when she'd got back to Granny Dolly's house that night she had run away. Everything had gone mental. She had heard Grandma Linda arguing and then, later on, Dad had explained that Tony was actually his dad, which meant he was her new granddad. And Holly thought it was brilliant. She liked Tony. So she had told Dad right away that this meant their name was Darling too. How mad was that? *Holly Darling*. She loved it. And had already altered all her social media stuff. Her friends thought it was just a thing, you know, change your name for a laugh … she had been Holls Horror for Halloween, with a cute pumpkin emoji. But this wasn't just a thing … it was for real. And Lauren, her diabetic friend from the hospital had Snapchatted her to say that Holly Darling was the perfect vlogger name … so she was definitely going to think about launching her own YouTube channel, and had even put it on her wish list. Everything was going to be great now. She just knew it.

Sam put his hand out to touch Chrissie's arm, relishing the moment he had thought would never come around again. After that night, when Holly had disappeared for those agonisingly long few hours, he and Chrissie had eventually managed to talk, just like he had hoped they would. Late into the night, once everyone had gone, they had sat in Dolly's sitting room, and talked. Properly talked.

Chrissie had told him how she really felt: that she was scared to let go, to trust him. She wanted to change, to open herself up to sharing life's responsibilities. And he had been honest too. He told her that he'd never felt he was good enough, that anything worth having would be taken away, ever since his father – yes, Rob would always be his father – had been snatched away from him and he'd been rejected by his mother. They didn't have all the answers, and they would always do things differently, but it was a start. There was no such thing as perfection and they couldn't return to how they were in the past. There was a lot of work still to do. But they had both agreed that they'd like to try to rebuild what they had. Together. Chrissie still loved him, and he loved her. It was like Rob had said in his letter, '*love is all you have at the end of the day …*' So Sam had got in touch with a marriage guidance counsellor and booked a course of sessions for them.

And Chrissie confirmed that there was never another man … 'Gavin from the choir is happily married to his husband, John, you idiot. We're friends, that's all. He's been a great support these last few months,' she had said when Sam asked. 'And he kindly gives me a lift because it's tricky to get to the village hall when there's only one bus *on the hour every hour*.' They had laughed at that, reminiscing how this quirk of country living had hindered their relationship in the early days before Sam could afford his first car. The times he spent sitting in the bus shelter in the village square, aching to see her, and a whole hour felt like an eternity. But she had lived at least three fields away from him and the narrow country lanes were pitch black without street lights, so there really was no alternative.

They had talked about Rob and the blood tests too, and the revelation that Sam had discovered about his family heritage.

'Why didn't you tell me you had all that going on too? I had no idea, and it must have been so difficult for you … I would have liked to have shared that, shouldered the burden with you,' she had said softly, when they'd broached the subject of Tony, who had been absolutely brilliant since finding out he was Sam's biological father. Of course, he had been devastated not to have known earlier, especially since his best friend, Rob, had died. Tony wasn't sure Rob ever knowing would have been fair on him, but he would have liked to have stepped up more, openly been more of the dad Sam hadn't had after

Rob passed away. But, now was now, Tony had said, and nothing could change what had happened to date, so ... and if Sam was in agreement, then he'd very much like the chance to be the best dad that he could be for him from now on.

'I was angry,' Sam had told her. 'And confused. And I felt like a failure. I wanted to do something, to show that I could take responsibility. But the blood results meant I wouldn't even be able to step up if Holly really needed me.'

'But don't you see?' Chrissie had said, taking both his hands in hers and drawing him to her. 'You've given Holly another chance ... she has two brand-new blood relatives who can't wait to get tested.'

Sam moved his arm around Chrissie's shoulders. He could see the maypole up ahead – its red, gold and green rainbow of satin ribbons fluttering around in the warm breeze, the only clouds in the sky mere wisps of candy floss. The trees at the entrance to the Blackwood Farm Estate were festooned with paper lanterns, looped from one to the other like bunting. As they got nearer, the air became full with the heady scent of coconut and lime from the numerous pomanders hanging on lengths of yellow ribbon from tall metal hooks pushed into the ground. A band playing kettledrums gave the fair a carnival atmosphere. Morris dancers waved tasselled batons in the air. They spotted jugglers deftly flicking balls and clubs, a machine jetting a cascade of giant bubbles everywhere; all of it here to welcome them as they walked on into the magical wonderland. Past big pots of petunias, buckets ablaze with exotic lilies – pink, blue and red. And, from the corner of his eye, Sam spotted a crimson-breasted robin perched on a branch in the woodland nearby. He pondered on whether it was the same one he'd seen on the five-bar gate when he'd pulled over into the layby on his first day back home in Tindledale. Signifying a new beginning. Or was that just fanciful thinking? Either way, it made him feel as if anything was possible ...

*

As Jude scooped Lulu up under her arm and stepped through the little Hobbit door, she gasped. It was just as she had imagined. And exactly as Myles had wanted. It was a veritable miracle that they had managed to pull it off in time. With a bit – well ... a lot, to be fair – of help from Billy Randall's Most Amazing Funfair and Theme Parks. The men had pulled out all the stops after Billy Randall's wife, Jackie, had turned out to be Myles King's Number 1 fan. She had even set up the fan club and everything back in the day. So Billy had had a word with Myles, and in exchange for an exclusive VIP performance by Myles of Jackie's favourite songs, he had taken charge of the whole event. Showing Myles and Jude exactly what needed to be done, and in what order ... there had been a lot of head shaking and muttering from Billy.

But it had all worked out well in the end, and now the grass all around the entrance to the swimming pool was covered in sand. Real sand. And there were lots of gorgeous little pastel-coloured beach huts too, selling all kinds of fare – candy floss, ice creams, lollies, smoothies, cakes, candles, jams, chutneys, sticks of rock, driftwood ornaments, nets of seashells and an assortment of deliciously aromatic food.

'I need one of those,' Tony laughed, pointing to a pink beach hut. Cooper the butcher was outside it, carving a giant side of beef into generous slices for the villagers to wedge into a roll with an equally generous portion of fried onions and a dollop of horseradish sauce.

'But what about this, Dad?' Jude grinned, tucking her hand through his crooked arm and leading him over to the hog roast stall. Cooper's wife, Molly, was supervising her four enormous sons in taking turns to rotate the spit over the hot coals. Sybs, from the haberdashery shop, was standing nearby with her husband, Dr Ben, and their adorable twin girls, each wearing blue polka-dot sundresses with cotton hats and flipflops. Coming to join them were Cher and Sonny from the Duck & Puddle pub, with their little boy, closely followed by a heavily pregnant Kitty from the Spotted Pig Café & Tearoom, and her partner, Mack, with little Teddie swinging on the end of his arm.

'Well, whatever we go for, we had better be quick,' Tony said, as he pointed to the sea of choristers heading over from the manor house, all wearing Hawaiian straw hula skirts and multicoloured lei garlands around their necks, singing 'Here Comes The Sun', creating a marvellous, tropical holiday feel. 'There will be nothing left after they've sung their hearts out and worked up an appetite.' Tony tilted his head up with an amused look on his face.

'Good point. And you need to go and get changed soon into your Willy Wonka velvet suit and top hat if you're to surprise all the children with your magic show.' Jude nudged and winked at her dad.

'Shuuushh, we don't want them hearing you, and it spoiling the magic,' Tony tapped the side of his nose.

'Very true. Come on then …' and she headed to the hog roast stall first.

In the queue, and she turned to Tony and leaned into him to create a smidgen of privacy while they chatted. 'Are you sure you're OK with it all, Dad? Everything that came out when Linda turned up? I mean, it was a massive shock.'

'Surprise, love! It's a wonderful surprise,' he confirmed resolutely, and smiled. 'And I know that I have no right in taking any credit whatsoever, but Sam is a great bloke.

He's a kind, caring man that any dad would be proud to call his son.'

'Oh Dad, you are so lovely. And Sam takes after you, obviously,' she grinned, still trying to get her head around the revelation of finding out that she had a half-brother. And someone she had grown up with, to boot. Went to school with, even. And there had been a moment years ago when they were about fourteen years old and she had very nearly had a kiss with Sam. Eeeep! She had been tipsy on Lambrini and Chrissie had dared her to kiss the first boy who came through the door of the village hall where they were having a disco. Luckily, thinking about it all now with hindsight, Sam had appeared in the doorway and then scarpered, meaning his mate Matt, the farrier, had ended up being the boy Jude first kissed on the actual mouth. Thankfully. That would have just been very awkward otherwise.

'I don't think he does take after me, love. He's very much like Rob. He was a great bloke too. Salt-of-the-earth type who would do anything for anyone, and I'm ashamed to this day for what I did ... with my mate's girlfriend.' Tony shook his head as his voice faded.

'But Dad, you mustn't feel like that,' Jude rubbed his arm, hating seeing him blame himself. 'It was years ago. And you must have been very young. We all make mistakes when we're that age. And you put a stop to it, right? ... As soon as you knew that Rob was serious about Linda.'

'I guess so. And I thought I had been careful, taken precautions. I never would have been deliberately irresponsible, we were just kids ourselves ...' He paused and looked away.

'Of course you wouldn't.'

'Doesn't stop me from feeling like the worst friend in the world now, though. Poor Rob never knew – and he would have hated me if he had.' Tony bowed his head and let out a long sigh.

'Then I think it's a good thing ... a blessing in disguise, Dad. You were a good friend to Rob and he died never knowing the pain that Linda's bombshell would have caused him.'

'I know, love. I know. And thank you for being so sensible about it all,' Tony nodded, wistfully.

'Well, I wasn't going to be an idiot about it. What's to be gained from that? You're a decent bloke, Anthony Darling, and I'm proud to have you as my dad, and Sam had better be too,' she laughed, 'or he'll have me to answer to. And I'm sure I could be a really annoying younger sister if I wanted to be.' And they both laughed.

'Ahh, surely not,' Tony gave his daughter a squeeze. 'And you know, I'm so pleased to have you home, love. Can't tell you what a world of difference it makes to this old man.'

'Stop that. You're not old. And a good job too ... ' Jude swapped Lulu onto her other hip, before straightening her little May Fair-themed Hawaiian shirt around her caramel-coloured curls. Lulu thanked Jude with a quick, cold, flyby lick on the cheek, which Jude instantly rubbed away with the back of a hand. She loved Lulu, but wasn't about to have her doggy slobber all over her face. Yuk.

'Why is that then?' Tony asked his daughter. She leaned into him.

'Well, Holly has got all of us now, but in a completely different way from before. I've got a new niece, and you've got a new granddaughter!'

*

Dolly, having recovered from the initial shock of that night, was determined not to let it spoil her granddaughter's upcoming birthday. Holly might not be related by blood, but that didn't change a thing. She still loved her and that was that. Now, if only Linda would leave and let them all get on with having a lovely time at the May Fair, but the blasted woman was determined to hang around like a bad smell. Dolly could see her hovering over by the carousel. The lovely carousel that glittered and flashed red, gold and green as the painted wooden horses went up and down and around and around. The jolly piped organ music bringing back memories of when she was a girl.

But enough was enough. Dolly knew that she needed to put this particular ghost to bed, for the sake of them all. Especially her dear Sam, who had been beside himself the day after Linda's nasty announcement, even though she had assured him it didn't change a thing between them. And when Colin had got home from the coach trip to Amsterdam, Dolly had let herself have a cry in her husband's arms up in the privacy of their bedroom. And now she was getting on with it. For Dolly had endured far worse upsets in her lifetime than the likes of Linda.

After taking a deep breath and adjusting her new lilac blouse, Dolly turned to Colin.

'Shan't be a moment, dear.' And she made her way over to where Linda was standing eying up the man tending the carousel. 'If I could tear you away for a moment?' Dolly said, raising one eyebrow.

'Hmm, I wondered when you were going to stick your oar in,' Linda huffed, unravelling herself from the post she'd been wrapped around in what Dolly could only assume she had thought was a provocative pose.

'Why do you insist on being so obnoxious? If cheating on my son wasn't bad enough, you have to turn up here all these years later and cause yet more heartache for everyone.'

'I don't know what you mean,' Linda said tartly, pushing her chin up in the air. 'And it wasn't like I was even married to your precious son, Rob, when I … err, um, had a bit of fun. Accidents happen, you know. I'm sure you've made a few in your lifetime …'

'Well, Linda, I guess you're never going to change. But thank God you did cheat on my dear son, Robert.' Dolly gave her daughter-in-law a look of death before pushing her handbag further into the crook of her elbow.

'What do you mean?' Linda looked taken aback.

'Don't you see?' Dolly smiled graciously. 'Jude or Tony may turn out to be a blood match for my Holly. And yes, she'll always be my great-granddaughter. And Sam my grandson. Because, do you know what, Linda …' she paused for maximum impact, before saying, 'Scraggen.' Linda's surname before she married her son. 'Yes, that's right, you aren't worthy of using my son's surname, Morgan, any more.'

'Flaming cheek!' Linda sniffed to interrupt.

'Anyway, as I was saying,' Dolly carried on regardless, 'my grandson and great-granddaughter mean the world to me, and they always will.'

'Good for you! But they're still my family,' Linda said nastily. 'You've always thought you were better than me. Looking down your nose when I was married to Rob—'

'No dear!' A short silence followed. 'That wasn't superiority. That was pity. Pity that you couldn't see what was right in front of you ... and you still don't!' Dolly held her gaze.

'What's that then?' Linda looked away.

'Just how important family is.'

'But, Sam and Holly ... they aren't *really* your family though, are they?' Linda retorted, her top lip curling into a spiteful grimace.

'Well, that's where you're wrong. Because blood isn't thicker than water. Not at all. It's just a different colour!'

And with that Dolly walked away to rejoin Colin. They were meeting Sam, Chrissie, Holly, Tony and Jude over by the swimming pool in precisely ten minutes to watch Holly and her little friend splash around in the fountains together before going in for a swim. And then, later, they were all going back to her cottage to enjoy a wonderful, big, family dinner of roast lamb with all the trimmings followed by strawberry pavlova and cream.

*

Jude had just dispatched her dad to the back entrance of the main marquee, and put Lulu in her little playroom, when an actual wooden canoe on wheels came hurtling across the sand towards her, complete with two giant paddles and a sail hoisted up to the top of the mast. She jumped out of the way as the canoe swerved in a big U-turn before slowing to a halt right beside her.

'Hop in!' It was Myles, grinning from ear to ear, wearing a long, curly black wig. His bare chest adorned in tribal tattoos. A bunch of shells on a length of string at his neck. He even had a grass skirt on over black swimming shorts too.

'What are you doing?' Jude spluttered, dusting sand from her mouth and hair as she gawped at him. He was toned and tanned all over. And made a very impressive Polynesian demi-god – a fitter, hotter version of Maui from that film, *Moana*.

'What does it look like?' he said, patting the plastic bench seat he was sitting on. 'I've come to rescue you!'

'Rescue me? But I don't need rescuing,' she laughed, shaking her head and bobbing her shoulders up and down.

'Well, not literally rescue you, as in … you know, properly *rescue* you,' he said, rolling his eyes and pulling a pretend exasperated look. 'I know you don't need rescuing. Come on, get in … I've got a surprise to show you.' And he patted the seat again. Jude, always up for a surprise, immediately put her foot inside the canoe and sat down beside him. Myles pressed two buttons – one to make the wheels spark into action, the other to spray a fine mist of salty-scented water all over them.

As they gathered speed, Jude felt as if she was riding along on the crest of a wave. It was incredible. The hot air in her hair, the close proximity of Myles's body pressed alongside hers as they surfed through the sand and into the forest surrounding the estate's perimeter ... it was sensational.

'Whoa,' Myles brought the canoe to a halt on the far side of the Blackwood Farm Estate. A section of ground that Jude hadn't been to before. Ahead of them was a little densely shaded wooded area illuminated with fairy lights. 'Follow me,' Myles jumped out of the canoe, ran around it and held out his hand to Jude.

'Where are we going?' she asked, intrigued.

'You'll see.' Moments later, and she was standing outside the door to a log cabin. Myles handed her a gold key with a scarlet ribbon looped through it.

'Unlock the door,' he prompted her, rubbing his hands together in glee. He really was like a big kid ... Jude slipped the key into the lock and tentatively pushed open the door. Directly in front of her was a luxurious gold velvet curtain which Myles quickly swept aside.

And she gasped.

'A studio?' She turned to look at him, unable to believe her own eyes – it was an exact replica of her workspace in LA. The base from where she had built her successful interior design business from scratch ... and it was now right here in Tindledale.

'It's yours. You like it?' he asked, eagerly.

'Like it? I love it,' she told him, taking in the luxurious décor, the sumptuous mink carpet, the creamy leather sofa, the walnut veneer-topped table on which she used to roll out her plan sheets to show clients. There was even a row of clocks on one wall for each of the different countries where her clients were based. 'But why?' she clasped her hands up under her chin.

'Why not?' Myles shrugged.

'Because ... because you can't just copy my LA office like this. And then give it to me. It's insane. And it must have cost you a fortune, for starters. And how did you even know about this?' She slipped off her sandals and dashed into the middle of the space. After twirling on the carpet that was at least four inches thick, she sunk down onto the sofa and practically caressed it as she drew in the exquisite fragrance of antique leather.

'I Googled it!'

'What?' she screamed, leaping up and laughing. 'But of course you did ... silly me.'

'Seriously though, I did Google you and I found out where your office was in LA and I called them, and well ... I figured that, seeing as that shop in the High Street of yours has kind of fizzled out ...' He paused and gave her a look, as if testing to see if he was overstepping the mark. She tilted her head and nodded to let him know that he had a point. She had already decided that closing the shop was going to be a necessity – her dream hadn't really worked out in the way she had hoped. The warm-hearted villagers of Tindledale just weren't that into antiques and high-end interiors and stuff. 'And you're working here on the estate most of the time … so I reckoned you'd like a proper space of your own. And you can resurrect your LA-based business from here too, if you like!' He stared at her, as if hesitant he'd done the right thing. 'No worries, if it's too much. I can get it dismantled when you've finished, you know … helping me do up the estate.' He ran a hand over his chin.

Jude smiled as she stared back at him, thinking what a wonderful man he was. That night when she had arrived here to bring Holly home, Myles had been amazing. He had guessed right away what Holly's intention had been, to run away, but he hadn't panicked or taken over and called in the cavalry. He had figured it more important that Holly felt safe, that she had someone there for her in that moment. To understand and not judge. Instead he had listened and helped her come to the realisation that things might turn out all right in the end, if she could be brave enough to stick around and give it all a go.

'But it's too much, Myles. Honestly, you don't need to do this.'

'Yes I do. Call it an apology, and a thank you, all rolled into one.'

'What do you mean?'

'An apology for being so obnoxious when I first got in

touch with you, for starters ... *Darling Antiques, what kind of a name is that, are you having a laugh?* Remember?' he grinned sheepishly. 'I guess I was a bit nervous. And the thank you ... is for all this,' and he waved a hand towards the window to indicate the grounds and the manor house.

'But it's my job,' Jude smiled.

'And you let me be part of it, and that's not something I've been able to do much of in the past. Anyway, you can't refuse it, as it's a present and nobody ever turns down one of those. That would just be rude.' And he laughed as he pulled the wig from his head and ruffled his hair. His eyes sparkling as he tugged the ridiculous straw skirt from his waist, he walked over to join her on the plush carpet.

'You're insufferable! Do you know that?' she said, and then quickly added, 'but in a lovely, nice way ... I know that now,' when his face momentarily dropped.

Silence followed as they stood together, watching the sun glimmer in between the trees outside. Then Myles turned towards Jude and pulled an envelope from the pocket of his shorts and handed it to her.

'What is it?'

'Open it and see,' he said, grinning from ear to ear.

'I don't believe it.' Jude scanned the letter inside. It was from Maggie!

Dear Jude,

I'm so looking forward to seeing you soon. Please thank that kind young man of yours for calling me and arranging such a lovely surprise.

Until then, lots of love,
Maggie x

'What? But how?' She read the letter again, dumbfounded, and then looked at Myles. 'This is amazing. You called Maggie and organised it all?' Nobody had ever done anything like this for her before. Certainly not a man.

'Yup,' Myles nodded, and then added, 'with a bit of help from your dad.' He shrugged.

'My dad?' Jude was almost speechless. 'When did you see him? And, more to the point, how did you know about Maggie?'

'I asked your dad when he was here painting the walls around the swimming pool,' Myles started, all matter of fact. '"What would be the best surprise for Jude?" And he said, "Probably to see Maggie." So I sorted it.'

'Just like that.' Jude felt overwhelmed as she shook her head in disbelief, her heart lifting at the prospect of giving Maggie a hug.

'Yes, just like that,' Myles laughed. 'So does this mean I can have a kiss?' Jude looked at him, his blond hair flopping forward, his sapphire blue eyes eager for her answer. And how could she refuse? The cocky, belligerent rock star was actually a very nice, kind, generous and thoughtful guy once you really got to know him. So she stood up on her tiptoes, inhaled his intoxicating scent and planted a kiss on his lips, wrapping her arms around his taut bare chest as his mouth lingered on hers, making a mountain of fireworks whoosh and explode inside her. Then, moments later, the opening line to that old country classic, 'Islands in the Stream', was blaring out through the many speakers erected around the estate. And Jude untangled herself from his embrace.

'Perfect timing. I love this song, Such an uplifting yet romantic tune,' she told him with a flourish.

'I thought you might.' And Myles grinned before pulling her in for another sumptuously long, lingering kiss.

*

Meanwhile, in another part of the estate, Holly fumbled inside her swimming bag, remembering the plastic karaoke microphones that Myles had given her when they had chatted on that evening. She grinned at the memory of the deal they had struck ... him telling her a secret, after they had eaten fish and chips and she was feeling much better. Myles told her that he had a big crush on her Aunty Jude. And it made her giggle, especially when he had asked her for advice ... he was a rock star after all. So she had told him that he really should already know about girls and how to make them want to kiss him and all that. Holly had then confided in him about the wish. Her Get Mum and Dad Back Together in Time for Her Birthday plan too ... and how it hadn't really worked out.

But there was still time!

So, with this in mind, Holly wiggled her way in between her parents so they were standing either side of her while they waited for the traditional May Fair tug-of-war battle to start. And then, after counting to three, she turned around in front of them, whipped the microphones from her pocket and thrust them into her parents' hands. Just as she and Myles had planned. Right on time. As Dolly Parton and Kenny Rogers reached the chorus bit. Holly had told him all about the song and her happy memories of Mum and Dad dancing and swooning along to it together. As far as she was concerned it was also the most perfect moment for him and Jude to kiss. And now she was going to make her mum and dad do it too. After they had joined in the song and had a laugh like they always had in the past.

'Sing. Sing. Sing,' she laughed, nudging her best friend, Katie, to join in, which she did, of course.

With the two young girls chorusing them on, Sam gave Chrissie's hand a squeeze as he searched her eyes to see if she was up for it. She hesitated, only momentarily, before lifting the microphone to her lips to sing. Sam, knowing how much this moment meant to Holly, put his heart and soul into the performance before scooping Chrissie up into his arms for the final chorus. When, to his overwhelming delight, she placed her arms around his neck and pressed her warm lips on to the side of his neck as he twirled her around and around all the while singing along to Dolly and Kenny.

And Holly thought her own heart really was going to burst right out of her chest this time, into a million, trillion, tiny, fluttery pieces of pure joy. Because seeing her mum and dad so happy together again meant the wish really did have a chance of coming true now ...

Epilogue

A year later

'Go on then,' Tony said, tapping the envelope that Jude had in her hand. The whole family had waited for what felt like an eternity for this day to arrive. They had already found out that he wasn't a match for Holly. Tony was a blood group A, the same as Sam, but Jude was an O, and therefore able to go on to the next stage for testing.

'I can't,' her voice quavered, as she nudged her dad in the arm, for she so hoped that she could do this for Holly. For her best friend, Chrissie, too, and her new brother, Sam. Their dad. And her whole family. Give them all the peace of mind of knowing that Holly would be OK, no matter what the future held for her.

'Shall I open it for you, love?' Tony offered, gently.

'It's OK. I can do this.' She nodded and pushed the tip of her fingernail under the flap of the envelope, silently wishing the contents would be the news they all hoped for. 'One. Two. Three.' She pulled the letter out and read it as fast as she could, all the while holding her breath.

Tears prickled in her eyes, making her vision all filmy. But there was no mistake.

She was a perfect match.

Blood and tissue.

One hundred per cent.

*

In another part of Tindledale, in the kitchen of The Forstal Farmhouse, Holly was laying the table for lunch. Knives, forks and spoons for eight people. Everyone was coming over to celebrate her fifteenth birthday. Granny Dolly and Colin, Aunty Jude, Granddad Tony and her best friend, Katie. Mum was cooking a special lunch for them all and was even making some sugar-free cupcakes especially for her. Everything was so much better now. The last year had been amazing. And she barely noticed the pump that was in her back pocket, silently but industriously working away, keeping her sugar levels stabilised. Dad had a new job with a construction company in Market Briar and was home for ever now. And Mum was happy again. Holly always knew she would be ...

'Holly, love. Can you give your dad a shout, please? I could do with his help.' Mum was standing on tiptoes trying to reach the bag of flour from the shelf. Holly went to dart into the hall where Dad was hanging a picture up on the wall.

And then she stopped.

Holly knew Mum would keep trying to get the bag down. She was just like that. Still a bit of a control freak who never gave up. So Holly crept really slowly up the stairs, taking as long as possible to reach Dad on the top landing.

'You OK, darling?' Dad asked when she got there.

'Yes, fine. I just wondered what you were up to,' she said, coyly, avoiding his gaze.

'Well, I've just finished. What do you think?' he stepped back to show her the framed photo.

'Ahh, it's lovely, Dad.' Holly took a look at the picture of the three of them together. Her family. Mum, Dad, and her last Christmas day at Granny Dolly's house, all wearing paper hats and smiling.

'Great, isn't it?'

'Sure is, Dad.'

She heard Mum yell out from downstairs.

With her heart soaring, Holly grinned at her dad.

'Come on.' Holly took her dad by the hand and led him down the stairs and into the kitchen. Mum was all covered in flour, with a massive grin on her face. And in that moment Holly Morgan knew that her Get Mum and Dad Back Together plan had definitely worked for good now. And the wish her thirteen-year-old unhappy self had made that day in her bedroom ... had now been granted. She had her mum and dad back together for ever ... and they were all going to live happily ever after.

Acknowledgments

Dear Friends

I really hope you enjoyed *The Wish*. It touches on several themes that I love to write about – multigenerational family life, triumph over adversity and finding the courage to try again. Everyone deserves a second chance! Whilst domestic dramas, particularly with a child in need, can be poignant at times, I do hope *The Wish* warmed your heart too and left you feeling uplifted.

My first thanks as always goes to all of you, my darling friends from around the world, who chat to me on my Facebook page and via my website. You're all magnificent and your kindness and continued cheerleading spurs me on every day – writing books can get lonely sometimes, but having you all there is like a wonderful family — our special community — and that is something very precious to me indeed. I couldn't do any of this without you. You mean the world to me and make it all worthwhile. Thank you so very much xxx

Special thanks and gratitude to my long-suffering agent, Tim Bates, for talking a lot of sense and always keeping me calm. Honestly, the man has the patience of a saint! An abundance of appreciation to my editor and dear friend, Kate Bradley, thank you for the laughs, love and unwavering support right from the start, back in the day. 'All riiiiiiise ....' ☺. Of course, none of the other stuff would happen without the wonderful team at HarperCollins, especially Kimberley Young, Lynne Drew, Charlotte Brabbin, Liz Dawson, Emilie Chambeyron (special thanks for sorting out the fabulous photoshoot) and Katy Blott. Special thanks to my copy editor Penny Isaac. As always, I couldn't write at all without my beloved Northern Soul music to evoke the right emotions, so thank you for helping me to keep the faith and keep on keeping on. Immense thanks to my kind friends Caroline Smailes, Kimberley Chambers and Rachel Forbes, your patience when I catastrophise, is what also keeps me going ☺xxx Aly Harrold for helping me find my voice and Niki Lawal for helping me find my dream. Ruth Mackay Langford for posting a picture on my Facebook page and sharing the details of her gorgeous Aga, aka Beryl the Peril. Katie Ferguson for winning my 'Name a Character' auction lot to raise funds for the CLIC Sargent charity supporting children and young people with cancer. Kaisha Holloway for kindly sending the gift to my cheeky Labradors.

To my husband Paul, aka Cheeks. See, your time at medical school and knowledge of bio chemistry has come in handy after all. Thank you for your endless patience in explaining how blood grouping works, how they are inherited and who can donate to who. Any mistakes are totally down to me for being clueless and quite uninterested in anything scientific. Thanks to my dad, the gypsy boy, for always cheering me on.

To my darling daughter, QT, not only the bravest little girl I know, but also a budding author too, for writing the original Magic Unicorn story that features in this book as Holly's story. I'm so proud of you every single day, my love.

Luck and love to you all,
Alex xxx

Jude's Delicious St Germain Prosecco Cocktail

Serves I

Ingredients

- 25ml Elderflower liqueur or cordial
- Prosecco
- Fresh mint leaves
- Cucumber
- Ice

Method

- Add the ice, mint leaves and a slice or two of cucumber to a tall glass.

- Pour in the elderflower liqueur or cordial and top up with chilled Prosecco. Stir with a straw, sip and bask in the afternoon sunshine.

The Duck & Puddle Pub
Special Lemon Meringue Pie

Serves 8

Ingredients

- 200g caster sugar
- 2 tablespoons plain flour
- 3 tablespoons cornflour
- ¼ teaspoon salt
- 350ml water
- 2 lemons, juiced and zested
- 30g butter
- 4 egg yolks, beaten
- 1 (23cm) shortcrust pastry case, already baked
- 4 egg whites
- 75g caster sugar

Method

- Heat the oven to 180 C / Gas 4.

To make the lemon filling:

- In a medium saucepan, whisk together the caster sugar, flour, cornflour and salt.
- Stir in the water, lemon juice and lemon zest.

- Cook over a medium-high heat, stirring frequently, until mixture comes to the boil.

- Stir in the butter.

- Place egg yolks in a small bowl and gradually whisk in 100ml of the hot sugar mixture.

- Then, whisk the egg yolk mixture back into remaining sugar mixture.

- Bring to the boil and continue to cook while stirring constantly until thick.

- Remove from heat.

- Pour filling into pastry case.

- To serve, pour the chocolate sauce over the pears.

To make the meringue:

- In a large glass or metal bowl, whip egg whites until foamy.

- Add sugar gradually, and continue to whip until stiff peaks form.

- Spread meringue over pie, sealing the edges.

- Bake in preheated oven for 10 minutes, or until meringue is golden brown.

- For best results, cool to room temperature and then chill in the fridge before serving.

Granny Dolly's
Fruit Scones

Makes 8 – 12 scones

Ingredients

- 225g self raising flour
- pinch of salt
- 55g butter
- 25g sultanas
- 25g caster sugar
- 150ml milk

Method

- Heat the oven to 220C/425F/Gas 7.
- Lightly grease a baking sheet.
- Mix together the flour and salt and rub in the butter.
- Stir in the sultanas, sugar and then the milk to get a soft dough.
- Turn on to a floured work surface and knead very lightly.
- Pat out to a round 2cm thick.
- Use a 5cm cutter to stamp out rounds and place on a baking sheet.
- Lightly knead together the rest of the dough and stamp out more scones to use it all up.
- Brush the tops of the scones with a little milk.
- Bake for 12-15 minutes until well risen and golden.
- Cool on a wire rack and serve slathered in strawberry jam and clotted cream with a nice mug of hot tea.